Lynne Graham _____ has been a keen rom_____ very happily married ~~to an understanding husband~~ who has learned to cook since she started to write! Her five children keep her on her toes. She has a very large dog who knocks everything over, a very small terrier who barks a lot, and two cats. When time allows, Lynne is a keen gardener.

After spending three years as a die-hard New Yorker, **Kate Hewitt** now lives in a small village in the English Lake District with her husband, their five children and a golden retriever. In addition to writing intensely emotional stories, she loves reading, baking and playing chess with her son—she has yet to win against him, but she continues to try.

Learn more about Kate at kate-hewitt.com.

Award-winning author **Jennifer Faye** pens fun, heart-warming romances. Jennifer has won the *RT Book Reviews* Reviewers' Choice Award, is a TOP PICK author, and has been nominated for numerous awards. Now living her dream, she resides with her patient husband, one amazing daughter (the other remarkable daughter is off chasing her own dreams) and two spoiled cats. She'd love to hear from you via her website: JenniferFaye.com

The Italian Mavericks

COLLECTION

January 2019

February 2019

March 2019

April 2019

May 2019

June 2019

Watch out for the Greek Mavericks collection coming soon!

Italian Mavericks:
In the
Italian's Bed

LYNNE GRAHAM

KATE HEWITT

JENNIFER FAYE

MILLS & BOON

First Published in Great Britain 2019
By Mills & Boon, an imprint of HarperCollins *Publishers*
1 London Bridge Street, London, SE1 9GF

ITALIAN MAVERICKS: IN THE ITALIAN'S BED
© 2019 Harlequin Books S.A.

Leonetti's Housekeeper Bride © 2016 Lynne Graham
Inherited by Ferranti © 2016 Kate Hewitt
Best Man for the Bridesmaid © 2015 Jennifer F. Stroka

ISBN: 978-0-263-27561-2

0119

Printed and bound in Spain
by CPI, Barcelona

LEONETTI'S HOUSEKEEPER BRIDE

LYNNE GRAHAM

CHAPTER ONE

GAETANO LEONETTI WAS having a very bad day. It had started at dawn, when his phone went off and proceeded to show him a series of photos that enraged him but which he knew would enrage his grandfather and the very conservative board of the Leonetti investment bank even more. Regrettably, sacking the woman responsible for the story in the downmarket tabloid was likely to be the sole satisfaction he could hope to receive.

'It's not your fault,' Tom Sandyford, Gaetano's middle-aged legal adviser and close friend, told him quietly.

'Of course it's *my* fault,' Gaetano growled. 'It was *my* house, *my* party and the woman in *my* bed at the time who organised the damned party—'

'Celia was that soap star with the cocaine habit you didn't know about,' Tom reminisced. 'Wasn't she sacked from the show soon after you ditched her?'

Gaetano nodded, his even white teeth gritting harder.

'It's a case of bad luck…that's all,' Tom opined. 'You can't ask your guests to post their credentials beforehand, so you had no way of knowing some of them weren't tickety-boo.'

'Tickety-boo?' Gaetano repeated, his lean, darkly handsome features frowning. Although he was born and raised in England, Italian had been the language of his home and he still occasionally came across English words and phrases that were unfamiliar.

'Decent upstanding citizens,' Tom rephrased. 'So, a handful of them were hookers? Well, in the rarefied and very privileged world you move in, how were you supposed to find that out?'

'The press found it out,' Gaetano countered flatly.

'With the usual silly "Orgy at the Manor" big reveal. It'll be forgotten in five minutes…although that blonde dancing naked in the fountain out front is rather memorable,' Tom remarked, scanning the newspaper afresh with lascivious intent.

'I don't remember seeing her. I left the party early to fly to New York. Everyone still had their clothes on at that stage,' Gaetano said drily. 'I really don't need another scandal like this.'

'Scandal does rather seem to follow you around. I suppose the old man and the board at the bank are up in arms as usual,' Tom commented with sympathy.

Gaetano compressed his wide sensual mouth in silent agreement. In the name of family loyalty and respect, he was paying in the blood of his fierce pride and ambition for the latest scandal. Letting his seventy-four-year-old grandfather Rodolfo carpet him like a badly behaved schoolboy had proved to be a truly toxic experience for a billionaire whose investment advice was sought by governments both in the UK and abroad. And when Rodolfo had settled into his favourite preaching session about Gaetano's womanising lifestyle, Gaetano had had to breathe in deeply several times and resist the urge to point out to the older man that expectations and values had changed since the nineteen forties for both men *and* women.

Rodolfo Leonetti had married a humble fisherman's daughter at the age of twenty-one and during his fifty years of devoted marriage he had never looked at another woman. Ironically, his only child, Gaetano's father, Rocco, had not taken his father's advice on the benefits of making an early marriage either. Rocco had been a notorious playboy and an incorrigible gambler. He had married a woman young enough to be his daughter when he was in his fifties, had fathered one son and had expired ten years later after over-exerting himself in another woman's bed. Gaetano reckoned he had been paying for his father's sins almost from the hour of his birth. At the age of twenty-nine and one of the world's leading bankers, he was tired of being continually forced to prove his worth and confine his projects to the narrow expectations of the board. He had made millions for the Leonetti Bank; he *deserved* to be CEO.

Indeed, Rodolfo's angry ultimatum that very morning had outraged Gaetano.

'You will *never* be the chief executive of this bank until you change your way of life and settle down into being a respectable family man!' his grandfather had sworn angrily. 'I will not support your leadership with the board and, no matter how brilliant you are, Gaetano, the board *always* listens to me... They remember too well how your father almost brought the bank down with his risky ventures!'

Yet what, realistically, did Gaetano's sex life have to do with his acumen and expertise as a banker? Since when were a wife and children the only measure of a man's judgement and maturity?

Gaetano had not the slightest interest in getting married. In fact he shuddered at the idea of being anchored to one woman for the rest of his life while living in fear of a divorce that could deprive him of half of his financial portfolio. He was a very hard worker. He had earned his academic qualifications with honours in the most prestigious international institutions and his achievements since then had been immense. Why wasn't that enough? In comparison his father had been an academically slow and spoiled rich boy who, like Peter Pan, had refused to grow up. Such a comparison was grossly unfair.

Tom dealt Gaetano a rueful appraisal. 'You didn't get the old "find an ordinary girl" spiel again, did you?'

"'An ordinary girl, *not* a party girl, one who takes pleasure in the *simple* things of life,'" Gaetano quoted verbatim because his grandfather's discourses always ran to the same conclusion: marry, settle down, father children with a home-loving female…and the world would then miraculously become Gaetano's oyster with little happy unicorns dancing on some misty horizon shaped by a rainbow. His lean bronzed features hardened with grim cynicism. He had seen just how well that fantasy had turned out for once-married and now happily divorced friends.

'Perhaps you could time travel back to the nineteen fifties to find this ordinary girl,' Tom quipped, wondering how the era of female liberation and career women had contrived to pass Rodolfo Leonetti by so completely that he still believed such women existed.

'The best of it is, if I did produce an *ordinary* girl and announce that I was going to marry her Rodolfo would be appalled,' Gaetano breathed impatiently. 'He's too much of a snob. Unfortunately he's become so obsessed by his conviction that I need to marry that he's blocking my progression at the bank.'

His PA entered and extended two envelopes. 'The termination of contract on the grounds of the confidentiality clause which has been breached and the notice to quit the accommodation that goes with the job,' she specified. 'The helicopter is waiting for you on the roof, sir.'

'What's going on?' Tom asked.

'I'm flying down to Woodfield Hall to sack the housekeeper who handed over those photos to the press.'

'It was the *housekeeper*?' Tom prompted in surprise.

'She was named in the article. Not the brightest of women,' Gaetano pointed out drily.

Poppy leapt off her bike, kicked the support into place and ran into the village shop to buy milk. As usual she was running late but she could not drink coffee without milk and didn't feel properly awake until she had had at least two cups. Her mane of fiery red-gold curls bounced on her slim black-clad shoulders and her green eyes sparkled.

'Good morning, Frances,' she said cheerfully to the rather sour-looking older woman behind the counter as she dug into her purse to pay.

'I'm surprised you're so bright this morning,' the shop owner remarked in a tone laden with suggestive meaning.

'Why wouldn't I be?'

The older woman slapped a well-thumbed newspaper down on the counter and helpfully turned it round to enable Poppy to read the headline. Poppy paled with dismay and snatched the publication up, moving on impatiently to the next page only to groan at the familiar photo of the naked blonde cavorting in the fountain. Her brother, Damien, had definitely taken that photo on the night of that infamous party. She knew that because she had caught him showing that particular one off to his mates.

'Seems your ma has been talking out of turn,' Frances remarked. 'Shouldn't think Mr Leonetti will appreciate that...'

Glancing up to meet the older woman's avidly curious gaze, Poppy hastily paid for the paper and left the shop. That photo? How on earth had the newspaper got hold of it? And what about the other photos? The heaving, fortunately unidentifiable bodies in one of the bedrooms? When invited to join the party by a drunken guest, had Damien taken other, even more risqué pictures? And her mother...what insanity had persuaded her to risk her job by trashing her employer to a tabloid journalist? Poppy's soft full mouth downcurved and her shoulders slumped as she climbed back on her bike. Unfortunately Poppy knew exactly why her mother might have been so foolish: Jasmine Arnold was an alcoholic.

Poppy had once got her mother to an AA meeting and it had done her good but she had never managed to get the older woman back to a second. Instead, Jasmine just drank herself insensible every day while Poppy struggled to do her mother's job for her as well as doing her own. What else could she do when the very roof over their heads was dependent on Jasmine's continuing employment? And after all, wasn't it *her* fault that her mother had sunk so low before Poppy realised how bad things had got in her own home and had finally come back to live with her family again?

It was very fortunate that Gaetano only visited the house once or twice a year. But then Gaetano was a city boy through and through and a beautiful Georgian country house an inconvenient distance from London was of little use or interest to him. Had he been a more regular visitor she would never have been able to conceal her mother's condition for so long.

Poppy pumped the bike pedals hard to get up the hill before careening at speed into the driveway of Woodfield Hall. The beautiful house had been the Leonetti family home in England since the eighteenth century when the family had first come over from Venice to set up as glorified moneylenders. And if there was one thing that family were good at it, it was making pots and pots of money, Poppy reflected ruefully, shying away from the challenge of thinking about Gaetano in an any more personal way.

She and Gaetano might have virtually grown up in the same household but it would be an outright lie to suggest that they were ever in any way friendly. After all, Gaetano was six years older and had spent most of his time in posh boarding schools.

But Poppy knew that Gaetano would go crazy about the publication of those photos. He was fanatical about his privacy and if his idea of fun was a sex party, she could perfectly understand why! Her spirits sank at the prospect of the trouble looming ahead. No matter how hard she worked life never seemed to get any easier and there always seemed to be another crisis waiting to erupt round the next corner. Yet how could she look after her mother and her brother when their own survival instincts appeared to be so poor?

The Arnold family lived in a flat that had been converted from part of the original stable block at the hall. Jasmine Arnold, a tall skinny redhead in her late forties, was sitting at the kitchen table when her daughter walked in.

Poppy slapped down the paper on the table. 'Mum? Were you out of your mind when you talked to a journalist about that party?' she demanded, before opening the back door and yelling her brother's name at the top of her voice.

Damien emerged from one of the garages, wiping oil stains off his hands with a dirty cloth. 'Where's the fire?' he asked irritably as his sister moved forward to greet him.

'You gave the photos you took at that party to a journalist?' his sister challenged in disbelief.

'No, I didn't,' her kid brother countered. 'Mum knew they were on my phone and she handed them over. She sold them. Got a pile of cash for them and the interview.'

Poppy was even more appalled. She could have excused stupidity or careless speech to the wrong person but she was genuinely shocked that her mother had taken money in return for her disloyalty to her employer.

Damien groaned at the expression on his sister's face. 'Poppy...you should know by now that Mum would do anything to get the money to buy her next drink,' he pointed out heavily. 'I told her not to hand over the photos or talk to the guy but she wouldn't listen to me—'

'Why didn't you tell me what she'd done?'

'What could you do about it? I hoped that maybe the photos wouldn't be used or that, if they were, nobody of any importance would see them,' Damien admitted. 'I doubt if Gaetano sits down to read every silly story that's written about him... I mean, he's never out of the papers!'

'But if you're wrong, Mum will be sacked and we'll be kicked out of the flat.'

Damien wasn't the type to worry about what might never happen and he said wryly, 'Let's hope I'm not wrong.'

But Poppy took after her late father and she was a worrier. It was hard to credit that it was only a few years since the Arnolds had been a secure and happy family of four. Her father had been the gardener at Woodfield Hall and her mother the housekeeper. At twenty years of age, Poppy had been two years into her training at nursing school and Damien had just completed his apprenticeship as a car mechanic. And then without any warning at all their much-loved father had dropped dead and all their lives had been shattered by that cruelly sudden bereavement.

Poppy had taken time out from her course to try and help her mother through the worst of her grief and then she had returned to her studies. Unhappily and without her knowledge, things had gone badly wrong at that point. Her mother had gone off the rails and Damien had been unable to cope with what was happening in his home. Her brother had then got in with the wrong crowd and had ended up in prison. That was when Poppy had finally come home to find her mother sunk in depression and drinking heavily. Poppy had taken a leave of absence from her course, hoping, indeed expecting, that her mother would soon pull round again. Unfortunately that hadn't happened. Although Jasmine was still drinking, Poppy's one consolation was that, after earning early release from prison with his good behaviour, her little brother had got his act together again. Sadly, however, Damien's criminal record had made it impossible for him to get a job.

Poppy still felt horribly guilty about the fact that she had left her kid brother to deal with her deeply troubled mother. Intent on pursuing her chosen career and being the first Arnold female in generations *not* to earn her living by serving the Leonettis, she had been selfish and thoughtless and she had been trying to make up for that mistake ever since.

When she returned to the flat her mother had locked herself in her bedroom. Poppy suppressed a sigh and dug out her work kit and rubber gloves to cross the courtyard and enter the hall. She turned out different rooms of the big house every week, dusting and vacuuming and scrubbing. It was deeply ironic that she had been so set against working for the Leonettis when she was a teenager but had ended up doing it anyway even if it was unofficial. Evenings she served drinks in the local pub. There wasn't time in her life for agonising when there was always a job needing to be done.

Disturbingly however she couldn't get Gaetano Leonetti out of her mind. He was the one and only boy she had ever hated but also the only one she had ever loved. What did that say about her? Self-evidently, that at the age of sixteen she had been really stupid to imagine for one moment that she could ever have any kind of a personal relationship with the posh, privileged scion of the Leonetti family. The wounding demeaning words that Gaetano had shot at her then were still burned into her bones like the scars of an old breakage.

'I don't mess around with staff,' he had said, emphasising the fact that they were not equals and that he would always inhabit a different stratum of society.

'Stop coming on to me, Poppy. You're acting like a slapper.' Oh, how she had cringed at that reading of her behaviour when in truth she had merely been too young and inexperienced to know how to be subtle about spelling out the fact that should he be interested, she was available.

'You're a short, curvy redhead. You could never be my type.'

It was seven years since that humiliating exchange

had taken place and apart from one final demeaning encounter she had not seen Gaetano since, having always gone out of her way to avoid him whenever he was expected at the hall. So, he didn't know that she had slimmed down and shot up inches in height, wouldn't much care either, she reckoned with wry amusement. After all, Gaetano went for very beautiful and sophisticated ladies in designer clothes. Although the one who had thrown that shockingly wild party had not been much of a lady in the original sense of the word.

Having put in her hours at the hall in the ongoing challenge to ensure that it was always well prepared for a visit that could come at very short notice, Poppy went back home to get changed for her bar work. Jasmine was out for the count on her bed, an empty bottle of cheap wine lying beside her. Studying her slumped figure, Poppy suppressed a sigh, recalling the busy, lively and caring woman her mother had once been. Alcohol had stolen all that from her. Jasmine needed specialised help and rehabilitation but there wasn't even counselling available locally and Poppy had no hope of ever acquiring sufficient cash to pay for private treatment for the older woman.

Poppy put on the Goth clothes that she had first donned like a mask to hide behind when she was a bullied teenager. She had been picked on in school for being a little overweight and red-haired. Heck, she had even been bullied for being 'posh' although her family lived in the hall's servant accommodation. Since then, although she no longer dyed her hair or painted her nails black, she had come to enjoy a touch of individuality in her wardrobe and had maintained the basic style. She had lost a lot of weight since she started working two jobs and she was convinced that her Goth-style clothes did a good job of disguising her skinniness. For work she had teamed a dark red net flirty skirt with a fitted black jersey rock print top. The outfit hugged her small full breasts, enhanced her waist and accentuated the length of her legs.

At the end of her shift in the busy bar that was paired with a popular restaurant, Poppy pulled on her coat and waited outside for Damien to show up on his motorbike.

'Gaetano Leonetti arrived in a helicopter this evening,' her brother delivered curtly. 'He demanded to see Mum but she was out of it and I had to pretend she was sick. He handed over these envelopes for her and I opened them once he'd gone. Mum's being sacked and we have a month's notice to move out of the flat.'

An anguished moan of dismay at those twin blows parted Poppy's lips.

'I guess he did see that newspaper.' Damien grimaced. 'He certainly hasn't wasted any time booting us out.'

'Can we blame him for that?' Poppy asked even though her heart was sinking to the soles of her shoes. Where would they go? How would they live? They had no rainy-day account for emergencies. Her mother drank her salary and Damien was on benefits.

But Poppy was a fighter, always had been, always would be. She took after her father more than her mother. She was good at picking herself up when things went wrong. Her mother, however, had never fully recovered from the stillbirth she had suffered the year before Poppy's father had died. Those two terrible calamities coming so close together had knocked her mother's feet from under her and she had never really got up again. Poppy swallowed hard as she climbed onto the bike and gripped her brother's waist. She could still remember her mother's absolute joy at that unexpected late pregnancy, which in the end had become a source of so much grief and loss.

As the bike rolled past the hall Poppy saw the light showing through the front window of the library and tensed. Gaetano was staying over for the night?

'Yeah, he's still here,' Damien confirmed as he put his bike away. 'So what?'

'I'm going to speak to him—'

'What's the point?' her brother asked in a tone of defeat. 'Why should he care?'

But Gaetano *did* have a heart, Poppy thought in desperation. At least he had had a heart at the age of thirteen when his father had run over his dog and killed it. She had seen the tears in Gaetano's eyes and she had been crying too. Dino had been as much her dog as his because Dino had hung around with her when Gaetano was away at school, not that he had probably ever realised that. Dino had never been replaced and when she had asked why not in the innocent way of a child, Gaetano had simply said flatly, 'Dogs die.'

And she had been too young to really understand that outlook, that raising of the barriers against the threat of being hurt again. She had seen no tears in his remarkable eyes at his father's funeral but he had been almost as devastated as his grandfather when his grandmother passed away. But then the older couple had been more his parents than his real parents had. Within a year of becoming a widow, his mother had remarried and moved to Florida without her son.

Poppy breathed in deep as she marched round the side of the big house with Damien chasing in her wake.

'It's almost midnight!' he hissed. 'You can't go calling on him now!'

'If I wait until tomorrow I'll lose my nerve,' she said truthfully.

Damien hung back in the shadows, watching as she rang the doorbell and waited, her hands dug in the pockets of her faux-leather flying jacket. A voice sounded somewhere close by and she flinched in surprise, turning her head as a man in a suit talking into a mobile phone walked towards her in the moonlight.

'I'm security, Miss Arnold,' he said quietly. 'I was telling Mr Leonetti who was at the door.'

Poppy suppressed a rude word. She had forgotten the tight security with which the Leonetti family surrounded themselves. Of course, calling in on Gaetano late at night wouldn't go unquestioned.

'I want to see your boss,' she declared.

The security man was talking Italian into the phone and she couldn't follow a word of what he was saying. When the man frowned, she knew he was about to deliver a negative and she moved off the step and snapped, 'I *have* to see Gaetano! It's really important.'

Somewhere someone made a decision and a moment later there was the sound of heavy bolts being drawn back to open the massive front door. Another security man nodded acknowledgement and stood back for her entrance into the marble-floored hall with its perfect proportions and priceless paintings. A trickle of perspiration ran down between her taut shoulder blades and she straightened her spine in defiance of it although she was already shrinking at the challenge of what she would have to tell Gaetano. At this juncture, coming clean was her sole option.

Poppy Arnold? Gaetano's brain had conjured up several time-faded images. Poppy as a little girl paddling at the lake edge in spite of his warnings; Poppy sobbing over Dino with all the drama of her class and no thought of restraint; Poppy looking at him as if he might imminently walk on water when she was about fifteen, a scrutiny that had become considerably less innocent and entertaining a year later. And finally, Poppy, a taunting sensual smile tilting her lips as she sidled out of the shrubbery closely followed by a young estate worker, both of them engaged in righting their rumpled, grass-stained clothing.

Bearing in mind the number of years the Arnold family had worked for his own, he felt that it was only fair that he at least saw Poppy and listened to what she had to say in her mother's defence. He hadn't, however, thought about Poppy in years. Did she still live with her family? He was surprised, having always assumed Poppy would flee country life and the type of employment she had soundly trounced as being next door to indentured servitude in the modern world. Touching a respectful forelock had held no appeal whatsoever for outspoken, rebellious Poppy, he acknowledged wryly. How much had she changed? Was she working for him now somewhere on the pay roll? His ebony brows drew together in a frown at his ignorance as he lounged back against the edge of the library desk and awaited her appearance.

The tap-tap of high heels sounded in the corridor and the door opened to reveal legs that could have rivalled a Vegas showgirl's toned and perfect pins. Disconcerted by that startlingly unexpected and carnal thought, Gaetano ripped his attention from those incredibly long shapely legs and whipped it up to her face, only to receive another jolt. Time had transformed Poppy Arnold into a tall, dazzling redhead. He was staring but he couldn't help it while his shrewd brain was engaged in ticking off familiarities and changes. The bright green eyes were unaltered but the rounded face had fined down to an exquisite heart shape to frame slanting cheekbones, a dainty little nose and a mouth lush and pink enough to star in any male fantasy. The pulse at Gaetano's groin throbbed and he straightened, flicking his jacket closed to conceal his physical reaction while thinking that Poppy might well get the last laugh after all because the ugly duckling he had once rejected had become a swan.

'Mr Leonetti,' she said as politely as though they had never met before.

'Gaetano, please,' he countered wryly, seeing no reason to stand on ceremony with her. 'We have known each other since childhood.'

'I don't think I ever *knew* you,' Poppy said frankly, studying him with bemused concentration.

She had expected to notice unappetising changes in Gaetano. After all, he was almost thirty years old now and lived a deskbound, self-indulgent and, by all accounts, *decadent* life. By this stage he should have been showing some physical fallout from that lifestyle. But there was no hint of portliness in his very tall, powerfully built frame and certainly no jowls to mar the perfection of his strong, stubbled jaw line. And his dense blue-black curly hair was as plentiful as ever.

An electrifying silence enclosed them and Poppy stepped restively off one foot onto the other, her slender figure tense as a drawn bow string while she studied him. Taller and broader than he had been, he was even more gorgeous than he had been seven years earlier when she had fallen for him like a ton of bricks. Silly, silly girl that she had been, she conceded ruefully, but there was no denying that even then she had had good taste because Gaetano was stunning in the way so very few men were. A tiny flicker in her pelvis made her press her thighs together, warmth flushing over her skin. His dark eyes, set below black straight brows, were locked to her with an intensity that made her inwardly squirm. He had eyes with incredibly long thick lashes, she was recalling dizzily, so dark and noticeable in their volume that she had once suspected him of wearing guy liner like some of the boys she had known back then.

'Do you still live here with your mother and brother?' Gaetano enquired.

'Yes,' Poppy admitted, fighting to banish the fog that had briefly closed round her brain. 'You're probably wondering why I've come to see you at this hour. I'm a bartender at the Flying Horseman down the road and I've only just finished my shift.'

Gaetano was pleasantly surprised that she had contrived to speak two entire sentences without spluttering the profanities which had laced her speech seven years earlier. Of course, right now she was probably watching her every word with him, he reasoned. A bartender? He supposed it explained the outfit, which looked as though it would be more at home in a nightclub.

'I saw the newspaper article,' she added. 'Obviously you want to sack my mother for talking about the party and selling those photos. I'm not denying that you have good reason to do that.'

'Where did the photos come from?' Gaetano asked curiously. 'Who took them?'

Poppy winced. 'One of the guests invited my brother to join the party when she saw him outside directing cars. He did what I imagine most young men would do when they see half-naked women—he took pictures on his phone. I'm not excusing him but he didn't sell those photos… It was my mother who took his phone and did that—'

'I assume I'll see your mother in person tomorrow before I leave. But I'll ask you now. My family has always treated your mother well. Why did she *do* it?'

Poppy breathed in deep and lifted her chin, bracing herself for what she had to say. 'My mother's an alcoholic, Gaetano. They offered her money and that was all it took. All she was thinking about was probably how she would buy her next bottle of booze. I'm afraid she can't see beyond that right now.'

Taken aback, Gaetano frowned. He had not been prepared for that revelation. It did not make a difference to his attitude though. Disloyalty was not a trait he could overlook in an employee. 'Your mother must be a functioning alcoholic, then,' he assumed. 'Because the house appears to be in good order.'

'No, she's not functioning.' Poppy sighed, her soft mouth tightening. 'I've been covering up for her for more than a year. I've been looking after this place.'

His lean, darkly handsome features tightened. 'In other words there has been a concentrated campaign to deceive me as to what was going on here,' he condemned with a sudden harshness that dismayed her. 'At any time you could have approached me and asked for my understanding and even my help—yet you chose not to do so. I have no tolerance for deception, Poppy. This meeting is at an end.'

A hundred different thoughts flashing through her mind, Poppy stared at him, her heart beating very fast with nerves and consternation. 'But—'

'No extenuating circumstances allowed or invited,' Gaetano cut in with derision. 'I have heard all I need to hear from you and there is nothing more to say. *Leave.*'

CHAPTER TWO

POPPY TOOK A sudden step forward. 'Don't speak to me like that!' she warned Gaetano angrily.

'I can speak to you whatever way I like. I'm in my own home and it seems that you are one of my employees.'

'No, I'm not!' Poppy contradicted with unashamed satisfaction. 'I donated my services free for my mother's sake!'

'Let's not make it sound as if you dug ditches,' Gaetano fired back impatiently. 'As I'm so rarely here there can't be that much work concerned in keeping the house presentable.'

'I think you'd be surprised by how much work is involved in a place this size!' Poppy snapped back firely.

Anger made her green eyes shine blue-green like a peacock feather, Gaetano noted. 'I'm really not interested,' he said drily. 'And if you donated your services free that was downright stupid, not praiseworthy.'

Poppy almost stamped an enraged foot. 'I'm not stupid. How dare you say that? I could hardly charge you for the work my mother was already being paid to do, could I?'

Gaetano shrugged a broad shoulder, watching her tongue flick out to moisten her red-lipsticked mouth, imagining her doing other much dirtier things with it and then tensing with exquisite discomfort as arousal coursed feverishly through his lower body. She was sexy, smoulderingly so, he acknowledged grimly. 'I'm sure you're versatile enough to have found some way round that problem.'

'But not dishonest enough to do so,' Poppy proclaimed with pride. 'Mum was being paid for the job and it was done, so on that score you have no grounds for complaint.'

'I don't?' An ebony brow lifted in challenge. 'An alcoholic has been left in charge of the household accounts?'

'Oh, no, that's not been happening,' Poppy hastened to reassure him. 'Mum no longer has access to the household cash. I made sure of that early on.'

'Then how have the bills been paid?'

Poppy compressed her lips as she registered that he truly did not have a clue how his own household had worked for years. 'I paid them. I've been taking care of the accounts here since Dad died.'

'But you're not authorised!' Gaetano slammed back at her distrustfully.

'Neither was my father but he took care of them for a long time.'

Gaetano's frown grew even darker. 'Your father had access as well? What the hell?'

'Oh, for goodness' sake, are you always this rigid?' Poppy groaned in disbelief. 'Mum never had a head for figures. Dad always did the accounts for her. Your grandmother knew. Whenever your grandmother had a query about the accounts she had to wait until Mum had asked Dad for the answer. It wasn't a secret back then.'

'And how am I supposed to trust you with substantial sums of money when your brother was recently in prison for theft?' Gaetano demanded sharply. 'My accountants will check the accounts and, believe me, if there are any discrepancies I will be bringing in the police.'

Having paled when he threw his knowledge of Damien's conviction at her, Poppy stood very straight and still, her facial muscles tight with self-control. 'Damien got involved with a gang of car thieves but he didn't actually *steal* any of the cars. He's the mechanic who worked on the stolen vehicles before they were shipped abroad to be sold.'

'What a very fine distinction!' Gaetano derided, unimpressed.

Poppy raised her head high, green eyes flashing defiance like sparks. 'You get your accountants in to check the books. There won't be any discrepancies,' she fired back with pride. 'And don't be snide about my brother.'

'I wasn't being snide.'

'You were being snide from the pinnacle of your rich, privileged, feather-bedded life. Damien broke the law and he was punished for it,' Poppy told him. 'He's paid his dues and he's learned his lesson. Maybe you've never made any mistakes, Gaetano?'

'My mistake was in allowing that party to be held

here!' Gaetano slung back at her grittily. 'And don't drag my background or my wealth into this conversation. It's unfair—'

'Then don't be so superior!' Poppy advised. 'But maybe you can't help being the way you are.'

'Do you really think hurling insults at me is likely to further your cause?'

'You haven't even given me the chance to tell you what my cause is,' she pointed out. 'You're so argumentative, Gaetano!'

'*I'm*...argumentative?' Gaetano carolled in disbelief.

'I want you to give Mum another chance,' Poppy admitted doggedly. 'I know you're not feeling very generous. I know that having your kinky party preferences splashed all over the media has to have been embarrassing for you—'

'I do not have kinky preferences—'

'It's none of my business whether you do or not!' Poppy riposted. 'I'm not being judgemental.'

'How very generous of you in the circumstances,' Gaetano murmured icily.

'And if you're not being argumentative, you're being sarcastic!' Poppy flared back at him with raw resentment. 'Can you even *try* listening to me?'

'If you could try to refrain from commenting about my preferences, kinky or otherwise,' Gaetano advised flatly.

'May I take my shoes off?' she asked him abruptly. 'I've been standing all night and my feet are killing me!'

Gaetano shifted an impatient hand. 'Take them off.

Say what you have to say and then go. I'm bored with this.'

'You're so kind and encouraging,' Poppy replied in a honeyed tone of stinging sweetness as she removed her shoes and dropped several crucial inches in height, unsettled by the reality that, although she was five feet eight inches tall, he had a good six inches on her and now towered over her in a manner she instinctively disliked.

As she flexed those incredible long legs sheathed in black lace, Gaetano watched, admiring her long toned calves, neat little knees and long slender thighs. A flash of white inner thigh as she bent in that short skirt and her small full breasts shifting unbound below the clinging top sent his temperature rocketing and made his teeth grit. Was she teasing him deliberately? Was the provocative outfit a considered invitation? What woman dressed like that came to see a man at midnight with clean intentions?

'Talk, Poppy,' he urged very drily, infuriated at the way his brain was rebelling against his usual rational control and concentration to stray in directions he was determined not to travel.

'Mum has had it tough the last few years—'

Gaetano held up a silencing hand. 'I know about the stillbirth and of course your father's death and I'm heartily sorry for the woman, but those misfortunes don't excuse what's been happening here.'

'Mum needs help, not judgement, Gaetano,' Poppy argued shakily.

'I'm her employer, not her family and not a therapist,' Gaetano pointed out calmly. 'She's not my responsibility.'

In a more hesitant voice, Poppy added, 'Your grandfather always said we were one big family here.'

'Please don't tell me that you fell for that old chestnut. My grandfather is an old-fashioned man who likes the sound of such sentiments but somehow I don't think he'd be any more compassionate than I am when it comes to the security of his home. Leaving an untrustworthy and unstable alcoholic in charge here would be complete madness,' he stated coolly.

'Yes, but…you could give Mum's job to me,' Poppy reasoned in a desperate rush. 'I've been doing it to your satisfaction for months, so you've actually had a free trial. That way we could stay on in the flat and you wouldn't have to look for someone new.'

Discomfiture made Gaetano tense. 'You never wanted to do domestic work… I'm well aware of that.'

'We all have to do things we don't want to do, particularly when it comes to looking out for family,' Poppy argued with feeling. 'After Dad died I went back to my nursing course and left Damien looking after Mum. He couldn't cope. He didn't tell me how bad things had got here and because of that he got into trouble. Mum is my responsibility and I turned my back on her when she needed me most.'

Gaetano, who was unsurprised that she had sought a career outside domestic service, thought she had a ridiculously overactive conscience. 'It wouldn't work, Poppy. I'm sorry. I wish you well and I'm sorry I can't help.'

'*Won't* help,' she slotted in curtly.

'You're not my idea of a housekeeper. It's best that you make a new start somewhere else with your family,' he declared.

No, he definitely didn't want Poppy with her incredibly alluring legs in his house, even though he didn't visit it very often. She would be a dangerous temptation and he was determined that he would never go there. *Never muck around with staff* was a maxim etched in stone in Gaetano's personal commandments. When a former PA had thrown herself at him one evening early in his career he had slept with her. For him it had been a one-night stand on a business trip and nothing more, but she had been far more ambitious and it had ended messily, teaching him that professional relationships should never cross the boundaries into intimacy.

'It's not that easy to make a new start,' Poppy told him tightly. 'I'm the only one out of the three of us with a job and if I have to move I'll lose that.'

Gaetano expelled his breath on an impatient hiss. 'Poppy... I am not going to apologise for the fact that your mother breached her employment contract and plunged me into a scandal. You cannot lay her problems at my door. I have every sympathy for your position and, out of consideration for the years that your family worked here and did an excellent job, I will make a substantial final payment—'

'Oh, keep your blasted conscience money!' Poppy flung at him, suddenly losing her temper, her fierce pride stung by his attitude. He thought that she and her mother and her brother were a sad bunch of losers and he was so keen to get them off his property that he was prepared to pay more for the privilege. 'I don't want anything from you. I won't *take* anything more from you!'

'Losing your temper is a very bad idea in a situation like this,' he breathed irritably as she bent down to scoop up her shoes and turned on her heel, her short skirt flaring round her pert behind.

Poppy turned her head, green eyes gleaming like polished jewels. 'It's the only thing I've got left to lose,' she contradicted squarely.

Gaetano threw up his hands in a gesture of frustration. 'Then why the hell are you *doing* it? Put yourself first and leave your family to sort out their own problems!'

'Is that what the ruthless, callous banker would do to save his own skin?' Poppy asked scornfully as she reached the door. 'Mum and Damien are my family and, yes, they're very different from me. I take after Dad and I'm strong. They're not. They crumble in a crisis. Does that mean I love them any less? No, it doesn't. In fact it probably means I love them *more*. I love them warts and all and as long as there's breath in my body I'll look after them to the best of my ability.'

Gaetano was stunned into silence by her emotive words. He couldn't imagine loving anyone like that. His parents had ~~been~~ both been weak and fallible in their different ways. His father had chased thrills and his mother had chased money and Gaetano had only learned to despise them for their shallow characters. His parents had not had the capacity to love him and

once he had got old enough to understand that he had
stopped loving them, ultimately recognising that only
his grandparents genuinely cared about him and his
well-being. For that reason, the concept of continuing
to blindly love seriously flawed personalities and still
feel a duty of care towards them genuinely shocked
Gaetano, who was infinitely more discerning and demanding of those closest to him. He had seen Poppy
Arnold's strength and he admired it, but he thought she
was a complete fool to allow her wants and wishes to be
handicapped by the double burden of a drunken mother
and a pretty useless kid brother.

He went for a shower, still mulling over the encounter with a feeling of amazement that grew rather than
dwindled. Rodolfo Leonetti would have been hugely
impressed by Poppy's speech, he acknowledged grimly.
His grandfather, after all, had wasted years striving
to advise and support his feckless son and his friv-
olous daughter-in-law. Rodolfo had overlooked their
faults and had compassionately made the best of a bad
situation. Gaetano, however, was much tougher than
the older man, less patient, less forgiving, less sympathetic. Was that a flaw in him? he wondered for the
very first time.

Thinking of how much Rodolfo would have ap-
plauded Poppy's family loyalty, Gaetano reflected
equally on her flaws that Rodolfo would have cringed
from. Her background was dreadful, the family un-
palatable. Mother an alcoholic? Brother a convicted
criminal? Poppy's provocative clothing and use of bad
language? And yet wasn't Poppy Arnold an ordinary

girl of the type Rodolfo had always contended would make his grandson a perfect wife?

Having towelled himself dry, Gaetano got into bed naked and lay there, lost in thought. A sudden laugh escaped him as he momentarily allowed himself to imagine his grandfather's horror if he were to produce a young woman like Poppy as his future wife. Rodolfo was much more of a snob than he would ever be prepared to admit and it was hardly surprising that he should be for the Leonettis had been a family of great wealth and power for hundreds of years. Yet the same man had risked disinheritance when he had married a fisherman's daughter against his family's wishes. Gaetano couldn't imagine that kind of love. He felt no need for that sort of excessive emotion in his life. In fact the very idea of it terrified him and always had.

He didn't want to get married. Maybe by the time he was in his forties he would have mellowed a little and would feel the need to settle down with a companion. At some point too he should have a child to continue the family line. He flinched from the concept, remembering his father's temper tantrums and his mother's tears and nagging whines. Marriage had a bad image with him. Why couldn't Rodolfo understand and accept that reality? He was just too young for settling down but not too young to take over as CEO of the bank.

The germ of an idea occurred to Gaetano and struck him as weird, so he discarded it, only to take it out again a few minutes later and examine it in greater depth. Suppose he quite deliberately produced a fiancée whom his grandfather would deem wrong for him?

In that scenario nobody would be the slightest bit surprised when the engagement was broken off again and Rodolfo would be relieved rather than disappointed. He would see that Gaetano had made an effort to commit to a woman and honour that change accordingly by giving his grandson breathing space for quite some time afterwards. A fake incompatible fiancée could get him off the hook...

In the moonlight piercing the curtains, Gaetano's lean, darkly handsome features were beginning to form a shadowy smile. Pick an ordinary girl and she would naturally have to be beautiful if his grandfather was to be convinced that his fastidious grandson had fallen for her. Pick a beautiful ordinary girl guaranteed to be an embarrassment in public. Poppy could drop all the profanities she liked, dress like a hooker and tell everybody about her sordid family problems. He wouldn't even have to prime her to fail in his exclusive world. It was a given that she would be so out of her depth that she would automatically do so.

A sliver of the conscience that Gaetano rarely listened to slunk out to suggest that it would be a little cruel to subject Poppy to such an ordeal merely for the sake of initially satisfying and then hopefully changing his grandfather's expectations. But then it wouldn't be a real engagement. She would know from the outset that she was faking it and she would be handsomely paid for her role. Nor would she need to know that he was expecting, no, *depending* on her to be a social embarrassment to get him out of the engagement again. It would sort of be like *Pygmalion* in reverse, he reasoned with quiet satisfaction. Pick an ordinary girl, who was an extraordinary beauty and extremely outspoken and hot-tempered... She would be absolutely perfect for his purposes because she would be an accident waiting to happen.

Poppy barely slept that night. Gaetano had said and done nothing unexpected. Of course he wanted them off his fancy property, out of sight and out of mind! His incredulous attitude to her attachment to her family had appalled her though. And where were they going to go? And how would they live when they got there? She would have to throw them on the tender mercies of the social services. My goodness, would they end up living in one of those homeless hostels? Eating out of a food bank?

She got up early as usual, relishing that quiet time of day before her mother or her brother stirred. Even better it was a sunny morning and she took her coffee out to the tiny square of garden at the back of the building that was her favourite place in the world. Making plants flourish, simply growing things, gave her great pleasure.

A riot of flowers in pots ornamented the tiny paved area with its home-made bench seat that was more than a little rickety. However, her Dad had made that bench and she would never part with it. With the clear blue sky above and birds singing in the trees nearby, she felt guilty for feeling so stressed and unhappy. When she had been a little girl working by her father's side she had wanted to be a gardener. Assuming that that would inevitably mean one day working for the Leonettis, she had changed her mind, ignorant of the reality that there were a host of training courses and jobs in the horticultural world far from Woodfield Hall that she could have aspired to. Well, so much for her planned escape, she thought heavily. Now that they were being evicted, she didn't want to leave.

'Miss Arnold?' One of Gaetano's security men looked over the fence at her. 'Mr Leonetti wants to see you.'

Poppy leapt upright. Had he had second thoughts about his decision? She smoothed down the thin jacket she wore over a black gothic dress. She had expected Gaetano to demand to see her mother again and she had dressed up in her equivalent of armour to tell him that her mother would be incapable of even speaking to him until midday. She walked round the side of the building and headed towards the house.

'Mr Leonetti is waiting for you at the helicopter.'

So, he was planning to toss a two-minute speech at her and depart, Poppy gathered ruefully. It didn't sound as though he'd had a change of heart, did it? She followed the path to the helipad at the far side of the hall, identifying Gaetano as the taller man in the small clump of waiting males who included the pilot and Gaetano's security staff. In a pale grey exquisitely tailored designer suit, his arrogant dark head held high, Gaetano looked like a king, and as she moved towards him he stood there much like a king waiting for her to come to him. So, what was new? Gaetano Leonetti didn't have a humble bone in his magnificent body.

No, no, less of the magnificent, she scolded herself angrily. No way was she going to look admiringly at the male making her and her family homeless, even if he did have just cause!

'Good morning, Poppy,' Gaetano drawled, smooth as glass, scanning her appearance in the form-fitting black dress that brushed her knees and what appeared to be combat boots with keen appreciation. The jacket looked as if it belonged to a circus ringmaster and he almost smiled at the prospect of his grandfather's disquiet. Clearly, Poppy always dressed strangely and he could certainly work with that eccentricity. In fact the more eccentricities, the better. And she looked amazingly well in that weird outfit with her freckle-free skin like whipped cream and her hair tumbling in silky bronzed ringlets round her slight shoulders, highlighting her alluring face.

He was not attracted to her, he told himself resolutely. He could appreciate a woman's looks without wanting to bed her. He wasn't that basic in his tastes, was he? The incipient throb of a hard-on, however, hinted that he might be a great deal more basic than he wanted to believe. Of course that was acceptable too, Gaetano conceded shrewdly. Rodolfo was no fool and would soon notice any apparent lack of sexual chemistry.

Poppy thought about faking a posh accent like his and abandoned the idea because Gaetano would be slow to see the joke, if he saw one at all. 'Morning,' she said lazily in her usual abbreviated style.

'We're going out for breakfast since there's no food in the house,' Gaetano murmured huskily.

Poppy blinked, catching the flick of censure but too caught up in the positive purr of his deep, slightly accented drawl, which was sending a peculiar little shiver down her taut spine. *'We?'* she queried belatedly, green eyes opening very wide.

Gaetano noted that her pupils were surrounded by a ring of tawny brown that merely emphasised the bright green of her eyes and said quietly, 'I have a proposition I want to discuss with you.'

'A proposition?' she questioned with a frown.

'Breakfast,' Gaetano reminded her and he bent to plant his hands to her hips and swing her up into the helicopter before she could even guess his intention.

'For breakfast we get into a helicopter?' Poppy framed in bewilderment.

'We're going to a hotel.'

A proposition? Her mind was blank as to what possible suggestions he might be able to put to her in her family's current predicament and, although she was far from entertained by his virtual kidnapping, she knew she was in no position to tell him to get lost. Even so, Poppy would very much have enjoyed telling Gaetano to get lost. His innate dominant traits set her teeth on edge, not to mention the manner in which he simply assumed that everyone around him would jump to do his bidding without argument. And he was probably right in that assumption, she thought resentfully. He had money, power and influence and she had none of those things.

The craft was so noisy that there was no possibility of conversation during the short flight. Poppy peered down without surprise as the biggest, flashiest country-house hotel in the area appeared below them. Only the very best would do for Gaetano, she thought in exasperation, wishing she'd had some warning of his plan. She had no make-up on and not even a comb with her and wasn't best pleased to find herself about to enter a very snooty five-star establishment where everyone else, including her host, would be groomed to perfection. And here she was wearing combat boots ready to cycle to the shop for a newspaper.

Deliberately avoiding Gaetano's extended arms, Poppy jumped down onto the grass. 'You could've warned me about where we were going... I'm not dressed—'

Gaetano dealt her a slow-burning smile, dark golden eyes brilliant in the sunshine. 'You look fabulous.'

Her mouth ran dry and suddenly she needed a deep breath but somehow couldn't get sufficient oxygen into her lungs. That shockingly appealing smile...when he had never smiled at her before. Gaetano was as stingy as a miser with his smiles. Why *was* he suddenly smiling at her? What did he want? What had changed? And why was he telling her that she looked *fabulous*? Especially when his raised-brow appraisal as she'd approached him at the helipad had told her that he knew about as much about her style as she knew about high finance.

At the door of the hotel they were greeted by the manager as though they were royalty and ushered to the 'Orangery' where Gaetano was assured that they would not be disturbed. Had there been a chaise longue, Poppy would have flopped down on it like a Victorian maiden and would have asked Gaetano if he was plan-

ning a seduction just to annoy him. But if he had a
proposition that might ease her family's current situation she was more than willing to listen without making
cheeky comments, she told herself. Unfortunately, her
tongue often ran ahead of her brain, especially around
Gaetano, who didn't have to do much to infuriate her.

CHAPTER THREE

'THAT...ER...' POPPY hastily revised the word she had been about to employ for a more tactful one. 'That remark you made about there being no food in the house... We didn't know you were coming to the hall,' she reminded him.

Gaetano watched a waiter pull out a chair for Poppy before taking his own seat. Sunshine was cascading through the windows, transforming her bright hair into a fiery halo. She clutched her menu and ordered chocolate cereal and a hot-chocolate drink. He was astonished that the vast number of menu options had not tempted her into a more adventurous order.

'The hall is supposed to be kept fully stocked at all times,' Gaetano reminded her, having ordered.

Poppy shifted in her seat. 'But this way is much more cost-effective, Gaetano. When I took over from Mum I was chucking out loads of fresh food every week and it hurt me to do it when there are people starving in this world. Until yesterday, someone always phoned to say you'd be visiting, so I cancelled the food deliveries... Oh, yes, and the flowers as well. I'm not into weekly flower arranging. I've saved you so much money,' she told him with pride.

'I don't need to save money. I expect the house to always be ready for use,' Gaetano countered drily.

Poppy gave him a pained look. 'But it's so wasteful...'

Gaetano shrugged. He had never thought about that aspect and did not see why he should consider it when he gave millions to charitable causes every year. Convenience and the ability to do as he liked, when he liked, and at short notice, were very important to him, because he rarely took time away from work. 'I'm not tight with cash,' he said wryly. 'If the house isn't prepared for immediate use, I can't visit whenever I take the notion.'

Poppy ripped open her small packet of cereal and poured it into the bowl provided. Ignoring the milk on offer, she began to eat the cereal dry with her fingers the way she always ate it. For a split second, Gaetano stared but said nothing. For that same split second she had felt slightly afraid that he might give her a slap across the knuckles for what he deemed to be poor table manners and she flushed pink with chagrin, determined not to alter her behaviour to kowtow to his different expectations. The rich were definitely different, she conceded ruefully.

'I will eat chocolate any way I can get it,' she confided nonetheless in partial apology. 'I don't like my cereal soggy. Now this proposition you mentioned...'

'My grandfather wants me to get married before I can become Chief Executive of the Leonetti Bank. As I don't want to get married, I believe a fake engagement would keep him happy in the short term. It will convince Rodolfo that I am moving in the right direction and assuage his fear that I'm incapable of settling down.'

'So, why are you telling me this?' Poppy asked him blankly.

'I want you to partner me in the fake engagement.' Gaetano lounged lithely back in his seat to study her reaction.

'You and me?' A peal of startled laughter erupted from Poppy's lush pink mouth beneath Gaetano's disconcerted gaze. 'You've got to be kidding. No one, but no one, would credit you and me as a couple!'

'Funny, you didn't see it as being that amusing when you were a teenager,' Gaetano derided softly.

'You are *such* a bastard!' Poppy sprang out of her chair, all pretence of cool abandoned as she stalked away from the table. She had never quite contrived to lose that tender, stinging sense of rejection and humiliation even though she knew she was being ridiculous. After all, she had been far too young and naïve for him as well as being the daughter of an employee, and for him to respond in any way, even had he wanted to, would have been inappropriate. But while her brain assured her of those facts, her visceral reaction was at another level.

A few weeks after his rebuff, the annual hall summer picnic had been held and Gaetano had put in his appearance with a girlfriend. Poppy had felt sick when she'd seen that shiny, beautifully dressed and classy girl who might have stepped straight out of a glossy modelling advertisement. She had seen how pathetic it had been to harbour even the smallest hope of ever attracting Gaetano's interest and as a result of that distress, that horrid feeling of unworthiness and mortification, she had plunged herself into a very unwise situation.

'Poppy...' Gaetano murmured wryly, wishing he had left that reminder of the past decently buried.

Poppy spun back to him, eyes wide and accusing. 'I was sixteen years old, for goodness' sake, and you were the only fanciable guy in my radius, so it's hardly surprising that I got a crush on you. It was hormones, nothing else. I wasn't mature enough to recognise that you were *totally* the wrong kind of guy for me—'

'Why?' Gaetano heard himself demand baldly, although no sooner had he asked than he was questioning why he had.

Poppy was equally surprised by that question. Her colour high, she stared at him, her clear green eyes luminescent in the sunlight. 'Why? Well, I've no doubt you're a great catch, being both rich and ridiculously good-looking,' she told him bluntly. 'You're a fiercely ambitious high achiever but you don't have heart. You're deadly serious and conventional too. We're complete opposites. People would only pair the two of us together in a comic book. Sorry, I hope I haven't insulted you in any way. That wasn't my intention.'

An almost imperceptible line of colour had fired along the exotic slant of Gaetano's spectacular cheekbones. He felt oddly as though he had been cut down to size and yet he couldn't fault what she had said because it was all true. There was an electric little silence. He glanced up from below his lashes and saw her standing there in the bright sunshine, her hair a blazing nimbus of red, bronze and gold in the light to give her the look of a fiery angel. Or in that severe black dress, a gothic angel of death? But it didn't matter because in that strange little instant when time stopped dead, Gaetano, rigid with raw arousal, wanted Poppy Arnold more than he had ever wanted any woman in his life and it gave him the chills like the scent of a good deal going bad. He breathed in slow and deep and looked away from her, battling to regain his logic and cool.

'I still want you to take on the role of playing my fake fiancée,' he breathed in a roughened undertone because just looking at her, drinking in that clear creamy skin, those luminous green eyes and that pink succulent mouth, was only making him harder than ever. 'Rodolfo always wanted me to choose an ordinary girl and you are the only one I know likely to fit the bill.'

Something in the way he was studying her made Poppy's mouth run dry and her breath hitch in her throat. She was suddenly aware of her body in a way she hadn't been aware of it in years. In fact, her physical reactions were knocking her right back to the discomfiting level of the infatuated teenager she had once been and that galled her, but the tight, prickling sensation in her breasts and the dampness between her thighs were uniquely memorable testaments to the temptation Gaetano provided. Falling for a very good-looking guy at sixteen and comparing every other man she had met afterwards to his detriment was not to be recommended

as a life plan for any sensible woman, she reflected ruefully, ashamed of the fact that she couldn't treat Gaetano
as casually as she treated other men.

'An ordinary girl?' she questioned with pleated
brows, returning to the table to succumb to the allure
of the melted marshmallows topping her hot chocolate.
While she sipped, Gaetano filled her in on his grandfather's fond hopes for his future.

Poppy almost found herself laughing again. Gaetano
would never genuinely *want* an ordinary girl and no ordinary girl would be able to cope with his essentially
cold heart.

'So, why me?' she pressed.

'You're beautiful enough to convince him that I
could be tempted by you—'

Guileless green eyes assailed his. 'Am I?'

'Yes, you're beautiful but, no, I'm not tempted,'
Gaetano declared with stubborn conviction. 'When I
say fake engagement I mean fake in *every* way. I will
not be touching you.'

Poppy rolled her eyes. 'I wouldn't let you. I'm very,
very picky, Gaetano.'

Gaetano resisted the urge to toss up the name of that
young estate worker she had entertained in the shrubbery. Odd how he had never forgotten those details, he
conceded, while recognising that such a crack would
be cruelly inappropriate because she was as entitled
to have enjoyed sex as any other woman. His perfect
white teeth clenched together. He loathed the way Poppy
somehow knocked him off-balance, tripping his mind
into random thoughts, persuading his usually controlled

tongue into making ill-advised remarks, turning him on when he didn't want to be turned on. Each and every one of those reactions offended Gaetano's pride in his strength of will.

'You've got to be wondering what would be in this arrangement for you,' Gaetano intoned quietly. 'Everything you want and need at present. Rehabilitation treatment for your mother, a fresh start somewhere, a new home for you all as security. I'll cover the cost of it all if you do this for me, *bella mia.*'

Straight off, Poppy saw that he was throwing her and her family a lifebelt when they were drowning and for that reason she didn't voice the refusal already brimming on her lips. Treatment for her mother. You couldn't put a price on such an offer. It was what she had dreamt about but knew she would never be able to afford.

'You've got to have a selfish bone somewhere in your body,' Gaetano declared. 'If you get your mother sorted out you can get your own life back and complete your nursing training, if that is still what you want to do.'

'I'm not sure I could be convincing as your ordinary-girl fiancée—'

'We'll cover that. Leave the worrying to me. I'm a skilled strategist,' Gaetano murmured, lush black lashes low over his beautiful dark golden eyes.

Her chest swelled as she dragged in a deep breath because really there was no decision to be made. Any attempt to sort out the mess her mother's life had become was worth a try. 'Then…where do I sign up?'

She had agreed. Having recognised that Poppy was pretty much between a rock and a hard place, Gaetano was not surprised by her immediate agreement. In his opinion she had much to gain and nothing at all to lose.

'So…er…' Poppy began uncertainly. 'You'll want me to dress up more…?'

A sudden wolfish smile flashed across Gaetano's lean, darkly handsome features. 'No, that's exactly what I don't want,' he assured her. 'Rodolfo would see straight through you trying to pretend to be something you're not. I don't want you to feel the need to change anything—just be yourself.'

'Myself…' Poppy repeated a tad dizzily as she collided with shimmering dark golden eyes fringed by those glorious spiky black lashes of his.

'Be yourself,' Gaetano stressed, severely disconcerting her because she had expected him to want to change everything about her. 'My grandfather, like me, respects individuality.'

Poppy wondered how it was then that, even in recent years, she had noticed from reading the papers, and catching a glimpse or two of past companions at the hall, Gaetano's women all seemed to be formed from the same identikit model. All were small, blonde and blue-eyed arm-clingers, who appeared to have no personality at all in his presence. The sort of women who simpered, hung on his every word and acted super-attentive to their man. No, Gaetano had definitely never struck her as a male likely to appreciate individuality.

'I would have another request,' she said daringly. 'My brother's a fully qualified mechanic. Find him a job.'

Gaetano frowned. 'He's an—'

'An ex-con. Yes, we are well aware of that, but he needs a proper job before he can hope to rebuild his life,' she pointed out. 'I'd be very grateful if there was anything you could do to help Damien.'

Gaetano's beautifully shaped mouth tightened. 'You drive a hard bargain. I'll make enquiries.'

Almost a full month after that breakfast, Poppy was sitting in the kitchen with her mother. Jasmine was studying her daughter and looking troubled, an expression that had become increasingly frequent on her face as she slowly emerged from the shrouding fog of alcoholic dependency and realised what had been happening in the world around her. Initial assessment followed by several sessions with trained counsellors and medication for her depression had brought about an improvement in Jasmine's state of mind. The older woman was trying not to drink, not doing very well so far but at least trying, something she had not even been prepared to contemplate just weeks earlier. This very afternoon Poppy and her mother were heading to London where Poppy would join Gaetano and take up her role as a fake fiancée while Jasmine embarked on a residential stay in a top-flight private clinic renowned for its success with patients.

'I just don't want to see you get hurt,' the older woman repeated, squeezing her daughter's hand. 'Gaetano is a real box of tricks. I appreciate his help, but I would never fully trust him. He's too clever and he hasn't got his granddad's humanity. I can't understand what's in this masquerade for Gaetano—'

'Climbing the career ladder at the bank—promotion. Seems that Rodolfo Leonetti is a real stick-in-the-mud about Gaetano still being single.' Poppy sighed, having already been through this dialogue several times with her mother and wishing the subject could simply be dropped.

'Yes, but how will it benefit Gaetano when your engagement is broken off again?' Jasmine prompted. 'That's the bit I don't get.'

Poppy didn't really get it either but kept that to herself. How was she supposed to know what went on in Gaetano's multifaceted brain? Apart from anything else she'd had hardly any contact with him since that hotel breakfast they'd shared. He had phoned her with instructions and information about arrangements for her mother and travel plans, but he had not returned to the hall. In the meantime, a new housekeeper had moved into Woodfield Hall and Poppy assumed that the giant refrigerator was being kept fully stocked and vases of flowers were now once again decorating the mansion for the owner who never visited. Gaetano had dismissed Poppy's opinions with an assurance that made it clear that his household arrangements were not and never would be any of her business.

The helicopter picked them up at two in the afternoon. Poppy had packed for both her and her mother, who was being taken to the clinic. Jasmine was nervous and not entirely sober when they boarded and fairly shaky on her legs by the time they landed in London, leaning on her daughter's arm for support.

Gaetano, however, didn't even notice Jasmine Ar-

nold. He was too busy watching Poppy stroll towards
him with that lithe, lazy walk of hers. She wore black
and red plaid leggings and a black tee, her hair falling
in wind-tousled curls round her heart-shaped face. He
saw other men taking a second glance at her and it annoyed him. She was unusual and it gave her a distinction that he couldn't quite put a label on but one quality
she had in spades and that was sex appeal, he acknowledged grimly, struggling to maintain control of what
lay south of his belt. He would get accustomed to her
and that response would fade because nothing, not one
single intimate thing, was going to take place between
them. This was business and he was no soft touch.

The staff member from the clinic designated to pick
up Jasmine intercepted Poppy and her mother. The
women parted with a hug and tears in their eyes, for
the guidelines of Jasmine's treatment plan had warned
that the clinic preferred there to be no contact between
their patients and families during the first few weeks of
treatment. That was why Poppy's first view of Gaetano
was blurred because she had been watching her mother
nervously walk away and, while knowing that she was
doing the best thing possible for her troubled parent,
she still felt horribly guilty about it.

'Poppy...' Gaetano murmured, one of his security
men taking immediate charge of her luggage trolley.

His lean, darkly handsome features swam through
the glimmer of tears in her wide eyes and sliced right
through her detachment. He looked utterly gorgeous,
sheathed in designer jeans and a casual white and blue
striped shirt that accentuated the glow of his bronzed

skin colour. For a split second, Poppy simply stared in search of a flaw in his classically beautiful face. At some stage she stopped breathing without realising it and, connecting with dark golden eyes the same shade as melting honey, she suddenly felt so hot she was vaguely surprised that people didn't rush up with fire extinguishers to put out the blaze. Her heartbeat thumped as the noise of their surroundings inexplicably ebbed. A little tweaking sensation in her pelvis caused her to shift her feet while her nipples pinched full and tight below her tee.

'G-Gaetano...' she stammered, barely able to find her voice as she fought a desperate rearguard reaction to what she belatedly realised was a very dangerous susceptibility to Gaetano's magnetic attraction.

Gaetano was taking in the tenting prominence of her nipples below her top and idly wondering what colour they were, arousal moving thickly and hungrily through his blood as he studied her lush pink mouth. 'We're going straight back to my house,' he told her brusquely, snapping back to full attention. 'You've got work to do this evening.'

'Work?' Poppy parroted in surprise as she fell into step by his side.

'I've made up some prompt sheets for you to cover the sort of details you would be expected to know about me if we were in a genuine relationship,' he explained. 'Once you memorise all that we'll be ready to go tomorrow.'

'*Tomorrow?*' She gasped in dismay because seemingly he wasn't giving her any time at all to practise her new role or even prepare for it.

'It's Rodolfo's seventy-fifth birthday and he's throwing an afternoon party. Obviously we will be attending it as an engaged couple,' Gaetano explained smoothly.

Nerves clenched and twisted in Poppy's uneasy tummy. She had probably met Rodolfo Leonetti at some stage but she had no memory of the occasion and could only recall seeing him in the distance at the hall when he had still lived there. She had known his late wife, Serafina, well, however, and remembered her clearly. Gaetano's grandmother had been a lovely woman, who treated everyone the same, be they rich or poor, family or staff. Alongside Jasmine, Serafina had taught Poppy how to bake. Recollecting that, Poppy knew exactly what she would be doing in terms of a gift for the older man's birthday.

Her cases were stowed in the sleek expensive car Gaetano had brought to the airport. Damien could probably have told her everything about the vehicle because he was a car buff, but Poppy was too busy marvelling that Gaetano had taken the time to come and pick her up personally and that he was actually driving himself.

His phone rang as they left the airport behind. It was in hands-free mode and the voluble burst of Italian that banished the silence in the car only made Poppy feel more out on a limb than ever. She had to toughen up, she told herself firmly, and regain her confidence. Gaetano had given her the equivalent of a high-paid job and she planned to do the best she could to meet his no doubt high expectations but secretly, deep down inside where only she knew how she felt, Poppy was totally terrified of doing something wrong and letting Gaetano down.

Gaetano was so incredibly particular, she reflected absently, recalling the look on his face when she'd eaten her chocolate cereal with her fingers. Even little mistakes would probably irritate Gaetano. He wasn't tolerant or understanding. No, Poppy knew it wasn't going to be easy to fake anything to Gaetano's satisfaction. In fact she reckoned she was in for a long, hard walk down a road strewn with endless obstacles. While the animated dialogue in Italian went on for what seemed a very long time, Poppy looked out at the busy London streets. Once or twice when she glanced in the other direction she noted the aggressive angle of Gaetano's jaw line that suggested tension and picked up on the hard edge to his dark-timbre drawl and clipped responses.

'Our goose has been cooked,' Gaetano breathed curtly when the phone call was over. 'That was Rodolfo. He wants to meet you now.'

'Now…like right now, *today*?' Poppy exclaimed in dismay.

'Like right now,' Gaetano growled. 'And you're not ready.'

Poppy's eyes flashed. 'And whose fault is that?'

'What do you mean?'

'You shouldn't have waited until the last possible moment to clue me up on what I'm supposed to know about you,' Poppy pointed out without hesitation. 'Sensible people prepare for anything important *more* than one day in advance.'

'Don't you dare start criticising me!' Gaetano erupted,

sharply disconcerting her as he flashed a look of angry, flaming censure. 'It's more than twenty-four hours since I even slept. We've had a crisis deal at the bank and this stupid business was the very last thing on my mind.'

'If it's so stupid you can forget about it again.' Poppy proffered that get-out clause stiffly. 'Don't mind me. This was, after all, *your* idea, *all* your idea.'

'I can't forget about it again when I've already told Rodolfo I'm engaged!' Gaetano launched back at her furiously. 'Whether I like it or not, I'm *stuck* with you and faking it!'

'Oh, goody…aren't I the lucky girl?' Poppy murmured in a poisonous undertone intended to sting. 'You're such a catch, Gaetano. All that money and success but not a single ounce of charm!'

'Be quiet!' Gaetano raked at her with incredulity.

'Go stuff yourself!' Poppy tossed back fierily as he shot the car to a halt outside a tall town house in a fancy street embellished with a central garden.

'And you're stuck with me,' Gaetano asserted with grim satisfaction as he closed her wrist in a grip of steel to prevent her leaping out of the car. He flipped open the ring box in his other hand and removed the diamond engagement ring to shove it onto her wedding finger with no ceremony whatsoever.

'Oh, dear…ugly ring alert,' Poppy snapped, studying the huge diamond solitaire with unappreciative eyes. 'Of course, it's one of those fake diamonds…right?'

'Of course it's not a fake!' Gaetano bit out, what little patience he had decimated by lack of sleep and her unexpectedly challenging behaviour.

'It's hard to believe that you can spend that much money and end up with something that looks like it fell out of a Christmas cracker.' Poppy groaned. 'I can't go in there, Gaetano.'

'Get out of the car,' he urged, leaning across to open the door for her. 'Of course you can go in there and wing it. Just look all intoxicated with your ring.'

'Yes, getting drunk in receipt of this non-example of good taste would certainly be understandable.'

'You're supposed to be in love with me!' Gaetano roared at her.

'Trouble is, you're about as loveable as a grizzly bear,' Poppy opined, walking round the bonnet and up onto the pavement. 'My acting skills may be poor but yours are a great deal worse.'

'What the hell are you talking about?' Gaetano squared up to her, six feet four inches of roaring aggression and impatience. 'It's time to stop messing about and start acting.'

Poppy lifted a hand and stabbed his broad muscular chest with a combative forefinger. 'But you *said* you wanted me to be myself. What exactly do you want, Gaetano?'

'*Porca miseria!* I want you to stop driving me insane!' Gaetano bit out wrathfully, backing her up against the wing of the car, long powerful thighs entrapping her. 'I will tell you only once. If you can't do as you're told you're out of here!'

'I'm only just resisting the urge to use some very rude words,' Poppy warned him, standing her ground with defiant green eyes. 'This is all *your* fault. You've dragged me here straight from the airport knowing I'm not remotely prepared for this meeting.'

And for Gaetano, whose aggressive need to dominate had emerged in the nursery when he had systematically bullied his first nanny into letting him do pretty much whatever he wanted, that resistance was like a red rag to a bull. Totally unaware of anything beyond the overwhelming desire to touch her while forcing her to do what he wanted her to do, Gaetano snapped an arm round her and kissed her.

His mouth slammed down on hers and it was as if the world stopped dead and then closed round that moment. She was in such a rage with him, it was a reflex reaction for Poppy to close her teeth together, refusing him entry. He shifted against her, all lean, sinuous, powerful male, and the erection she could feel nudging against her stomach sent the most overwhelming awareness shimmying through her like a dangerous drug. The heat and strength of him against her was even more arousing and she unclamped her teeth for him, helpless in the grip of the driving hunger that had captured her and destroyed her opposition.

With a hungry groan, his tongue eased into her mouth and it was without a doubt the most heart-stopping instant of sensation she had ever experienced as his tongue teased and tangled with hers before plunging deep. An ache she had never felt in a man's arms before hollowed almost painfully at the heart of her and she was pushing instinctively against him even as he urged her back against the car, so that they were welded together so tight a card couldn't have slid between them.

Her arms went round him, massaging up over his wide shoulders before sliding up to lace into his luxuriant black hair and then raking down again over his muscled arms to spread across his taut masculine ass. It was a mindless, addictive, totally visceral embrace.

In an abrupt movement, Gaetano stepped back from her, his breathing audible, sawing in and out of his big chest as if he had run a marathon. Poppy was all over the place mentally and she blinked, literally struggling to return to the real world while fighting a shocking desire to yank him bodily back to her. He was so hot at kissing she was ready to spontaneously combust. He might not have an ounce of charm but when it came to the sex stuff he was out at the front of the field, she decided, a burning blush warming her face as she too worked to get her breath back.

'Well…that was interesting,' she remarked shakily, feeling the need to say something, anything that might suggest that she had regained control when she had not.

Gaetano, who never, *ever* did PDAs with women, was horribly aware of his bodyguards standing by staring as if a little Martian had taken his place. In short, Gaetano was in shock but he also knew that if he had been parked somewhere private he would have had Poppy spread across the bonnet while he plunged into her lithe body hard and fast and sated the appalling level of hunger coursing through his lower body. He ached; he ached so bad he wanted to groan out loud. Dark colour etched the line of his high cheekbones.

'Let's go inside,' he suggested in a driven undertone. 'Just take your lead from me, *bella mia*.'

And won't doing exactly as Gaetano tells you be fun? a little devil enquired inside Poppy's bemused head. If it had related to kissing, she would have been queuing up, she conceded numbly. Nobody had ever made her feel so much with one kiss. In fact she hadn't known it was even possible to be that turned on by a man after just one kiss. Gaetano had hidden depths, dark, sexy depths, but she had not the smallest intention of plumbing those depths…

CHAPTER FOUR

'I SAW YOU ARRIVE,' Rodolfo Leonetti volunteered, disconcerting his grandson. 'It looked as though you were having words.'

Poppy almost froze by Gaetano's side, her discomfiture sweeping through her like a tidal wave. Gaetano's grandfather didn't look his age. With his head of wavy grey hair and the upright stature of a much younger man, not to mention a height not far short of Gaetano's, he still looked strong and vital. He greeted her with a kiss on both cheeks and smiled warmly at her before unleashing that unsettling comment on Gaetano.

'We were having a row,' Poppy was taken aback to hear Gaetano admit. 'Poppy doesn't like her engagement ring. Perhaps I should have taken her with me to choose it...'

Rodolfo widened his shrewd dark eyes. 'My grandson left you out of that selection?'

Pink and flustered by the speed with which Gaetano plotted and reacted in a tight corner, Poppy said, 'I'm afraid so...' In an uncertain movement she extended her hand for the older man to study the ring.

'You could see that diamond from outer space,' Rodolfo remarked, straight-faced.

'It's beautiful,' Poppy hastened to add.

'Be honest, you hate it,' Gaetano encouraged, having told the story, clearly happy to go with the flow.

'It's too bling for me,' she murmured dutifully, sinking down into the comfortable seat Rodolfo had indicated. Her nerves were strung so tight that her very face felt stiff with tension. She barely had the awareness to take in the beautiful big reception room, which strongly resembled the splendour of the reception rooms at Woodfield Hall.

'I was very sorry to hear about your mother's problems,' Gaetano's grandfather said while Poppy was pouring the tea, having been invited to do the hostess thing for the first time in her life. She almost dropped the teapot at Rodolfo's quietly offered expression of sympathy. Evidently Gaetano had been honest about her mother's predicament. 'I'm sure the clinic will help her.'

'I hope so.' Poppy compressed her lips as Rodolfo got to his feet and excused himself. As the door swung in his wake, Poppy groaned out loud. 'I'm no good at this, Gaetano—'

'You'll improve. He must've seen us kissing. That will have at least made us look like a proper couple,' he pointed out soft and low. 'Sometimes not having a script is better.'

'I would work better from a script.' She slanted a glance at him, encountering smouldering dark golden eyes, and pink surged into her cheeks.

Rodolfo reappeared and sank back into his seat. He

had a small box in his hand, which he opened. 'This was your grandmother's ring. As all her jewellery will go to your wife I thought it would be a good idea to let Poppy have a look at Serafina's engagement ring now.'

Poppy stared in astonished recognition at the fine diamond and ruby cluster on display. 'I remember your wife taking it off when she was baking,' she shared quietly. 'It's a fabulous ring.'

'It belongs to you now,' Rodolfo said with gentle courtesy and the sadness in his creased eyes made her eyes sting.

'She was a lovely person,' Poppy whispered shakily.

Gaetano couldn't credit what he was seeing. His fake fiancée and Rodolfo were having a mutual love-in, full of exchanged glances and sentimental smiles of understanding. His grandfather was sliding his beloved late wife's ring onto Poppy's finger as if she were Cinderella having the glass slipper fitted.

'I believe she would have been happy for you to wear it,' the old man said fondly, admiring it on Poppy's hand, the giant diamond solitaire purchased by Gaetano now abandoned on the coffee table.

'Thank you very much,' Poppy responded chokily. 'It's gorgeous.'

'And it comes with a very happy history in its back story,' Rodolfo shared mistily.

Gaetano wanted to groan out loud. He wanted his grandfather to disapprove of Poppy, not welcome her with open arms and start patting her hand while he talked happily about his late wife, Serafina. Of course, a little initial enthusiasm was to be expected, he reasoned shrewdly, and Rodolfo would hardly feel critical in the first fine flush of his approval of the step that Gaetano had taken.

Afternoon tea stretched into dinner, by which time Gaetano was heartily bored with family stories. With admirable tact and patience, however, Poppy had listened with convincing interest to his grandfather recount Leonetti family history. She had much better manners than Gaetano had expected and her easy relaxation with the older man was even more noteworthy because few people relaxed around Rodolfo, who was considerably more clever and ruthless than he appeared. If Poppy had been his real fiancée, Gaetano would have been ecstatic at the warmth of her reception. Indeed one could have been forgiven for thinking that Rodolfo had waited his entire life praying for the joy of seeing his grandson bring the housekeeper's daughter home and announce that he was planning to marry her. Only when Poppy began smothering yawns did Gaetano's torture end.

'Time for us to leave.' Gaetano tugged a drooping Poppy out of her seat with a powerful hand.

'Hope we don't have to go far,' she mumbled sleepily.

Encountering the older man's startled glance at his bride-to-be's ignorance, Gaetano straightened and smiled. 'She hasn't been here before,' he pointed out. 'I wanted to surprise her.'

'What surprise?' Poppy pressed as he walked her out of the drawing room.

'Rodolfo had an entire wing of this house converted

for me to occupy ten years ago,' he told her, throwing wide a door at the foot of the corridor. 'All we have to do is walk through a connecting door and we're in my space.'

And even drowsy as she was it was very obvious to Poppy that Gaetano's part of the house was a hugely different space. Rich colours, heavy fabrics and polished antiques were replaced by contemporary stone floors, pale colours and plain furniture. It was as distinct as night was to day from his grandfather's house. 'Elegant,' she commented.

'I'm glad you think so.' Gaetano showed her upstairs into the master bedroom. 'This is where we sleep…'

Poppy froze, her brain snapping into gear again. *'We?'*

'We can't stay this close to Rodolfo and pretend to be engaged *without* sharing a room,' Gaetano fired back at her impatiently. 'His staff service this place as well as his.'

'But you didn't *warn* me about this!' Poppy objected. 'Naturally I assumed you had an apartment somewhere on your own where I'd have my own room.'

'Well, you can't have your own room here,' Gaetano informed her without apology. 'Doubtless Rodolfo would like to think you're the vestal-virgin type, but he wouldn't find it credible that I had asked you to marry me…'

Poppy studied the huge divan sleigh bed and her soft mouth compressed. 'For goodness' sake, there's only one bed…and I'm not sharing it with you!'

'You have to sleep in here with me. There's a downside for both of us in this arrangement,' Gaetano countered grimly.

'And what's *your* downside?' Poppy asked with interest.

'Celibacy,' Gaetano intoned very drily. 'I can't risk being seen or associated with any other woman while I'm supposed to be engaged to you.'

'Oh, dear…' Poppy commented without an atom of sympathy. 'From what I've read about your usual pursuits in the press, that will be a character-building challenge for you.'

Exasperation laced Gaetano's lean, darkly handsome features. He would never ever hurt a woman but there were times when he wanted to plunge Poppy head first into a mud bath. 'There's a lot of rubbish talked about my private life in the newspapers.'

'That line might work with one of your socialites, Gaetano…but *not* with me. I know that party *did* take place and what happened at it.'

Gaetano fought the urge to defend himself and collided with her witchy green eyes and momentarily forgot what he had been about to say. 'I'm going for a shower,' he said instead and began to undress.

Leonetti flesh alert! screamed a little voice in Poppy's head as Gaetano shed his shirt without inhibition. And why would he be inhibited when he was unveiling a work of art? He was all sleek muscle from the vee above his lean hips to the corrugated muscular flatness of his abdomen and the swelling power of his pectoral muscles. Her mouth ran dry. She might not be the vestal-virgin type but she *was* a virgin and she had never shared a room with a half-naked male before. That was not information she planned to share with Gaetano, especially as she pretty much blamed him for the reality that she had yet to take that sexual plunge in adulthood.

At sixteen, after his rejection, she had almost decided to have sex with someone else but had realised what she was doing in time and had called a halt before things got out of hand. She wasn't proud of that episode, well aware that she had acted like a bit of a tease with the boy concerned. Her real lesson had been grasping that going off to have mindless sex with someone else because Gaetano didn't want her was pathetic and silly. While she was at college doing her nursing training she had had boyfriends and occasional little moments of temptation but nobody had tempted her as much as Gaetano had once tempted her. And Poppy was stubborn and had decided that she would only sleep with someone when she really, *really* wanted to. She wasn't going to have sex just because some man expected it of her, nor was she planning to have sex just for the sake of it.

Poppy opened one of her cases and only then appreciated that her luggage had already been unpacked for her. So this was how the rich lived, she thought ruefully, wondering what she was going to use as pyjamas when she didn't ever wear them because she preferred to sleep naked. She had nothing big enough to cover her decently in mixed company and she rifled through Gaetano's drawers to borrow a big white tee shirt that was both large and sexless. He might have forgotten that kiss, that terrifying surge of limitless hunger…but she hadn't and she had no plans to tempt fate.

* * *

Gaetano was thinking about sex in the shower and wondering if Poppy would consider broadening their agreement. He wanted her and she wanted him. To his outlook that was a simple balanced equation and it made sense that they should make the most of each other for the duration of their relationship. It was the practical solution and Gaetano was always practical, particularly when it came to his high sex drive.

A towel knotted round his lean hips, Gaetano trod back into the bedroom. Poppy took one look at all that bronzed skin still sprinkled with drops of water and re-alised that she wanted to lick him like a postage stamp. With a stifled groan at her own atrocious weakness, she pushed past him and went into the bathroom to get changed.

Gaetano pulled on boxers on the grounds that it never paid to take anything for granted with women and that doing so only annoyed them. Poppy emerged from the bathroom wearing what could only be one of his tee shirts because it hung off her slender frame in loose folds. Even so, it still couldn't hide the promi-nent little peaks of her breasts, the womanly curve of her hips or the perfection of the long shapely legs below the hem.

'I have a suggestion to make,' Gaetano murmured huskily.

'Do I want to hear this?' Poppy wisecracked, pushing back the bedding and scrambling into the bed, feeling her limbs settle into an incredibly soft and supportive mattress that was a far cry from the ancient lumpy bed of her youth. Wearing only silk boxers Gaetano was an outrageously masculine presence and very hard for Poppy to ignore. She was trying to respect his space by not looking at him and hoping he would award her the same courtesy of acting as though she were still fully clothed.

'We have to pretend to be lovers,' Gaetano pointed out.

Wondering in what possible direction that statement could be travelling, Poppy prompted, 'Yes...so?'

'Why don't we make it real?' Gaetano drawled, smooth as melted honey.

Her vocal cords went into arrest and respecting his space suddenly became much too challenging. *'Real?'* Poppy exclaimed loudly. 'What exactly do you mean by real?'

'You're not that innocent,' Gaetano assured her lazily as he sprang into bed beside her.

'So, you're suggesting that we have sex because you don't fancy celibacy?' Poppy enquired, delicate auburn brows raised in disbelief.

'We are stuck in this situation,' Gaetano reminded her.

'I can live without sex,' Poppy told him tightly, feeling colour climb hotly towards her hairline because even saying 'sex' in Gaetano's presence made her feel horribly self-conscious.

'I can as well but not happily,' Gaetano told her bluntly. 'We're very attracted to each other. We might as well make the most of it.'

'Any port in a storm?' Poppy remarked without

amusement. 'I'm here in the bed and, as you see it, available, so I should be interested?'

Gaetano leant closer, his stubbled jaw line propped on the heel of his upraised hand as he gazed down at her with absolutely gorgeous dark golden eyes. 'I'm good, *bella mia*. You wouldn't be disappointed.'

Poppy was as frozen with fear as a woman facing a hungry cannibal might be. But insidious heat and dampness were welling in the tender place between her thighs, striving to work their wicked seductive magic on her resistance. In fact she could feel her whole body literally wake up, sit up and take notice of Gaetano's offer. He was offering her what she had once desperately wanted but on terms she could never accept. 'I don't want to be used.'

'I'm surprised you're so narrow in your outlook. Wouldn't you be using me to scratch the same itch?' Gaetano enquired softly.

Her whole face flamed and she flipped over on her side, turning her narrow back defensively on him. Get thee behind me, Satan, she thought helplessly. 'No, thanks,' she said chokily, unsure whether she wanted to laugh or cry at his blunt proposition. 'If I want meaningless sex I imagine I can get it just about anywhere.'

Gaetano stroked a long brown forefinger down her taut spinal cord. 'Sex with me wouldn't be meaningless. It would be amazing. You set me on fire, *gioia mia*.'

Poppy rolled her eyes. He was so slick and full of confidence but that caressing touch lingered with her, lighting up little pockets of melting willingness inside her treacherous body. 'I'll keep it in mind. If my itch has to be scratched I will seriously consider you,' she lied stonily.

'What more do you want from me?' Gaetano asked silkily. 'I'm honest. I'm clean. I don't lie or cheat.'

'It doesn't stop you from being a four-letter word of a man,' Poppy told him roundly. 'I thought Italian lovers were supposed to be the last word in seduction. You just turned me off big time.'

'I was respecting your intelligence by not shooting you a line,' Gaetano traded with husky amusement that laced through his dark deep drawl in a sexy, accented purr.

Poppy pictured herself flipping over and slapping him so hard his perfect teeth rattled in his too ingenious head. Her own teeth gritted aggressively. Without warning she was also imagining easing back into the hard, allmale heat of him while his arms closed round her and his hips moved against hers. And that sensual imagery was so energising that she felt boiling hot all over. Her nipples swelled and prickled and the heat in her pelvis mushroomed. Her face burned with shame in the darkness. Wanting was wanting, she reasoned with the sexual side of her nature, but it wasn't enough on its own. Gaetano wasn't the man for her, she reminded herself doggedly.

'You know, if you were a nice guy—'

'When did I ever say I was a nice guy?' Gaetano cut in sharply.

'You didn't,' Poppy conceded grudgingly, turning over to pick out the powerful silhouette of his head and shoulders in the dim light. 'But you shouldn't be thinking about your sex life. Right now you should be worrying more about how your grandfather is going to feel when this engagement falls through. Because he's making such an effort to be welcoming and accepting of someone like me, I think he'll be devastated when our relationship comes to nothing.'

'Allow me to know my own grandfather better than you.'

'You're too focused on your career plan to see beyond it. What I saw today was that Rodolfo was incredibly happy about you getting engaged. How could he be anything other than upset when it breaks down?'

Gaetano grimaced and flung his dark head back against the pillows. She didn't understand. How could she? He could hardly tell her that she was supposed to bomb as a fiancée so that her disappearance from his life again would be more worthy of celebration than disappointment. Time would take care of that problem. After all, she had most likely been on her very best behaviour at her first meeting with his grandfather and sooner rather than later she would probably let herself down.

'You used to swear a lot,' he remarked out of the blue.

'I picked it up at school because everyone used bad language. For a while I did it deliberately because I was being bullied and I was desperate to fit in,' she confided.

'Did it make a difference?'

'No,' she admitted with a wry laugh. 'Nothing I wore or did or said could make me cool. Being plump with red hair and living at Woodfield Hall with "those posh bastards" was a supreme provocation to the other pupils.'

'What did the bullies do?'

Thinking of her getting bullied, Gaetano was experiencing an extraordinary desire to pull her into his arms and comfort her. But he didn't do comforting. Indeed he was downright unnerved by that perverse impulse and he actually shifted as far away from her as he could get and still be in the same bed.

'All the usual. Name calling, tripping me up, nasty rumours and messages and texts,' she recited wearily. 'I hated school, couldn't wait to get out of there. Once I was out, I stopped swearing as soon as I realised it offended people.'

He was tempted to tell her that she had never been plump. She had simply developed her womanly curves before she shot up in height. But right then he didn't want to talk and he didn't want to think about curves, womanly or otherwise. His hunger for her was making him uncomfortable and that infuriated him because Gaetano had never hungered that much for one particular woman. Beautiful women had always been pretty much interchangeable for him. It was the challenge, he told himself impatiently. He only wanted her because she was saying no. But that simplistic belief didn't ease his tension in the slightest. It was, he decided grimly, likely to feel like a *very* long engagement.

First thing in the morning, Poppy looked amazing, Gaetano conceded hours later, studying her from across the bedroom. Her red hair streamed like a banner across the pale bedding, framing her delicate face and the rose-bud pout of her lips. A narrow shoulder protruded from below his slipped tee shirt and the sheet was pushed back to bare one leg from knee to slender ankle. And that easily, that quickly, Gaetano had a hard-on again and gritted his teeth in annoyance. What the hell was it about her? He felt like a man trying to fight an invisible illness!

'Poppy…?'

She shifted in the bed, lashes fluttering up on luminous green eyes. 'Gaetano…?' she whispered drowsily.

'I left that prompt sheet I meant you to study last night on the desk in my home office. I'll see you at Rodolfo's party at three.'

Poppy sat up in a panic. 'What will I wear?'

'Your usual clothes. Be yourself,' he reminded her as he vanished out of the door.

Poppy scrambled out of bed to follow him. 'Where are you going?'

Gaetano swung round and sent her a pained appraisal. 'Work…the bank.'

'Oh…' Having asked what appeared to be a stupid question, Poppy ducked hastily back into the bedroom and went for a shower while planning her own day.

First of all she had to go and buy the ingredients for her present for Rodolfo's seventy-fifth. She could only hope that she wasn't getting it wrong in the gift department. After that she had a rather more pressing need to attend to: finding work for herself. She had just about enough money in her purse to make Rodolfo's cake but she had nothing more and no savings to fall back on.

The sleek granite-topped kitchen had a fridge packed with food and a very large selection of chocolate cereals that made her smile. Gaetano had remembered her preference. She ate while she studied the prompt sheets he had mentioned. It was like a CV written for a job: qualifications listed, sports pursuits outlined, not a single reference to any memorable moments. He just had no idea of the sort of things that a woman in love would want to know about him, Poppy reflected ruefully. When was his birthday? What was his favourite colour?

She texted him to ask.

Gaetano suppressed a groan when his phone buzzed yet again and lifted it to see what the latest irrelevant question was.

Who was the first woman you fell in love with?

He had never been in love and he was proud of it.

What do you value most in a woman?

Independence, he texted back.

As Poppy walked round the supermarket with her shopping list she raised her brows. If he liked independent women why did he always date clingy airheads? So, she asked that too and they began to argue by text until she was laughing. Gaetano had an image of himself that did not always match reality. She could have told him that he dated clingy airheads because they did as they were told, accepted his workaholic schedule and made few demands.

Noticing a 'help wanted' sign in the window of a café she called in, enjoyed an interview on the spot and was hired to work a shift that very evening. Relieved to have solved the problem of being broke, she returned to the town house by the separate entrance at the side and proceeded to mess up Gaetano's basically unused kitchen with her baking session. She settled the cake into the cake carrier she had bought for the purpose and set the birthday card on top of it before going to get changed.

She wore a tartan skirt with black lace stockings and high heels. Gaetano wolf-whistled the instant he saw her. 'Wow...' he breathed with quiet masculine appreciation. 'Your legs are to die for...'

'Really?' Poppy grinned and then frowned doubtfully. 'Is this phase one of the Italian seduction routine?'

'You're very suspicious.'

'I don't trust you,' Poppy told him truthfully. 'I think being sneaky would come naturally to you.'

'I've never had to be sneaky with women,' Gaetano told her truthfully.

The drawing room was crowded with guests when they arrived. The instant Poppy saw the fancy cocktail-type frocks and delicate jewellery that the other women sported and the stares that her informal outfit attracted, she paled in dismay. She stuck out like a sore thumb and hated the feeling, squirming discomfiture taking her by storm and reminding her of her days at school when no matter how hard she'd tried she had always failed to fit in. Remembering that Gaetano had urged her to be herself was not a consolation because her unconventional appearance *had* to be an embarrassment to him. How could it be anything else?

Gaetano's grandfather made a major production out of welcoming them and announcing their engagement. Poppy's guilt over their deception sent colour flying into her cheeks but she saw only satisfaction in Gaetano's brilliant smile and from it she deduced that everything was going the way he had planned.

But Poppy was wrong in that assumption. She served Rodolfo with the strawberry layer cake with mascarpone-cheese icing that was his favourite and which she had learned to bake at his wife's side. His eyes went all watery and he gave her an almost boyish grin as he took up the cake knife she passed him and cut himself a large helping.

'So, when's the big day?' he asked Poppy within Gaetano's hearing.

Gaetano tensed. 'We haven't set a date as yet…'

'You don't want to risk a treasure like Poppy getting away,' his grandfather warned him softly, shrewd eyes resting on his grandson's lean, darkly handsome face. 'I don't believe in long engagements.'

'We don't want to rush in either,' Poppy remarked carefully, instinct sending her to Gaetano's rescue.

'Next month would be a good time for me before I head off to Italy for the summer,' Rodolfo pointed out calmly.

'We'll talk it over,' Gaetano fielded smoothly.

'And when you get back from your honeymoon,' the old man delivered cheerfully, 'it will be as CEO.'

Gaetano nodded, thoroughly disconcerted and fighting not to betray the fact that he knew that his promotion was now a *marriage* step away from him. He studied Poppy from below his black lashes. Against all the odds, Rodolfo adored her. Trust Poppy to bake his grandmother's signature cake. She couldn't have done anything more likely to please and impress. She had ticked his grandfather's every box. Not only was she beautiful, kind and thoughtful, she could actually *cook*. Gaetano experienced a hideous 'hoist with his own petard' sensation and wondered how the hell he was going to climb back out of the hole he had dug.

CHAPTER FIVE

'WHY ARE YOU in such a hurry?' Gaetano frowned as Poppy sped away from him towards the bedroom. His grandfather had outmanoeuvred him and he needed to have a serious conversation with his fake fiancée.

'I have to get changed and get out in the next…er… ten minutes!' she exclaimed in dismay, hastening her step after checking her watch.

Gaetano took his time about strolling down to the bedroom where Poppy was engaged in pulling on a pair of jeans, lithe long legs topped by a pair of bright red knickers on display. Her face flushing, she half turned away, wriggling her shapely hips to ease up the jeans. The enthusiastic stirring at his groin was uniquely un-welcome to Gaetano at that moment. 'Where do you have to be in ten minutes?' he asked quietly.

'Work. I picked up a waitressing shift at the café round the corner. I'll be back by midnight,' she told him chirpily.

In the doorway, Gaetano went rigid, convinced that he could not have heard her correctly. 'You applied for a job as a *waitress*…' his dark deep drawl climbed tellingly in volume and emphasis as he spoke that word '…while you're pretending to be engaged to me?'

'Why not? Bartending is better paid but the café was closer and the hours are casual and flexible and that would probably suit you better.'

Brilliant dark eyes landed on her with the chilling effect of an ice bath. 'You working as a waitress doesn't suit me in *any* way.'

'I don't see why you should object,' Poppy reasoned, thrusting her feet into her comfy ankle boots. 'I mean, you're still working and what am I supposed to do with myself while you're busy all day? It's not even as if pretending to be your fiancée is a full-time job.'

'As far as I'm concerned, it *is* full-time and you will go to the café now and tell them that you're sorry but you won't be working there tonight,' Gaetano told her with raking impatience. '*Diavelos!* Do I have to spell every little thing out to you? I'm a billionaire banker. You can't work in a café or a bar for peanuts while you're purportedly engaged to me!'

An angry flush had lit up Poppy's cheeks. 'Then what am I supposed to do for money?'

'If you need money, I'll give it to you,' Gaetano declared, pulling out his wallet, relieved that the problem could be so easily fixed. But seriously, where was her brain? Working as a waitress while living in a mansion?

Poppy backed away a step and then snaked past him in the doorway to trudge down to the hall. 'I don't want your money, Gaetano. I *work* for my money. I don't take handouts from anyone.'

'But I'm the exception to that rule,' Gaetano slotted

in grimly as he followed her with tenacious resolve. 'While you are engaged to me, you are not allowed to embarrass me by working in a low-paid menial job.'

Outraged by that decree, Poppy whirled round to face him again, the hank of hair from her ponytail falling over her shoulder in a bright colourful stream. 'Is that a fact?' she prompted. 'Well, I'm sorry, you're out of luck on this one. As far as I'm concerned, any kind of honest work is preferable to living off charity and I don't care if you think waitressing is menial—'

'We have a deal!' Gaetano raked at her with raw bite. 'You're breaking it!'

'At no stage did you ever mention that I would not be able to take paid work,' Poppy flung back at him in furious denial. 'So, don't try to deviously change the rules to suit yourself. I'm sorry if you see me working as a waitress at Carrie's coffee shop as a major embarrassment. Don't you have enough status on your own account? Does it really matter what I do? I would remind you that I am an ordinary girl who needs to work to live and that's not about to change for you or anyone else!'

'It's totally unnecessary for you to work...in fact it's *preposterous*!' Gaetano slammed back at her loudly, dark eyes flaring as golden as the heart of a fire now, his anger unconcealed. 'Particularly when I have already assured you that I will cover your every expense while you are staying in London.'

'Just as I've already told you,' Poppy proclaimed heatedly, 'I will *not* accept money from you. I'm an independent woman and I have my pride. If our positions were reversed, would you want me keeping you?'

'Don't be ridiculous!' Gaetano roared back, all control of his temper abandoned in the face of her continuing refusal to listen to him and respect his opinion. Never before in his life had a woman opposed him in such a way.

More intimidated than she was prepared to admit or show by the depth of his anger and the sheer size of him towering over her while he gave forth as if he were voicing the Ten Commandments, Poppy brought up her chin. 'I'm not being ridiculous,' she countered obstinately. 'I'm standing up for what I believe in. I don't want your money. I want my own. And as only a few people know I'm engaged to you, I don't see how it's going to embarrass you. Especially as you don't embarrass that easily.'

'And what's that supposed to mean?' he demanded.

Poppy dealt him an accusing look. 'You should've given me some pointers on what to wear at the birthday party. Once I saw how the other women were dressed, I felt stupid.'

Gaetano shrugged. 'It wasn't important. I want you to be yourself,' he repeated dismissively. 'As for the waitress job—'

'I'm keeping it!' Poppy incised, lifting her chin combatively because she was needled by his assurance that being the odd one out in the fashion stakes at the party was something she should simply be able to shrug off. Had that been a rap on the knuckles? Was she oversensitive? Too prone to feeling inadequate?

'And that's your last word on the subject?' Gaetano growled as she yanked open the front side door, which serviced his wing of the house.

'I'm afraid so,' Poppy declared before she raced off at speed, pulling the door shut behind her.

'If you don't watch out, you'll lose her,' a voice said from behind Gaetano.

In consternation, he swung round to focus on his grandfather, who was wedged in the doorway communicating between the two properties. 'How much of that did you hear?' Gaetano asked tautly.

'With this door open I couldn't help overhearing the last part of your argument,' Rodolfo Leonetti advanced. 'I'll admit to hearing enough to appreciate that my grandson is a hopeless snob. She was correct, Gaetano. There can never be shame in honest work. Your grandmother insisted on selling her father's fish at a stall until the day she married me.'

'Your wife was raised on a tiny backward island in a different era. Times have changed,' Gaetano parried thinly.

Rodolfo laughed with sincere appreciation. 'Women don't change that much. Poppy's not interested in your money. Do you realise how very lucky you are to have found such a woman?'

In silence, Gaetano jerked his aggressive chin in acknowledgement. He was still climbing back down from the dizzy heights of the unholy rage Poppy's defiance had lit inside him, marvelling at how angry she had made him while being disconcerted by his loss of control. His lean hands flexed into fists before slowly loosening again.

'And as her temper seems to be as hot as your own it may well take some very nifty moves on your part to keep her,' his grandfather opined with quiet assurance as he strolled back through the communicating door.

Gaetano struck the wall with a knotted fist and swore long and low beneath his breath. Poppy set his temper off like a rocket, not a problem he had ever had with a woman before. That's because you date 'clingy airheads', a voice chimed in the back of his mind, an exact quote of Poppy's text that sounded remarkably like her. He gritted his teeth, tension pulling like tight strings in his lean, powerful body to tauten every muscle group. It was stress caused by the lack of sex, he decided abruptly. A wave of relief for that rational explanation for his recent irrational behaviour engulfed him. Gaetano didn't like anything that he couldn't understand. Yet Poppy fell into that category and he knew he didn't dislike her.

Poppy worked her shift in the café, her mind buzzing like a busy bee throughout. Had she been too hard on Gaetano? It was true that he was a snob but what else could he be after the over-privileged life he had led since birth? But Rodolfo's clear desire to rush his grandson into marriage had shocked Gaetano and naturally that had put him in a bad mood, she conceded ruefully. Evidently when Gaetano had suggested their fake engagement he had seriously underestimated the extent of his grandfather's enthusiasm for marrying him off. Only an actual wedding was going to satisfy Rodolfo Leonetti and move Gaetano up the last crucial step of his career ladder. An engagement wasn't going to achieve that for

him, which pretty much meant that everything Gaetano
had so far done had been for nothing.

When Poppy finished work, she was astonished to
glance out of the window and see Gaetano waiting outside for her. Street light fell on his defined cheekbones,
strong nose and stubbled jaw line. One glance at his
undeniable hotness and he took her breath away. Why
had he come to meet her? Colour washing her face,
she pulled her coat out of the back room and waited
for the manager to unlock the door for her exit. Gaetano's gaze, dark, deep-set and pure gold, flamed and he
moved forward.

'What are you doing here?' she asked to fill the tense
silence.

'You can't walk back to the house on your own at
this time of night,' Gaetano told her.

'Well, I suppose you would think that way,' Poppy
remarked, inclining her head to acknowledge his bodyguards ranged across the pavement mere yards from
them. Gaetano was never ever alone in the way that
other ordinary people were alone. 'Why didn't you just
send one of them to look out for me?'

'I owed you,' Gaetano breathed, unlocking the sleek
sports car by the kerb. 'I was out of line earlier.'

'You get out of line a lot…but that's the first time
you've admitted it,' Poppy said uncertainly.

Gaetano swung in beside her and in the confined
space she stared at him, her breath hitching in her
throat, heartbeat thumping very loudly in her eardrums.
Black-lashed eyes assailed hers and she fell still, her
mouth running dry. He lifted a hand, framed her face

with spread fingers and kissed her. Her hand braced on a strong masculine thigh as she leant closer, helplessly hungry for that connection and the heat and pressure of his strong sensual mouth on hers. Her body went haywire, all liquid heat and response as his tongue delved and tangled with hers, and a deep quiver thrummed through her slender length. The wanting gripping her was all powerful, racing through her to swell her breasts and ignite a feverish damp heat between her thighs. In a harried movement, Poppy yanked her head back and forced her trembling body back into the passenger seat. 'What was that for?' she asked shakily.

'I have no excuse or reason. I can't stop wanting to touch you.'

'It wasn't supposed to be like this...with us,' she mumbled accusingly through her swollen lips.

Long brown fingers circled over the top of her knee and roved lazily higher, skating up her inner thigh. 'Tell me, no,' Gaetano urged in a harsh undertone.

'No,' she framed without conviction, legs involuntarily parting because with every fibre of her being she craved his touch.

'You're pushing me off the edge of sanity,' Gaetano growled, shifting position to claim her mouth again. With little passionate nips and licks and bites he took her mouth in a way it had never been taken and sent hot rivers of excitement rolling into her pelvis.

Long fingers stroked over the taut triangle of fabric stretched tight between her thighs, lingering to circle over her core. A warm tingling sensation of almost unbearable excitement gripped her and she bucked beneath his hand, helplessly, wantonly inviting more. Give me more, her body was screaming, shameless in the grip of that need. The fabric that separated her most sensitive flesh from him was a torment but he made no attempt to remove or circumvent its presence. She ground her hips down on the seat, nipples straining and stiff and prickling, the hunger like a voracious animal clawing for more inside her. That hunger was so terrifyingly strong and her brain felt so befogged with it she shivered, suddenly cold and scared of being overwhelmed.

'This is not cool,' Gaetano whispered against her lips. 'We're in a car in a public street. This is not cool at all, *bella mia*.'

'It's just lust,' she tried to say lightly, dismissively, and she tried to summon a laugh but found she couldn't because there was nothing funny about the power of the physical urges engulfing her or the nasty draining aftermath of blocking and denying those urges.

'Lust has never made me behave like a randy teenager before,' Gaetano growled. 'Around you I have a constant hard-on.'

'Stop it…*stop* talking about it!' Poppy snapped, ramming her trembling hands into the pockets of her flying jacket.

'That's impossible when it's all I can think about.' With a stifled curse he fired the engine of the car. 'But we have more important things to discuss.'

'Yes. Rodolfo called your bluff,' she breathed heavily, struggling to return to the real world again.

'That's not how I would describe what he did. I've been mulling it over all evening,' Gaetano admitted grittily. 'I'm afraid you hit the target last night when you accused me of ignoring the human dimension. I'm great with figures and strategy, not so good with people. But this afternoon looking at Rodolfo and listening to him talk I saw a man aware of his years and afraid he wouldn't live long enough to see the next generation. All my adult life I've read him wrong. I thought all I had to do to please him was to become a success and be everything my father wasn't but it wasn't enough.'

'How wasn't it enough?'

'Rodolfo would have been a much happier man if I'd married straight out of university and given him grand-children,' Gaetano breathed wryly.

'Why regret what you can't change? Obviously you didn't meet anyone you wanted to marry.'

'No, I didn't *want* to get married,' Gaetano contradicted drily. 'I've seen too many of my friends' marriages failing and my own parents fought like cat and dog.'

Poppy grimaced and said nothing. Gaetano was very literal, very black and white and uncompromising in his outlook. He had probably decided as a teenager that he would not get married and had never revisited the decision. But it did go some way towards explaining why he never seemed to stay very long with any woman because clearly none of his relationships had had the option of a future.

'At some stage you must have met at least *one* woman who stood out from the rest?' she commented.

'I did…when I was at university. Serena ended up marrying a friend and I was their best man. They divorced last year,' Gaetano volunteered with rich scorn. 'When I heard about that, I was relieved I had backed off from her.'

'That's very cold and cynical. For all you know you and she could have made a success of marriage,' Poppy commented tongue in cheek, mad with curiosity to know who Serena had been and whether he still had feelings for her now that she was free. Her face burned because she was so grateful he had not persevered with the wretched woman. She was just then discovering in consternation that she couldn't bear to think of Gaetano with *any* other woman, let alone married to one. When had she become that sensitive, that possessive of him? She had no right to feel that way and that she did mortified her. Was this some pitiful hangover from her infatuation with him as a teenager?

As she walked into the hall Gaetano pushed the door open into a dimly lit reception room. 'Before I went out I ordered supper for us. I thought you'd be hungry because unless you ate while you were working, you missed dinner.'

She was strangely touched that it had even occurred to Gaetano to consider her well-being. But then Poppy wasn't used to anyone looking out for her. In recent years she had acted as counsellor and carer for her family. Neither her mother nor her brother had ever had the inclination to ask her how she was coping working two jobs or whether she needed anything. Removing her coat, she sank down into a comfy armchair, glancing round at the stylish appointments of the spacious room. An interior designer had probably been employed, she suspected, doubting that such classy chic was attainable in any other way. She poured the tea and filled her plate with sandwiches.

For a few minutes she simply ate to satisfy the gnawing hunger inside her. Only slowly did she let her attention roam back to Gaetano. The black stubble framed his jaw, accentuating the lush curve of his full mouth, and he could work magic with that mouth, she conceded, inwardly squirming at that intimate thought and the longing behind it while ducking her head to evade the cool gold intensity of his gaze. Her body, still taut and tender from feverish arousal, recalled the stroke of his fingers and she tingled, dying inside with chagrin that she had lost her control to that extent.

'So, what do you want to talk about?' she prompted in the humming silence.

'I think you already know,' Gaetano intoned very drily.

'You have to decide what to do next,' Poppy clarified reluctantly, disliking the fact that he read her with such accuracy and refused to allow her to play dumb when it suited her to do so.

After all, so much hung on the coming discussion and it was only natural that she should now be nervous. Of what further use could she be to Gaetano? Their fake engagement was worthless because Rodolfo Leonetti wanted much more than a fake couple could possibly deliver. They couldn't set a wedding date because they weren't going to get married. And if she was of no additional value to Gaetano, maybe he wanted her to leave his home and maybe, quite understandably, he would also expect to immediately stop paying the bills for her mother's treatment at the clinic? A cold trickle of nervous perspiration ran down between Poppy's breasts and suddenly she was furious with herself for not thinking through what Rodolfo's declaration would ultimately mean to her and the lives of those who depended on her.

'I had no problem deciding what to do next. I'm very decisive but unfortunately what I do next is heavily dependent on what you decide to do,' Gaetano admitted quietly, disconcerting her while his extraordinarily beautiful eyes rested on her full force.

'What I decide...?'

'Only a fake fiancée can become a fake bride!' Gaetano derided, watching her pale.

'You can't seriously be suggesting that we carry this masquerade as far as a wedding!' Poppy exclaimed with a look of disbelief.

'Rodolfo likes you. He's really excited and happy about our relationship,' Gaetano breathed grimly. 'In fact it's many years since I saw him this enthusiastic about anything or anyone. I would like to give him what he wants even if it's not real and even though it can't last.'

'You love your grandfather. I understand that you don't want to disappoint him, but—'

'We could get married for a couple of years while I continue to pay for your mother's care.'

Poppy leant forward to say sharply, 'If Mum does well, she will probably be released from the clinic next month.'

Gaetano shook his handsome dark head slowly as if in wonder at her naivety. 'Poppy... Jasmine is most probably a long-term rehabilitation project. To stay off alcohol for the foreseeable future she's going to need regular ongoing professional support.'

It was true, Poppy conceded painfully. What Gaetano was saying was true, *horribly* true, but until that moment Poppy had not thought that far ahead. Indeed she had dreamt only of the day when she hoped and prayed that her newly sober parent would walk out of the clinic and back into the real world. Sadly, however, the real world offered challenges Jasmine Arnold might struggle to handle. And Poppy already knew that she did not have the power to stop her mother drinking because she had already tried that and had failed abysmally.

'If you agree to marry me I will faithfully promise to take care of your mother's needs for however long it takes for her to regain her health and sobriety,' Gaetano swore. 'At the same time I will make it possible for you to return to further education. That would mean that by the time we divorce you would be in a position to pursue any career you chose.'

Poppy sucked in a steadying breath because he was offering to deliver momentous benefits and security. But she still didn't want to sell herself out for the money that would empower her to transform her mother's life and give them both the best possible chance of a decent future. 'I can't take your money or your support. It's immoral,' she argued jaggedly. 'Stop trying to tempt me into doing what I know would be wrong.'

'I'm offering you the equivalent of a job. All right...'

Gaetano shifted an expressive bronzed hand in the air with the fluid arrogance that came as naturally as breathing to him. 'Taking on the role of being my wife would be an unusual job but it's not a job you *want*, so why shouldn't you be paid for sacrificing your freedom? Because make no mistake—you *would* be giving up your freedom while you were pretending to be my wife.'

'Fooling your grandfather, faking and pretending. It wouldn't be right,' Poppy protested vehemently.

'If it makes Rodolfo genuinely happy, why is it wrong?' Gaetano fired back at her in challenge. 'It's the best I've got to offer him. I can't give him the real thing. I can't give him a real marriage when I don't want one. Marrying you, a woman he has readily accepted and approved, is as good as it's likely to get from his point of view.'

Poppy was pale and troubled. 'You're good in an argument,' she allowed ruefully. 'But I'm never going to win a trophy for my acting skills.'

'You don't need to act. Rodolfo likes you as you are. Think about what I'm offering you. You can reclaim your life and return to being a carefree student,' Gaetano pointed out, his persuasion insidious. 'No more fretting about your mother falling off the wagon again, no more scrubbing floors or serving drinks.'

'Shut up!' Poppy told him curtly, leaping to her feet to walk restively round the room while she battled the tempting possibilities he had placed in front of her.

Gaetano studied her from below heavily lashed eyelids. She would surrender, of course she would. She had had a very tough time coping with her mother over the past couple of years and it had stolen her youthful freedom of choice. As a teenager she had been ambitious and he could still see that spirited spark of wanting more than her servant ancestors had ever wanted glowing within her.

'And how long would this fake marriage have to last to be worthwhile?' she demanded without warning.

Gaetano almost grinned and punched the air because that was when he knew for sure that he had won. 'I estimate around two years with three years being the absolute maximum. By that stage both of us will be eager to reclaim our real lives and I would envisage that divorce proceedings would already have begun.'

'And you think a divorce a couple of years down the road is less of a disappointment for Rodolfo than a broken engagement?'

'At least he'll believe I *tried*.'

'And of course your ultimate goal is becoming CEO of the Leonetti Bank and marrying me will deliver that,' Poppy filled in slowly, luminous green eyes skimming to his lean, darkly handsome features in wonderment. 'I can't believe how ambitious you are.'

'The bank is my life, it always has been,' Gaetano admitted without apology. 'Nothing gives me as much of a buzz as a profitable deal.'

'If I were to agree to this…and I'm not saying I *am* agreeing,' Poppy warned in a rush, 'when would the marriage take place?'

'Next month to suit Rodolfo's schedule and, for that matter, my own. I won't be here much over the next few weeks,' Gaetano explained. 'I have a lot of pressing business to tie up before I can take the kind of honeymoon which Rodolfo will expect.'

At that disconcerting reference to a honeymoon a tension headache tightened in a band across Poppy's brow and she lifted her fingers to press against her forehead. 'I'm very tired. I'll sleep on this and give you an answer in the morning.'

Gaetano slid fluidly out of his seat and approached her. 'But you already know the answer.'

Poppy settled angry green eyes on his lean, strong face. 'Don't try to railroad me,' she warned him.

'You like what I do to you,' Gaetano husked with blazing confidence, running a teasing forefinger down over her cheek to stroke it along the soft curve of her full lower lip.

In all her life Poppy had never been more aware of anything than she was of that finger caressing the still-swollen surface of her mouth. But then, as she was learning, Gaetano couldn't touch any part of her body without every nerve ending standing to attention and screaming for more of the same. Her breathing fractured in her throat and sawed heavily in and out of her chest. His fingertip slid into her mouth and before she could even think about what she was doing she laved it with her tongue, sucked it, watched his brilliant eyes smoulder and then his outrageous long black lashes lower over burning glints of gold.

'Are you offering to let me have you tonight?' Gaetano enquired, startling and mortifying her with that direct question.

Her luminous eyes flew wide. 'I can't believe you just asked me that!'

'And I can't believe that you can still try to act the innocent when you're teasing me,' Gaetano riposted.

'You touched me first,' she reminded him defensively, her cheeks scarlet as she thought of what she had done with his finger and the expectation he had developed as a result. 'Are you always this blunt?'

'Pretty much. Sex requires mutual consent and I naturally dislike confusing signals, which could lead to misunderstandings.'

Poppy stared up at him, momentarily lost in the tawny blaze of his hot stare. He wanted her and he was letting her see it. Her whole body seized up in response, her nipples prickling while that painful hollow ached at the heart of her. She tore her gaze from his, dropped her eyes and then, noticing the sizeable bulge in his jeans, felt pure unashamed heat curling up between her thighs.

'If you're not going to let me have you, sleep in one of the spare rooms tonight,' Gaetano instructed. 'I'm not a masochist, *bella mia*.'

'Spare room,' Poppy framed shakily, the only words she could get past her tight throat because it hurt her that she wanted to say yes so badly. She didn't want to be used 'to scratch an itch', not her first time anyway. Surely some day somewhere some man would want her for more than that? Gaetano only wanted the release of sex and would probably not have wanted her at all had they not been forced into such proximity.

Gaetano let her reach the door. 'If I marry you, I'll expect you to share my bed.'

Wide-eyed, Poppy whirled round to gasp, 'But…'

'I'm too well-known to get away with sneaking around having affairs for a couple of years,' Gaetano asserted silkily. 'If we get married it should look like a happy marriage, at least at the start, and there's no way I'd be happy in a sex-free marriage. Is that likely to be a deal-breaker?'

'I'll think it over.' Her heart-shaped face expressionless, Poppy studied the polished floor. She wanted to discover sex with Gaetano but she wasn't about to confess that to him. *That* was private, strictly private. Her body burned inside her clothing at the thought of that intimacy. Meaningless, sexual intimacy, she reminded herself doggedly. And it disturbed her that even though she knew it would mean nothing to him she still wanted him…

CHAPTER SIX

POPPY SANK INTO the guest-room bed and rolled over to hug a pillow. She was incredibly tired but so wired she was convinced that she would not sleep a wink.

She was going to marry Gaetano Leonetti. Gorgeous, filthy rich, super-successful Gaetano. Who sent her body into spasms of craving with a single kiss. If she was honest with herself, she really hadn't needed a night to think it over. He would help her protect her mother and he would support her getting back onto a career path. Really, marrying Gaetano would be win-win whichever way she looked at it, wouldn't it be?

As long as she didn't get too carried away and start acting as if it were a real marriage. As long as she didn't fall for Gaetano. Well, she wasn't about to do that, was she? He was almost thirty years old and had never been in love. The closest he had come to love was with a woman who had married his friend. And he had acted as best man at their wedding, which didn't suggest to her that it had been very close to love at all. Gaetano might be planning to marry her but he wasn't going to love her and he wasn't going to keep her either. It would be a temporary marriage and it would make Rodolfo happy...at least for a while, she thought guiltily, because faking it for the older man's benefit still troubled her conscience. He was such a kind, genuine sort of man and so unlike Gaetano, who kept the equivalent of a coffin lid slammed down hard on his emotions.

While Poppy was ruminating over her bridegroom's lack of emotional intelligence, Gaetano was subjecting himself to yet another cold shower. She *had* to marry him. There was no alternative. Just at that moment in the grip of a raging inferno of frustrated lust he felt as though he would spontaneously combust if he didn't get Poppy spread across his bed as the perfect wedding gift. The definitive wedding gift, with those ballerina legs in lace stockings, those pert little breasts in satin cups, that voluptuous pink mouth pouting as she looked up at him with those witchy green spellbinding eyes. He groaned out loud. He couldn't credit that he had barely touched her when he wanted so much more.

But if they married, a few weeks down the matrimonial road he'd be back to normal, he told himself bracingly. The challenge would be gone. The lust would die once he could have her whenever he wanted her. He would soon be himself again, cooler, calmer, back in control, fully focussed on the bank. How was it possible that just the fantasy of sinking into Poppy's wet, willing body excited him more than he had ever been excited? What was it about her?

Maybe it was the weird clothes, maybe he had a secret Goth fetish. Maybe it was her argumentative nature, because he had always thrilled to a challenge. Maybe it was her cheeky texts that made him laugh. The fact she could still blush? That was strange. Every time he mentioned sex she went red, as if he had said something outrageous. She couldn't possibly be that innocent, although he was willing to allow that she might well have considerably less experience between the sheets than he had acquired.

Gaetano shook Poppy awake at the ungodly hour of six in the morning, obstinately and cruelly ignoring her heartfelt moans to insist that she join him for breakfast. After a quick shower and the application of a little make-up, Poppy teamed a black dress enlivened with a red rose print with high heels and sauntered down to the dining room. Gaetano was already ensconced with black coffee, a horrendously unhealthy fry-up and the *Financial Times*.

She was gloriously conscious of his attention as she helped herself to cereal and took a seat at the other end of the table, her ruby cluster ring catching the light. Gaetano put down the newspaper and regarded her levelly, dark golden eyes steady as a rock and full of an impatience he didn't need to voice.

'Yes, I'll marry you,' Poppy told him straight off.

'Does that mean I get to share my bed with you tonight?' was Gaetano's first telling question.

'You are incredibly goal-orientated about entirely the wrong things!' Poppy censured immediately. 'You can wait until we're married.'

'Nobody waits until they're married these days!'

'I haven't had sex before. I want it to feel special,' she told him stubbornly.

His expressive dark eyes flared with incredulity. 'I refuse to credit that. I saw you with Toby Styles…'

'I hate you!' Poppy launched at him in a sudden tempest of furious embarrassment, her pale skin flushed to her hairline. 'Of all the moments I don't *want* to be reminded of, you have to bring that one up and throw it at me!'

'Well, it was one of those unforgettable moments that did seem fairly self-explanatory. I saw you sidling out of the shrubbery covered in blushes and grass stains,' Gaetano commented with grudging amusement. 'So, why lie about it? This is purely about sex, *bella mia*, and I'm all for full bedroom equality. Whether or not you're a virgin or a secret slut matters not a damn to me.'

Poppy compressed her lips. 'If you must know—although it's none of your blasted business—I did plan to have sex that day with Toby but I changed my mind because it wasn't what I really wanted.' No, what she had really, *really* wanted that day, she acknowledged belatedly, was to wander off into the shrubbery and be ravished by Gaetano, who had dominated her every juvenile fantasy. Sadly, however, Gaetano hadn't been an option.

'Poor Toby…' Gaetano frowned.

'He was very decent about it,' Poppy muttered in mortification. 'He's married to one of my friends now.'

'But there must have been someone since then?'

'No.'

Gaetano continued to stare at her as if she were a circus freak. 'But you're so full of passion…'

Only with you. The words remained unspoken.

Gaetano lifted his coffee with a slightly dazed expression in his shrewd gaze. 'I'll be the first...*really*?'

Poppy shrugged a shoulder. 'But if you think it's likely to be a turn-off I can always go and look for a one-night stand.'

'Don't even think about it,' Gaetano growled.

'That was a joke.'

'It's not a turn-off, simply a surprise,' Gaetano admitted flatly. 'OK, I'll wait until we're married if it's so significant to you. But I think you're making an unnecessary production out of it.'

Her body was all he wanted from her, Poppy interpreted painfully. At least if she was his legal wife, it would feel less demeaning, wouldn't it?

'I'll organise a gynae appointment for you,' Gaetano continued briskly. 'Reliable birth control is important. We don't want any slip-ups in that department when we're not planning to stay together.'

'Obviously not,' she agreed, sipping with determination at her hot-chocolate drink while thinking for the very first time in her life about having a baby. She had always liked children, always assumed that she would become a mother one day, but she reckoned that day lay a long way ahead in her future.

'And whatever you do,' Gaetano warned with chilling precision, 'don't go falling for me.'

'And why would I do that?' Poppy demanded baldly, her cheeks hotter than hell in fear of him mentioning that so mortifying teenaged crush again. 'Having sex with you is not going to make me fall in love with you.

I know you think you're fantastic in bed, Gaetano, *but* you're not fantastic enough *out* of bed.'

Infuriatingly, Gaetano did not react badly to that criticism. 'That's good because that's one complication I can do without. I hate it when women fall for me and make me feel that it's my fault.'

Well, that was frank, and forewarned was forearmed, Poppy told herself squarely. 'It's probably your money they're falling for,' she suggested in a tone of saccharine sweetness. 'You have yet to show me a single loveable trait.'

'*Grazie al cielo*...thank goodness,' Gaetano responded in a tone of galling relief. 'I don't want you to get the wrong idea about me *or* this marriage.'

'I won't. This marriage will be like one of those business mergers. You are *so* safe,' Poppy declared brightly. 'You will merely be the first stepping stone on my sexual path.'

Gaetano was taken aback to discover that he didn't want to think of a string of other men enjoying her along that particular path. In fact it gave him a slightly nauseated sensation in the pit of his stomach. The acknowledgement bemused him and he put it down to the simple fact that as yet he had not enjoyed her either. He was thinking too much about something relatively unimportant, he reflected impatiently. Sex was sex and his wedding night would provide the cure for what was currently afflicting him. Since when had he ever attached so much consequence to sex? Even so, it had been entirely right to have the conversation with

Poppy to ensure that they perfectly understood each other's expectations.

'I'll make a start on the wedding arrangements today,' Gaetano completed smoothly.

'You look beautiful,' Jasmine Arnold told her daughter warmly as she emerged from her bedroom in her wedding dress.

The older woman was attending her daughter's wedding with a member of the clinic support staff. Although Poppy could see a big improvement in her mother's appearance and mood, she knew how hard it was for Jasmine to return to Woodfield Hall where she had been so depressed. And while Poppy had asked her mother to walk her down the aisle, her brother was doing it instead because Jasmine could not face being the centre of that much attention.

Poppy quite understood the older woman's reluctance because hundreds of guests were attending the wedding being staged to celebrate Gaetano's marriage at Woodfield Hall. The Leonetti men had always got married in the church in the grounds of their ancestral home and neither Rodolfo nor Gaetano had seen any reason to flout tradition. Indeed Gaetano had expected Poppy to move straight into the main house as though she already belonged there but Poppy had returned to the small service flat where she had grown up, determined to move back and forth as required.

'I'm still hoping that you know what you're doing,' Damien muttered in an admission intended only for Poppy's ears as he emerged from his own room, smartly clad in his hired morning suit. He looked relieved when he registered that his mother and her companion had already left for the church. 'You've always had a thing for Gaetano...'

'As I've already explained, this is only a business arrangement.'

'Maybe it is...for him.' Her brother sighed. 'But if it's only business why are you always checking your phone and texting him?'

'He expects regular updates on the wedding arrangements.'

'Yeah...like his staff can't do that for him,' Damien responded, unimpressed.

But it was true, Poppy reflected ruefully. Gaetano was hyper about details and had a surprising number of strong opinions about bridal matters that she had mistakenly assumed he wouldn't be interested in. Although, as he had warned her, she had barely seen him since the month-long countdown to the wedding had begun, they had stayed in constant contact by phone while Gaetano flew round Europe. Poppy had ignored his opinion of the casual job she had taken and had kept up regular shifts at the café.

Now she climbed into the limousine waiting in the courtyard to collect the bride and her brother. The chapel was barely two hundred yards away and she would have much preferred to walk there but Gaetano had vetoed that option, saying it lacked dignity.

In the same way he had vetoed the flowers she'd wanted to wear in her hair and had had a family diamond tiara delivered to her. He had also picked the

bridal colour scheme as green, arguing that that particular shade would match her eyes, which had struck
Poppy as ridiculously whimsical for so practical a male.
And to crown his interference he had acted as though he
were her Prince Charming by buying her wedding shoes
the instant he saw them showcased in some high-fashion
outlet in Milan. Admittedly they were gorgeous, even
if they were over-the-top dramatic—delicate leather
sandals ornamented with pearls and opals that glim-
mered and magically shone in the light. In fact Gaetano
had embarrassed his bride with his choice of shoes because her selections had been considerably less fanci-
ful. Her dress was cap-sleeved and fitted to the waist,
flaring out over net underskirts to stop above her slender knees. In comparison to the Cinderella shoes, the
dress, while being composed of beautiful fabric, was
plain and simple in style.

'Are you nervous?' Damien prompted.

'Why would I be? Well, only because the Leonettis
have invited hundreds of people,' she admitted.

'Including most of the estate staff and locals, so you
can't fault Gaetano there. The rich are going to have to
rub shoulders with the ordinary folk.' Damien laughed.

Poppy smiled because Gaetano had kept the last
promise he had made before their engagement. Within
a week Damien would be starting work as a mechanic in
a London garage staffed by other former offenders. Her
brother's happiness at the prospect of a complete new
start somewhere he would no longer be pilloried for his
past had lifted her heart. Not that her heart needed lifting, she told herself urgently. If her family was happy,

she was happy. In stray moments between the wedding arrangements and spending time with Rodolfo, who got lonely in his big empty mansion, she had started looking into the option of training as a garden designer and that gem of an idea looked promising.

Closing her hand into the crook of her brother's arm, she looked down the aisle to where Gaetano had turned round to see her arrival and she grinned. My goodness, how ridiculous all this pomp and ceremony were for a couple who weren't remotely in love, she thought helplessly. But Gaetano certainly looked the part of bridegroom, all tall, dark and handsome, black curls cropped to his head in honour of the wedding, the usual stubble round his jaw line dispensed with, his bronzed, handsome features clean-shaven. His dark eyes glittered gold as precious ingots in the sunlight filtered by the stained-glass window behind him. He looked downright amazing, she conceded with a sunny sensation of absolute contentment.

When Poppy came into view, she took Gaetano's breath away. Her waist looked tiny enough to be spanned by his hands and, as he had requested, her glorious hair tumbled loose round her shoulders in vibrant contrast to the white dress that displayed her incredible legs. And she was wearing the shoes, the shoes *he* had bought for her, having known at a glance and feeling slightly smug at the knowledge that they were the sort of theatrical feminine touch the unconventional Poppy would appreciate.

The priest rattled through the ceremony at a fair old pace. Rings were exchanged. Poppy trembled as

Gaetano eased the ring down over her knuckle, glancing up to encounter smouldering golden eyes that devoured her. Colour surged into her face as she thought of the night ahead but there was anticipation and excitement laced with that faint sense of apprehension. She had decided that she was glad that Gaetano would become her first lover. Who better than the male she had fallen for as a teenager? After all, no other man had yet managed to wipe out her memory of Gaetano. There would be someone else some day, she told herself bracingly as Gaetano retained her hand and his thumb gently massaged the delicate skin of her inner wrist with the understated sensuality that seemed so much a part of him.

'You made me wait ten minutes at the altar but you were definitely worth waiting for,' Gaetano quipped as they walked down the aisle again.

'I warned you I'd be late,' Poppy reminded him. 'Knowing you, you'd have preferred to find me waiting humbly for you.'

'No, waiting naked would have been sufficient, late or otherwise,' Gaetano whispered only loud enough for her ears. 'As for humble—are you kidding? You've never been the self-effacing type.'

Rodolfo hugged her outside the chapel, his creased face wrinkled into a huge smile. 'Welcome to the family,' he said happily.

A beautiful blonde watched with raised brows of apparent surprise as, urged on by the photographer, Poppy wound her arms round Gaetano's neck and gazed at him as if he were her sun, her moon and her stars. She was great at faking it, she thought appreciatively as Gaetano smiled down at her with that wonderful, charismatic smile that banished the often forbidding austerity from his lean, darkly handsome features.

'Congratulations, Gaetano,' the blonde intercepted them as they made their way to the limo to be wafted back to the hall.

'Poppy…meet Serena Bellingham. We'll catch up later, Serena,' Gaetano drawled.

'Is she the one you almost married?' Poppy demanded, craning her neck to look back at the smiling blonde who rejoiced in the height, perfect figure and face of a top model.

'Oh, don't do it. Don't make something out of nothing the way women do!' Gaetano groaned in exasperation. 'I didn't *almost* marry Serena and, even if I did, what business is it of yours? This isn't a real wedding.'

The colour ebbed from below Poppy's skin to leave her pale. She felt oddly as though she had been slapped down and squashed and she felt enormously hurt and humiliated but didn't understand why. But, unquestionably, he was right. Theirs was not a normal wedding and she was not entitled to ask nosy personal questions about exes.

As if he recognised that he had been rude, Gaetano released his breath in a slow measured hiss. 'I'm sorry. I shouldn't have said that.'

'No, it's OK. I'm just naturally nosy,' Poppy muttered in an undertone.

'Serena is a very talented hedge-fund manager. She may come and work for Leonettis now that she's single again. Her ex was envious of her success, which is—apparently—the main reason their marriage failed.'

Poppy pictured Serena's cloyingly bright smile and her tummy performed a warning somersault. It sounded as though Gaetano had spoken to Serena recently to catch up. Confidences had been exchanged and that sent the oddest little current of dismay through Poppy. She suspected that if the beautiful blonde went to work for Gaetano, it wouldn't entirely be a career move. But even if that was true, what business was it of hers to judge or speculate? She was Gaetano's wife and soon she would also be Gaetano's lover yet she had not, it seemed, acquired any relationship rights over Gaetano, which suddenly struck her as a recipe for disaster.

Woodfield Hall was awash with guests and caterers. Jasmine Arnold approached her daughter to ask if it would be all right if she took her leave. Newly sober, Poppy's mother did not want as yet to be in the vicinity of alcohol. Understanding, Poppy hugged the older woman and they agreed to talk regularly on the phone. As Gaetano joined her Poppy smiled at one of her few school friends, Melanie, who was now married to Toby Styles, the estate gamekeeper.

Overpowered by Gaetano's presence, the small brunette gushed into speech. 'You and…er… Mr Leonetti? It's so romantic, Poppy. You know,' Melanie said, addressing Gaetano directly, 'the whole time we were growing up Poppy never had eyes for anyone but you.'

Gaetano responded wittily but Poppy was already trying not to cringe before Toby grinned at her. 'Nobody knows that better than me,' he teased.

Kill me now, Poppy thought melodramatically when Gaetano actually laughed out loud and chatted to the couple about their work on the estate as if nothing the slightest bit embarrassing had been shared. And of course, why would it embarrass Gaetano to be reminded of Poppy's adolescent crush?

As they mingled she noticed Rodolfo chatting to Serena Bellingham. The blonde was wreathed in charming smiles. Poppy scolded herself for thinking bitchy thoughts. And why? Just because Serena had once shared a bed with Gaetano? Just because Serena had the looks, the social background and the education that would have made her the perfect wife for Gaetano? Or because Gaetano had once freely chosen to have a relationship with Serena when he had merely ended up with Poppy by accident and retained her for convenience?

Deliberately catching her eye, Serena strolled over to Poppy's side. 'I can see that you're curious about me,' she drawled in her cut-glass accent. 'I'm Gaetano's only serious ex, so it's natural...'

'Possibly,' Poppy conceded, determined to be very cautious with her words and ashamed of the explosive mixture of inexcusable envy and resentment she was struggling to suppress.

'We were too young when we first met,' Serena declared. 'That's why we broke up. Gaetano wasn't ready to commit and I was, so I rushed off and married someone else instead.'

'Everyone matures at a different rate,' Poppy remarked non-committally.

'Maturity is immaterial,' Serena responded with

stinging confidence. 'You and Gaetano won't last five minutes. You don't have anything to offer him.'

Disconcerted by that sudden attack coming at her out of nowhere, Poppy froze. 'That's a matter of opinion.'

'But you'll do very well for a short-lived *first* marriage. Gaetano is the last man alive I would expect to stay married to a Goth bride. You don't fit in and you never will…'

As that bitingly cold forecast hit her Poppy was silenced by Gaetano's arm closing round her spine. She encountered a suspicious sidewise glance and her temper flared inside her. Evidently, Gaetano was so far removed from the reality of Serena's barracuda nature that it was Poppy he didn't trust to behave around Serena. Entrapped there in Gaetano's controlling hold, Poppy silently seethed and brooded over what Serena had said.

Sadly, the blonde's assurance that Poppy would never fit in as Gaetano's wife had cut deep—particularly because Poppy had quite deliberately made conventional choices when it came to what to wear for her wedding day. Why had she done that? she suddenly asked herself angrily. And there it was—the answer she didn't want. She had done it for Gaetano's benefit in an effort to please him and make him proud of her, make him appreciate that the housekeeper's daughter could get it right for a big occasion. Serena's automatic dismissal of all that Poppy had to offer had seriously hurt and humiliated her.

Fortunately from that point on their wedding day seemed to speed up and race past. Poppy's throat was sore and she put that down to the amount of talking she had to do. She ate little during the meal even though she was trying to regain the weight she had lost in recent months while she had worked two jobs. Unfortunately her appetite had vanished.

She changed into white cropped trousers and a cool blue chiffon top for their flight to Italy. The luxurious interior of the Leonetti private jet stunned her into silence. She studied the glittering ruby cluster nestling next to the wedding band on her finger and Serena's wounding forecast of her marriage seemed to reverberate in her ears. *You don't fit in and you never will.*

And why should that matter when they didn't plan to stay married? Poppy asked herself wearily, unsettled by the nagging insecurities tugging at her. Why should she care what Serena thought? Or what Serena truly wanted from Gaetano? She reckoned that Serena was already planning to be Gaetano's second, rather more permanent wife. So what?

It wasn't as though she had any feelings for Gaetano beyond tolerance, Poppy reminded herself. Lust was physical, not cerebral.

CHAPTER SEVEN

'*STOP... STOP THE CAR!*' Poppy yelled as the Range Rover wound down the twisting Tuscan country road.

Startled, Gaetano jumped on the brake. He frowned in astonishment as Poppy leapt out of the car at speed and assumed that she felt sick. But to his surprise and that of the security men climbing out of the car behind, Poppy ran back down the road and crouched down.

Bloodstains and dust had smeared her white cropped jeans by the time she stood up again cradling something hairy and still in her arms as tenderly as if it were a baby. 'It's a dog…it must've been hit by a passing car.'

'Give it to my security. They'll deal with this,' Gaetano advised.

'No, we will,' Poppy told him. 'Where's the closest veterinary surgery?'

The dog, a terrier mix with a pepper and salt coat and a greying snout, licked weakly at her fingers and whined in pain. Fifteen minutes later they were in the waiting room at the local surgery while Gaetano spoke with the vet in Italian.

'The situation is this…' Gaetano informed Poppy.

'The animal is not microchipped, has no collar and has not been reported missing. Arno can operate and I can obviously afford to cover the cost of the treatment but it may be more practical simply to put the animal to sleep.'

'*Practical?*' Poppy erupted.

'Rather than put the dog through the trauma of surgery and a prolonged recuperation when the local pound is already full, as is the animal rescue sanctuary. If there is no prospect of the dog going to another home—'

'I'll keep him,' Poppy cut in curtly.

Gaetano groaned. 'Don't be a bleeding heart for the sake of it.'

'I'm not. I *want* Muffin.'

His gorgeous dark eyes widened in surprise, black lashes sky-high. '*Muffin?*'

'Ragamuffin... Muffin,' she explained curtly.

'But I can buy you a beautiful pedigreed puppy if you want one,' Gaetano murmured with unconcealed incredulity. 'Muffin is no oil painting and he's old.'

'So? He needs me much more than a beautiful puppy ever would,' Poppy pointed out defiantly. 'Think of him as a wedding gift.'

Having made arrangements for Muffin's care, they drove off again.

'You've become so cold-hearted,' Poppy whispered ruefully, studying his lean dark classic profile. 'What happened to you?'

'I grew up. Don't be a drama queen,' Gaetano urged. 'When you care too much you get hurt. I learned that from a young age.'

'But you're shutting yourself off from so many good things in life,' she argued.

'Am I? Rodolfo enjoyed a long and happy marriage but he was so wretched after my grandmother passed that he too wanted to die.'

'That was grief. Think of all the happy years he enjoyed with his wife,' Poppy urged. 'Everything has a downside, Gaetano. Love brings its own reward.'

Gaetano voiced a single rude word of disagreement in Italian. 'It didn't reward my mother when the husband she once adored ran round snorting cocaine with hookers. It didn't reward me as her son when her super-rich second husband persuaded her to forget that she had left a child behind in England. But you'll be glad to know that my mother's second husband *loved* her,' Gaetano continued with raw derision. 'As she explained when she tried to foolishly mend fences with me a few years ago, Connor loved her so much that he was jealous of her first marriage and the child born from it.'

Poppy had paled. 'That's a twisted kind of love.'

'And there's a lot of that twisted stuff out there,' Gaetano completed in a chilling tone of finality. 'That's why I never wanted anything to do with that kind of emotion.'

Poppy knew when to keep quiet. Of course, his outlook was coloured by his background, she reflected ruefully. Her parents had been happily married but his had not been. And his mother's decision to turn her back on her son to please her second husband had done even more damage. Poppy had been surprised that Gaetano's mother had not been invited to the wedding but Rodolfo had simply shrugged, saying only that his former daughter-in-law rarely returned to England.

Gaetano turned off the winding road onto a lane that threaded through silvery olive groves. Woods lay beyond the groves, occasionally parting to show views of rolling green hills and vineyards and an ancient walled hilltop village. Gaetano indicated another track to the left. 'That leads down to the guest house where Rodolfo spends his summers.'

'We'll have to be careful to stay in role with your grandfather staying so close,' Poppy remarked.

'La Fattoria, the main house, is over a mile away. He won't see us unless we visit. He is very keen not to intrude in any way on what he regards as our honeymoon,' Gaetano said drily.

'So this property has belonged to your family for a long time,' she assumed.

'Rodolfo bought it before I was born, fondly picturing it as the perfect spot for wholesome family holidays with at least half a dozen children running round.' Gaetano sounded regretful on the older man's behalf rather than scornful. 'Sadly I was an only child and my parents only ever came here with parties of friends. The house was signed over to me about five years ago and I had it fully renovated.'

A magnificent building composed of creamy stone appeared round the next corner. It was larger than Poppy had expected but she was learning to think big or bigger when it came to Leonetti properties, for, while the family might only consist of Rodolfo and his one grandson, the older man did not seem to think in terms of small or convenient. Glorious urns of flowers adorned the terrace and a rotund little woman in an apron, closely followed by a tall lanky man, appeared at the front door.

'Dolores and Sean look after La Fattoria.' Gaetano introduced the friendly middle-aged Irish couple and their cases were swept away.

Poppy accepted a glass of wine and sat down on the rear terrace to enjoy the stupendous view and catch her breath in the sweltering heat. She was feeling incredibly tired and had tactfully declined Dolores's invitation to do an immediate tour of the house. Worse still, she was getting a headache and she had an annoying tickle in her sore throat that had made her cough several times and was giving her voice a rough edge. It was just her luck, she thought ruefully. She was on her honeymoon in Tuscany in the most gorgeous setting, with an even more gorgeous man, and she was developing a galloping bad cold.

The master bedroom was a huge airy space with a tiled floor and a bed as big as a football pitch. The bathroom was fitted out like a glossy magazine spread and she revelled in the wet room with the complex jet system. Everything bore Gaetano's contemporary stamp and the extreme shower facilities were not a surprise. She had been feeling very warm and the cold water gushing over her before she managed to work out how to operate the complicated controls cooled her off wonderfully. Clad in a light cotton sundress, she wandered back downstairs.

Black hair curling and still damp from the shower, Gaetano joined her on the terrace to slot another glass of wine into her hand. 'From our own award-winning winery,' he told her wryly. 'Rodolfo takes a personal interest in the vineyard.'

Poppy surveyed him from below her lashes. He was so beautiful, she found it a challenge to look anywhere else. His spectacular black-lashed eyes were reflective as he leant gracefully up against a stone pillar support to survey the panoramic landscape, his lithe, lean, powerful body indolently relaxed. A faint shadow of black stubble roughened his strong jaw line, accentuating the wide sensual curve of his mouth. A tiny nerve snaked tight somewhere in her pelvis as she thought of how long it had been since he kissed her and whether a kiss could possibly be as unbelievably good as she remembered it being. Likely not, she told herself, for she had always been a dreamer. How else could she have imagined even as a teenager that Gaetano Leonetti would ever be seriously interested in her?

And yet, here she was, a little voice whispered seductively, Gaetano's wedding ring on her finger, and mortifyingly that awareness went to her head like the strongest alcohol. But their marriage still wasn't real; it was *still* a fantasy, the same little voice added. She had been a fake fiancée and a fake bride and now she was a fake wife. In fact just about the only thing that wouldn't be fake between them was their wedding night.

The very blood in her veins seemed to be coursing slowly, heavily. She finished her wine and set down the glass, insanely aware of the tightening prominence of her nipples. She lifted the tiny handwritten menu displayed on the table, glancing with a sinking heart through the several courses that were to be served.

'You know, I'm not remotely hungry and I don't think I *could* eat anything,' Poppy confided truthfully. 'I hope that's not going to offend Dolores...'

Gaetano glanced at her, eyes flaming golden as a lion's in the sunset lighting up the sky in an awesome display of crimson and peach. Mouth suddenly dry, she stopped breathing, frowning as he strode back into the house and disappeared from view. A few minutes later she heard a noisy little car start up somewhere and drive away. Gaetano reappeared to close a hand over hers and tug her gently back indoors.

'Do we have to eat in some stuffy dining room?' She sighed.

'No, we don't have to do anything we don't want to do,' Gaetano told her, bending down to lift her up into his arms. 'I've sent Sean and Dolores home. We're on our own until tomorrow and I am much hungrier for you than for food.'

'You can't possibly carry me up those stairs!' Poppy exclaimed.

'Right at this moment I could carry you up ten flights of stairs, *bellezza mia*,' Gaetano admitted, darting his mouth across her collarbone so that her head fell back to expose her slender white throat and her bright hair cascaded over his arm. 'Congratulations on being the only woman smart enough to make me wait...'

'Wait for what? *Oh*...' Poppy registered with a wealth of meaning in her tone while distinctly revelling in being carried as though she were a little dainty thing, which, in her own opinion, she was not.

Gaetano settled her down on the bed. Helpfully she kicked off her shoes and wished she had taken a painkiller for her sore throat and head. But she couldn't possibly take the gloss off the evening by admitting that she was feeling under par, could she? And she would have to admit it to get medication because she had packed nothing of that nature, indeed had only brought her contraceptive pills with her. She wasn't about to make a fuss about a stupid cold, was she?

He ran down the zip on her dress but only after kissing a path across her bare shoulders and lingering at the nape of her neck where her skin proved to be incredibly sensitive and she quivered, her insides turning to liquid heat beneath his attention.

'I have died and gone to heaven…' Gaetano intoned thickly as the dress dropped unnoticed to the carpet, exposing his bride in her ice-blue satin corset top and matching knickers.

'This is your wedding present,' Poppy announced, stretching back against the smooth white bedding with a confidence that she had never known she could possess.

Of course it would be different once he started removing stuff and nudity got involved, she conceded ruefully. For now, however, having guessed that Gaetano would be the type of male who found sexy lingerie that enhanced a woman's figure appealing, Poppy felt like a million dollars. Why? Simply because somehow Gaetano always contrived to look at her as if she had the most amazing female body ever and that had done wonders for her self-image.

'No, *you* are my wedding present,' Gaetano told her with conviction. 'I've been counting down the hours until we were together.'

Her luminous green eyes widened in surprise and she bit back the tactless retort that anyone would consider that a romantic comment. After all, Gaetano was fully focused on sex and neither romance nor commitment would play any part in their marriage. And wasn't that all she was focused on as well? As Gaetano came down on the bed beside her, his shirt hanging loose and unbuttoned to display a sleek, bronzed, muscular six-pack, Poppy was entranced by the view. He was stunning and, for now, he was hers. Why look beyond that? Why try to complicate things?

Loosening the corset one hook at a time, Gaetano ran a long finger down over the delicate spine he had exposed and then put his mouth there, tracing the line below her smooth ivory skin. 'You are so beautiful, *gioia mia.*'

Poppy hid a blissed-out smile behind her tumbling hair and closed her eyes as he eased off the light corset and lifted his hands to cup her breasts. Her back arched, her straining nipples pushing against his fingers until he tugged on the tender buds and an audible gasp escaped her.

Gaetano lifted her and turned her round to face him. 'I want to be your first,' he breathed in a roughened undertone. 'It will be my privilege.'

'Careful, Gaetano...you're sounding nice.' Now outrageously aware of her naked breasts, Poppy crossed her arms to hide them.

'I may be many things, but nice isn't one of them,' Gaetano growled, pulling her down on the bed beside him and covering her pouting mouth hungrily with his own. Unbridled pleasure snaked through her as his tongue merged with hers. An electrifying push of hunger gripped her as his hands shifted to toy with her breasts. He pushed her back against the pillows and lowered his mouth to her pouting nipples.

'Palest pink like pearls,' Gaetano mused, stroking a tender tip with appreciation as he gazed down at her.' I wondered what colour they would be...'

Her green eyes widened. 'Seriously?' she prompted.

'And they're perfect like the rest of you,' he groaned, lowering his head to lick a distended crest. 'You were so worth waiting for at the church.'

Poppy wasn't quite as pleased as she would have assumed she would be by having that much appreciation directed at her physical attributes. Gaetano was interfering with her fantasy, that fantasy that she had not even acknowledged was playing at the back of her mind, the fantasy in which Gaetano loved her and appreciated her for all sorts of other reasons that went beyond lust.

'And so were you,' Poppy told Gaetano, deciding to turn the tables as she sat up to dislodge him and pushed him back against the pillows. He studied her with questioning dark golden eyes semi-veiled by black curling lashes. She spread her fingers across his hard pectoral muscles, stroking down over his sleek ribcage to his flat abdomen.

'Don't stop now,' he husked.

Her fingers were clumsy on his belt buckle and the button on the waistband of his trousers, her knuckles nudging against the little furrow of dark hair that disappeared below his clothing. She reached for the zip. Her lack of expertise was obvious to Gaetano and the oddest sensation of tenderness infiltrated him as he noted the tense self-consciousness etched in her flushed face.

'Why do I get the feeling this is a first for you?'

'Everyone is a learner at some stage...' she framed jerkily.

Gaetano yanked down his zip for himself and then tossed her back flat on the bed again while he divested himself of his trousers and his boxers. 'If you touched me now, it would all be over far too fast,' he told her thickly. 'That's why I'm going to do most of the touching and you will lie back and let me do the work.'

'If you think of it as work, I don't think you should bother.'

'Nothing would stop me now. I can hardly wait to be inside you.' Gaetano leant over her, his urgent erection pushing against her hip. 'Having you in my bed has been my fantasy for weeks.'

'Fantasy never lives up to reality,' Poppy said nervously. 'I don't want to be a fantasy.'

'Sorry, it's *my* fantasy,' Gaetano traded, stroking a wondering hand down over the slender curve of her hip to the hot, damp secret at the heart of her.

Her hips jerked and her eyes shut as he traced between her thighs. Her breath snarled in her throat. She was so sensitised that she shuddered when he circled her clitoris with his fingertip. Her whole body was climbing of its own volition into a tight, tense spiral of growing need. Even the brush of a finger against her tight entrance was almost too much to bear. Her hips pushed against the mattress, her heart thumping like thunder inside her chest as he shimmied down the bed, fingertips delicately caressing her inner thighs as he pushed her legs back, opening her.

'No, you can't do that!' she gasped in consternation.

'Stai zitto...' he told her softly. 'You don't get to tell me what to do in bed.'

The flick of his tongue across torturously tender nerve endings deprived her of voice and then of thought. Her head shifted back and forth on the pillows, the thrum of hunger building up through her body to a siren's scream of need. She gasped, she cried his name, she moaned, she lost control so completely and utterly that when the explosive release of orgasm claimed her it took her by storm. And the world stopped turning for long minutes, her body still quaking with wondrous aftershocks while Gaetano looked down at her with satisfaction.

As Gaetano tilted her back she felt the smooth steel push of him against her still-throbbing core. The tight knot low in her pelvis made its presence felt again, the hollow ache of hunger stirring afresh. He slid against her, easing into her by degrees, straining her delicate sheath.

'You're so tight,' he groaned, pulling back again and then angling his hips for another, more forceful entrance.

The sharp stinging pain made Poppy flinch for a millisecond and then her body was pushing on past that fleeting discomfort to linger on the satisfying stretch and fullness of his invasion. A little moan broke low in her throat and she moved her hips to luxuriate in the throbbing hardness of his bold masculinity.

Gaetano swore in Italian. 'You feel like heaven,' he growled in her ear. 'Am I hurting you now?'

'Oh, no,' she told him truthfully.

And then he moved again, withdrawing and spearing deep enough to wring a cry of startled enjoyment from her. From that moment on her eagerness climbed in tune with Gaetano's every measured thrust. Her heart raced, her legs clamping round his lean hips as she lifted to him, matching his driving rhythm while the electrifying excitement continued to build. And when she reached that peak for the second time she plunged over it in a fevered delirium of intense quivering release and lay adrift in pleasure.

'That was amazing,' Gaetano muttered thickly, rolling over onto his back while curving an arm round her trembling body. '*You* were amazing, *bella mia*.'

Poppy felt totally exhausted and she was content to lie there in the circle of his arms and marvel at the sublime sense of peace she was experiencing. Belatedly, she acknowledged that her throat and head had now become seriously sore. She hoped that Gaetano wouldn't catch her cold and felt guilty for not warning him.

In fact she was just about to mention her affliction when Gaetano sat up to say quietly, 'Possibly part of the reason it felt so amazing was that it was the very first time I've had sex bareback.'

'Bareback?' she queried.

'I didn't use protection. I had a health check a couple of weeks ago to ensure that I'm clean and you're guarded against pregnancy,' he reminded her. 'I couldn't resist the temptation to try it.'

Poppy made no comment because she knew that he would be ultra-careful with her in the protection stakes because to be careless and risk a pregnancy would come at too high a price for either of them.

'I'm really hungry now...aren't you?' Gaetano admitted, thrusting back the sheet and vacating the bed.

'Not really, no.' Indeed the thought of forcing food past her aching throat made her wince. 'But I could murder a cup of tea.'

'You'll have to make it for yourself,' he warned her. 'I sent the staff home.'

'I've been making tea for myself since I was a child,' she told him wryly.

'I forgot.' Faint colour enhancing the exotic slant of his cheekbones, Gaetano frowned. 'Your voice sounds funny...'

'I'm getting a cold.' Poppy sighed. 'I hope you don't get it too.'

'I never catch colds.' Gaetano vanished into the bathroom and a moment later she heard the shower running.

Poppy was so exhausted that she really didn't want to move, but exhaustion was something she had become practised at shaking off and working through in recent months when she had spent all day cleaning Woodfield Hall and then had stood at the bar serving drinks all evening. Sliding out of bed, she went into the dressing room to pick an outfit and padded off to find another bathroom to use.

Gaetano hadn't hurt her much, she thought tiredly as she dressed. He had been considerate. He had made it incredibly enjoyable. Why did the knowledge that he had learned how to make sex enjoyable with other women stab her like a knife? She blinked, feeling hot and more than a little dizzy. Clearly she had caught an absolute doozy of a cold but she didn't want to be a burden by admitting to Gaetano that she felt awful. A good night's sleep would make her feel much better.

Casually clad in cotton palazzo pants and a tee shirt, she went downstairs, located the kitchen and put on the kettle. She heard Gaetano talking to someone and her brow pleated as she walked to the doorway to see who it was. She almost groaned out loud when she finally realised that he was talking into his phone in tones that sounded angry. As his brilliant dark golden eyes landed on her she froze at the chilling light in his gaze.

'What's wrong?' she asked, her voice fracturing into roughness.

Gaetano thrust his phone back in the pocket of his jeans and stared at her angrily, almost as if he'd never seen her before. 'That was Rodolfo calling to warn me about something some tabloid newspaper plans to print tomorrow. One of his old friends in the press tipped him off…'

'Oh..?' Poppy heard the kettle switching off behind

her and turned away, desperate to ease her sore throat with a hot drink.

Gaetano bit out a sharp, unamused laugh. 'When were you planning to tell me that you once worked as a nude model?'

Poppy spun back, wide-eyed with astonishment. 'What on earth are you talking about?'

'That filthy rag is going to print photos of you naked tomorrow. My wife *naked* in a newspaper for the world to see!' Gaetano launched at her in outrage. '*Madonna diavolo*...how could you cheapen yourself like that?'

'I've never worked as a nude model. There couldn't possibly be photos of me naked anywhere...' Poppy protested and then she stilled, literally freezing into place, sudden anxiety filling her eyes.

'Oh, you've just remembered doing it, have you?' Gaetano derided harshly. 'Well, thanks for warning me. If I'd known I would've bought the photos to keep them off the market.'

'It's not like you think,' Poppy began awkwardly, horrified at the idea that illegal shots might have been taken of her at the photographic studio while she was unaware. But what else could she think?

As something akin to an anxiety attack claimed her already overheated body Poppy found it very hard to catch her breath. She dropped dizzily down into the chair by the scrubbed pine table. 'I'm not feeling well,' she mumbled apologetically.

'If you think that feigning illness is likely to get you out of this particular tight corner, it's not,' Gaetano asserted in such a temper that he could hardly keep his voice level and his volume under control.

The mere idea of nude photos of Poppy being splashed all over the media provoked a visceral reaction from Gaetano. It offended him deeply. Poppy was his wife and the secrets of her body were his and not for sharing. He wanted to punch walls and tear things apart. He was ablaze with a dark, violent fury that had very little to do with the fact that another scandal around his name would once again drag the proud name of the Leonetti Bank into disrepute. In fact his whole reaction felt disturbingly personal.

'Not feigning,' Poppy framed raggedly, pushing her hands down on the table top to rise again.

'I want the truth. If you had told me about this, I would never have married you,' Gaetano fired at her without hesitation.

Poppy flopped back down into the seat because her legs refused to support her. She felt really ill and believed she must have caught the flu. He would never have married her had he known about the photo. Who would ever have thought that Gaetano, the notorious womaniser, would be that narrow-minded? And why should she care? And yet she *did* care. A lone stinging tear trickled from the corner of her eye and once again she tried to get up and leave but she couldn't catch her breath. It was as though a giant stone were compressing her lungs. In panic at that air deprivation her hands flailed up to her throat, warding off the darkness that was claiming her.

Gaetano gazed in disbelief at Poppy as she virtually

slithered off the chair down onto the floor and lay there unconscious, as pale and still as a corpse. And all of a sudden the publication of nude photos of *his* wife was no longer his most overriding concern...

CHAPTER EIGHT

'No, I DON'T think that my wife has an eating disorder,' Gaetano bit out between gritted teeth in the waiting room.

'Signora Leonetti is seriously underweight, dehydrated…in generally poor physical condition,' the doctor outlined disapprovingly. 'That is why the bacterial infection has gained such a hold on her and why we are still struggling to get her temperature under control. That she contrived to get through a wedding and travel in such a state has to be a miracle.'

'A miracle…' Gaetano whispered, sick to his stomach and, for the very first time in his brilliantly successful, high-achieving life, feeling like a failure.

How else could he feel? Poppy had collapsed. His wife was wearing an oxygen mask in the IC unit, having drugs pumped into her. All right, she hadn't told him how she was feeling but shouldn't a normal, decent human being have *noticed* that something was wrong?

Unfortunately he clearly couldn't claim to be a normal, decent human being. And his analytical mind left him in no doubt of exactly where he had gone wrong.

He had been too busy admiring his bride's tiny waist to register that she was dangerously thin. He had been too busy dragging her off to bed to register that she was unwell. And when she had tried to tell him, what had he done? *Porca miseria*, he had shouted at her and accused her of feigning illness!

'May I see her now?' he asked thickly.

He stood at the foot of the bed looking at Poppy through fresh eyes, rigorously blocking the sexual allure that screwed with his brain. Ironically she had always impressed him as being so lively, energetic and opinionated that he had instinctively endowed her with a glowing health that she did not possess. Now that she was silent and lying there so still, he could see how vulnerable she really was. It was etched in the fine bones of her face, the slenderness of her arms, the exhaustion he could clearly see in the bluish shadows below her eyes.

And what else would she be but exhausted? he asked himself grimly. For months she had worked two jobs, managing the hall and working at the bar. She had been so busy looking after her mother and her brother that she had forgotten to look after herself. He suspected that she had got out of the habit then of taking regular meals and rest. And even when both food and rest had been on offer in London she had *still* chosen to work every day at that café. In truth she was as much of a workaholic in her proud and stubborn independence as he was, he acknowledged bleakly. He could only hope that he was correct in believing that she did not suffer from an underlying eating disorder.

'Your grandfather is waiting outside...' a nurse informed him.

'There was no need for you to leave your bed,' Gaetano scolded the older man. 'I only texted you so that you would know where I was.'

'How is she?' Rodolfo asked worriedly.

And Gaetano told him, withholding nothing. 'I've been a pretty lousy husband so far,' he breathed in grim conclusion, conceding the point before it could be made for him.

'You have a steep learning curve in front of you.' His grandfather sighed. 'But she's a wonderful girl and well worth the effort. And it's not where you start out that matters, Gaetano...it's where you end up.'

Rodolfo could not have been more wrong in that estimate, Gaetano reflected austerely. Where you started out mattered very much if you had previously blocked the road to journey's end. His marriage was not a marriage and the relationship was already faltering. He had put up a roadblock with the word divorce on it and used that as an excuse to behave badly. He had screwed up. He had been shockingly selfish and with Poppy of all people, Poppy who had trailed round after him and his dog, Dino, on the estate when they were both kids. And what had she been like then?

Like an irritating little kid sister. Kind, madly affectionate, his biggest fan. He exhaled heavily. He had had more compassion as a boy than he had retained as an adult and he had not lived up to Poppy's high expectations. Worse still, he had taken advantage of her

LYNNE GRAHAM   137

despair over her family's predicament. He had forced
through the terms he wanted, terms she should have
denied for her own sake, terms only a complete selfish
bastard would have demanded. But it was a little too
late to turn that particular clock back.

Was the selfishness a Leonetti trait? His father had
been the ultimate egotist and his mother had never in
her life, to his knowledge, put anyone's needs before her
own. Had his dysfunctional parents made him the ruthless predator that he was at heart? Or had wealth and
success and boundless ambition irrevocably changed
him? Gaetano asked himself grimly.

Poppy surfaced to appreciate that her head had stopped
aching. She discovered that she could swallow again
and that her breath was no longer trapped in her chest.
She opened her eyes on the unfamiliar room, taking
in the hospital bed and the drip attached to her arm
before focusing on Gaetano, who was hunched in the
chair in the corner.

Gaetano looked as if he had been dragged through
hell and far removed from the sophisticated, exquisitely
groomed image that was the norm for him. His black
curls were tousled, his jaw line heavily stubbled. His
jacket was missing. His shirt was open at his brown
throat and his sleeves were rolled up. As she stared
he lifted his head and she collided with glorious dark
golden eyes.

Snatches of memory engulfed her in broken bits and
pieces. She remembered the passion and the pleasure
he had shown her. Then she remembered his fury about

the nude photos, his refusal to credit that she was ill. But she remembered nothing after that point.

Gaetano stood up and pressed the bell on the wall. 'How are you feeling?'

'Better than I felt when I fainted…er…did I faint?'

'You passed out. Next time you feel ill, *tell me*,' he breathed with grim urgency.

Poppy grimaced. 'It was our first night together.'

'That's irrelevant. Your health comes first…*always*,' he stressed. 'I'm not a little boy. I can deal with disappointment.'

She was relieved to see that his anger had gone. A nurse came in and went through a series of checks with her.

'Why did I pass out?' Poppy asked Gaetano once the nurse had departed.

'You had an infection and it ran out of control. Your immune system was too weak to fight it off,' he shared flatly. 'From here on in you have to take better care of yourself. But first, give me an honest answer to one question…do you have an eating disorder?'

'No, of course not. I'm naturally skinny…well, I have lost weight over the last few months,' she conceded grudgingly.

'You have to eat more,' Gaetano decreed. 'No more skipping meals.'

'I didn't eat on our wedding day because I wasn't feeling well,' she protested.

'Am I so intimidating that you couldn't tell me that?' Gaetano asked, springing restively upright again to pace round the spacious room.

'Come on, Gaetano. All those guests, all that fuss. What bride would have wanted to be a party pooper?'

'You should have told me that night,' Gaetano asserted.

Poppy's lashes lowered over her strained eyes. 'You weren't in the mood to hear that I was ill.'

'*Dio mio!* It shouldn't have mattered how I felt!'

A flush drove away her pallor but she kept her gaze firmly fixed on the bed. 'We had an agreement.'

'That's over, forget about it,' Gaetano bit out in a raw undertone.

She wondered what he meant and would have questioned him but the doctor arrived and there was no opportunity. Gaetano spoke to the older man at length in Italian. Breakfast arrived on a tray and she ate with appetite, mindful of the doctor's warning that she needed to regain the weight she had lost. She was smothering a yawn when Gaetano lifted the tray away.

'Get some sleep,' he urged. 'I'm going back to the house to shower and change and bring you back some clothes. As long as you promise to eat and rest, I can take you out of here this evening.'

'I'm not an invalid...' Uneasy with his forbidding attitude, Poppy fiddled with her wedding ring, turning it round and round on her finger. 'What's happened about the photos you mentioned?'

Gaetano froze and then he reached for the jacket on the chair and withdrew a folded piece of paper. 'It was a hoax...'

The newspaper cutting depicted a reproduction of a calendar shot headed Miss July. In it Poppy was reclining on a chaise longue with her bare shoulders and long legs on display while a giant floral arrangement was sited to block any more intimate view of her body.

'I kept my knickers on,' she told him ruefully. 'But I had to take my bra off because the straps showed. I was a student nurse on the ladies' football team. We did the charity calendar to raise funds for the children's hospice. There was nothing the slightest bit raunchy about the shots. It was all good, clean fun...'

Dark colour now rode along Gaetano's cheekbones. 'I know and I accept that. I'm sorry I shouted at you. When Rodolfo showed me that photo in the newspaper I felt like an idiot.'

'No, you're not an idiot.' Just very *very* possessive in a way Poppy had not expected him to be. *My* wife, he had growled, outraged by the prospect of anyone else seeing her naked.

'You have an old-fashioned streak that I never would have guessed you had,' Poppy remarked tentatively.

'What is mine is mine and you are mine,' Gaetano informed her in a gut reaction that took control of him before he could even think about what he was saying.

That gut reaction utterly unnerved him. What the hell was wrong with him? *Mine?* Since when? Only weeks earlier he would have leapt on the excuse of inappropriate nude photos to break off their supposed engagement. He had not intended to stay engaged to Poppy for very long at all, had actually been depending on her to do or say something dreadful to give him a good reason to reclaim his freedom. How had he travelled from that frame of mind to his current one? All of a sudden she felt like his wife, his *real* wife. Why was that? Sex had never meant that much to Gaetano and had certainly never opened any doors to deeper connections. But he had wanted Poppy as he had never wanted any woman before and that hunger had triumphed.

Poppy went pink. 'Not really…'

'For as long as you wear that ring you're mine,' Gaetano qualified.

Poppy hadn't needed that reminder of her true status, hadn't sought that more detailed interpretation. Her heart sank and she closed her eyes to shut out his lean, darkly handsome features. It was no good because she still saw his beautiful face in her mind's eye.

'Lie down, relax,' Gaetano urged. 'You're exhausted. I'll be back later.'

You're mine. But she wasn't. She was a fake bride and a temporary wife. Casual sex didn't grant her any status. Suppressing a groan, she shut down her brain on her teeming thoughts and fell asleep.

Late that afternoon, she left the hospital in a wheelchair in spite of her protests. In truth she still felt weak and woozy. Gaetano lifted her out of the chair and stowed her carefully in the passenger seat before joining her.

She was wearing the faded denim sundress Dolores had packed for her.

'I need to organise new clothes for you,' Gaetano told her.

'No, you don't. When this finishes we go our separate ways and I won't have any use for fancy threads.'

'But *this* isn't going to finish any time soon,' Gaetano pointed out softly.

Poppy studied his bold bronzed profile. So far they had enjoyed the honeymoon from hell but he was bearing up well to the challenge. His caring, compassionate husband act was off-the-charts good but she guessed that was purely for Rodolfo's benefit. They were supposed to be in love, after all, and a loving husband would be upset when his bride fell ill on their wedding day. Lush black lashes curled up as he turned his head to look at her, blue-black hair gleaming in the bright light, spectacular golden eyes wary.

'What's wrong?' he prompted.

'I should compliment you. You can fake nice to the manner born,' she quipped.

His wide sensual mouth compressed. For once there was no witty comeback. 'Dolores is planning to fatten you up on pasta. I also mentioned that you're passionate about chocolate.'

Chocolate and Gaetano, she corrected inwardly.

She collided with his eyes and hurriedly looked away, struggling not to revel in the sound of his dark, deep, accented drawl and the high she got from the sheer charisma of his smile. Awareness shimmied through her like an electrical storm. Something low in her tummy had turned molten and liquid while her breasts were swelling inside her bra. He had taught her to want him, she thought bitterly, and now the wanting wouldn't conveniently go away. That hunger was like a slow burn building inside her.

When they returned to La Fattoria, Gaetano insisted

that she went straight to bed and dined there. He ignored her declaration that she was feeling well enough to come downstairs and urged her to follow medical advice and rest. A large collection of books and DVDs were delivered mid-evening for her entertainment and although Poppy was tired she deliberately stayed awake waiting for Gaetano to come to bed. She drifted off around one in the morning and wakened to see Gaetano switching out the light and walking back to the door.

'Where are you going?' she mumbled.

'I'm sleeping next door,' he said wryly.

'That's not necessary.' Poppy had to fight to keep the hurt note out of her voice. She had been looking forward to Gaetano putting his arms around her again and she was disappointed that it wasn't going to happen.

'I'm a restless sleeper. I don't want to disturb you,' Gaetano countered smoothly.

Poppy's heart sank as if he had kicked it. Maybe if sex wasn't on the menu, Gaetano preferred to sleep alone. And why would she argue about that? It was possible that Gaetano had already had all he really wanted from her. She had heard about men who lost sexual interest once the novelty was gone. One night might have been enough for him. Was he that kind of lover? And if he was, what did it matter to her? It wasn't as if she were about to embarrass herself and chase after him, was it? Why would she do that when their eventual separation and divorce were already set in stone?

So, it didn't make sense that after he had gone she curled up in the big bed feeling lonely and needy and rejected. Why on earth was she bothered?

* * *

'You shouldn't be down here keeping an old man company,' Rodolfo reproved as Poppy poured his coffee and her own. 'No cake?'

'Cinzia's putting it on a fancy plate to bring it out. You're getting spoiled,' Poppy told him fondly, perching on the low wall of the terrace.

His bright dark eyes twinkled. 'Nothing wrong with being spoiled. You spoil me with your cakes but Gaetano's supposed to be spoiling you.'

Poppy's luminous green eyes shadowed. 'He does but I've let him off the honeymoon trail for a few hours to work. It keeps him happy...'

'You look well,' Gaetano's grandfather said approvingly. 'On your wedding day you looked as though a strong breeze would blow you over, now you look...'

'Fatter?' Poppy laughed. 'You can say it. I'd got too thin and I look better carrying a little more weight. Dolores has been feeding me up like a Christmas turkey.'

Hands banded round her raised knees, Poppy gazed out over the valley, scanning the marching rows of bright green vines. The property referred to as the guest house was a substantial building surrounded by trees and it had a spectacular view. It had always been Rodolfo's favourite spot and when he had tired of his late son's constant parties at the main house he had built his own bolt-hole.

Cinzia, who looked after the guest house and its elderly occupant, brought out the lemon drizzle cake that Poppy had baked.

Poppy and Gaetano had been in Tuscany for a whole

month, days fleeing past at a speed she could barely register. As soon as she had regained her strength, Gaetano had begun taking her out sightseeing. Her brain was crammed to bursting point by magnificent artworks and architectural wonders. But the memories that lingered were of a rather more personal variety.

Her delicate gold earrings were a gift from Gaetano, purchased from one of the spectacular goldsmiths on the Ponte Vecchio in Florence. In Pisa they had strolled through the magical streets to dine after the daily visitors had left and he had told her that in bright light her red hair reminded him of a gorgeous sunset. In Lucca they had walked the city walls in the leafy shade of the overhanging trees and Gaetano had briefly held her hand to steady her. In Siena she had proved Gaetano wrong when he'd told her that climbing more than four hundred steps to the top of the Torre del Mangia would be too much for her and he had laughed and given her that special heart-stopping smile that somehow always rocked her world. And in the Grotta del Vento he had whipped off his jacket and wrapped it round her when he'd seen her shiver in the coolness of the underground cave system.

Personal memories but not the romantic memories of a newly married couple, Poppy conceded unhappily. There was no sex. There had been no sex since she had taken ill and he refused to take hints. And she refused to count as romantic all the many evenings they had talked long and late at the farmhouse after a beautiful leisurely meal because every evening had ended with them occupying separate beds.

Indeed, Gaetano only got close to her in his grand-father's presence, clearly as part of his effort to keep up the pretence that they were a normal couple, and then he would close his arms round her, kiss her shoulder or her cheek, act as if he were a touchy-feely loving male even though he wasn't. His determined detachment often made Poppy want to scream and slap him into a normal reaction. What had happened to the sex-hungry male who couldn't keep his hands off her?

And while Poppy was lying awake irritating herself by wondering how to tempt Gaetano without being too obvious about it and scolding herself for being so defensive, another bigger worry slowly began to percolate in the back of her mind. At first she had told herself off for being foolish. After all, they had only had sex once and she had conscientiously taken the contraceptive pill from the first day it was prescribed to her. When her period was late she had believed that her illness or even the change of diet or stress could have messed up her menstrual cycle. As the days trickled past her sub-dued sense of panic had steadily mounted and she was very glad that she was visiting the doctor the following day for an official review following her release from hospital a month earlier. She would ask for a pregnancy test then just to be on the safe side. And of course she would soon realise that she had been foolishly worrying over nothing. There was no way she could possibly be pregnant.

Leaving Rodolfo snoozing in the shade, Poppy clicked her fingers to bring Muffin gambolling to her side as she strolled back to the main house.

Muffin had made a full recovery from his injuries and had been inseparable from Poppy from the day Gaetano had brought him back from the vet's and settled the little terrier in his wife's lap. The dog ran ahead as Poppy walked below the trees enjoying the cool shade rather than the heat of late afternoon. She smiled at the colourful glimpses of poppy-and-sunflower-studded fields visible through the gaps between the trees.

Since the wedding she had talked to her mother and brother every week on the phone. Damien was happy in his new job while her mother had renewed contact with Poppy's aunt, Jess, who had stopped seeing her sister when she became an alcoholic. Now there was talk of Poppy's mother going to live with her sister in Manchester after she was released.

That idea left Poppy feeling oddly abandoned and she told herself off for her selfishness because it was not as if she herself would be in a position to set up home with her mother any time soon. No, Poppy was very conscious that she had a long, hard haul ahead of her faking being happily married to Gaetano for at least a couple of years. And if she was miserable, well, she accepted that that was her own fault as well. If her emotions made her miserable it was because she had failed to control them. Her craving for Gaetano's attention had been the first warning sign, missing him in bed after only one night the second. From that point on the warning signs had simply multiplied into a terrifying avalanche.

If Gaetano held her hand, she felt light-headed. If he touched her she lit up inside like a firework. If he smiled her heart soared. Her adolescent crush had grown into something much more dangerous, something she couldn't control and that occasionally overwhelmed her. She had fallen madly, insanely in love with the husband who wasn't a husband. It wasn't fair that Gaetano should be so beautiful that she found intense pleasure in simply looking at him. It was even less fair that he was such entertaining company and had wonderful manners. Nor did it help that he took great pains to ensure that she ate well and rested often, revealing a caring side she had only previously seen in play around his grandfather. It was all a cheat, she kept on telling herself. It was a cheat because he wasn't available to her in any way even though she loved him.

She *loved* Gaetano. She was ashamed of that truth when he had warned her not to make that mistake long before he'd even married her. How had she turned out so predictable? It was not as if she believed in the pot of gold at the end of the rainbow. She was not a dreamer now that she had grown up. She knew that no happy ending awaited her and she would cope as long as she contrived to keep her emotional attachment to herself because she would die a thousand deaths before she allowed Gaetano to even suspect how she felt. He hadn't asked for love from her and he didn't want her love. No way was he getting her love for free so that he could pity her.

A fancy sports car that didn't belong to Gaetano's collection was parked outside La Fattoria. Poppy smoothed down her exotic black and red sundress, one of the designer garments Gaetano had purchased for her weeks ago. It was cutting-edge style and edgy enough to feel comfortable to her, so she had acquiesced to the new wardrobe, mortified by the suspicion that for her to insist on continuing to wear cheap clothing would embarrass Gaetano. No, he might deserve a kick for seducing her with unforgettable enthusiasm and then stopping that intimacy in its tracks, but she still cringed at the idea of embarrassing him in public.

Gaetano saw his wife from the front window, her show-stopping long legs silhouetted beneath the thin fabric of her dress. It was see-through, and it killed him to see her legs and recall that one indescribably hot night when he had slid between them. Feeling his trousers tighten, he gritted his teeth. The sooner he was out of their marriage and free again, the more normal he would feel.

In truth nothing had felt normal since their wedding. Being around Poppy without being able to touch her was driving him insane. He had a high sex drive and he had never tried to suppress it before. But for the first time in his life with a woman he was trying to do the right thing and it was hurting like a bitch. Poppy deserved more than he had to give. But inexplicably Poppy had got under his skin and since he had laid eyes on her no other woman had attracted him. Although he'd satisfied himself sexually with her, he still desired her, which was a first for him. The thrill of the chase had gone, but the hunger lingered, ever present, ever powerful. There was something about her that affected him differently from other women. She didn't irritate him, she didn't make demands, she didn't care about his money. In the strangest of ways she reminded him of his grandmother, who had been as at home with staff as she was with visitors. Poppy's easy charm was spread wide and he no longer marvelled that Rodolfo idolised her and the household staff couldn't do enough for her. Even that ugly little dog was her devoted slave.

'Sorry... I needed to freshen up,' Serena announced as she walked back into the drawing room. 'I got blown to bits. I forgot to tie my hair back before I drove over.'

Gaetano studied the smooth golden veil of Serena's hair. He had never seen her with a hair out of place. Poppy's hair got madly tangled, but she didn't care. It had been wild that night in bed, he recalled, fighting off arousal as he pictured that vibrant mane tumbled across the pillows, her lovely face flushed and full of satisfaction, satisfaction *he* had given her.

Poppy entered and froze at the sight of Serena. 'Sorry, I didn't realise you had company.'

'Oh, I'm not company. I'm one of Gaetano's oldest friends,' Serena reminded her. 'How are you, Poppy? I would have called in sooner, but it is your honeymoon, after all.'

'Are you staying round here?'

'Didn't Gaetano tell you that my parents have had a house near here for years and years? We first met at one of his parents' parties when we were teenagers,' Serena told her with a golden-girl smile of fond familiarity aimed at Gaetano.

Serena was the wicked witch in the disguise of a beautiful princess, Poppy decided bleakly. Serena knew exactly where to plunge the knife and twist it in another's woman's flesh. She loved to boast of how well,

how intimately and how long she had known Gaetano.
'Fancy that,' she said non-committally.

'I'm actually here to beg for a favour,' Serena confided cutely. 'I met Rodolfo in the village last week and
he told me that Gaetano was flying to Paris for a conference tomorrow. May I come too? As you know I'm
looking for a new job and I could use the introductions
you'd give me.'

'Of course. I'll pick you up on the way to the airport,'
Gaetano suggested calmly.

Hell no, Poppy thought, watching Serena look at
Gaetano with a teasing girly smile and a shake of her
golden head that sent the silken strands tossing round
her perfect face. Her teeth ground together.

'Are you coming too?' Serena asked Poppy.

But Poppy could see that somehow Serena had already established that Gaetano would be travelling to
Paris alone. 'No, I'm afraid I have an appointment to
keep,' Poppy admitted.

'I wish you'd agreed to reschedule that. I wanted to
accompany you,' Gaetano reminded her with detect-
able exasperation.

Poppy wrinkled her nose. 'It's only a check-up.'

And she didn't want him attending the doctor's surgery with her because she didn't want him present for
the discussion of the pregnancy possibility.

'I could cancel and come to Paris with you,' she heard
herself offer abruptly, because she really didn't want
Serena getting the chance to be alone with Gaetano.

'You need to keep that appointment,' Gaetano countered levelly. 'In any case, I'll be back by evening.'

'I'll look after him,' Serena assured her smugly and Poppy wondered unhappily if the other woman somehow sensed that Gaetano's marriage was not quite normal. Or was it simply that the beautiful blonde could not imagine a male as well educated and sophisticated as Gaetano marrying an ordinary woman without there being some hidden agenda?

She had paled at Serena's self-satisfaction. Gaetano had not been with a woman in a month. Naturally Poppy didn't want him on board his private jet with a man-eater like Serena. Serena was already putting out willing and welcome signals as bright as traffic lights. But what could Poppy possibly say to Gaetano to inhibit him in such a marriage as theirs? He didn't belong to her. She didn't own him.

There were other ways of holding onto a man's attention though, she reasoned abstractedly. There was using sex as a weapon, exactly the sort of manipulative behaviour she had looked down on *before* she fell in love with Gaetano. Now, all of a sudden confronted by Serena studying Gaetano as though he were one of the seven wonders of the world, Poppy's stance on the moral high ground felt foolish and dangerous. Pride wouldn't keep her warm at night if Gaetano succumbed to Serena's advances and embarked on an affair with her. An affair that Poppy suspected would soon be followed by divorce and remarriage because she didn't believe that Serena would accept being hidden in the background or that Gaetano would resist the chance to acquire a woman who would make a much more suitable wife.

* * *

Gaetano released his breath in a slow hiss when Poppy joined him for dinner in a black halter-necked dress that outlined her lithe, slender figure. His intense dark gaze rested briefly on the taut little buds of her breasts that were clearly defined by the thin fabric and he compressed his lips round his wine glass. Look, *don't* touch, he told himself grimly.

'I've been wondering,' he remarked. 'What made you choose nursing?'

Surprised by the topic, Poppy lifted and dropped her bare shoulders. 'I like caring for people. Being needed makes me feel useful.'

'Your family certainly needed you,' Gaetano said drily.

The main course was served. After eating in silence for a few minutes Poppy said, 'I'm thinking of doing something other than nursing when the time comes.'

'Such as?' Gaetano prompted impatiently.

'Gardening,' she admitted in a defensive tone.

'Gardening?' Gaetano repeated with incredulity.

'I always discounted my interest in growing things because I come from several generations of gardeners. But I suppose it's in my blood,' Poppy opined wryly. 'Of course if I'd ever mentioned it I would have found myself working for your family and I didn't want that.'

'I've never understood why not. We're good employers.'

'Yes, but working on the estate means real old-fashioned service.'

'And what is bartending but service?' Gaetano watched her turn to lift her water glass and his attention dropped to the firm, full, pouting curve of her breast revealed by her dress. He shifted tensely in his seat.

'There's not that same sense of inequality between employer and employee that there is on the estate. I can't explain it but I've never accepted that you are superior to me simply because you were born into wealth and privilege.'

'Have I ever made you feel that way?'

Poppy pushed away her plate and stood up. 'You can't help it. Your parents raised you like that.'

'Where are you going?'

'For a walk—it's a beautiful evening. I'll have space for dessert by the time I come back,' she told Sean, who was hovering to remove their plates.

'I'll come too.' Gaetano sprang upright.

Poppy was as restless as a cat on hot bricks, which was hardly surprising when she had set herself the objective of somehow seducing Gaetano before his flight to Paris. Sadly discussing her career aspirations and the class system wouldn't get her any closer to him and she wasn't very deft at flirting. If all else failed, she thought ruefully, she would simply slip into bed with him and pray that his libido cracked his detachment.

'That's a daring dress,' Gaetano observed. 'The split in the skirt shows me your thighs at every step and I can see the curve and shape of your breasts. Don't wear it anywhere more public…'

Poppy was relieved that he had actually noticed the provocative outfit because it meant that she wasn't yet fading into the wallpaper as far as he was concerned. Her high heels crunched through the gravel. A finger danced up her exposed spine like a flame licking at her bare skin and she shivered, snatching in a breath as he flicked the knot at the nape of her neck. 'If I pulled that loose...'

'The whole thing would probably fall off,' she completed.

Gaetano groaned out loud. 'Don't tempt me.'

'I didn't think you could be tempted any more.'

'Temptation runs on a continuous loop around you.'

Poppy glanced at him with disbelieving eyes. 'Then why have you been keeping your distance?'

'It should've been that way from the start, *bellezza mia*. I was a selfish bastard to insist on sex.'

'So, tell me something new,' Poppy invited.

After a moment of telling silence, Gaetano's stunning dark golden gaze locked to her flushed face in near wonderment at that response before he burst out laughing. 'Well, that's telling me...'

'If you wanted lies you married the wrong girl.'

'Obviously,' Gaetano conceded, lounging back against an aged stone pedestal table at the viewpoint where the land fell away to reveal the panoramic landscape beyond the garden. Poppy gazed out at the beautiful countryside, her hair glowing like a live flame against her ivory skin as the sun went down.

'I'm not being fair to you,' Poppy muttered with sudden awkwardness. 'I wanted sex too!'

'Maybe when we were actually having it but not before,' Gaetano qualified.

'Oh, for goodness' sake, Gaetano... I couldn't *wait* to rip your clothes off!' Poppy flung back at him in exasperation. 'I didn't stay a virgin until this age by not knowing what I wanted. I'm not some easily led little rag doll. Stop talking as if you took advantage of a naïve kid!'

'But I *did* take advantage of you.' Gaetano reached out to grip both her hands in emphasis and prevent her from her constant pacing back and forth in front of him. 'You were a virgin and I'm a natural predator. What I want I take. And I very much wanted you.'

Poppy took a step closer to his lean, powerful body. 'How much is "very much"?'

He brought her hands down lightly to the revealing bulge at his groin. Her fingertips fluttered appreciatively over the hard jut of his erection and he jerked in surprise at that intimate caress. His golden eyes smouldering with erotic heat, he pulled her up against him and crushed her ripe pink mouth beneath his, his tongue darting and delving deep to send tiny shudders of shocking arousal coursing through her lower body. Liquid heat pooled between her thighs.

'You're a tease,' Gaetano told her darkly.

'No, I'm a sure thing,' Poppy contradicted, helpless in the grip of the need throbbing and pulsing through her trembling length.

She felt the sudden give at her neck as he tugged loose the tie of her dress. As the bodice dropped to her waist his hands closed to her hips and he lifted her up onto the stone table before reaching below the skirt to close his hands into the waistband of her lace knickers and yank them down.

'Out here?' she whispered, shaken by the concept as he dug her discarded underwear into his pocket with single-minded efficiency.

'Out here because I couldn't make it back indoors… and I believe I can promise you a very active night,' he husked, bending her backwards to capture a rosy nipple between his lips and lash it with his tongue while his fingers stroked and teased the delicate pink folds at her core.

'I want you,' she framed jaggedly, her breath strangled in her throat by a responsive gasp as his thumb rubbed over her and then a long finger tested her readiness.

He slid a single digit into her lush opening and her body jackknifed, spine arching, hips lifting off the cold stone surface. And the coldness below her only added to the intense heat punching through her quivering body, steamrollering over her inhibitions and heightening every sensation to an unbearable level.

'So wet, so tight,' Gaetano growled, yanking down his zip with a lack of cool that even in the state he was in astounded him. On some level the hunger was so all-consuming that he honestly thought he might die of overexcitement if he didn't get inside her.

His mouth roved between the straining mounds of her perfect breasts, tugging at the swollen buds, arrowing lower, letting her feel the long, slow glide of his tongue while he pulled her to the edge of the table to position her.

He plunged in and drove the breath from her body with the intensity of his entrance. She whimpered as he stretched her, her body clenching round him like a hot velvet glove.

'*So* good,' Gaetano ground out between gritted teeth as he pulled back and slammed back into her with delicious force.

Poppy couldn't think, she could only feel and she was riding a torrent of excitement she couldn't control, her entire being pitched to crave the peak of his every powerful thrust. The heat and the hunger and the pleasure all melded together into one glorious, overwhelming rush of sexual ecstasy. Her climax claimed her in an explosive surge of intense sensation and her teeth bit into his shoulder as the exquisite convulsions shook her violently in his arms.

In the aftermath she was as limp as a floppy doll. He fed her feet back into her underwear, retied her dress and lifted her down to the ground again where she swayed, utterly undone by the sheer primal wildness of their joining.

'Did I hurt you?'

'No, you blew me away,' she whispered truthfully.

'You bring out the animal in me, *delizia mia*,' he admitted raggedly, pressing his sensual mouth to the top of her down-bent head in what felt like a silent apology.

'And I like it,' Poppy admitted shakily. 'I like it very much.'

'What the hell have we been playing at, then, for the last few weeks?' he demanded.

Poppy shot him a teasing glance. 'You were depriving me of sex. Why, I have no idea.'

But Gaetano was ♞ not in the mood to talk. He was already painfully aware of the lack of logic in his recent behaviour. He couldn't answer his own questions, never mind explain or defend his decisions to her. He had honestly believed that for once he was doing the honourable thing and that she would appreciate his restraint. Evidently he had got that badly wrong. She was accusing him of depriving her. *Diavelos*...no doubt it was sexist but he was the one who had felt most deprived. And being deprived of the joy of her body had eased his conscience.

His brooding silence nagged at Poppy's nerves. Perhaps even though he enjoyed the physical release of her body he had preferred the distance provided by their lack of intimacy. Maybe he was worried she was getting too attached. Maybe she wasn't as good an actress as she liked to believe.

'It was just sex, you know,' she mumbled as lightly as she could. 'It doesn't have to mean anything.'

'I know,' Gaetano fielded drily while also knowing that he could never, ever have imagined having a wife who would admit that she had just used him for sex.

It felt wrong to him and downright offensive but he was willing to admit that getting married to Poppy and living with her while struggling to stay out of her bed had played merry hell with his values. One hint of encouragement from her and he had shelved honour without a backward glance. In fact he'd been a pushover, he conceded grimly. He craved her like a drug. He was already thinking of early nights, dawn takeovers and afternoon siestas, hopefully the kinkier, the better, because his bride was still on a wonderful learning curve. Did it really matter if she only wanted him for sex?

Why complicate something simple? She was right. It was just sex, not something he had ever felt the need to agonise over or attach labels to. *Maledizione!* What was she doing to his brain? Why was he dwelling on something so basic?

CHAPTER NINE

'I BELIEVE THE medication you received in hospital may have disrupted your birth control. Of course, no contraceptive pill is foolproof either. It's an interesting conundrum,' Mr Abramo remarked as if the development were purely one of academic interest. 'Fortunately you're in much better health than you were a month ago...absolutely blooming, in fact!'

Poppy's smile felt stiff because she was still in shock. She was pregnant, one hundred per cent with no room for error pregnant and Gaetano was likely to go into even greater shock over that reality. One night, one bout of passion, one baby. Obviously, Gaetano would feel that he had been very unlucky. What were the odds of such a development? What would he want to do? How would he react? She was already praying that he would not hope that she might be willing to consider a termination.

While it was true that she hadn't planned on a baby, she still wanted the child that was now on its way. Her baby and Gaetano's, a little piece of Leonetti heritage that even Gaetano couldn't take off her again, divorce or otherwise. A little boy, a little girl, Poppy wasn't fussy about the gender. Indeed she was getting excited about the prospect of motherhood and feeling guilty about the fact. How could she dare to look forward happily to an event that would probably seriously depress and infuriate Gaetano, who preferred to plan everything and liked to believe that he could control everybody and everything in his life? The baby would be a wildly out-of-control event. And Gaetano had been frank from the outset that he did not want to risk a conception when they were planning to part. Having foreseen that scenario, he had set out to prevent that situation arising.

Before her conscience could claim her and stifle her natural impulses, Poppy paid a visit to a very exclusive baby shop in Florence where without the smallest encouragement she purchased an incredibly expensive shawl and a tiny pair of exquisite white lace bootees. When she emerged again, clutching a cute beribboned bag, she saw her pair of bodyguards exchanging knowing looks and, scolding herself for her mindless compulsion, made a hurried comment about needing wrapping paper for her gift.

When she returned to La Fattoria for lunch, Gaetano was still in Paris. But he might well have fallen asleep during the flight there, Poppy thought with a wicked little smile. Quite deliberately she had exhausted him. A sexually satiated tired male was unlikely to be tempted by the offer of sex on the side. She had kept him up half the night and had awakened him at dawn in a manner that he had sworn was the ultimate male fantasy.

His response had been incredibly enthusiastic. But then Gaetano had remarkable stamina, she reflected sunnily. She ached all over. She ached in places she hadn't known she could ache but it had all been in a good cause. Surely Serena could no longer be considered a threat?

Given the smallest excuse, Gaetano would have abandoned Serena at the airport. Her incessant flirtatiousness had begun to irritate him during the flight back. Raunchy jokes about bankers and the mile-high club had fallen on stony ground. Gaetano had partied on board when he'd acquired his first private jet but those irresponsible days were far behind him now that he was in the act of becoming the new CEO of the Leonetti Bank. He was quietly satisfied by the attainment of that long-held ambition but he had spent far more time choosing a gift for Poppy during a break between meetings than he had spent considering his lofty rise in status. Ironically now that he had that status it meant less than he had expected to him. His focus in life had definitely shifted in a different direction.

Poppy got sleepy in the late afternoon and went for a nap. She lay on the bed wondering about how best to share her news with Gaetano and tears prickled her eyes because she feared his reaction. He wasn't likely to be happy about her pregnancy and she had to accept that. It would drive them apart, not keep them together. Fate had thrown them something that couldn't be easily worked around.

Gaetano was strangely disappointed when Poppy didn't greet him downstairs as Muffin did. Muffin hurled himself cheerfully at Gaetano's legs, refused to sit when told and barked like mad. Muffin didn't discriminate. Everyone who came through the front door received the same boisterous, undisciplined welcome. Dolores informed Gaetano that Poppy had gone up to lie down and concern quickened the long strides with which he mounted the stairs. Suddenly Gaetano was worrying about what the doctor might have told his wife about her health because taking forty winks in the evening was more Rodolfo's style.

As Gaetano entered the bedroom, Poppy, roused by Muffin's barks, pushed herself up on her elbows and smiled, tousled red hair falling round her sleep-flushed face.

'I exhausted you last night,' Gaetano assumed with a wolfish grin of all-male satisfaction as he stood at the foot of the bed. 'I wondered what you were doing in bed and started worrying about what Mr Abramo might have said but that was before I remembered that you had another very good reason to need some extra rest.'

'It's the heat. It makes me feel drowsy.' Butterflies danced to a jungle beat in her tummy while she studied him.

In his beautifully tailored designer suit, Gaetano was a vision of masculine elegance and sex appeal. He was gorgeous with dark stubble outlining his strong jaw line and those intense dark eyes below his extraordinary lashes. Her breasts tingled and heat simmered low in her pelvis.

'It's weird because I've only been away a few hours…

but I missed you,' Gaetano confided in a constrained undertone. 'What did Mr Abramo have to say?'

Poppy tensed and swung her legs off the side of the bed so that she was half turned away from him. 'He had some news for me after the tests,' she told him tautly.

'What sort of news?' Gaetano prompted, shedding his jacket and jerking loose his tie while wondering if she would consider him excessively demanding and greedy if he joined her on the bed.

'Unexpected news,' Poppy qualified tightly. 'You're going to be surprised.'

'So, go ahead and surprise me,' Gaetano urged, unsettled by her uncharacteristic reluctance to meet his eyes and shelving the sexual trail to force his brain to focus.

'I'm pregnant.' She framed the words curtly, refusing to sound apologetic or nervous, putting it out there exactly like the fact of life it was.

'How could you possibly be pregnant?' Gaetano shot at her with an incredulous frown. 'If it had only just happened, it would be too soon to know and the one and only other time…it isn't possible…'

'It *is* possible. I fell ill that same day and I missed taking my pill. Mr Abramo also believes the drugs I was given could have interfered with my birth control,' she told him flatly.

'You got pregnant on our wedding night?' Gaetano queried in astonishment. 'From *one* time? What are you? The fertility queen?'

'You didn't use a condom,' she reminded him.

'There shouldn't have been a risk.'

'If you're having sex there's always a risk,' she pointed out ruefully. 'The odds weren't good that night because I ended up in hospital. In any other circumstances we'd probably have got away with it.'

'Pregnant,' Gaetano repeated, expelling his breath on a long slow hiss as he paced over to the windows, the taut muscles in his lean behind and long, powerful legs braced rigid with tension. 'You're pregnant.'

Although there was little expression in his dark, deep drawl Poppy took strength from his lack of anger and his ability to joke. Gaetano was dealing with it, *wasn't he*? He was good in a crisis, very cool-headed and logical and what they had right now was undeniably a *huge* crisis. A baby nobody had counted on was on the way, a baby she would nonetheless love and protect to the best of her ability.

Gaetano was still feeling light-headed with shock. A baby! He was going to be a father? *Dio mio*…he was in no way prepared to be a parent. Having a child was a massive responsibility. It had proved a challenge too much for his own parents and even Rodolfo had struggled with the test of raising Gaetano's good-for-nothing father. How the hell would he manage? What did he have to offer a child?

'Gaetano?' Poppy probed in the tense silence.

He swung round and raked long brown fingers through his cropped black hair in a gesture of frustration. 'A baby… I can't believe it. That's some curve ball to be thrown.'

'Yes,' Poppy agreed stiffly. 'For both of us.'

'In fact it's a nightmare,' Gaetano framed, shocking

her with that assessment, which was so much more pessimistic than her own.

Poppy stiffened but fought not to take that comment too personally. 'Not much I can do to change your outlook if that's how you feel.'

'I don't like the unexpected, the spontaneous,' he admitted grimly. 'A baby will turn our lives upside down.'

'But there's a positive side as well as a negative side,' Poppy murmured.

'Is there?' Gaetano traded in stark disagreement. 'We had a divorce planned.'

Poppy lost colour and screened her eyes. A *nightmare*? That had been a body blow but that his second comment on their situation should refer to their divorce was even tougher. But what had she expected from him? A bottle of champagne and whoops of satisfaction? It could have been a lot worse, she told herself urgently. Gaetano could have lost his temper. He could have tried to imply that the pregnancy was somehow more her fault than his. But then possibly he hadn't reached that stage yet. After all, he was still pretty much stunned, studying her with brilliant dark eyes that had an unusually unfocused quality. *We had a divorce planned.* He had gone straight for the jugular.

'But, obviously I couldn't possibly leave you to raise my child alone,' Gaetano completed without skipping a beat. 'Looks like we're staying together, *bella mia*.'

Poppy stiffened at his bleak intonation. 'So, you're suggesting that we should forget about getting a divorce now?'

'What else would I suggest?' Gaetano asked very

drily. 'You're carrying the next generation of the Leonetti dynasty. Nobody expects you to do that alone, least of all me. Even though I had two parents they did a fairly rubbish job of raising me. To thrive, our child will need both of us and a stable home to grow up in.'

'But it's not what we planned,' Poppy reminded him while anger simmered like a pot bubbling on the hob beneath her careful surface show of calm.

There was nothing to be gained from losing her temper, she told herself fiercely, but his practical approach was downright insulting. Yes, she agreed that ideally a child should have both parents and a steady home but at what cost? If the parents themselves made sacrifices that resulted in unhappiness how could that be good for anyone? Poppy did not want an unwilling husband and reluctant father by her side. That was not a cross she was prepared to bear for years knowing that it wouldn't benefit anyone. If that was the best Gaetano had to offer, he could keep it and the wedding ring, she thought painfully. She wanted more, she *needed* more than a man who would only keep her as a wife because she had fallen pregnant.

'We couldn't possibly make a bigger mess of our marriage than my parents did,' he pointed out wryly. 'We can only try our best.'

'As a goal, that just depresses me, Gaetano,' Poppy admitted.

'How? We'll continue on as we are now but at least we won't be living a lie for Rodolfo's benefit any longer.'

'No, *you* won't need to live a lie any longer,' Poppy agreed tightly as she walked towards the door.

'Where are you going?'

Powered by a furious mix of anger and pain, Poppy ignored the question and stalked up the stairs to the next floor where the luggage was stored. From the room used for that purpose she grabbed up two cases.

From his stance on the landing, Gaetano stared at her in bewilderment. 'What on earth are you doing?'

'Your nightmare is leaving you!' Poppy bit out squarely.

'I did not call you a nightmare,' Gaetano argued vehemently.

'No, you called the baby I'm having a nightmare, which was worse,' Poppy countered fiercely. 'This baby may be unplanned and a big unexpected surprise but I love it already!'

'*Dio mio*, Poppy!' Gaetano exclaimed as she yanked garments out of the built-in closets in the dressing room, hangers falling in all directions. 'Will you please calm down?'

'Why would I calm down? I'm pregnant and my husband thinks it's a nightmare!'

'I didn't mean it that way.'

'And you seem to believe that I have no choice but to stay married to you. Well, here's some news for you, Gaetano... I can have a baby and manage perfectly well without you!' Poppy slung at him from between gritted teeth. 'I don't *need* you. I deserve more. I don't intend to stay married to a guy who's only with me because he thinks it's his duty!'

'That's not what I said.'

'That's exactly what you said!' Poppy slammed a case

down on the bed and wrenched it open. 'Well, this particular nightmare of yours is taking herself off. There's got to be better options than you waiting for me.'

Standing very still, Gaetano lost colour and watched her intently. 'There probably is. But I want very badly for you to stay.'

'No, you don't, not really,' Poppy reasoned thinly. 'You think our baby would be the icing on the cake for Rodolfo but you don't want to be married and you don't want to be a father.'

'I *do* want to be married to you.' Gaetano flung back his shoulders and studied her with strained dark eyes. 'And I know that I can learn how to be a good father. I meant that the situation of being unprepared for a child was a nightmare. I'm not good with surprises but I can roll fast with the punches that come my way. And believe me, watching you pack to leave me *is* a hell of a punch.'

The firm resolution in that response surprised her. She paused to roughly fold up a dress before thrusting it into the case, sending an unimpressed glance at his lean, darkly handsome face. She wasn't listening to him, she told herself urgently. She had made her decision. It was better for her to leave him with her head held high than to consider giving him another chance… wasn't it?

'Is it? Are you really capable of changing your outlook to that extent? Accepting being married without feeling that you're somehow doing me a favour and settling for second best?' she queried with scorn. 'Accepting our child as the gift that a child is?'

'I know that I was difficult when I married you.' Gaetano compressed his lips on that startling admission. 'I'm not easy-going but I am adaptable and I do learn from my mistakes. *Dio mio, bella mia*…my attitude to you has changed most of all.'

'How?' Poppy prompted, needing him to face up to the major decision he was trying to make for both of them. She didn't want Gaetano deciding that they should stay married and then changing his mind again because he felt trapped by the restrictions. She had to know and understand exactly what he was thinking and feeling and expecting. How else could she make a decision?

His wide sensual mouth twisted. 'I don't want to discuss that.'

'Why not?'

'Because sometimes silence is golden and honesty can be the wrong way to go,' he framed grudgingly. 'And knowing my luck, I'll say the wrong thing again.'

'But you should be able to tell me anything. We shouldn't *have* secrets between us. How has your attitude to me changed?' Poppy persisted, curiosity and obstinacy combining to push her on.

Gaetano glanced heavenward for a brief moment and then drew in a ragged breath. 'I asked you to pretend to be engaged to me because I thought you would be a huge embarrassment as a fiancée.'

Shock gripped Poppy in a debilitating wave only to be swiftly followed by a huge rush of hurt. 'In what way?'

'I was the posh bloke who made unjustified assumptions about you,' Gaetano admitted, his deep voice raw-edged with regret. 'I assumed you'd still be using a lot of bad language. I expected you to be totally lost and unable to cope in my world. In fact I believed that your eccentric fashion sense and everything about you would horrify Rodolfo and put him off the idea of me getting married, so that when the engagement broke down he would be relieved rather than disappointed...'

Gaetano had finished speaking but his every word still struck through the fog of Poppy's shell-shocked state like lightning on a dark stormy night. She felt physically sick.

Gaetano had watched the blood drain from below her skin and fierce tension now stamped his lean dark features. 'So that's the kind of guy I really am, the kind of guy you get to stay married to and the father of your future child. I know it's not pretty but you have earned the right to know the truth about me. Most of the time I'm an absolute bastard,' he stated bleakly. 'I tried to use you in the most callous way possible and it didn't once occur to me to wonder how that experience would ultimately affect you...or Rodolfo.'

Poppy wrapped her arms round her slim body as if she were trying to hold the dam of pain inside her back from breaking its banks. She couldn't bear to look at him any longer. He had seen from the outset how unworthy she was to be even his fiancée and he had planned to use her worst traits and the handicap of her poor background as an excuse to dump her again without antagonising his grandfather. In short he had handpicked her as the fake fiancée most likely to mortify him.

Poppy cringed inside herself. His prior assumptions appalled her, for she had not appreciated how prejudiced he had still been about her. Shattered by his admission, she felt humiliated beyond bearing. He had seen her flaws right at the beginning and had pinned his hopes on her shaming him. How could he then adapt to the idea of staying married to her for years and years? Raising a child with her? Taking her out in public?

'The moment I picked you to fail was the moment that I sank to my all-time personal low,' Gaetano confessed in a roughened undertone. 'I got it horribly wrong. You *showed* me how wrong my expectations were. You proved yourself to be so much more than I was prepared for you to be and I became ashamed of my original plan.'

'But you didn't need to tell me this once we went as far as getting married,' she whispered brokenly, backing in the direction of the door, desperate to lick her wounds in private.

'You've always been honest with me. I'm trying to give you the same respect.'

'Only a couple of months ago you had *no* respect for me!' Poppy condemned with embittered accuracy.

'That changed fast,' Gaetano fielded, moving a step closer, wanting to hold her so badly and resisting the urge with a frustration that coiled his big hands into fists. 'I *learned* to respect you. I learned a lot of other stuff from you as well.'

Feeling as though he were twisting a knife in her heart, Poppy voiced a loud sound of disagreement and snapped, 'You didn't learn anything…you never do. You're dumb as a rock about everything that really matters from giving Muffin a second chance at life to raising our child!' she accused. 'How could I ever trust you again?'

Poppy stalked out of the door and he fought his need to follow her. He didn't want her racing down the stairs and falling in an effort to evade him. 'Muffin trusts me,' he murmured flatly to the empty room. *Muffin?* Muffin who couldn't even tell him and Rodolfo apart? Admittedly, Muffin wasn't the sharpest tool in the box.

Gaetano groaned out loud. Maybe he should have kept on pretending to be a better man than he was but Poppy would only have found him out in the end. Poppy had a way of cutting through the nonsense to find the heart of an issue and see what really mattered. Just as Gaetano had finally seen what really mattered. Unfortunately that single instant of inner vision and comprehension had arrived with him pretty late in the day. He wasn't dumb as a rock about emotional stuff. He simply wasn't very practised at it. It wasn't something he'd ever bothered with until Poppy came along.

Poppy pelted out into the cool night. She needed air and space and silence to pull herself back together. The garden was softly lit, low-sited lights shining on exotic leaves and casting shadows in mysterious corners. Her face was wet with tears and she wiped her cheeks with angry hands. Damn him, damn him, damn him! What he had confessed had wounded her deeply. She loved Gaetano and he had always been her dream male. Handsome, brilliant, rich and glitzy, he had met

every requirement for an adolescent fantasy. Now for
the first time she was seeing herself through his eyes
and it was so humiliating she wanted to sink into the
earth and stay hidden there for ever.

He had only remembered the highly unsuitable bold
girl with the potty mouth, and eccentric clothes, who
could be depended on to embarrass him. And being
Gaetano, who was never ever straightforward when he
could be devious, manipulative and complicated instead, he had hoped to utilise her very obvious faults
to frighten Rodolfo out of demanding that his grandson
marry. And ironically, Rodolfo himself had set Poppy
up for that fall by advising Gaetano to marry 'an ordinary girl'. And just how many ordinary girls did a jet-
setter like Gaetano know?

None. Until Poppy had stumbled in that night at
Woodfield Hall, to demand his attention and his nonexistent compassion.

An embarrassment to him? No conventional dress
sense, a dysfunctional family, no idea how to behave in
rich, exclusive circles. Well, nothing had changed and
she would never reach the high bar of social acceptabil-
ity. Poppy shuddered, sick to her stomach with a galling
sense of defeat and failure. She had never cared about
such things but evidently Gaetano did. Even worse,
Gaetano was currently offering to stay married to his
unsuitable bride because she was pregnant.

She sat down on one of the cold stone seats sited
round the table and her face burned hot in spite of the
cool evening air when she remembered what had happened on that table only the day before. Gaetano was

like an addiction, toxic, dangerous. He had gone from
infuriating her to charming her to making her fall very
deeply in love with him. And yet she had still never
guessed how he really saw her. The gardener's daughter with the unfortunate family. It hurt—oh, my goodness, it *hurt*. But he had been right to tell her because
she had needed to know the truth and accept it before
she could stop weaving silly dreams about their future.
So, how did she stay married to a male who had handpicked her to be an embarrassment?

The answer came swiftly. In such circumstances she
could *not* stay married to Gaetano. Regardless of her
pregnancy, she needed to leave him and go ahead with
a divorce.

'Poppy...'

Poppy stiffened. He must have walked across the
grass because she would have heard his approach had
he used the gravel paths. She breathed in deep, stiffening her facial muscles before she lifted her head.

'Should I have kept it a secret?' he asked her in a
raw undertone.

He knew she was upset. His dark eyes were lingering
on her, probably picking up on the dampness round her
eyes even though she had quickly stopped crying. He
noticed too much, *knew* too much about women. 'No,'
she said heavily. 'It was better to tell me. I don't like
you for it and it'll be hard to live with what I now know
but you can't build a relationship on lies and pretences.'

Gaetano stilled in the shadow of the trees, his white
shirt gleaming, his spectacular bone structure accentuated by the dim light. 'Don't leave me,' he framed un-

evenly. 'Even the idea of being without you scares me. I wouldn't like my life without you in it.'

Poppy couldn't imagine Gaetano being scared and she imagined his life would be a lot more normal and straightforward without her in it. Their child deserved better than to grow up with unhappily married and ill-matched parents. A divorce would be preferable to that. She would give Gaetano as much access as he wanted to their child but she didn't have to live with him or hang round his neck like an albatross to be a good parent. They could both commit to their child while living separately.

'I can't stay married to you,' she told him quietly. 'What would be the point?'

'I'm not good with emotions. I'm good at being angry, at being passionate, at being ambitious but I'm no good at the softer stuff. I lost that ability when I was a kid,' Gaetano admitted grittily. 'I loved my parents but they were incapable of loving me back and I saw that. I also saw that in comparison to them I felt *too* much. I learned to hide what I feel and eventually it became such a habit I didn't have to police myself any more. Emotion hurts. Rejection hurts, so I made sure I was safe by not feeling anything.'

Involuntarily, Poppy was touched that he was talking about his parents in an effort to bridge the chasm that had opened up between them. He never ever talked about his childhood but she would never forget his determined non-reaction when his dog had died, his stark refusal to betray any emotion. 'That makes sense,' she conceded.

'The only woman I ever loved after my mother left was my grandmother.'

'I thought at some stage you and *Serena*...'

'No. I walked away from her because I felt nothing and I knew there should be more.'

Poppy bowed her head, wondering why he was trying to stop her from walking away from him.

'I'm not quite as dumb as a rock,' Gaetano asserted heavily. 'But I was all screwed up about you long before we even got to the wedding. Unfortunately marrying you only made me ten times more screwed up.'

'Screwed up?' Poppy queried, shifting uncomfortably on her hard stone seat.

'I got really involved with the wedding.'

'Yes, that was a surprise.'

'I wanted it to be special for you. I became very possessive of you. I assumed it was because we hadn't had sex.'

'Obviously,' Poppy chimed in because he seemed to expect it.

'In fact I was really only thinking in terms of sex.'

Poppy sent him a rather sad smile. 'I know that... it's basically your only means of communication in a relationship.'

'You're the only woman I've ever had a relationship with.'

Poppy stared at him, green eyes luminous in the light. 'How can you say that with your reputation?'

'All those weeks after your illness when I didn't touch you but we were together all the time...that was like my version of dating,' Gaetano told her darkly. 'The affairs I had with women before you went no further than dinner followed by sex or the theatre followed by sex or—'

'OK… I've got the picture,' she cut in hurriedly, her gaze clinging to the dark beauty of his bronzed features with growing fascination. 'So…your version of dating?'

'I wanted to get to know you—'

'No, you were on a massive guilt trip because I fell ill. That's why you didn't sleep with me again and why you spent so much time entertaining me.'

'I'm not a masochist. I spent so much time with you because I was enjoying myself,' Gaetano contradicted. 'And I didn't touch you again because I didn't want to be selfish. I thought you would be happier if I made no further demands.'

Poppy sent him a withering appraisal. 'You got it wrong.'

'Poppy…let's face it,' Gaetano muttered heavily. 'I got *everything* wrong with you.'

Her tender heart reacted with a first shard of genuine sympathy. 'No, the sex was ten out of ten and your version of dating was amazingly engaging. You made me happy, Gaetano. You definitely win points for that.'

'I bought you something today and it wasn't until I bought it and realised what it symbolised that I finally understood myself,' he framed harshly, pulling a tiny box from his pocket.

Poppy studied the fancy logo of a world-famous jeweller with surprised eyes and opened the box. It was a ring, a continuous circlet of diamonds that flashed like fire in the artificial light. She blinked down at it in confusion.

'It's an eternity ring,' Gaetano pointed out very quietly.

A laugh that wasn't a laugh at all was wrenched from Poppy. 'Kind of an odd choice when before you came home and I made my announcement you were set on eventually getting a divorce,' she pointed out.

'But it expresses how I feel.' Gaetano cleared his throat in obvious discomfiture. 'When you talk about leaving me, it tears me apart. Because somewhere along the line, somehow, I fell in love with you, Poppy. I know it's love because I've never felt like this before and the idea of losing you terrifies me.'

'Love...' Poppy whispered shakily.

'Never thought it could happen to me,' Gaetano confided in a rush. 'I didn't want it to happen either. I didn't want to get attached to anyone and then you came along and you were so perfect I couldn't resist you.'

'P-perfect?' she stammered in a daze.

Gaetano dropped down on his knees in the dew-wet grass and reached for her hand. He tugged off the engagement ring and threaded on the eternity ring so that it rested beside her wedding ring. 'You're perfect for me. You get who I am, even with my faults. The money doesn't get in the way for you, doesn't impress you. You keep me grounded. You make me unbelievably happy. You make me question my actions and really think about what I'm doing,' he bit out. 'With you, I'm something more, something better, and I need that. I need you in my life.'

Her lashes fluttered. She could hear him but she couldn't quite believe him, there on his knees at her feet, his hand trembling slightly in hers because he was scared, he was scared she wouldn't listen, wouldn't accept that he really loved her. And that fear touched her down deep inside, wrapping round her crazy fears about Serena and the terrible insecurities that had sent her running out of the house and sealing them for ever. Suddenly none of that existed because Gaetano *loved* her, Gaetano *needed* her...

'I love you so much. I couldn't stand to lose you and my first thought when you told me you were pregnant was, "She'll stay now," and it was a massive relief to think that even though you didn't love me you would stay so that we could bring up our child together.'

'I do love you,' Poppy murmured intently, leaning forward to kiss him.

'You're not just saying it because I said it first?' Gaetano checked.

'I really, *really* love you.'

'Even though I don't have a single loveable trait?' he quoted back at her quick as a flash.

'You grew on me like mould,' Poppy told him deadpan.

Gaetano burst out laughing and sprang upright, pulling her up into the circle of his arms. 'Like mould?' he queried.

Poppy looked up into his beautiful eyes and her heart did a happy dance inside her. 'I like cheese,' she proclaimed defensively.

'Do you like your ring?'

'Very much,' she told him instantly, smiling up at him with a true sense of joyful possessiveness. 'But I like what it symbolises most of all. You didn't want to let me go, you wanted to keep me.'

'And I intend to keep you for ever and ever. Anything less than eternity wouldn't be enough, *amata mia*.'

'The baby was a shock, wasn't it?' She sighed, walking back towards the house with him hand in hand.

'A wonderful one. Our little miracle,' Gaetano said with sudden rueful humour. 'It took one hell of a baby to get in under my radar, so I'll be expecting a very determined personality in the family.'

Gaetano halted at that point to claim a kiss. And Poppy threw herself into that kiss with abandon. He pressed her back against a tree trunk, his body hard and urgent against hers and a rippling shudder of excitement shimmied through her slender length.

'Let's go to bed,' she suggested, looking up at him with bold appreciative eyes.

'We haven't had dinner yet and a mother-to-be needs sustenance,' Gaetano told her lazily, trailing her indoors and out to the terrace where the table awaited them.

But neither of them ate very much. Between the intense looks exchanged and the suggestive conversation, it wasn't very long before they headed upstairs at a very adult stately pace, which broke down into giggles and a clumsy embrace as Poppy rugby-tackled Gaetano down onto the floor of their bedroom. By the time they made it to the bed and he had moved the suitcase she had left there they were kissing passionately and holding each other so tightly that it was a challenge to remove clothes. But they managed through kisses and caresses and mutual promises to make love with all the fire and excitement that powered them both and afterwards they lay with their arms wrapped round each other, secure in their love and talking about their future.

Poppy glanced out of the front window and saw her children with Rodolfo. Sarah was holding his hand and chattering, her little face animated below her halo of red curls. Benito was pedalling his trike doggedly in front of them, ignoring the fact that the deep gravel on the path made cycling a challenge for a little boy.

Sarah was four years old and took after her mother in looks and her father in nature. She already knew all her numbers, was very much a thinking child and tended to look after her little brother in a bossy way. Benito was two, dark of hair and eye and as lively as a jumping bean. He was on the go from dawn to dusk and generally fell asleep during his bedtime story in his father's arms.

Sometimes, or at least until she looked at her expanding family, Poppy found it hard to credit that she had been married for five years. Gaetano might have been a late convert to family life but he had taken to it like the proverbial duck to water. He adored his children and rushed home to be with them and it was thanks to his persuasion that Poppy was carrying their third child. Third and last, she had told him firmly even though she liked the way their family had developed. In retro-

spect she was glad they hadn't waited and that Sarah
had taken them by surprise and not having too big a
gap between the children meant that they could grow
up with each other.

But, at the same time, Poppy was also looking forward to having more time to devote to her own interests.
She had taken several landscape designer courses over
the years and was planning to set up a small landscaping
firm. She had redesigned the gardens at La Fattoria to
make them more child-friendly and had already taken
several private commissions from friends, one of which
had won an award. The gardens at the London town
house and at Woodfield Hall both bore her stamp and
when she wanted to relax she was usually to be found
in a greenhouse tending the rare orchids she collected.

Gaetano was CEO of the Leonetti Bank and when he
travelled, Poppy and the children often went with him.
He put his family first and at the heart of his life, ensur-
ing that they took lengthy breaks abroad to wind down
from their busy lives. Poppy's mother, Jasmine, had
made a good recovery and was now training as an addiction counsellor to help others as she had been helped.
She lived in Manchester with her sister but she was
a frequent visitor in London, as was Poppy's brother.
Damien, backed by Gaetano, had recently started up a
specialist motorcycle repair shop.

In fact there wasn't a cloud in Poppy's sky because
she was happy. Sadly, Muffin had passed away of old
age the year before and he had been replaced by a res-
cued golden Labrador who enjoyed rough and tumble
games with the children.

'Guess who...' A pair of hands covered her eyes while a lean, hard body connected with hers.

Poppy grinned. The familiar scent of Gaetano's cologne assailed her while his hands travelled places nobody else would have dared. 'You're the only sex pest I know,' she teased, suppressing a moan as the hand that had splayed across her slightly swollen belly snaked lower and circled, sending sweet sensation snaking through her responsive body.

Gaetano spun his wife round and she reached up to wind her arms round his neck. 'Sorry, I slept in this morning and missed seeing you.'

'You were up with Benito last night when he had a nightmare, *amata mia*,' he reminded her. 'That's why I didn't wake you.'

Poppy teased the corner of his wide sensual mouth with her own, heat warming her core. She wanted to drag him to the bed and ravish him. Her hunger for him never went entirely away. He shrugged off his jacket and stared down at her with smouldering dark golden eyes. 'Share the shower with me...'

'Promise not to get my hair wet,' she bargained.

'You know I can't.' An unholy grin slashed Gaetano's lips. 'Sometimes you get carried away. Is that my fault?'

'Absolutely your fault,' his wife told him as she peeled off her dress.

Gaetano treated her to a fiercely appreciative appraisal. 'Did I ever tell you how amazingly sexy you look when you're pregnant?'

'You may have mentioned it once or twice—'

'Sometimes I can hardly believe you're mine. I love

you so much, *amata mia*,' Gaetano swore passionately, gathering her up into his arms with care and kissing her breathless.

'I love you too,' she said between kisses, happiness bubbling through her at the sure knowledge that she was going to get her hair very wet indeed.

* * * * *

INHERITED
BY FERRANTI

KATE HEWITT

CHAPTER ONE

TOMORROW WAS HER wedding day. Sierra Rocci gazed at the fluffy white meringue of a dress hanging from her wardrobe door and tried to suppress the rush of nerves that seethed in her stomach and fluttered up her throat. She was doing the right thing. She had to be. She had no other choice.

Pressing one hand to her jumpy middle, she turned to look out of the window at the darkened gardens of her father's villa on the Via Marinai Alliata in Palermo. The summer night was still and hot, without even a breath of wind to make the leaves of the plane trees in the garden rattle. The stillness felt expectant, even eerie, and she tried to shake off her nervousness; she'd *chosen* this.

Earlier that night she'd dined with her parents and Marco Ferranti, the man she was going to marry. They'd chatted easily, and Marco's gaze had rested on her like a caress, a promise. She could trust this man, she'd told herself. She had to. In less than twenty-four hours she would promise to love, honour and obey him. Her life would be in his hands.

She knew the hard price of obedience. She prayed Marco truly was a gentle man. He'd been kind to her so far, in the three months of their courtship. Gentle and patient, never punishing or pushing, except perhaps for that one time, when they'd gone for a walk in the gardens and he'd kissed her in the shadow of a plane tree, his mouth hard and insistent and surprisingly exciting on hers.

Another leap in her belly, and this was a whole different kind of fear. She was nineteen years old, and she'd only been kissed by her fiancé a handful of times. She was utterly inexperienced when it came to what happened in the bedroom, but Marco had told her, when he'd stopped his shockingly delicious onslaught under the plane tree, that he would be patient and gentle when it came to their wedding night.

She believed him. She'd chosen to believe him—an act of will, a step towards securing her future, her freedom. And yet… Sierra's unfocused gaze rested on the darkened gardens as nerves leapt and writhed inside her and doubt crept into the dark corners of her heart, sly and insidious as that old serpent. Did she really know Marco Ferranti? When she'd first glimpsed him in the courtyard of her father's *palazzo*, she'd watched as one of the kitchen cats had wound its scrawny body around Marco's legs. He'd bent down and stroked the cat's ears and the animal had purred and rubbed against him. Her father would have kicked the cat away, insist its kittens be drowned. Seeing Marco exhibit a moment of unthinking kindness when he thought no one was looking had lit the spark of hope inside Sierra's heart.

She knew her father approved of the marriage between her and Marco; she was not so naïve not to realise that it was his strong hand that had pushed Marco towards her. But she'd encouraged Marco; she'd made a choice. As much as was possible, she'd controlled her own destiny.

On that first evening he'd introduced himself, and then later he had asked her out to dinner. He'd wooed her gently, always courteous, even tender. She wasn't in love with him; she had no interest in that deceitful, dangerous emotion, but she wanted a way out of her father's house and marriage to Marco Ferranti would provide it…if she could truly trust him. She would find out tomorrow, when the vows were said, when the bedroom door closed…

Heaven help her. Sierra bit her knuckles as a fresh wave of fear broke coldly over her. Could she really do this? How could she not? To back out now would be to incur her father's endless wrath. She was marrying in order to be free, and yet she was not free to cry off. Perhaps she would never be truly free. But what other choice was there for a girl like her, nineteen years old and completely cut off from society, from life? Sheltered and trapped.

From below she heard the low rumble of her father's voice. Although she couldn't make out the words, just the sound of his voice had her tensing, alarm prickling the nape of her neck. And then she heard Marco answer, his voice as low as her father's and yet somehow warm. She'd liked his voice the first time she'd heard it, when he'd been introduced to her. She'd liked his smile, too, the quirking of one corner of his mouth, the slow way it lit up his face. She'd trusted him instinctively, even though he worked for her father. Even though he was a man of great power and charm, just as her father was. She'd convinced herself he was different. But what if she'd been wrong?

Before she could lose her nerve Sierra slipped out of her bedroom and hurried halfway down the front stairs, the white marble cold under her bare feet. She paused on the landing, out of view of the men in the foyer below, and strained to listen.

'I am glad to welcome you into my family as a true son.' Her father was at his best, charming and authoritative, a benevolent *papà*, brimming with good will.

'And I am glad to be so welcomed.'

Sierra heard the sound of her father slapping Marco's back and then his good-humoured chuckle. She knew that sound so well. She knew how false it was.

'*Bene*, Marco. As long as you know how to handle Sierra. A woman needs a firm hand to guide her. Don't be too gentle or they get notions. You can't have that.' The words were abhorrent and yet so terribly familiar, the tone gentle, almost amused, her father as assured as ever and completely in control.

Every muscle in Sierra's body seemed to turn to iron as she waited for Marco's response.

'Don't worry, *signor*,' Marco said. 'I know how to handle her.'

Sierra shrank back against the wall, horror and fear churning inside her. *I know how to handle her.* Did he really think that way, like her father did? That she was some beast to be guided and tamed into subservience?

'Of course you do,' Arturo Rocci said, his voice smug with satisfaction. 'I've groomed you myself, chosen you as my son. This is what I wanted, and I could not be more pleased. I have no doubts about you, Marco.'

'You honour me, *signor*.'

'Papà, Marco. You may call me Papà.'

Sierra peeked around the edge of the landing and saw the two men embracing. Then her father gave Marco one more back slap before disappearing down the corridor, towards his study.

Sierra watched Marco, a faint smile curving that mobile mouth, the sharp angle of his jaw darkened with five o'clock shadow, his silvery-grey eyes hooded and sleepy. He'd loosened his tie and shed his suit jacket, and he looked rumpled and tired and overwhelmingly male. *Sexy.*

But there was nothing sexy about what he'd just said. Nothing romantic or loving or remotely attractive about a man who thought women needed to be *handled*. Her stomach clenched hard with fear and, underneath, anger. Anger at Marco Ferranti, for clearly thinking as her father did, and anger at herself for being so naïve to think she actually knew a man after just three months, a handful of arranged dates, all of them carefully orchestrated evenings where Marco was at his best, guiding her gently towards the inevitable conclusion. She'd thought she'd chosen him, but now she wondered how well she'd been manipulated. *Handled.* Perhaps her fiancé was as false as her father, presenting a front she wanted to see while disguising the true man underneath. Would she ever know? Yes, when it was too late. When she was married to him and had no way to escape.

'Sierra?' Marco's silvery gaze flicked upwards, one eyebrow lifted as he gazed at her peeking around the landing, his faint smile deepening, revealing a dimple in one cheek. When Sierra had first seen that dimple it had made him seem friendlier. Kinder. She'd liked him more because of a *dimple.* She felt like such a child, naïve to the point of stupidity, thinking she'd wrested some control for herself when in fact she'd been the merest puppet.

'What are you doing hiding up there?' he asked, and he stretched one hand towards her.

'I…' Sierra licked dry lips as her mind spun. She could not think of a single thing to say. The only thing she could hear on an endless, awful reel was Marco's assured, indulgent words. *I know how to handle her.*

Marco glanced at his watch. 'It's after midnight, so technically I suppose I shouldn't see you. It's our wedding day, after all.'

Wedding day. In just a few hours she would marry this man. She would promise to love him. To honour and obey him…

I know how to handle her.

'Sierra?' Marco asked, concern sharpening his voice.
'Is something wrong?'

Everything was wrong. Everything had been wrong for
ever, and she'd actually thought she'd been fixing it. She'd
thought she was finally escaping, that she was choosing
her own destiny. The thought seemed laughable now. How
could she have fooled herself for so long? 'Sierra?' Impatience edged his voice now, and Sierra heard it. Heard how
quickly the façade of concern fell away, revealed the true
man underneath. Just as it did with her father.

'I'm only tired,' she whispered. Marco beckoned her towards him and on shaking legs she came down the stairs
and stood before him, trying not to tremble. Not to show
her fear. It was one small act of defiance she'd nurtured
for most of her life, because she knew it infuriated her father. He wanted his women to cower and cringe. And Sierra had done her fair share of both, to her shame, over the
years. But when she had the strength to stand tall, to act
cool and composed, she did. Cloaking herself in numbness had been a way of coping since she was small. She
was glad of it now.

Marco cupped her cheek with one hand. His palm was
warm and dry and even now the tender gesture sent sparks
shooting through her belly, and her legs shook.

'It's not long now,' he murmured, and his thumb brushed
her lips. His expression was tender, but Sierra couldn't
trust it any more. 'Are you nervous, little one?'

She was terrified. Wordlessly she shook her head.
Marco chuckled, the sound indulgent, perhaps patronising.
The assumptions she'd made about this man were proving
to be just that: assumptions. She didn't really know who he
was, what he was capable of. He'd been kind to her, yes,
but what if it had just been an act, just like her father's

kindness in public was? Marco smiled down at her, his dimple showing. 'Are you certain about that, *mi amore*?'

Mi amore. My love. But Marco Ferranti didn't love her. He'd never said he did, and she didn't even want him to. Looking back, she could see how expedient their relationship had been. A family dinner that led to a walk in the gardens that led to a proper date that led to a proposal. It had been a systematic procedure orchestrated by this man—and her father. And she hadn't realised, not completely. She'd thought she'd had some say in the proceedings, but now she wondered at how well she'd been manipulated. Used.

'I'm all right, Marco.' Her voice came out in a breathy whisper, and it took all the strength she possessed to step away from him so his hand dropped from her cheek. He frowned, and she wondered if he didn't like her taking even that paltry amount of control. She'd let him dictate everything in the three months of their courtship, she realised now. When and where they went, what they talked about—everything had been decided by him. She'd been so desperate to get away, and she'd convinced herself he was a kind man.

'One last kiss,' Marco murmured and before Sierra could think to step farther away he was pulling her towards him, his hands sliding up to cup her face as his lips came down on hers. Hard and soft. Hot and cold. A thousand sensations shivered through her as her lips parted helplessly. Longing and joy. Fear and desire. All of the emotions tangled up together so she couldn't tell them apart. Her hands fisted in his shirt and she stood on her tiptoes to bring his body closer to hers, unable to keep herself from it, not realising how revealing her response was until Marco chuckled and eased her away from him.

'There will be plenty of time later,' he promised her. 'Tomorrow night.'

When they were wed. Sierra pressed her fingers to her lips and Marco smiled, satisfied by her obvious response.

'Goodnight, Sierra,' he said softly, and Sierra managed to choke out a response.

'Goodnight.' She turned and hurried up the stairs, not daring to look back, knowing Marco was watching her.

In the quiet darkness of the upstairs hallway she pressed a hand to her thundering heart. Hated herself, hated Marco, for they were both to blame. She never should have let this happen. She should have never thought she could escape.

Sierra hurried down the hallway to the far wing of the house, knocking softly on the door of her mother's bedroom.

Violet Rocci opened the door a crack, her eyes wide with apprehension. She relaxed visibly when she saw it was Sierra, and opened the door wider to let her daughter in.

'You shouldn't be here.'

'Papà's downstairs.'

'Even so.' Violet clutched the folds of her silk dressing gown together, her face pale with worry and strain. Twenty years ago she'd been a beautiful young woman, a world-class pianist who played in London's best concert halls, on the cusp of major fame. Then she'd married Arturo Rocci and virtually disappeared from the public, losing herself in the process.

'Mamma…' Sierra stared helplessly at her mother. 'I think I may have made a mistake.'

Violet drew her breath in sharply. 'Marco?' Sierra nodded. 'But you love him…' Even after twenty years of living with Arturo Rocci, cringing under his hand, Violet believed in love. She loved her husband desperately, and it had been her destruction.

'I've never loved him, Mamma.'

'What?' Violet shook her head. 'But Sierra, you said…'

'I trusted him. I thought he was gentle. But the only reason I wanted to marry him was to escape…' Even now she couldn't say it. *Escape Papà.* She knew the words would hurt her mother; Violet hid from the truth as much as she could.

'And now?' Violet asked after a moment, her voice low.

'And now I don't know.' Sierra paced the room, the anxiety inside her like a spring that coiled tighter and tighter. 'I realise I don't know him at all.'

'The wedding is tomorrow, Sierra.' Violet turned away from her, her hand trembling at the throat of her dressing gown. 'What can you do? Everything has been arranged—'

'I know.' Sierra closed her eyes as regret rushed through her in a scalding wave. 'I'm afraid I have been very stupid.' She opened her eyes as she blinked back useless tears and set her jaw. 'I know there's nothing I can do. I have to marry him.' Powerlessness was a familiar feeling. Heavy and leaden, a mantle that had weighed her down for far too long. Yet she'd made her own trap this time. In the end she had no one to blame but herself. She'd agreed to Marco's proposal.

'There might be a way.'

Sierra glanced at her mother in surprise; Violet's face was pale, her eyes glittering with uncharacteristic determination. 'Mamma…'

'If you are certain that you cannot go through with it…'

'Certain?' Sierra shook her head. 'I'm not certain of anything. Maybe he is a good man…' *A man who was marrying her for the sake of Rocci Enterprises? A man who worked hand in glove with her father and insisted he knew how to handle her?*

'But,' Violet said, 'you do not love him.'

Sierra thought of Marco's gentle smile, the press of his lips. Then she thought of her mother's desperate love for her father, despite his cruelty and abuse. She didn't love Marco Ferranti. She didn't want to love anyone. 'No, I don't love him.'

'Then you must not marry him, Sierra. God knows a woman can suffer much for the sake of love, but without it…' She pressed her lips together, shaking her head, and questions burned in Sierra's chest, threatened to bubble up her throat. How could her mother love her father, after everything he'd done? After everything she and her mother had both endured? And yet Sierra knew she did.

'What can I do, Mamma?'

Violet drew a ragged breath. 'Escape. Properly. I would have suggested it earlier, but I thought you loved him. I've only wanted your happiness, darling. I hope you can believe that.'

'I do believe it, Mamma.' Her mother was a weak woman, battered into defeated submission by life's hardships and Arturo Rocci's hand. Yet Sierra had never doubted her mother's love for her.

Violet pressed her lips together, gave one quick nod. 'Then you must go, quickly. Tonight.'

'Tonight…?'

'Yes.' Swiftly, her mother went to her bureau and opened a drawer, reached behind the froth of lingerie to an envelope hidden in the back of the drawer. 'It's all I have. I've been saving it over the years, in case…'

'But how?' Numbly, Sierra took the envelope her mother offered her; it was thick with euros.

'Your father gives me housekeeping money every week,' Violet said. Spots of colour had appeared high on each delicate cheekbone, and Sierra felt a stab of pity. She knew her mother was ashamed of how tied she was to her husband, how firmly under his thumb. 'I rarely spend it. And so over the years I've managed to save. Not much…a thousand euros maybe, at most. But enough to get you from here.'

Hope and fear blazed within her, each as strong as the other. 'But where would I go?' She'd never considered such a thing—a proper escape, unencumbered, independent, truly free. The possibility was intoxicating and yet terrifying; she'd spent her childhood in a villa in the country, her adolescent years at a strict convent school. She had no experience of anything, and she knew it.

'Take the ferry to the mainland, and then the train to Rome. From there to England.'

'England…' The land of her mother's birth.

'I have a friend, Mary Bertram,' Violet whispered. 'I have not spoken to her in many years, not since…' Since she'd married Arturo Rocci twenty years ago. Wordlessly, Sierra nodded her understanding. 'She did not want me to marry,' Violet said, her voice so low now Sierra strained to hear it, even when she was standing right next to her mother. 'She didn't trust him. But she told me if anything happened, her door would always be open.'

'You know where she lives?'

'I have her address from twenty years ago. I am afraid that is the best I can do.'

Sierra's insides shook as she considered what she was about to do. She, who did not venture into Palermo without an escort, a guard. Who never handled money, who had never taken so much as a taxi. How could she do this?

How could she not? This was her only chance. Tomorrow she would marry Marco Ferranti, and if he was a man like her father, as his wife she would have no escape. No hope.

'If I leave…' she whispered, her voice thickening. She could not continue, but she didn't need to.

'You will not be able to return,' Violet said flatly. 'Your father would...' She swallowed, shaking her head. 'This will be goodbye.'

'Come with me, Mamma—'

Violet's expression hardened. 'I can't.'

'Because you love him?' The hurt spilled from her like a handful of broken glass, sharp and jagged with pain. 'How can you love him, after everything...?'

'Do not question my choices, Sierra.' Violet's face was pale, her mouth pinched tight. 'But make your own.'

Her own choice. Freedom at last. Overwhelming, frightening freedom, more than she'd ever had before, more than she'd even know what to do with. Instead of shackling herself to a man, even a good man, she would be her own person. Free to choose, to live.

The realisation made her feel sick with fear, dizzy with hope. Sierra closed her eyes. 'I don't know, Mamma...'

'I cannot choose for you, Sierra.' Her mother brushed her cheek lightly with her fingertips. 'Only you can decide your own destiny. But a marriage without love...' Her mother swallowed hard. 'I would not wish that on anyone.'

Not every man is like Arturo Rocci. Not every man is cruel, controlling, hard. Sierra swallowed down the words. Marco Ferranti might not be like her father, but he might very well be. After what she'd heard and realised tonight, she knew she couldn't take the risk.

Her hand clenched on the envelope of euros. Violet nodded, seeing the decision made in Sierra's face. 'God go with you, Sierra.'

Sierra hugged her mother tightly, tears stinging her eyes. 'Quickly now,' Violet said, and Sierra hurried from the room. Down the hall to her own bedroom, the wedding dress hanging from the wardrobe like a ghost. She dressed quickly and then grabbed a bag and stuffed some clothes into it. Her hands shook.

The house was quiet, the night air still and silent. Sierra glanced at the violin case under her bed and hesitated. It would be difficult to bring, and yet…

Music had been her only solace for much of her life. Leaving her violin would be akin to leaving a piece of her soul. She grabbed the case and swung the holdall of clothes over her shoulder. And then she tiptoed downstairs, holding her breath, her heart pounding so hard her chest hurt. The front door was locked for the night, but Sierra slid the bolt from its hinges without so much as a squeak. From the study she heard her father shift in his chair, rustle some papers. For a terrible moment her heart stilled, suspended in her chest as she froze in terror.

Then he let out a sigh and she eased the door open slowly, so slowly, every second seeming to last an hour. She slipped through and closed it carefully behind her before glancing at the dark, empty street. She looked back at the house with its lit windows one last time before hurrying into the night.

CHAPTER TWO

Seven years later

'SHE MIGHT NOT COME.'

Marco Ferranti turned from the window and his indifferent perusal of Palermo's business district with a shrug. 'She might not.' He glanced at the lawyer seated behind the large mahogany desk and then strode from the window, every taut, controlled movement belying the restlessness inside him.

'She didn't come to her mother's funeral,' the lawyer, Roberto di Santis, reminded him cautiously.

Marco's hands curled into fists and he unclenched them deliberately before shoving them into the pockets of his trousers and turning to face the man. 'I know.'

Violet Rocci had died three years ago; cancer had stalked her and killed her in a handful of months. Sierra had not come back for her mother's illness or funeral, despite Arturo's beseeching requests. She had not even sent a letter or card, much to her father's sorrow. The last time Marco had seen her had been the night before their wedding, when he'd kissed her and felt her trembling, passionate response.

The next morning he'd waited at the front of the church of Santa Caterina for his bride to process down the aisle. And waited. And waited. And waited.

Seven years later he was still waiting for Sierra Rocci to show up.

The lawyer shuffled some papers before clearing his throat noisily. He was nervous, impatient, wanting to get the ordeal of Arturo Rocci's will over with. He'd assured Marco it was straightforward if uncomfortable; Marco had seen the document himself, before Arturo had died. He knew what it said. He didn't think Sierra did, though, and he grimly looked forward to acquainting her with its details.

Surely she would come?

Marco had instructed the lawyer to contact her personally. Marco had known where Sierra was for a while; about five years ago, when the first tidal wave of rage had finally receded to a mist, he'd hired a private investigator to discover her whereabouts. He'd never contacted her, never wanted to. But he'd needed to know where she was, what had happened to her. The knowledge that she was living a seemingly quiet, unassuming life in London had not been satisfying in the least. Nothing was.

'She said she would come, didn't she?' he demanded, although he already knew the answer.

When di Santis had called her at her home, she'd agreed to meet here, at the lawyer's office, at ten o'clock on June fifteenth. It was now nearing half past.

'Perhaps we should just begin...?'

'No.' Marco paced the room, back to the window where he gazed out at the snarl of traffic. 'We'll wait.' He wanted to see Sierra's face when the will was read. He wanted to see the expression in her eyes as realisation dawned of how much she'd lost, how much she'd sacrificed simply to get away from him.

'If it pleases you, *signor*,' di Santis murmured and Marco did not bother to answer.

Thirty seconds later the outer door to the building

opened with a telling cautious creak; di Santis's assistant murmured something, and then a knock sounded on the office door.

Every muscle in Marco's body tensed; his nerves felt as if they were scraped raw, every sense on high alert. It had to be her.

'Signor di Santis?' the assistant murmured. 'Signorina Rocci has arrived.'

Marco straightened, forcing himself to relax as Sierra came into the room. She looked exactly the same. The same long, dark blond hair, now pulled back into a sleek chignon, the same wide blue-grey eyes. The same lush mouth, the same tiny, kissable mole at its left corner. The same slender, willowy figure with gentle curves that even now he itched to touch.

Desire flared through him, a single, intense flame that he resolutely quenched.

Her gaze moved to him and then quickly away again, too fast for him to gauge her expression. She stood straight, her shoulders thrown back, her chin tilted at a proud, almost haughty angle. And then Marco realised that she was not the same.

She was seven years older, and he saw it in the faint lines by her eyes and mouth. He saw it in the clothing she wore, a charcoal-grey pencil skirt and a pale pink silk blouse. Sophisticated, elegant clothing for a woman, rather than the girlish dresses she'd worn seven years earlier.

But the inner sense of stillness he'd always admired she still possessed. The sense that no one could touch or affect her. He'd been drawn to that, after the tempest of his own childhood. He'd liked her almost unnatural sense of calm, her cool purpose. Even though she'd only been nineteen she'd seemed older, wiser. *And yet so innocent.*

'Signorina Rocci. I'm so glad you could join us.' Di

Santis moved forward, hands outstretched. Sierra barely brushed her fingertips with his before she moved away, to one of the club chairs. She sat down, her back straight, her ankles crossed, ever the lady. She didn't look at Marco.

He was looking at her, his stare burning. Marco jerked his gaze from Sierra and moved back to the window. Stared blindly out at the traffic that crawled down the Via Libertà.

'Shall we begin?' suggested di Santis, and Marco nodded. Sierra did not speak. 'The will is, in point of fact, quite straightforward.' Di Santis cleared his throat and Marco felt his body tense once more. He knew just how straightforward the will was. 'Signor Rocci, that is, your father, *signorina*—' he gave Sierra an abashed smile that Marco saw from the corner of his eye she did not return '—made his provisions quite clear.' He paused, and Marco knew he was not relishing the task set before him.

Sierra sat with her hands folded in her lap, her chin held high, her gaze direct and yet giving nothing away. Her face looked like a perfect icy mask. 'Could you please tell me what they are, Signor di Santis?' she asked when di Santis seemed disinclined to continue.

The sound of her voice, after seven years' silence, struck Marco like a fist to the gut. Suddenly he was breathless. Low, musical, clear. And yet without the innocent, childish hesitation of seven years ago. She spoke with an assurance she hadn't possessed before, a confidence the years had given her, and somehow this knowledge felt like an insult, a slap in his face. She'd become someone else, someone stronger perhaps, without him.

'Of course, Signorina Rocci.' Di Santis gave another apologetic smile. 'I can go through the particulars, but in essence your father left the bulk of his estate and business to Signor Ferranti.'

Marco swung his gaze to her pale face, waiting for her

reaction. The shock, the regret, the acknowledgement of her own guilt, the realisation of how much she'd chosen to lose. *Something.*

He got nothing.

Sierra merely nodded, her face composed, expressionless. 'The bulk?' she clarified quietly. 'But not all?'

At her question Marco felt a savage stab of rage, a fury he'd thought he'd put behind him years ago. So she was going to be mercenary? After abandoning her family and fiancé, offering no contact for seven long years despite her parents' distress and grief and continued appeals, she still wanted to know how much she'd get.

'No, not all, Signorina Rocci,' di Santis said quietly. He looked embarrassed. 'Your father left you some of your mother's jewellery, some pieces passed down through her family.'

Sierra bowed her head, a strand of dark blond hair falling from her chignon to rest against her cheek. Marco couldn't see her expression, couldn't tell if she was overcome with remorse or rage at being left so little. Trinkets, Arturo had called them. A pearl necklace, a sapphire brooch. Nothing too valuable, but in his generosity Arturo had wanted his daughter to have her mother's things.

Sierra raised her eyes and Marco saw that her eyes glistened with tears. 'Thank you,' she said quietly. 'Do you have them here?'

'I do…' Di Santis fumbled for a velvet pouch on his desk. 'Here they are. Your father left them into my safekeeping a while ago, when he realised…' He trailed off, and Sierra made no response.

When he realised he was dying, Marco filled in silently. Had the woman no heart at all? She seemed utterly unmoved by the fact that both her parents had died in her absence, both their hearts broken by their daughter's running away. The only thing that had brought her to tears was knowing she'd get nothing more than a handful of baubles.

'They won't be worth much, on the open market,' Marco said. His voice came out loud and terse, each word bitten off. Sierra's gaze moved to him and he felt a deep jolt in his chest at the way she looked at him, her gaze opaque and fathomless. As if she were looking at a complete stranger, and one she was utterly indifferent to.

'Is there anything else I need to know?' Sierra asked. She'd turned back to the lawyer, effectively dismissing Marco.

'I can read the will in its entirety...'

'That won't be necessary.' Her voice was low, soft. 'Thank you for my mother's jewels.' She rose from the chair in one elegantly fluid movement, and Marco realised she was leaving. After seven years of waiting, wondering, wanting a moment where it all finally made sense, he got nothing.

Sierra didn't even look at him as she left the room.

Sierra's breath came out in a shudder as she left the lawyer's office. Her legs trembled and her hands were clenched so tightly around the little velvet pouch that her knuckles ached.

It wasn't until she was out on the street that her breathing started to return to normal, and it took another twenty minutes of driving out of Palermo, navigating the endless snarl of traffic and knowing she'd left Marco Ferranti far behind, before she felt the tension begin to unknot from her shoulders.

The busy city streets gave way to dusty roads that wound up to the hill towns high above Palermo, the Mediterranean glittering blue-green as she drove towards the Nebrodi mountains, and the villa where her mother was

buried. When di Santis had rung her, she'd thought about
not going to Sicily at all, and then she'd thought about simply going to his office and returning to London on the very
same day. She had nothing left in Sicily now.

But then she'd reminded herself that her father couldn't
hurt her any longer, that Sicily was a place of ghosts and
memories, and not of threats. She'd forgotten about Marco
Ferranti.

A trembling laugh escaped her as she shook her head
wryly. She hadn't forgotten about Marco; she didn't think
she could ever do that. She'd simply underestimated the
effect he'd have on her after seven years of thankfully
numbing distance.

When she'd first caught sight of him in the office, wearing an expensive silk suit and reeking of power and privilege, looking as devastatingly attractive as he had seven
years ago but colder now, so much colder, her whole body
had trembled. Fortunately she'd got herself under control
before Marco had swung that penetrating iron-grey gaze
towards her. She had forced herself not to look at him.

She had no idea how he felt about her seven years on.
Hatred or indifference, did it really matter? She'd made the
right decision by running away the night before her wedding. She'd never regret it. Watching from afar as Marco
Ferranti became more ingrained in Rocci Enterprises, always at her father's side and groomed to be his next-in-line,
told her all she needed to know about the man.

The road twisted and turned as it climbed higher into
the mountains, the air sharper and colder, scented with
pine. The hazy blue sky she'd left in Palermo was now
dark with angry-looking clouds, and when Sierra parked
the car in front of the villa's locked gates she heard a distant rumble of thunder.

She shivered slightly even though the air was warm; the

wind was picking up, the sirocco that blew from North Africa and promised a storm. The pine trees towered above her, the mountains seeming to crowd her in. She'd spent most of her childhood at this villa, and while she'd loved the beauty and peace of its isolated position high above the nearest hill town, the place held too many hard memories for her to have any real affection for it.

Standing by the window as dread seeped into her stomach when she saw her father's car drive up the winding lane. Fear clenching her stomach hard as she heard his thunderous voice. Cringing as she heard her mother's placating or pleading response. No, she definitely didn't have good memories of here.

But she wouldn't stay long now. She'd see her mother's grave, pay her respects and then return to Palermo, where she'd booked into a budget hotel. By this time tomorrow she'd be back in London, and she'd never come to Sicily again.

Quickly, Sierra walked along the high stone wall that surrounded the estate. She knew the property like her own hand; she and her mother had always stayed here until Arturo called them into service, to play-act at being the perfect family for various engagements or openings of the Rocci hotels that now graced much of the globe. Her mother had lived for her husband's summons; Sierra had dreaded them.

Away from the road she knew the wall had crumbled in places, creating a gap low enough for her to climb over. She doubted her father had seen to repairs in the last seven years; she wondered if he'd come to the villa at all. He'd preferred to live his own life in Palermo except when he needed his wife and daughter to play at happy families for the media.

She stepped into the shelter of a dense thicket of pine

trees, the world falling to darkness as the trees overhead shut out any remnant of sunlight. Thunder rumbled again, and the branches snagged on her silk blouse and narrow skirt, neither a good choice for walking through woods or climbing walls.

After a few moments of walking she came to a crumbled section of wall and with effort, thanks to her pencil skirt, she managed to clamber over it. Sierra let out a breath of relief and started towards the far corner of the estate, where the family cemetery was located.

She skirted the villa, not wanting to attract attention to herself; she had no idea if anyone was in residence. Arturo had installed a housekeeper when she'd lived here with her mother, a beady-eyed old woman who had been her father's henchman and spy. If she was still here, Sierra had no wish to attract her attention.

In the distance the ghostly white marble headstones of the Rocci family plot appeared through the stormy gloom like silent, still ghosts, and Sierra's breath caught in her throat as she approached. She knew where her mother's marker lay, in the far corner; it was the only one that hadn't been there when she'd left.

Violet Rocci, Beloved Wife

She stared at the four words written starkly on the tombstone until they blurred and she blinked back tears. Beloved mother, yes, but *wife*? Had her father loved her mother at all? Sierra knew Violet believed so, but Sierra wanted to believe love was better and bigger than that. Love didn't hurt, didn't punish or belittle. She wanted to believe that, but she didn't know if she could. She certainly had no intention of taking the risk of finding out for herself.

'*Ti amo*, Mamma,' she whispered, and rested her hand on top of the cool marble. She'd missed her mother so much over these past seven years. Although she'd written Violet a few letters over the years, her mother had discouraged contact, fearing for Sierra's safety. The few letters she'd had were precious and all too rare, and had stopped completely well before Violet's illness.

She drew a deep breath and willed the tears away. She wouldn't cry now. There had been enough sadness already. Another deep breath and her composure was restored, as she needed it to be. Cloak herself in coolness, keep the feelings at bay. She turned away from the little cemetery plot and started walking back towards her car. She hoped Violet Rocci was at peace now, safe from her husband's cruelty. It was the smallest comfort, but the only one she could cling to now.

Thunder rumbled and forked lightning split the sky as the first heavy raindrops fell. Sierra ducked her head and started hurrying back to the section of wall she'd climbed over. She didn't want to be caught in a downpour, and neither did she relish the drive back down the steep mountain roads in this weather.

She climbed over the wall and hurried through the stand of pines, the branches snagging on her blouse and hair as the rain fell steadily, soaking her. Within seconds her pink silk blouse was plastered to her skin and her hair fell out of its chignon in wet rat's tails.

She cursed under her breath, thankful to emerge from the trees, only to have her insides freeze as she caught sight of a second car, a dark SUV, parked behind her own. As she came onto the road the door to the car opened, and an all too familiar figure emerged.

Marco Ferranti strode towards her, his white dress shirt soon soaked under the downpour so every well-defined

muscle was outlined in glorious detail. Sierra flicked her
gaze upwards, but the anger she saw snapping in his eyes,
the hard set of his mouth and jaw, made her insides quell
and she looked away. The rain was sheeting down now
and she stopped a few feet from him, sluicing rainwater
from her face.

'So.' Marco's voice was hard, without a shred of warmth.
'What the bloody hell do you think you're doing here?'

CHAPTER THREE

SIERRA DREW A deep breath and pushed the sodden mass of her hair away from her face. 'I was paying my respects.' She tried to move past him to her car but he blocked her way. 'What are *you* doing here?' she challenged, even though inside she felt weak and shaky with fear. Here was the real man Marco had hidden from her before, the angry, menacing man who loomed above her like a dark shadow, fierce and threatening. But, just as with her father, she wouldn't show her fear to this man.

'It's my home,' Marco informed her. 'As of today.'

She recoiled at that, at the triumph she heard in his tone. He was glad he'd got it all, and that she'd got almost nothing. Of course he was. 'I hope you enjoy it then,' she bit out, and his mouth curved in an unpleasant smile.

'I'm sure I will. But you were trespassing on private property, you do realise?'

She shook her head, stunned by the depth of his anger and cruelty. So this was the true face of the man she'd once thought of marrying. 'I'm leaving anyway.'

'Not so fast.' He grabbed her arm, his powerful fingers encircling her wrist, making her go utterly still. The commanding touch was so familiar and instinctively she braced herself for a blow. But it didn't come; Marco simply stared at her, and it took Sierra a moment to realise the fingers around her wrist were actually exerting only a gentle pressure.

'I want to know why you were here.'

'I told you,' she bit out. 'To pay my respects.'

'Did you go inside the villa?'

She stared at him, nonplussed. 'No.'

'How do I know that? You might have stolen something.'

She let out an incredulous laugh. If she'd had any doubts about whether jilting Marco Ferranti had been the right thing to do, he was dispelling them with dizzying speed.

'What on earth do you think I stole?' She shook his hand off her wrist and spread her arms wide. 'Where would I hide it?' She saw Marco's gaze flick down to her breasts and too late she realised the white lace bra she wore was visible through the soaked, near-transparent silk. Sierra kept her head held high with effort.

'I can't be sure of anything when it comes to you, except that you can't be trusted.'

'Did you follow me all the way from Palermo?'

His jaw tightened. 'I wanted to know where you were going.'

'Well, now you know. And now I'm going back to Palermo.' She started to move away but Marco stilled her with one outflung hand. He nodded towards the steep, curving road that led down the mountain.

'The road will be impassable now with flash flooding. You might as well come into the villa until it is over.'

'And you'll frisk me for any possible stolen goods?' Sierra finished. 'I'll take my chances with the flooding.'

'Don't be stupid.' Marco's voice was harsh, dismissive, reminding her so much of her father. Clearly, he'd decided to emulate his mentor.

'I'm not being stupid,' she snapped. 'I mean every word I say.'

'You'd rather risk serious injury or even death than come into a dry house with me?' Marco's mouth twisted. 'What did I ever do to deserve such disgust?'

'You just accused me of *stealing*.'

'I simply wanted to know why you were here.'

Above them an ear-splitting crack of thunder sounded, making Sierra jump. She was completely soaked and unfortunately she knew Marco spoke the truth. The roads would be truly impassable, most likely for some time.

'Fine,' she said ungraciously and got into her car.

Marco unlocked the gates with the remote control in his car, and they swung silently back, revealing the villa's long, curving drive.

Taking a deep breath, Sierra drove up with Marco following like her jailer. As soon as his car had passed, the gates swung closed again, locking her inside.

She parked in front of the villa and turned off the engine, reluctant to get out and face Marco again. And to face all the unwelcome memories that crowded her brain and heart. Coming back to Sicily had been a very bad idea.

Her door jerked open and Marco stood there, glowering at her. 'Are you going to get out of your car?'

'Yes, of course.' She climbed out, conscious of his nearness, of the animosity rolling off him even though he'd sounded cold and controlled. After seven years, did he still hate her for what she'd done? It seemed so.

'Is anyone living in the villa?' she asked as he pressed the security code into the keypad by the front door.

'No. I've left it empty for the time being, while I've been in Palermo.' He glanced back at her, his expression opaque. 'While your father was in hospital.'

Sierra made no reply. The lawyer, di Santis, had told her

that her father had died of pancreatic cancer. He'd had it for several years but had kept it secret; when the end came it had been swift. After the call she'd tried to dredge up some grief for the man who had sired her; she'd felt nothing but a weary relief that he was finally gone.

Marco opened the front door and ushered her into the huge marble foyer. The air was chilly and stale, the furniture shrouded in dust cloths. Sierra shivered.

'I'll turn the hot water on,' Marco said. 'I believe there are clothes upstairs.'

'My clothes…?'

'No, those were removed some time ago.' His voice was clipped, giving nothing away. 'But some of my clothes are in one of the guest bedrooms. You can borrow something to wear while your own clothes dry.'

She remained shivering in the foyer, dripping rainwater onto the black and white marble tiles, while Marco set about turning on lights and removing dust covers. It felt surreal to be back in this villa, and she couldn't escape the clawing feeling of being trapped, not just by the locked gates and the memories that mocked her, but by the man inhabiting this space, seeming to take up all the air. She felt desperate to leave.

'I'll light a fire in the sitting room,' Marco said. 'I'm afraid there isn't much food.'

'I don't need to eat. I'm going to leave as soon as possible.'

Marco's mouth twisted mockingly as he glanced back at her. 'Oh, I don't think so. The roads will be flooded for a while. I don't think you'll be leaving before tomorrow morning.' His eyes glinted with challenge or perhaps derision as he folded his powerful arms across his chest. Even angry and hostile, he was a beautiful man, every taut muscle radiating strength and power. But she didn't like brute strength. She hated the abuse of power. She looked away from him.

'Why don't you take a bath and change?'

Sierra's stomach clenched at the prospect of spending a night under the same roof as Marco Ferranti. Of taking a bath, changing clothes…everything making her feel vulnerable. He must have seen something in her face for he added silkily, 'Surely you're not worried for your virtue? Trust me, *cara*, I wouldn't touch you with a ten-foot bargepole.'

She flinched at both the deliberate use of the endearment and the contempt she saw in his face. The casual cruelty had been second nature to her father, but it stung coming from Marco Ferranti. He'd been kind to her once.

'Good,' she answered when she trusted her voice. 'Because that's the last thing I'd want.'

His gaze darkened and he took a step towards her. 'Are you sure about that?'

Sierra held her ground. She knew her body had once responded to Marco's, and even with him emanating raw, unadulterated anger she had a terrible feeling it would again. A single caress or kiss and she might start to melt, much to her shame. 'Very sure,' she answered in a clipped voice, and then she turned towards the stairs without another word.

She found Marco's things in one of the guest bedrooms; he hadn't taken the master bedroom for himself and she wondered why. It was all his now, every bit of it. The villa, the *palazzo* in Palermo, the Rocci business empire of hotels and real estate holdings. Her father had given everything to the man he'd seen as a son, and left his daughter with nothing.

Or almost nothing. Carefully she took the velvet pouch out from the pocket of her skirt. The pearl necklace and sapphire brooch that had been her mother's before she married were hers now. She had no idea why her father had allowed her to have them; had it been a moment of kindness on his deathbed, or had he simply been saving face, trying to seem like the kind, grieving father he'd never been?

It didn't matter. She had a keepsake to remind her of her mother, and that was all she'd wanted.

Quickly, Sierra slipped out of her wet clothes and took a short, scaldingly hot shower. She dressed in a soft grey T-shirt and tracksuit bottoms of Marco's; it felt bizarrely intimate to wear his clothes, and they swam on her. She used one of his belts to keep the bottoms from sliding right off her hips, and combed her hair with her fingers, leaving it hanging damply down her back.

Then, hesitantly, she went downstairs. She would have rather hidden upstairs away from Marco until the storm passed but, knowing him, he'd most likely come and find her. Perhaps it would be better to deal with the past, get that initial awful conversation out of the way, and then they could declare a silent truce and ignore each other until she was able to leave.

She found him in the sitting room, crouched in front of the fire he was fanning into crackling flame. He'd changed into jeans and a black T-shirt and the clothes fitted him snugly, emphasising his powerful chest and long legs, every inch of him radiating sexual power and virility.

Sierra stood in the doorway, conscious of a thousand things: how Marco's damp hair had started to curl at the nape of his neck, how the soft cotton of the T-shirt she wore—*his* T-shirt—rubbed against her bare breasts. She felt a tingling flare of what could only be desire and tried to squelch it. He hated her now, and in any case she knew what kind of man he was. How could she possibly desire him?

He glanced back at her as she came into the room, and with a shivery thrill she saw an answering flare of awareness in his own eyes. He straightened, the denim of his jeans stretching across his powerful thighs, and Sierra's gaze was drawn to the movement, to the long, fluid length of his legs, the powerful breadth of his shoulders. Once he would have been hers, a thought that had filled her with apprehension and even fear. Now she felt a flicker of curiosity and even loss for what might have been, and she quickly brushed it aside.

The man was handsome. Sexy. She'd always known that. It didn't change who he was, or why she'd had to leave.

'Come and get warm.' Marco's voice was low, husky. He gestured her forward and Sierra came slowly, reluctant to get any closer to him. Shadows danced across the stone hearth and her bare feet sank into the thick, luxuriously piled carpet.

'Thank you,' she murmured without looking at him. The tension in the room was thick and palpable, a thousand unspoken words and thoughts between them. Sierra stared at the dancing flames, having no idea how to break the silence, or whether she wanted to. Perhaps it would be better to act as if the past had never happened.

'When do you return to London?' Marco asked. His voice was cool, polite, the question that of an acquaintance or stranger.

Sierra released the breath she'd bottled in her lungs without realising. Maybe he would make this easy for her. 'Tomorrow.'

'Did you not think you'd have affairs to manage here?'

She glanced at him, startled, saw how his silvery eyes had narrowed to iron slits, his mouth twisted mockingly. His questions sounded innocuous, but she could see and feel the latent anger underneath the thin veneer of politeness.

'No. I didn't expect my father to leave me anything in his will.'

'You didn't?' Now he sounded nonplussed, and Sierra shrugged.

'Why would he? We've neither spoken nor seen each other in seven years.'

'That was your choice.'

'Yes.'

They were both silent, the only sound the crackling of the fire, the settling of logs in the grate. Sierra had wondered how much Marco guessed of her father's abuse and cruelty. How much he would have sanctioned. The odd slap? The heaping of insults and emotional abuse? Did it even matter?

She'd realised, that night she'd left, that she could not risk it. She'd been foolish to think she could, that she could entrust herself to any man. Leaving Marco had been as much about her as about him.

'Why did you come back here, to this villa?' Marco asked abruptly, and Sierra looked up from her contemplation of the fire.

'I told you—'

'To pay your respects. To what? To whom?'

'To my mother. Her grave is in the family plot on the estate.'

He cocked his head, his silvery gaze sweeping coldly over her. 'And yet you didn't return when your mother was ill. You didn't even send a letter.'

Because she hadn't known. But would she have come back, even if she had known? Could she have risked her father's wrath, being under his hand once more? Sierra swallowed and looked away.

'No answer?' Marco jibed softly.

'You know the answer. And anyway, it wasn't a question.'

He shook his head slowly. 'You are certainly living up—or should I say down—to my expectations.'

'What does that mean?'

'For seven years I've wondered just how cold a bitch I almost married. Now I know.'

The words felt like a slap, sending her reeling. She blinked past the pain, told herself it didn't matter. 'You can think what you like.'

'Of course I can. It's not as if you've ever given me any answers, have you? Any possible justification for what you did, not just in leaving me, but in deserting your family?'

She didn't reply. She didn't want to argue with Marco, and in any case he hadn't really been asking her a question. He'd been stating a fact, making a judgement. He'd made his mind up about her years ago, and nothing she could say would change it now, not even the truth. Besides, he'd been her father's right-hand man for over a decade. Either he knew how her father had treated his family, or he'd chosen not to know.

'You have nothing to say, Sierra?'

It was the first time he'd called her by her first name and it sent a shiver of apprehensive awareness rippling through her. He sounded so *cold*. For one brief blazing second she remembered the feel of his lips on hers when he'd kissed her in the garden. His hands on her body, sliding so knowingly up to cup her breasts; the electric tingle of excitement low in her belly, kindling a spark she hadn't even known existed, because no man had ever touched her that way. No man had ever made her feel so desired.

Mentally, Sierra shrugged away the memory. So the man could kiss. Marco Ferranti no doubt had unimaginable sexual prowess. He'd probably been with dozens— hundreds—of women. It didn't change facts.

'No,' she told him flatly. 'I have nothing to say.'

* * *

Marco stared at Sierra, at the cool hauteur on her lovely face, and felt another blaze of anger go off like a firework in his gut. How could she be so cold?

'You know, I admired how cool you were, all those years ago,' he told her. Thankfully, his voice sounded as flat as hers, almost disinterested. He'd given away too much already, too much anger, too much emotion. He'd had seven years to get over Sierra. In any case, it wasn't as if he'd ever loved her.

'Cool?' Sierra repeated. She looked startled, wary.

'Yes, you were so self-possessed, so calm. I liked that about you.' She didn't reply, just watched him guardedly. 'I didn't realise,' Marco continued, his tone clipped as he bit off each word precisely, 'that it was because you had no heart. You were all ice underneath.' Except she hadn't been ice in his arms.

Still she said nothing, and Marco could feel the anger boiling inside him, threatening to spill out. 'Damn it, Sierra, didn't you ever think that I deserved an explanation?'

Her gaze flicked away from his and her tongue darted out to touch her lips. Just that tiny gesture set lust ricocheting through him. He felt dizzy from the excess of emotion, anger and desire twined together. He didn't want to feel so much. After seven years of cutting himself off from such feelings, the force of their return was overwhelming and unwelcome.

'Well?' Marco demanded. Now that he'd asked the question, he realised he wanted an answer.

'I thought it was explanation enough that I left,' Sierra said coolly.

Marco stared at her, his jaw dropping before he had the presence of mind to snap it shut, the bones aching. 'How on earth could you think that?'

Her gaze moved to his and then away again. 'Because it was obvious I'd changed my mind.'

'Yes, I do realise. But I've never understood why, and your father didn't, either. He was devastated when you left, you know. Utterly bereft.' He still remembered how Arturo had wept and embraced him when he'd told him, outside the church, that Sierra was gone. Marco had been numb, disbelieving; he'd wanted to send search parties until the truth of what Arturo was saying slammed home. She wasn't missing. She'd *left*. She'd left him, and for a second he wasn't even surprised. His marriage to Sierra, his acceptance into the Rocci family, it had all been too good—too wonderful—to be true.

Now Sierra's mouth firmed and she folded her arms, her blue-grey eyes turning as cold as the Atlantic on a winter's day. 'Why did you want to marry me, Marco, if we're going to rake through the past? I never quite understood that.' She paused, her cool gaze trained on him now, unflinching and direct, offering an unspoken challenge. 'It's not because you loved me.'

'No.' He could admit that much. He hadn't known her well enough to love her, and in any case he'd never been interested in love. Love meant opening yourself up to emotional risk, spreading your arms wide and inviting someone to take a shot. In his mother's case, she'd sustained a direct hit. Not something he'd ever be so foolish or desperate to do.

'So?' Sierra arched an eyebrow, and it disconcerted him how quickly and neatly she'd flipped the conversation. He was no longer the one on the attack. How dare she put him on the defensive—she, who'd walked away without a word?

'I could ask the same of you,' he said. 'Why did you agree to marry me?' *And then change your mind?*

Sierra's mouth firmed. 'I'd convinced myself I could be happy with you. I was wrong.'

'And what made you decide that?' Marco demanded.

She sighed, shrugging her slim shoulders. 'Do we really want to go through all this?' she asked. 'Do you think it will help? So much has happened. Seven years, Marco. Maybe we should just agree to—'

'Disagree? We're not talking about a little spat we had, Sierra. Some petty argument.' His voice came out harshly—too harsh, ragged and revealing with the force of his emotion. Even so, he couldn't keep himself from continuing. 'We're talking about *marriage*. We were a few hours away from pledging our lives to one another.'

'I know.' Her lips formed the words but he could barely hear her whisper. Her face had gone pale, her eyes huge and dark. Still she stood tall, chin held high. She had strength—more strength than he'd ever realised—but right now it only made him angry.

'Then why…?'

'You still didn't answer my question, Marco.' Her chin tilted up another notch. 'Why did you want to marry me?'

He stared at her for a moment, furious that he felt cornered. 'I need a drink,' he said abruptly, and stalked into the kitchen. She didn't follow him.

He yanked a bottle of whisky from the cupboard and poured a healthy measure that he downed in one swallow. Then he poured another.

Damn it, how dare she ask him, accuse *him*, when she was the one who should be called to account? What did it matter why he'd wanted to marry her, when she'd agreed?

He drained his second glass and then went back to the sitting room. Sierra had moved closer to the fire and the flames cast dancing shadows across her face. Her hair was starting to dry, the ends curling. She looked utterly delectable wearing his too-big clothes. The T-shirt had slipped off one shoulder, so he could see how golden and smooth her skin was. The belt she'd cinched at her waist showed off its narrowness and the high, proud curve of her breasts. He remembered the feel of them in his hands, when he'd given his desire free rein for a few intensely exquisite moments. He'd felt her arch into him, heard her breathy gasp of pleasure.

The memory now had the power to stir the embers of his desire and he turned away from her, willing the memories, the emotion, back. He didn't want to feel anything, not even simple lust, for Sierra Rocci now.

'Damn it, Sierra, you have some nerve asking me why I behaved the way I did. You're the one who chose to leave without so much as a note.'

'I know.'

'And you still haven't given me a reason why. You changed your mind. Fine. I accept that. It was patently obvious at the time.' His voice came out sharp with bitterness and he strove to moderate it. 'But you still haven't said why. Don't you think I deserve an explanation? Your parents are no longer alive to hear why you abandoned them, but I am.' His voice hardened, rose. 'So why don't you just tell me the truth?'

CHAPTER FOUR

A LOG SETTLED in the grate and popped, sparks scattering across the hearth before turning to cold ash. The silence stretched on and Sierra let it. What could she say? What would Marco believe or be willing to hear?

It was obvious he'd manufactured his own version of events, no doubt been fed lies by her father, who would have pretended to grieve for her. Marco wouldn't believe the truth now, even if she fed it to him with a spoon.

'Well?' His voice rang out, harsh and demanding. 'No reply?'

She shrugged, not meeting his gaze. 'What do you want me to say?'

'I told you—the truth. Why did you leave, Sierra? The night before our wedding?'

Sierra took a deep breath and forced herself to meet his hard gaze; looking into his eyes felt like slamming into a wall. 'Fine. The truth is I had second thoughts. Cold feet. I realised I was putting my life in the hands of a virtual stranger, and that it was a mistake. I couldn't do it.'

He stared at her, his gaze like concrete, a muscle flickering in his jaw. 'You realised all this the night before our wedding? It didn't occur to you at any point during the month of our engagement?'

'I'd thought I was making the right decision. That night I realised I wasn't.'

He shook his head derisively. 'You make it sound so simple.'

'In some ways it was, Marco.' Another deep breath. 'We didn't love or even know each other, not really. We'd had a handful of dates, everything stage-managed by my father. Our marriage would have been a disaster.'

'You can be so sure?'

'Yes.' She looked away, wanting to hide the truth she feared would be reflected in her eyes. She *wasn't* sure. Not completely. Maybe their marriage would have worked. Maybe Marco really was a good and gentle man. Although the fact that he'd remained at her father's right hand since then made her wonder. Doubt. How much of her father's shallow charm and ruthless ways had rubbed off on her ex-fiancé? Judging from the cold anger she'd seen from him today, she feared far too much. No, she'd made the right choice. She had to believe that.

'Fine.' Marco exhaled in one long, low rush of breath. 'You changed your mind. Why didn't you tell me, then? Talk to me and tell me what you were thinking? Did I not deserve that much courtesy? A note, at the very least? Maybe I could have convinced you…'

'Exactly. You would have convinced me.' He stared at her, nonplussed, and she continued, 'I was nineteen, Marco. You were a man of nearly thirty, sophisticated and worldly, especially compared to me. I had no life experience at all, and I was afraid to stand up to you, afraid that you'd sweep my arguments aside and then I'd marry you out of fear.'

'Did I ever give you any reason to be afraid of me?' he demanded. 'What a thing to accuse me of, Sierra, and with 'no proof.' His voice vibrated with anger and she fought not to flinch.

Now was the time to say it. To admit what she'd over-heard, how it had made her feel. Why shouldn't she? What did she have to lose? She'd lost it all already. She'd gained a new life—a small, quiet life that was safe and was *hers*. She had nothing she either needed or wanted from this man. 'I heard you,' she said quietly.

His gaze widened and his mouth parted soundlessly before he finally spoke. 'You *heard* me? Am I supposed to know what that means?'

'The night before our wedding, I heard you talking to my father.'

He shook his head slowly, not understanding. Not wanting to understand. 'I'm still in the dark, Sierra.'

A deep breath, and she let it buoy her lungs, her cour-age. 'You said, "I know how to handle her", Marco.' Even after all the years the memory burned. 'When my father told you how women get notions. You spoke about me as if I were a dog, a beast to be bridled. Someone to be man-aged rather than respected.'

A full minute passed where Marco simply stared at her. Sierra held his gaze even though she ached to look away. To hide. The fire crackled and a spark popped, the loud sound breaking the stillness and finally allowing her to look somewhere else.

'And for this, this one statement I can't even remember,' Marco said in a low voice, 'you condemned me? Damned me?'

'It was enough.'

He swore, a hiss under his breath. Sierra flinched, tried not to cringe. A man's anger still had the power to strike fear into her soul. Make her body tense as she waited to ward off the blow.

'How could you—' He broke off, shaking his head. 'I don't even want to know. I'm not interested in your excuses.' He stalked into the kitchen. After a moment Sierra followed him. She'd rather creep back upstairs but she felt the conversation needed to be finished. Maybe then the past would be laid to rest, or at least as much as it could be.

She stood in the doorway while he opened various cupboards, every movement taut with suppressed fury.

He took out a packet of dried pasta and tossed it onto the granite island. 'I'm afraid there's not much to eat.'

'I'm not hungry.'

'Don't be perverse. You probably haven't eaten anything all day. You should keep up your strength.'

The fact that he was right made Sierra stay silent. She was being perverse because she didn't want to spend any more time with him than necessary. Her stomach growled loudly and Marco gave her a mocking look.

Sierra forced a smile. 'Very well, then. Let me help.' He shrugged his indifferent assent and Sierra moved awkwardly through the kitchen, conscious how this cosy domestic scene was at odds with the tension and animosity that still tautened the air.

They worked in silence for a few minutes, concentrating on mundane things; Sierra found a large pot and filled it with water, plonking it on the huge state-of-the-art range as Marco retrieved a tin of crushed tomatoes and various herbs from the cupboards.

This was his home now, and yet it once had been hers. She glanced round the huge kitchen, the oak table in the dining nook where she'd eaten breakfast while her mother moped and drank espresso. Sierra had enjoyed a cautious happiness at the villa, but Violet had always been miserable away from Arturo.

Sierra shook her head at the memory, at the regret she still felt for her mother's life, her mother's choices.

Marco noticed the movement and stilled. 'What is it?'

She turned to him. 'What do you mean?'

'You're shaking your head. What are you thinking about?'

'Nothing.'

'Something, Sierra.'

'I was just thinking about my mother. How I missed her.'

His eyebrows rose in obvious disbelief. 'Why didn't you ever come back, then?'

The question hung in the air, taunting her. She could tell him the truth, but she resisted instinctively. Sierra didn't know if it was because she didn't want to be pitied, or because she suspected he wouldn't believe her. Or, worse, an innate loyalty to her father, a man who had shown her so much contempt and disgust.

She drew a deep breath. 'I couldn't.'

'Why not?'

'My father would not want me back, after…everything.'

'You're wrong.' She recoiled at the flatly spoken statement. He could be so sure? 'You judge people so quickly, Sierra. Me and your father both. He would have welcomed you back with open arms, I know it. He told me as much, many times.'

She leaned against the counter, absorbing his statement. So her father had been feeding him lies all along, just as she'd suspected. She could tell Marco believed what he said, deeply and utterly. And he would never believe her.

'I suppose I wasn't prepared to risk it.'

'You broke his heart,' Marco told her flatly. 'And your mother's. Neither of them were ever the same.'

Guilt curdled her stomach like sour milk. She'd always

known, even if she hadn't wanted to dwell on it, that her leaving would cost her mother. It hurt to hear it now. 'How do you know? Did you see my mother very much?'

'Often enough. Arturo invited me to dinner many times. Your mother became reclusive—'

'She was always reclusive,' Sierra cut in sharply. She could not let every statement pass as gospel. 'We lived here, at the villa, except when my father called us into action.'

'A country life is better for children.' He glanced round the huge kitchen, spreading one arm wide to encompass the luxurious villa and its endless gardens. 'This would be a wonderful place to raise children.' His voice had thickened, and with a jolt Sierra wondered if he was thinking about their children. The thought made her feel a strangely piquant sense of loss that she could not bear to consider too closely.

'So how was she more reclusive?'

'She didn't always join us for meals. She didn't come to as many social events. Her health began to fail...'

Tears stung Sierra's eyes and she blinked rapidly to dispel them. She didn't want Marco to see her cry. She could guess why her mother had retreated more. Her father must have been so angry with her leaving, and he would have taken it out on her mother. She'd have had no choice but to hide.

'The truth hurts, does it?' Marco said, his voice close to a sneer. He'd seen her tears and he wasn't impressed. 'I suppose it was easy to forget about them from afar.'

'None of it was easy,' Sierra choked out. She drew a deep breath and willed the grief back. Showing Marco how much she was affected would only make him more contemptuous. He'd judged her long ago and nothing she could do or say would change the way he felt about her.

And it shouldn't matter, because after today she would never see him again.

A prospect that caused her an absurd flash of pain; she forced herself to shrug it off.

'It seemed easy from where I stood,' Marco answered. His voice was sharp with bitterness.

'Maybe it did,' Sierra agreed. 'But what good can it do now, to go over these things? What do you want from me, Marco?'

What did he want from her? Why was he pushing her, demanding answers she obviously couldn't or didn't want to give? Did it even matter which? It was seven years ago. She'd had cold feet, changed her mind, whatever. She'd treated both him and her parents callously, and he was glad to have escaped a lifetime sentence with a woman as cold as she was. They'd both moved on.

Except when he'd seen her standing in the doorway of di Santis's office, when he'd remembered how she'd tasted and felt and even more, how he'd enjoyed being with her, seeing her shy smile, the way those blue-grey eyes had warmed with surprised laughter...when he'd been looking forward to the life they would build together... It didn't feel as if he'd moved on. At all. And that realisation infuriated him.

Marco swung away from her, bracing his hands against the counter. 'I don't want anything from you. Not any more.' He busied himself with opening the tin of tomatoes and pouring the contents into a pan. 'Seeing you again has made me ask some questions,' he answered, his voice thankfully cool. 'And want some answers. Since I never had any.'

'I can understand that.' She sounded sad.

'Can you?' *Then why...?* But he wouldn't ask her anything more. He wouldn't beg. Wordlessly, he turned back to their makeshift meal. Sierra watched him, saying nothing, but Marco felt the tension ease slightly. The anger that had been propelling him along had left in a defeated rush, leaving him feeling more sad than anything else. And he didn't want to feel sad. God help him, he was *over* Sierra. He'd never loved her, after all—he'd desired her, yes. He'd wanted her very much.

But love? No. He'd never felt that and he had no intention of feeling it for anyone.

He slid his gaze towards her, saw the way her chest rose and fell under the baggy T-shirt. He could see the peaks of her nipples through the thin fabric, and desire arced through him. He still wanted her.

And did she want him? The question intrigued him and, even though he knew nothing would happen between them now, he realised he wanted to know the answer—very much.

There was only one way to find out. He reached for the salt, letting his arm brush across her breasts for one tantalising second. He heard her draw her breath in sharply and step back. When he glanced at her, he saw the colour flare into her face, her eyes widen before she quickly looked away.

Marco only just suppressed his smile as satisfaction surged through him. She wanted him. Seducing her would be easy…and such sweet revenge. But was that all he wanted from Sierra now? A moment's pleasure? The proof that she'd missed out? It felt petty and small, and more exposing of him than her.

And yet it would be so satisfying.

'What will you do with the estate?' She cleared her throat, her gaze flicking away from his as she stirred the pasta. 'Will you live here? Or sell it?'

'I haven't decided.' His thoughts of revenge were replaced by an uncomfortable flicker of guilt for taking Sierra's inheritance from her. Not that he'd actually wanted to; Arturo had insisted, claiming Marco had been far more of a son to him than Sierra had ever been a daughter. And, in his self-righteous anger and hurt, Marco had relented. Sierra had walked away from the family that had embraced him. He'd believed she deserved what she'd got: nothing.

'Is there anything you want from the villa?' he asked. 'Or the *palazzo* in Palermo? Some heirlooms or pictures?'

She shook her head, her certainty shocking him even though he knew it shouldn't. She'd turned her back on all of it seven years ago. 'No. I don't want anything.'

'There's nothing?' he pressed. 'What about a photograph of your parents? There's a wedding picture in the front hall of the *palazzo*. It's lovely.' He watched her, searching for some sign of softness, some relenting towards her family, towards him.

'No,' she said, and her voice was firm. 'I don't want anything.'

They worked in silent tandem, preparing the simple meal, and it wasn't until they were seated at the table in the alcove with steaming plates of pasta that Sierra spoke again.

'I always liked this spot. I ate breakfast here. The cook was an old battleaxe who thought I should eat in the dining room but I couldn't bear it, with all the stuffy portraits staring down at me so disapprovingly. I much preferred it here.' She smiled, the gesture touched with sorrowful whimsy.

Marco imagined her as a child sitting at the table, her feet not even touching the floor. He imagined their daughter doing the same, and then abruptly banished the thought. Dreams he'd once had of a proper family, a real life, and now they were nothing but ashes and smoke. He'd never live here with Sierra or anyone.

'You can have the villa.' His voice came out abrupt, ungracious. Marco cleared his throat. 'I won't be using it. And it was your family home.'

She stared at him, her eyes wide. 'You're offering me the *villa*?'

He shrugged. 'Why shouldn't I? I didn't need any of your inheritance. The only thing I wanted was your father's shares in Rocci Enterprises.' Which gave him control of the empire he'd helped to build.

'Of course.' Her mouth curved in a mocking smile. 'That's why you wanted to marry me, after all.'

'What do you mean?' He stared at her in surprise, shocked by her assumption. 'Is that what you think? That I wanted to marry you only for personal gain?'

'Can you really deny it? What better way to move through the ranks than marry the boss's daughter?' She held his gaze and even though her voice was cool he saw pain in her eyes. Old, unforgotten pain, a remnant of long past emotion, and strangely it gratified him. So this was why she'd left—because she'd assumed he had been using her?

'I won't deny that there were some advantages to marrying you,' he began, and she let out a hard laugh.

'That's putting it mildly. You wouldn't have looked twice at me if my last name hadn't been Rocci.'

'That's not necessarily true. But I was introduced to you by your father. I always knew you were a Rocci.'

'And he stage-managed it all, didn't he? The whole reason he introduced you to me was to marry me off.'

Marco heard the bitterness in her voice and wondered at it. 'But surely you knew that.'

'Yes, I knew.' She shook her head, regret etched on her

fine-boned features. Marco laid down his knife and fork and stared at her hard.

'Then how can you object? Your father was concerned for your welfare. It made sense, assuming we got along, for him to encourage the match. He'd provide for his daughter and secure his business.'

'Which sounds positively medieval—'

'Not medieval,' Marco interjected. 'Sicilian, perhaps. He was an old-fashioned man, this is an old-fashioned country, with outdated ideas about some things. Trust me, I know.'

She looked up, the bitterness and regret sliding from her face, replaced by curiosity. 'Why do you say that? Why should you know better than another?'

He shouldn't have said that at all. He had no intention of telling Sierra about the shame of his parentage, the sorrow of his childhood. The past was best left forgotten, and he knew he could not stomach her pity. 'We've both encountered it, in different ways,' he answered with a shrug. 'But if you knew your father intended for us to marry, why do you fault me for it now?'

Sierra sighed and leaned back in her chair. 'I don't, not really.'

'But…' He shook his head, mystified and more than a little annoyed. 'I don't understand you, Sierra. Perhaps I never did.'

'I know.' She was quiet then, her face drawn in sorrowful lines. 'If it helps, I'm truly sorry for the way it all happened. If I'd had more courage, more clarity, I would have never let it get as far as it did. I would have never agreed to your proposal.'

And that was supposed to make him feel *better*? Marco's chest hurt with the pressure of holding back his anger and hurt. He was not going to show Sierra how her words wounded him. She saw their entire relationship as a mistake, an error of judgement. Until she hadn't come down the aisle, he'd been intending to spend the rest of his life with her. The difference in their experiences, their feelings, was too marked and painful for him to remark on it.

'I didn't intend to marry you simply because it was good business,' he finally managed, his voice level. He would not have her accuse him of being mercenary.

'I suppose it helped that I didn't have a face like an old boot,' Sierra returned before he could continue. 'And I was so biddable, wasn't I? So eager to please, practically fawning over you.' She shook her head in self-derision.

Marco cocked his head, surprise sweeping over him. 'Is that how you saw it?'

'That's how it was.'

He knew there was truth in what she said, but it hadn't been the whole truth. Yes, she'd been pretty and he'd been physically attracted to her. Overwhelmingly physically attracted to her, so his palms had itched to touch her softness, to feel her body yield to his. *And they still did.*

And yes, he'd liked how much she'd seemed to like him, how eager and admiring she'd been. What man wouldn't?

She'd been young and isolated, but so had he, even though he'd been almost thirty. Back then he hadn't had many, if any, people who looked up to him. He'd been a street rat from the dusty gutters of Palermo, a virtual orphan who had worked through half a dozen foster homes before he'd finally left at sixteen. No one had missed him.

Seeing Sierra Rocci look at him with stars in her eyes had felt *good.* Had made him feel part of something bigger than himself, and he'd craved that desperately. But Sierra made it sound as if he'd been calculating and cold, and it had never been like that for him.

'You are painting only part of the picture,' Marco finally said.

'Oh, I'm sure you felt an affection for me,' Sierra cut in. 'An amused tolerance, no doubt. But eventually you would have tired of me and I would have resented you. It would have been a disaster, like I said.'

He opened his mouth to object, to tell her what he'd hoped would have happened. That maybe they would have liked each other, grown closer. No, he hadn't loved her, hadn't wanted to love her. Hadn't wanted that much emotional risk. But he'd hoped for a good marriage. A real family.

She stared at him with challenge in her eyes and he closed his mouth. Why would he say all that now? Admit so much pathetic need? There was nothing between them now, no hope of any kind of future. Nothing but an intense physical awareness, and one he could use to his own ruthless advantage. Why shouldn't he? Why shouldn't he have Sierra Rocci in bed? Surely she wasn't the innocent she'd once been, and he could tell she desired him. Even if she didn't want to.

'Perhaps you're right,' he said tonelessly. 'In any case, you never gave us the opportunity to discover what might have happened. And, as you've said, it's all in the past.'

Sierra's breath left in a rush. 'Yes.' She sounded wary, as if she didn't trust his words, that he could be so forgiving.

'I'm glad you've realised that,' she said, her voice cool, and Marco inclined his head. 'I think I'll go to bed.' She rose gracefully and took her plate to the sink. Marco watched her go. 'It's been a long day and I have to get up early tomorrow for my flight.'

'Very well.'

She turned to him, uncertainty flashing in her eyes. 'Goodnight.'

Marco smiled fleetingly, letting his gaze rest on hers with intent, watching with satisfaction as her pupils flared and her breath hitched. 'Let me show you to your room.'

'It's not necessary—'

He rose from the table and strode towards her, his steps eating up the space in a few long strides. 'Oh,' he assured her with a smile that had become feral, predatory, 'but it is.'

CHAPTER FIVE

SHE COULDN'T SLEEP. Sierra lay in the double bed in the guest room Marco had shown her to a few hours ago and stared up at the ceiling. The rain drummed against the roof and the wind battered the shutters. And inside her a tangle of fear and desire left her feeling restless, uncertain.

She didn't think she'd been imagining the heightened sense of expectation as Marco had led her from the kitchen and up the sweeping marble staircase to the wing of guest bedrooms. She certainly hadn't been imagining the pulse of excitement she'd felt low in her belly when he'd taken her hand to guide her down the darkened corridor.

She hated how immediate and overwhelming her response to him was, and yet she told herself it was natural. Understandable. He was an attractive, virile man, and she'd responded to him before. She couldn't control the way he made her body feel, but she could certainly control her actions.

And so with effort she'd pulled her hand from his. The gesture seemed only to amuse him; he'd glanced back at her with a knowing smile, and Sierra had had the uncomfortable feeling that he knew exactly what she was thinking—and feeling.

But he hadn't acted on it. He'd shown her into the bedroom and she'd stood there, clearly *waiting*, while he'd turned on lights and checked that the shutters were bolted.

For an exquisite, excruciating second Sierra had thought he was going to do something. Kiss her. He'd stood in front of her, the lamplight creating a warm golden pool that bathed them both, and had looked at her. And she'd waited, ready, expectant...

If he'd kissed her then, she wouldn't have been able to resist. The realisation should have been shaming but she'd felt too much desire for that.

But Marco hadn't kissed her. His features had twisted in some emotion she couldn't discern, and then he'd simply said goodnight and left her alone. *Thank God.*

There was absolutely no reason whatsoever to feel disappointed about that.

Now Sierra rose from the bed, swinging her legs over so her bare feet hit the cold tiles. Music. Music was what she needed now. Music had always been both her solace and her inspiration. When she was playing the violin, she could soar far above all the petty worries and cruelties of her day-to-day life. But she didn't have her violin here; she'd left it in London.

Still, the villa had a music room with a piano. It was better than nothing. And she needed to escape from the din inside her own head, if only for a few minutes. Quietly, she crept from her bedroom and down the long darkened hallway. The house was silent save for the steady patter of rain, the distant rumble of thunder as the storm thankfully moved off.

Sierra tiptoed down the stairs, feeling her way through the dark, the moonless night not offering even a sliver of light. Finally, she found her way to the small music room with its French windows opening onto the terrace that was now awash in puddles.

She flicked on a single lamp, its warm glow creating a pool of light across the dusty ebony of grand piano. Gently she eased up the lid; the instrument was no doubt woefully out of tune. She quietly pressed a key and winced at the discordant sound.

Never mind. She sat at the piano and softly played the opening bars to Debussy's *Sarabande*, not wanting to wake Marco in one of the rooms above. Even with the piano out of tune, the music filled her, swept away her worries and regrets and left only light and sound in their wake. She closed her eyes, giving herself up to the piece, to the feeling. Forgetting, for a few needful moments, about her parents, her past, *Marco*.

She didn't know when she became aware that she wasn't alone. A prickling along her scalp, the nape of her neck. A shivery awareness that rippled through her and caused her to open her eyes.

Marco stood in the doorway of the music room, wearing only a pair of pyjama bottoms, his glorious chest bare, his gaze trained on her. Sierra's fingers stilled on the piano, plunging the room into an expectant silence.

'I didn't know you played piano.' His voice was low, husky with sleep, and it wove its sensual threads around her, ensnaring her.

'I don't, not really.' She put her hands in her lap, self-conscious and all too aware of Marco standing so near her, so bare and so beautiful. Every muscle of his chest was bronzed and perfectly sculpted; he looked like an ad for cologne or clothes or cars. Looking the way he did, she thought he could sell anyone anything. 'I had a few lessons,' Sierra continued stiltedly, 'but I'm mostly self-taught.'

'That's impressive.'

She shrugged, his surprising praise unnerving her. Having Marco standing here, wearing next to nothing, acting almost as if he admired her, sent her senses into hyperdrive and left her speechless.

'I never even knew you were musical.' He'd taken a step closer to her and she could feel the heat from his body. When she took a breath the musky male scent of him hit her nostrils and made her stomach clench. Hard.

'The violin is actually my chosen instrument, but it's not something I usually tell people. It's a private thing.' She forced herself to meet his sleepy, silvery gaze. She'd been a fool to come out of her bedroom tonight, and yet a distant part of her recognised she'd done it because she'd wanted this. Him. And even though desire was rushing through her in a torrent, both nerves and common sense made her back off. 'I'm sorry I disturbed you. I must have got carried away.' She half rose from the piano bench, halting inexplicably, pinned by his gaze.

'It sounded lovely.'

'The piano is out of tune.'

'Even so.'

He held her gaze, and inwardly Sierra quaked at how intent he looked. How utterly purposeful. So she wasn't even surprised when he reached a hand out and cupped her cheek, the pad of his thumb stroking the softness of her lower lip. Her breath caught in a gasp that lodged in her chest. Her heart started to pound. She'd been waiting for this, and even though she was afraid she knew she still wanted it.

'Almost,' he said softly, 'as lovely as you. Do you know how beautiful you are, Sierra? I've always thought that. You undid me, with your loveliness. I was caught from the moment I saw you, at your father's *palazzo*. Do you remember? You were standing in the drawing room, wearing a pink dress. You looked like a rose.'

She stared at him, shocked by how much he had admitted, how much he'd felt. 'I remember,' she whispered. Of course she remembered. She'd glimpsed him from the window, seen him gently stroke that silly cat, and felt her heart lift in both hope and desire. How quickly she'd fallen for him. How completely. Not in love, no, but in childish hope and longing. He'd overwhelmed her senses, even when she'd thought she'd been acting smart, playing safe.

'Do you remember when I kissed you?' Marco asked. His thumb pressed her lip gently, reminding her of how his lips had felt on hers. Hard, hot, soft, cool. Everything, all at once.

'Yes,' she managed in a shaky whisper. 'I remember.'

'You liked my kisses.' It was a statement, and he waited for her to refute it, confident that she couldn't. Sierra tried to look away but Marco held her gaze as if he were holding her face in place with his hands. He was that commanding, that forceful, and he hadn't even moved.

'You don't deny it.'

'No.' The word was drawn from her with helpless reluctance.

'You still like them, I think,' he said softly, and her silence condemned her. Slowly, inexorably, Marco drew her to him. She knew he was going to kiss her, and she knew she wanted him to. She also knew it was a bad idea, a *dangerous* idea, considering all that had—and hadn't— happened between them and yet she didn't resist.

His lips brushed hers once, twice. A shuddering sigh escaped her and she reached up to clutch his shoulders and steady herself. His skin felt hot and hard under her palms and she couldn't keep herself from smoothing her hands down his back, revelling in the feel of him. How could a man's skin feel so silky?

Marco's hands framed her face as he deepened the kiss,

his tongue sliding sweetly into her mouth as he tasted and explored her. He slid his hands from her face to her shoulders and then, wonderfully, to her breasts, cupping them as he had that day under the plane tree. She remembered how exciting it had felt, or at least she thought she had, but the reality of his touch now was so intense, so exquisite, she almost cried out as his thumbs brushed over her nipples. She hadn't remembered this, not enough.

'Marco.' His name came on a breath, and she didn't even know why she said it. Was she asking him to continue or telling him to stop?

He moved his mouth to her jaw, blazing kisses along her neck and collarbone as he slid his hand under her T-shirt and cupped her bare breast, the feel of his rough palm against her soft flesh, the gentle abrasion of it, making every nerve-ending blaze almost painfully to life. It was too much, and yet she wanted more.

'I want you.' He spoke hoarsely, firmly, declaring his intent. Sierra could only nod. He touched her chin with his fingers, forcing her to meet his blazing gaze. 'Say it. Say you want me, Sierra.'

'I want you,' she whispered, the words drawn from her, falling into the stillness, creating ripples.

Triumph blazed in his eyes as he pulled the T-shirt off her. She hadn't bothered with the tracksuit bottoms for pyjamas, so in one fluid movement she'd become naked. She sucked in a hard breath when he pulled her towards him, her breasts colliding and then crushed against his chest. The feel of their bare skin touching sent another tingling quiver of awareness shooting through her. Marco's hands were on her waist and then her hips as he fitted her against him. She could feel his arousal through the thin pyjama bottoms and it made her gasp. So many sensations all at once; she could barely acknowledge one before another came crashing over her.

Marco eased her back onto the piano bench, spreading her legs so he could stand between them. Her head fell back as he kissed his way from her collarbone to her breasts, and Sierra moaned as his tongue flicked across her sensitive flesh. She'd never realised you could feel this way, that a man could make you feel this way. He glanced up at her, his grey eyes blazing with triumph, and then he moved his head from her breasts to between her thighs and her breath came out in a shaky moan as he touched her centre.

'Oh.' She arched against his mouth, astonished at how sharp and intense the pleasure was, how consuming as his tongue found the very heart of her. *'Oh.'* She threaded her hands through his silky hair as her body arched helplessly against his mouth and his hands gripped her hips. It only took a few exquisite moments for her world to explode in glittering fragments around her and she cried out, one jagged note that echoed through the stillness of the villa.

She *really* had no idea.

She sagged against the piano as her body trembled with the aftershocks of her climax and Marco lifted his head to gaze at her with blatant—and smug—satisfaction. Realisation thudded sickly through her; his look said it all. He'd been trying to prove something, and he'd just proved it—in spades.

Shakily, colour rushing to her face, Sierra pushed her tangle of hair from her hot cheeks and closed her legs, pushing him away from her. The intensity of the moment had splintered, leaving her feeling raw and exposed. Wounded and ashamed. She'd been so wanton, so shameless, and Marco had been utterly in control. *As always.*

'Now at least you know a little of what you've missed,' he said and her mouth opened on a soundless gasp.

'You've proved your point, then, I suppose,' she managed and on shaking legs she grabbed her T-shirt and rushed from the room.

Marco stalked upstairs, his whole body throbbing with unfulfilled desire—and worse, regret. He'd behaved like a cad. A heartless, cruel cad. And he needed an icy-cold shower. Swearing under his breath, he strode into his bedroom and went straight to the en suite bathroom, turning the cold on full blast. He stepped beneath the needling spray, sucking in a hard breath as the icy water hit his skin and chilled him right through. And even then he couldn't quench the fire that raged in his veins, heated his blood, born of both shame and lust.

He'd wanted her so much, more than he'd ever wanted another woman. More than he'd ever thought possible. The sweetness of her response, the *innocence* of it... Marco braced his hands against the shower stall. He could almost believe she was still untouched. She'd seemed so surprised by everything, so enthralled. And when she'd fallen to pieces beneath his mouth...

Forcefully he pushed the memory away. The last thing he needed now was to remember how that had felt. Better to remember the sudden look of uncertainty on her face, of shame. The realisation that he'd been low enough to exact some kind of revenge, using her body against her. Forcing her to respond to him, even though she'd once rejected him.

He'd been tempted to seduce her, yes, and he could have had her earlier, when he'd shown her to her bedroom. He'd seen the uncertainty and desire in her eyes, how she had hesitated. But he'd resisted the temptation, had told himself he was better than that.

Apparently he wasn't.

His body numb with cold, his blood still hot, Marco

turned off the shower and wrapped a towel around his hips. Sleep would not come for him tonight, not when too many emotions still churned through him. He went to his laptop instead, powered it up and prepared to work.

By dawn his eyes were gritty, his body aching, but at least the rain had stopped. Marco stood at the window and gazed out at the rain-washed gardens. The once manicured lawns and groomed beds were a wild tangle of shrubs and trees; he hadn't looked after the estate in the last few years, when Arturo had been too ill to do so himself. He'd hire a gardener to clean it up before he sold it. He didn't want to have anything more to do with the place.

When he came downstairs Sierra was already in the kitchen, dressed in the silk blouse and pencil skirt she'd worn yesterday. Both were creased but dry; she'd put her hair back up in its sleek chignon and all of it felt like armour, a way to protect herself against him.

Marco hesitated in the doorway, wondering whether to mention last night. What would he even say? In any case Sierra looked as if she wanted to pretend it hadn't happened, and maybe that was best.

'We should get on the road if your flight is this afternoon.'

'We?' She shook her head firmly. 'I'll drive myself.'

'The mountain roads still aren't passable, and your rental car looks like little more than a tin can on wheels,' Marco dismissed. 'I'll drive you. My car can handle the flooding.'

'But what about my rental…?'

'I'll have someone pick it up and deliver it to the agency. It's not a problem.'

She licked her lips, her eyes wide, her expression more than a little panicked. 'But…'

'It makes sense, Sierra. And, trust me, you don't have

to worry about some kind of repeat of last night. I don't intend to touch you ever again.' He hadn't meant to sound quite so harsh, but he saw the surprised hurt flicker in her eyes before she looked away.

'And I have no intention of letting you touch me ever again.'

He was almost tempted to prove her wrong, but he resisted the impulse. The sooner Sierra was out of his life, the better. 'It seems we're agreed, then. Now, we should get ready to go.' Marco grabbed his keys and switched off the lights before ushering Sierra out of the kitchen. He followed her, locking the villa behind him, and then opened the passenger door to his SUV. As Sierra slid inside the car he breathed in her lemony scent, and his gut tightened. It was going to be a long three hours.

They drove in silence down the sweeping drive, the villa's gates closing silently behind them. Sierra let out a sigh of relief as Marco turned onto the mountain road.

'You're glad to leave?'

'Not glad, exactly,' she answered. 'But memories can be…difficult.'

He couldn't argue with that. He had a truckload of difficult memories, from his father's retreat from his life, to his mother leaving him at the door of an orphanage run by monks when he was ten years old, to the slew of foster homes he'd bounced through, to the endless moment when he'd stood at the front of the church, the smile slipping from his face as Arturo came down the aisle, his face set in extraordinarily grim lines.

Sierra was staring out of the window; it was as if she'd dismissed him entirely. As he would dismiss her. For better or worse, last night's episode would serve as a line drawn across the past. Perhaps he had evened the score between them. In any case, his tie to Sierra Rocci was cut—firmly and for ever.

Setting his jaw, Marco stared straight ahead as he drove in silence all the way to Palermo.

CHAPTER SIX

'YOU NEED SIERRA ROCCI.'

Marco swivelled around in his chair to gaze out of the window at Palermo's business district as everything in him resisted that flatly spoken statement. 'I've been Arturo's right-hand man for nearly ten years. I don't need her.'

Paolo Conti, his second-in-command and closest confidant, sighed. 'I'm afraid you do, Marco. The board isn't happy without a Rocci to front the business, at least at first. And with the hotel opening in New York in a few weeks...'

'What about it? Everything is going according to plan.' He'd overseen the work on Rocci Enterprises' first hotel in North America himself; it had been his idea to expand, and to take the exclusive chain of hotels in a new direction. His credibility as CEO rested on The Rocci New York succeeding.

'That's true,' Paolo replied, 'but in the seventy years of Rocci Enterprises, a Rocci has always headed the board.'

'Things change.'

'Yes,' Paolo agreed patiently, running his hand through his silver hair, 'but for the last seventy years a Rocci has opened each hotel. Palermo, Rome, Paris, Madrid, London, Berlin.' He ticked them off on his fingers. 'A Rocci at every one.'

'I know.' He'd seen a few of the grand openings himself. He'd started work for Rocci Enterprises when he was sixteen years old, as a bellboy at the hotel in Palermo. He'd seen Sierra walking with her parents up the pink marble steps to eat in the hotel's luxurious dining room. He'd watched her walk so daintily, her hands held by both her mother and father. The perfect family.

'Change is a part of life,' Marco dismissed, 'and Arturo Rocci willed his shares to me. The board—and the public—will simply have to adjust.' It had been nearly a month since he'd left Sierra at the Palermo airport. Four weeks since he'd watched her walk away from him and told himself he was glad, even as he felt the old injustice burn. She hadn't looked back.

He wasn't angry with her any more, but he didn't know what he felt. Whatever emotion raged through him didn't feel good.

'It's not that simple, Marco,' Paolo said. He'd been with Rocci Enterprises for decades, always quietly serving and guiding. As Arturo had become more and more ill, Marco had relied increasingly on Paolo's help and wisdom.

'It can be,' he insisted.

'If the board feels there is too much separation from the Rocci name and values, they might hold a vote of no confidence.'

Marco tensed. 'I've been with this company for over ten years. And I hold the controlling shares.'

'The board needs to see you in public, acting as CEO. They need to believe in you.'

'Fine. I'll appear at any number of events.'

'With a Rocci,' Paolo clarified. 'And, as you know, Sierra is the only Rocci left.' Arturo's brother, a bachelor, had died a dozen years ago, his parents before then. 'There needs to be a smooth transition,' Paolo insisted. 'For the board *and* the public. Arturo wasn't able to manage it while he was alive—'

'He was ill.'

'I know. I'm sure he would have addressed this himself if he could have.'

But Arturo hadn't made Marco the beneficiary of his will until the very end. Marco suspected the old man had been hoping for Sierra to come back, to keep the business in the family. Restlessly, Marco rose from his chair and paced his office. Damn it, he'd given his life to Rocci Enterprises. He could still remember the sense of incredulous joy he'd had when Arturo had moved him from hefting suitcases to working in an office. Arturo Rocci had seen his potential and helped him to rise. And he'd paid his mentor back tenfold, by increasing Rocci Enterprises' revenue and expanding its business concerns. But he feared that all his board saw was a street rat from Palermo's gutters who had got ideas far above his station.

Sighing, he sank back into his chair. He could see the sense in what Paolo was saying. A smooth transition from him being the second-in-command who worked invisibly behind the scenes to being the public face of Rocci Enterprises. All it would take was a few key appearances, some stage-managed events...with Sierra.

Considering how they'd parted, he doubted Sierra Rocci was going to want to help him out in any fashion. He might not be angry with her any more, but she could very well still harbour a grudge for his ruthless semiseduction of her at the villa. Sighing, he closed his eyes and rubbed his temples, fighting off the tension headache that felt like a band of iron encircling his head.

He didn't want to need Sierra. He certainly didn't want to go begging for favours. But Rocci Enterprises meant everything to him. He couldn't afford to risk its well-being.

'Well?' Paolo asked. 'Do you think Sierra Rocci will agree? I know the two of you have a history...' He paused delicately, and Marco opened his eyes.

'I'll make her agree,' he stated flatly. Already his mind was racing through the possibilities. How could he get Sierra to come to New York? She'd accused him of being manipulative seven years ago, of engaging her affections so he could secure his position with Rocci Enterprises. She'd been wrong then, or at least that hadn't been the whole truth. But now it would be.

Marco's mouth curved coldly. 'Don't worry,' he told Paolo. 'I know how to handle her.'

'Play it again please, Chloe.'

Sierra shifted in her hard chair as her pupil sawed her way through 'Twinkle, Twinkle, Little Star' for the third time. Sierra tried not to wince. She loved her job tutoring children in music for a variety of after-school clubs, but it wasn't always easy on the ears.

Her mind drifted, as it had these last few weeks, to Marco Ferranti. It irritated and unnerved her that he was so often in her thoughts; the passionate interlude in the music room had haunted her dreams and left her aching with both desire and shame.

There was so much she didn't understand about Marco. He seemed like a tangle of unsettling contradictions: his anger at her abandonment of him seven years ago, and then the sudden moments of generosity and even tenderness that he'd shown her. Which was the real man? Which was the act? And why on earth was she still thinking about him?

'Miss Rocci?'

Sierra's unfocused gaze settled on the little girl in front of her. 'Yes, Chloe?'

'I finished.'

'Yes, of course you did,' Sierra murmured. 'Well done.'
She leafed through the music she'd brought before select-
ing another piece. 'Why don't you try this one now that
you've managed "Twinkle, Twinkle" so well?'

An hour later Sierra packed up her things and headed
out of the school where she'd been running music lessons.
It had taken a few years, but she'd managed to build up a
regular business, offering lessons to schoolchildren across
London's schools.

After her tumultuous and panicked flight from Sicily,
she'd found her mother's friend Mary Bertram living in
London; she'd moved house but, with the help of the internet, Sierra had managed to track her down. Mary had
sheltered her, helped her find her feet along with her first
job. She'd died three years ago, and Sierra had felt as if
she'd lost another mother.

Outside the school, she started down the pavement towards the Tube station, the midsummer evening sultry
and warm. People were spilling out of houses and offices,
laughing as they slung bags over their shoulders and made
plans for the pub.

Sierra regarded them with a slight pang of envy. She'd
never been able to make friends easily; her isolated childhood and her innate quietness had made it difficult. Her
job was isolated, too, although she'd become friendly
with a few of the other extracurricular teachers at various schools. But in the seven years she'd lived in London,
no one had got close. She'd never had a lover or even a
boyfriend, nothing more than a handful of dates that had
gone nowhere.

'Hello, Sierra.'

Sierra came to a shocked halt as Marco Ferranti stepped
out in front of her. Her mouth opened soundlessly; she
felt as if she'd conjured him from thin air, from her lonely

thoughts. He quirked an eyebrow, his mouth curving in the gentle quirk of a smile she recognised from seven years ago.

'What…what are you doing here?' she finally managed.

'Looking for you.'

A thrill of illicit pleasure as well as of apprehension shivered through her. He'd come to London just for her? 'How did you know where I was?'

He shrugged, the movement assured, elegant. 'Information is always easy to find.'

And just like that she was unnerved again, realising once more how little she knew him, the real him. How powerful he was. 'I don't know why you'd want to talk to me, Marco.'

'Is there somewhere private we could go?'

She glanced around the busy city street and shrugged. 'Not really.'

'Then let me find a place.' Marco slid his phone from the pocket of his suit jacket and thumbed a few buttons. Within seconds he was issuing instructions and then he returned his phone to his pocket and put his hand on the small of Sierra's back, where it rested enticingly, his palm warm through the thin fabric of her summer blouse. 'I've found a place.'

'Just like that?' Sierra hadn't heard what he'd said into the phone; his Italian had been low and rapid, inaudible over the sounds of traffic.

'Just like that,' Marco answered with a smile and guided her down the street, his hand never leaving her back.

A few minutes later they were entering a wine bar with plush velvet sofas and tables of polished ebony and teak. Sierra gaped to see a sofa in a private alcove already prepared for them, a bottle of red wine opened and breathing next to two crystal wine glasses.

'Some service,' she remarked shakily.

'As a Rocci, you must be used to such service,' Marco replied. He gestured for her to sit down while he poured the wine.

'Perhaps, but it's been a while.' In the seven years since she'd come to London she'd lived on little more than a pittance. She rented a tiny flat in Clapham and she bought everything second-hand. The days of luxury and privilege as Arturo Rocci's daughter were long over.

As she sank into the velvet sofa and watched Marco pour her a glass of wine, Sierra couldn't help but enjoy the moment. Even if Marco's presence overwhelmed and unnerved her. She had no idea why he'd come to London to find her, or what he could possibly want.

'Here.' He pressed a glass of wine into her hand and she took a much-needed sip.

'What do you want from me?' she asked, and then steeled herself for his answer.

Whatever they were, Marco wasn't going to reveal his intentions so easily. 'I didn't realise you were a music teacher.'

So he'd done some digging. She took another sip of wine. 'I teach children in after-school clubs.'

'And you play the piano and violin yourself.'

'Only in private.' Her cheeks heated as Marco's knowing gaze locked with hers. She knew they were both remembering the last time she'd played, and just how private it had been.

'I'd like to hear you play the violin.' His gaze seemed to caress her, and she felt goosebumps rise on her arms as a familiar ache started in her centre. 'I'd like you to play it for me.' His voice was low, sensuous, his gaze never leaving hers, his words making images and ideas leap into her mind in a vivid and erotic montage.

Sierra shook her head slowly, forcing the feelings back. 'Why are you acting this way, Marco?'

He took a sip of wine, one eyebrow arched. 'What way?'

'Like…like a lover,' she blurted, and then blushed. 'The last time we saw each other you seemed glad to be shot of me.'

'And I must confess you seemed likewise.'

'Considering the circumstances, not to mention our history, yes.'

'I'm sorry for the way I acted,' Marco said abruptly. His gaze was still locked on hers, his expression intent. 'In the music room. When I made love to you. I was trying to prove you still desired me and it was a petty, stupid thing to do. I'm sorry.' His lips curved in a tiny smile. 'Even if it seemed you enjoyed it.'

His words were gently teasing, and they made her blush all the more. She had no idea how to respond.

'Thank you,' she finally muttered. 'For your apology. But I still don't know why you're here.'

Marco shifted in his seat, his powerful thigh brushing her leg. The contact sent sizzling arrows of remembered sensation firing through her, and Sierra only just resisted pulling away. She wouldn't show him how much he affected her. In any case, he undoubtedly already knew.

'I've been thinking about you, Sierra.' His voice flowed over like her melted chocolate, warm and liquid, enticing but also a way to drown. 'A lot.'

Her mouth had dried, her lungs emptying of air, and yet suspicion and doubt still took hold of her heart. She shook her head slowly. 'Marco…'

'I've been thinking that it's unfair you didn't receive anything from your father's will.'

The abrupt reality check felt like falling flat on her face. Left her breathless, smarting. Of course he wasn't

thinking about her *that* way. She shouldn't even want to
be thinking of him *that* way. Good grief, where was her
backbone? Her resolve? She'd spent the last seven years
telling herself she'd done the right thing in walking away
from this man, and now she was panting and dreaming
like some lovesick teenager.

'I don't care about my father's will.'

'You should. You had a birthright, Sierra.'

'Even though I walked away from my family? In di
Santis's office you seemed to think I was getting exactly
what I deserved. Almost nothing.' She hadn't cared about
her father's inheritance, but Marco's smug triumph had
rankled. More than rankled, if she was honest. It had hurt.

'I was angry,' Marco admitted quietly. 'I'm sorry.'

So many apologies. She didn't know what to do with
them. She didn't entirely trust them—or him. And her own
feelings were cartwheeling all over the place, which made
sounding and feeling logical pretty difficult. 'It's all in the
past, Marco. Let's leave it there.'

'I think you should have a part in Rocci Enterprises.'

She drew back, truly startled. If anything, she'd been
expecting him to offer her the villa again, or perhaps some
family heirlooms she had no need for. Not her father's
business. 'I've never had a part in Rocci Enterprises.' Her
father had been very much of the persuasion that women
didn't need to be involved in business. She'd left school at
sixteen at her father's behest.

'A new hotel is opening in New York City,' Marco continued as if she hadn't spoken. 'It will be the most luxurious Rocci hotel yet, and I think you should be there. You
deserve to be there.'

'In New York?' She stared at him in disbelief.

'You opened four hotels before you were nineteen,'

Marco reminded her. 'People are used to seeing a Rocci cut the ribbon. You should be the one to do it.'

'I had nothing to do with that hotel, or any of them.' She was filled with sudden and utter revulsion at the thought of opening one of her father's hotels. Playing happy families, and this time from the grave. How many times had she smiled and curtsied for the crowds, how many times had her mother waved, wearing a long-sleeved dress to hide the bruises? She had no desire whatsoever to revisit those memories or play that part again. 'I appreciate your consideration,' she said stiffly, 'but I don't need to open the hotel. I have no wish to.' Some of her distaste must have shown on her face because Marco frowned.

'Why not?'

Sierra hesitated, stalling for time by taking a sip of wine. She was still hesitant to tell Marco the truth of her father, her family, because she didn't think he'd believe her and even if he did she didn't want his pity. It was shaming to admit she'd allow herself to be abused and used for so long, even if she'd only been a child. And if he didn't believe her? If he accused her of lying or exaggerating to sully her father's name? Or maybe he *would* believe her, and think her father had been justified. Maybe he countenanced a little rough handling. The truth was, she had no idea what his response would be and she had no intention of finding out.

'Sierra?' He leaned forward, covering her hand with his own. She realised she was trembling and she strove for control.

'Like I said, the past is in the past, Marco. I don't need to be part of Rocci Enterprises. I left it behind when I left Sicily.' She forced a smile, small and polite, definitely strained. 'But, as I said, thank you for thinking of me.'

His hand still rested on hers; it felt warm and strong.

Comforting, even if it shouldn't be. Even if she still didn't understand or trust this man. She didn't pull away.

Confused frustration surged through him as Marco gazed at Sierra, tried to figure out what she was thinking. His magnanimous approach had clearly failed. He'd hoped that Sierra would embrace his suggestion, that she'd be glad to have a chance to mend a few bridges, be a Rocci again. More fool him.

He sat back, letting go of her hand, noticing the loss even as his mind raced for another way forward. 'You don't seem to bear much good will for Rocci Enterprises,' he remarked, 'even though you were obviously close to your family at one time.'

Her mouth twisted. 'I don't feel anything for Rocci Enterprises,' she said flatly. 'I was never part of it.'

'You were at every hotel opening—'

'For show.' She turned away, her expression closing, her gaze downcast so he could see her blond lashes fanning her cheeks.

'For show?' He disliked the thought instinctively. 'It looked real to me.'

'It was meant to.'

'What are you saying? I know your parents loved you very much, Sierra. I saw how they reacted when you left. They were devastated, both of them. Your father couldn't speak of you without tears coming into his eyes. And you never even wrote them a letter to say you were safe.' His voice throbbed with intensity, with accusation, and Sierra noticed. Her gaze narrowed and her lips pursed.

'You don't think my father could have found me if he wanted?'

'Of course he could have. He was a very powerful man.'

'So why do you think he didn't?'

Marco hesitated, trying to assess Sierra's tone, her mood. 'Sierra,' he said finally, 'I am under no illusions about your father. He was a proud and sometimes ruthless man, but he was honourable. *Good.*' Sierra pressed her lips together and said nothing. 'You hurt him very much by leaving. Even if he'd never admit it.'

'Of course.' She shook her head. 'Why did you ask me to come to New York?' she said. 'Really?'

Unease spiked in his gut. 'What do you mean?'

'I mean you're not telling me the truth. Not the whole truth,' she amended when he opened his mouth to object. 'Just like always. This isn't some act of chivalry, is it, Marco? It isn't some benevolent impulse you've had out of the goodness of your heart.' She shook her head slowly. 'I almost bought it. I almost bought the whole act, because I was almost so stupid. Again.'

'Again?'

'I trusted you seven years ago—'

'I wasn't the one who betrayed a trust,' Marco snapped.

Sierra leaned forward, her eyes glittering icy-blue now, two slits of arctic rage. 'And you say you're not angry any more? Why are you here? Why am *I* here?' She folded her arms, levelling him with her glare. 'What do you really want from me?'

CHAPTER SEVEN

SHE COULDN'T BELIEVE how gullible she'd been—*again*. Wanting to believe the best of Marco Ferranti. Wanting, instinctively, to trust him. Hadn't she learned *anything*? No matter how kind he could seem, he'd been her father's apprentice for ten years. He'd wanted to marry her to further his business interests. And yet some part of her still wanted him to be kind.

'Well?' she demanded. 'Have I actually managed to render you speechless?'

'You're jumping to conclusions,' Marco said, an edge entering his voice. The charm was gone, dropped like the flimsy, false mask it was. She knew how it went. Fear spiked through her and she tamped it down. She would be no man's punching bag, emotional or physical, again.

'Then why don't you try being honest?'

'I was being honest. I do think you should have some part in Rocci Enterprises. In fact, if you'd given me a chance, I would have told you I'm prepared to give you most of your inheritance back.' He eyed her coolly, as if waiting for her to trip over herself with gratitude.

'That's very big of you,' she answered, sarcasm spiking her voice. 'You're *prepared* to give me *most*. That's so very, very noble.'

Marco's lip curled. 'You want more?'

'I don't want anything but the truth. Stop trying to manipulate me. Just tell me what you want.'

A muscle ticked in his jaw as their gazes clashed. Even
with the anger simmering between them, Sierra felt an un-
welcome kick of desire. A sudden sharp memory of the
way he'd plundered her mouth, her body…and how good
it had felt.

She saw an answering spark of awareness in Marco's
eyes and knew he was remembering, too.

Good grief, what was *wrong* with her? How could she
still want a man whom she couldn't trust, didn't like? Why
did she have to have this intense physical reaction to him?

'I'm still waiting,' she snapped.

'Having you open the New York hotel is of some benefit to me, too,' Marco finally bit out. 'Fine, I'll admit it.
The public would like to see a Rocci cut the damn ribbon.'

She sat back against the sofa, strangely deflated by his
admission. 'So you were trying to make it seem like you
were being nice. Thoughtful. When really you just wanted
me to come for your sake.'

'For the company's sake. You might have no great interest in Rocci Enterprises, but do you want to see it fail?
Seventy years of history, Sierra, and most of my life.'

'I don't care about Rocci Enterprises,' she said flatly.
'I don't care if it fails.'

'You don't care about your family's livelihood?'

'The only family left is me, and I make my own living,'
she retorted. 'Stop trying to guilt me into this.'

'What about the livelihood of all the employees? Five
hundred people are going to be employed by Rocci New
York. If the hotel fails—'

'The hotel is not going to *fail* if I'm not there,' Sierra
declared. 'My father has opened several hotels in the last

seven years. I haven't been at any of them. I'm not needed, Marco.'

'As you pointed out yourself, you're the only Rocci left and people want to see you.' He paused. 'The board wants to see you.'

'Ah.' It was starting to make more sense now. 'Your job is in jeopardy.'

His mouth tightened. 'I have the controlling shares of the company.'

'But if you lose the confidence of the board as well as the public?' She shook her head. 'It won't look good.'

Fury flared in his eyes and Sierra felt an answering alarm. She was baiting him, and why? Because she was angry. She was furious and hurt that he'd been using her. Again. And she'd almost let him.

'I'm leaving.' She shoved her wine glass onto the coffee table with a clatter and rose from the sofa, grabbing her bag. 'Thanks for the drink,' she tossed over her shoulder, and then she strode from the wine bar.

She was halfway down the street, her heels clicking loudly on the pavement, when she heard his voice from behind.

'I need you, Sierra. I admit it.'

She slowed but didn't stop. Was this simply more manipulation?

'I don't want to need you, God knows.' There was a note in his voice that she hadn't heard before, a weary defeat that touched her even though she knew it shouldn't. 'I don't want to be at your mercy. I was once before and it didn't feel all that great.'

She turned around slowly, shocked when she saw him standing there, his expression unguarded and open in a way she'd never seen before.

'When were you at my mercy?'

'When I stood at the front of the church and waited for you to show up at our wedding.' He took a step towards her. People had been streaming past them but now a few slowed, curious about the drama that was being enacted on a London street. 'Why would you help me?' he asked. 'I didn't feel I could simply ask. I didn't want to simply ask, because I didn't want to be refused. Rejected.' His mouth twisted in a grimace and Sierra realised how hard this was for him. This—here, now—was real honesty. 'Again.'

'Marco...'

'I poured my life into Rocci Enterprises,' he said, his voice low and intense. 'Everything I had. I've worked for the company since I was sixteen. I started as a bellboy, which is something you probably didn't know.'

'A bellboy...' Sierra shook her head. She'd assumed Marco had come in on the executive level. She'd never asked, and he'd never spoken about his history, his background or his family. A painful reminder of how little she knew about him.

'Your father saw my potential and promoted me. He treated me like a son from the beginning. And I gave everything in return. Everything.'

'I know you did.' And Marco's unwavering loyalty was, Sierra surmised, why her father had chosen him in the first place, both as business associate and prospective son-in-law. Because her father had wanted someone who would forever be in his debt.

Marco closed his eyes briefly. 'The company is my family, my life. Losing it...' His voice choked and he ran a hand through his hair. 'I can't bear the thought of it. So I am sorry I tried to manipulate you. I apologise for not being honest. But you have my life in your hands, Sierra, whether you want to or not. I know you bear no love or even affection for me, and I accept that my behaviour recently hasn't deserved it. But all I have left, all I can do now, is to throw myself on your mercy.' His gaze met hers, bleak, even hopeless. 'Not a position I ever wanted to be in, and yet here I am.'

He hadn't meant to say all of that. He'd come into this meeting wanting to keep his pride intact, and instead he'd had everything stripped away. Revealed. He might as well be standing by the damned altar, waiting for his bride. If she refused him now...

He couldn't tell what she was thinking or feeling. She'd cloaked herself in that cool composure he'd once admired. He waited, breath held, having no idea what he could say or do if she told him *no*. If she walked away. Then she spoke.

'I'll go to New York,' she said. 'And I'll open the hotel.'

Relief poured through him, made him nearly sag with the force of it. 'Thank you.'

She nodded stiffly. 'When is it?'

'In two weeks.'

'You can forward me the details,' she said, and for a second her expression wobbled, almost as if she was going to cry. Then she nodded her farewell and turned and walked down the street, away from him.

Sierra peeked out of the window of her ground floor flat at the sleek black limo that had just pulled up to the kerb. Marco had said he would send a car, and she supposed she shouldn't be surprised that it was a limo.

But she was surprised when he stepped out, looking as devastatingly sexy as ever in a crisply tailored navy blue suit. She'd assumed she would meet him at the airport. Apparently Marco had other ideas.

Nervously, she straightened the pale grey sheath dress

she'd chosen for travel. She didn't have too many fancy clothes and after she'd agreed to Marco's suggestion, out on the street, she'd realised she didn't have anything to wear to the ball on the night of the hotel's opening. She'd used some of her paltry savings to buy a second-hand dress at a charity shop and hoped that in the dim lighting no one would notice the fraying along the hem.

Marco rapped on the front door and, taking a deep breath, Sierra willed her shoulders back and went to answer it.

'Hello, Sierra.' His voice felt like a fist plunging inside her soul. Ever since she'd seen him out on that street, admitting everything, being honest and open, she'd been plagued by doubts, filled with hope. *Here* finally was the man she could trust and like. The man she'd glimpsed seven years ago. And she didn't know whether to be glad or fearful of the fact. In some ways it had been easier, simpler, to hate Marco Ferranti.

'You're ready?' His gaze swept over her in one swift assessment as she nodded.

'Yes, I'll just fetch my case.'

'I'll get it.' He shouldered past her so she could breathe in the scent of his aftershave and hefted her single suitcase easily. 'This is all you're bringing?'

'I don't need much.'

He frowned, his straight eyebrows drawing together as his gaze moved around the tiny sitting room with its shabby sofa and rickety chairs. She'd tried to make it homely with some throws and framed posters, but it was a far cry from the luxury Marco was used to. 'What about a hanging case, for your evening clothes?'

She thought of the second-hand dress folded in her suitcase. 'It's fine.'

Marco didn't answer; he just took her suitcase and

walked out of the flat. Sierra expelled a shaky breath and then followed him, locking the door behind her.

In the two weeks since she'd agreed to accompany Marco to New York, she'd questioned her decision many times. Wondered why on earth she was entangling herself with Marco again, when things between them were complicated enough. Surely it would be better, or at least easier, to walk away for good. Draw a final line across the past.

But there on the street she'd seen Marco as she'd never seen him before. She'd seen him being open and honest, *vulnerable*, and she'd believed him. For once suspicion hadn't hardened her heart or doubt clouded her mind. She'd known Marco was speaking the truth even when he didn't want to, when it made him feel weak.

And so she'd said yes.

And not just because he'd been so honest, Sierra knew. It was more complicated than that. Because she felt she owed him something, after the way she'd walked away seven years ago. And, if she was as honest as he had been, because she wanted to see him again. And that was very dangerous thinking.

The driver of the limo took her suitcase from Marco and stowed it in the back as Marco opened the door and ushered her inside the car.

Sierra slid inside the limo, one hand smoothing across one of the sumptuous leather seats that faced each other. She scooted to the far side as Marco climbed inside, and suddenly the huge limo with its leather sofa-like seats and coffee table seemed very small.

It was going to be a long three days. An exciting three days. Maybe that was another reason she'd agreed; as much as she liked her life in London, it was quiet and unassuming. The thought of spending three days in luxury in New

York, three days with Marco, was a heady one. Even if it shouldn't be.

The door closed and Marco settled in the seat across from her, stretching his legs out so his knee nudged hers. Sierra didn't move, not wanting to be obvious about how much he affected her. Just that little nudge sent her pulse skyrocketing, although maybe it was everything all at once that was affecting her: the limo, the scent of his after-shave, the real and magnetic presence of the man oppo-site her, and the fact that she'd be spending the next three days with him.

She looked out of the window, afraid all her apprehen-sion and excitement would be visible on her face.

'Are you all right?'

She turned back, startled and a little embarrassed. 'Yes, I'm fine.'

'Have some water.' He handed her a bottle of water and after a moment Sierra uncapped it and took a drink, con-scious of Marco's eyes on her as she swallowed. 'I do ap-preciate you agreeing to do this,' he said quietly.

She lowered the bottle to look at him; his expression was shuttered, neutral, all the openness and honesty he'd shown two weeks ago tucked safely away. 'It's no hard-ship, spending a few days in New York,' she said.

'You seemed quite opposed to the idea initially.'

She sighed and screwed the cap back on the bottle of water. 'Revisiting everything in the past has been hard. I want to move on with my life.'

'After this you can, I promise. I won't bother you again, Sierra.'

Which should make her feel relieved rather than disap-pointed. Not trusting herself to speak, Sierra just nodded.

They kept the conversation light after that, speaking only of innocuous subjects: travel and food and films. By the time they reached the airport Sierra was starting to feel more relaxed, although her nerves jumped to alert when Marco took her arm as they left the limo.

He led her through the crowds, bypassing the queue at check-in for private VIP service.

'This is the life,' Sierra teased as they settled in the private lounge and a waiter brought a bottle of champagne and two flutes. 'Are we celebrating?'

'The opening of The Rocci New York,' Marco answered easily. 'Surely you've travelled VIP before?'

She shook her head. 'No, I've hardly travelled at all. Going to London was the first time I'd left the mainland of Europe.'

'Was it?' Marco frowned, clearly surprised by this information, and Sierra wondered just how rosy a view he had of her family life. Had he not realised how her father had tucked his family away, bringing them out only when necessary? But she didn't want to dwell on the past and neither, it seemed, did Marco, for after the waiter had popped the cork on the champagne and poured them both glasses, he asked, 'So how did you get into teaching in London?'

'I volunteered at first, and took some lessons myself. It started small—I took a slot at an after-school club and then word spread and more schools asked.' She shrugged. 'I'm not grooming too many world-class musicians, but I enjoy it and I think the children do, as well.'

'And you like London?'

'Yes. It's different, of course, and I could do without the rain, but...' She shrugged and took a sip of champagne, enjoying the way the bubbles zinged through her. 'It's become home.'

'You've made friends?' The innocuous lilt to his voice belied the sudden intensity she saw spark in his eyes. What was he really asking?

'I've made a few. Some teachers, a few neighbours.' She shrugged. 'I'm used to being solitary.'

'Are you? Why?'

'I spent most of my childhood in the mountains or at convent school. Company was scarce.'

'I suppose your father was strict and old-fashioned about that kind of thing.'

Her stomach tightened, memory clenching inside her. 'You could say that.'

'But he had a good heart. He always wanted the best for you.'

Sierra didn't reply. Couldn't. Marco sounded so sincere, so sure. How could she refute what he said? Now seemed neither the time nor the place. 'And for you,' she said after a moment, when she trusted her voice to sound measured and mild. 'He loved you like a son. More than I ever even realised.'

Marco nodded, his expression sombre, the corners of his mouth pulled down. 'He was like a father to me. Better than my own father.'

Curiosity sharpened inside her. 'Why? What was your own father like?'

He hesitated, his glass halfway to his lips, his mouth now a hard line. 'I don't really know. He was out of my life by the time I was seven years old.'

'He was? I'm sorry.' She paused, feeling her way through the sudden minefield of their conversation. It was obvious from his narrowed eyes and his tense shoulders, that Marco didn't like talking about his past. And yet Sierra wanted to know. 'I've realised how little I knew about you. Your childhood, your family.'

'That's because they're not worth knowing.'

'What happened to your father when you were seven?'

He was silent for a moment, marshalling his thoughts,

and Sierra waited. 'I'm illegitimate,' he finally stated flatly. 'My mother was a chambermaid at one of the hotels in Palermo—not The Rocci,' he clarified with a small, hard smile. 'My father was an executive at the hotel. Married, of course. They had an affair, and my mother became pregnant. That old story.' He shrugged dismissively, as if he wasn't going to say anything more.

'And then what happened?' Sierra asked after a moment.

'My mother had me, and my father set her up in a dingy flat in one of Palermo's slums. Gave her enough to live on—just. He'd visit us on occasion, a few times a year, perhaps. He'd bring some cheap trinkets, things guests left behind.' He shook his head, remembrance twisting his features. 'I don't think he was a truly bad man. But he was weak. He didn't like being with us. I could see that, even as a small child. He always looked guilty, miserable. He kept checking his watch, the whole time he was there.' Marco sighed and drained his flute of champagne. 'The visits became less frequent, as did the times he sent money. Eventually he stopped coming altogether.'

Sierra's mouth was dry, her heart pounding strangely. Marco had never told her any of this before. She'd had no idea he'd had such a childhood; he'd suffered loss and sorrow, just as she had, albeit in a different way. 'He never said goodbye?'

Marco shook his head. 'No, he just stopped coming. My mother struggled on as best as she could.' He shrugged. 'Sicily, especially back in those days, wasn't an easy place to be a single mother. But she did her best.' His mouth firmed as his gaze became distant. 'She did her best,' he repeated, and he almost sounded as if he were trying to convince himself.

'I'm sorry,' Sierra said quietly. 'That must have been incredibly difficult.'

He shrugged and shook his head. 'It was a long time ago. I left that life behind when I was sixteen and I never looked back.'

Just like she had, except he would never understand her reasons for leaving, for needing to escape. *Not unless she told him.*

Considering all he'd just told her, Sierra felt, for the first time, that she could tell Marco the truth of her childhood. She wanted to. She opened her mouth to begin, searching for the right words, but he spoke first.

'That's why I'm so grateful to your father for giving me a chance all those years ago. For believing in me when no one else did. For treating me more like a son than my own father did.' He shook his head, his expression shadowed with grief. 'I miss him,' he said quietly, his tone utterly heartfelt.

Bile churned in her stomach and she nodded mechanically. The memories Marco spoke of were so far from her own reality of a man who had only shown her kindness in public. He'd chuck her under the chin, heft her onto his shoulders, tell the world she was his little *bellissima*. And everyone had believed it. Marco had believed it. Why shouldn't he?

And in that moment she knew she could never tell him the truth. Not when his own family life had been so sadly lacking, not when her father had provided the love and support he'd needed. She'd had her own illusions ripped away once. She wouldn't do the same to him, to anyone, and for what purpose? In three days she'd be back in London, and she and Marco need never see each other again.

CHAPTER EIGHT

By the time they were settled in the first-class compartment on the flight to New York, Sierra had restored her equilibrium. Mostly. She felt as if she were discovering a whole new side to Marco, deeper and intriguing layers, now that they'd laid aside the resentment and hostility about the past.

She was remembering how kind and thoughtful he could be, how he saw to her small comforts discreetly, how he cocked his head, his mouth quirking in a smile as he listened to her, making her feel as if he really cared what she said.

She didn't think it was an act this time. She hoped it wasn't. The truth was she still didn't trust herself. Didn't trust anyone. But the more time she spent with Marco, the more her guard began to lower.

And she was enjoying simply chatting to him over an amazingly decadent three-course meal, complete with fine crystal and china and a bottle of very good wine. She liked feeling important and interesting to him, and she was curious about his life and ambitions and interests. More curious than she'd been seven years ago, when she'd seen him as little more than a means to an end—to escape. Now she saw him as a man.

'It was your idea to bring Rocci Hotels to North Amer-

ica?' she asked as she spooned the last of the dark chocolate mousse they'd been served for dessert.

He hadn't said as much, but she'd guessed it from the
way he'd been describing the New York project. He'd
clearly been leading the charge.

'The board wasn't interested in expansion,' Marco answered with a shrug. 'They've never liked risk.'

'So it's even more important that this succeeds.'

'It will. Especially since you've agreed.' His warm gaze
rested on her, and Sierra felt her insides tingle in response.
It would be so easy to fall under Marco's charm again, especially since this time it felt real. But where would any of
it lead? They had no future. She knew that. But she still
enjoyed talking to him, being with him. She even enjoyed
that tingle, dangerous as it was.

The steward dimmed the lights in the first-class cabin
and Marco leaned over her seat to let it recline. Sierra
sucked in a hard breath at the nearness of his body, the
intoxicating heat of him. His head was close to hers as he
murmured, 'You should get rest while you can. Tomorrow
will be a big day.'

She nodded wordlessly, her gaze fastened on his, and
gently Marco tucked a strand of hair behind her ear. It was
the merest of touches, it meant nothing, and yet still she
felt as if he'd given her an electric shock, her whole body
jolting with longing. Marco smiled and then settled back
in his own seat, stretching his long legs out in front of him
as his seat dipped back. 'Get some sleep if you can, Sierra.'

Marco shifted in his seat, trying to get comfortable. It was
damned difficult when desire was pulsing in his centre,
throbbing through his veins. It had been nearly impossible
to resist touching Sierra as they'd talked. And he'd enjoyed
the conversation, the sharing of ideas, the light banter. He'd

even been glad, in a surprising way, to have told her more about his past. He hadn't been planning to reveal the deprivations of his childhood and he'd kept some of it back, not wanting to invite her pity. But to see her face softened in sympathy...to know that she cared about him, even in that small way, affected him more than he was entirely comfortable with.

He'd been glad to move on to lighter topics, and Sierra had thankfully taken his cue. He'd enjoyed talking with her seven years ago, but she'd been a girl then, innocent and unsophisticated. The years had sharpened her, made her stronger and more interesting. And definitely more desirable.

In the end he hadn't been able to resist. A small caress, his fingers barely grazing her cheek as he'd tucked her hair behind her ear. He could tell Sierra was affected by it, though, and so was he. He longed to take her in his arms, even here in the semiprivacy of their seats, and plunder her mouth and body. Lose himself in her sweetness and feel her tremble and writhe with pleasure.

Stifling a groan, Marco shifted again. He needed to stop thinking like this. Stop remembering what Sierra's naked body had looked like as she'd been splayed across the piano bench, her skin golden and perfect in the lamplight. Stop remembering how silky she'd felt, how delicious she'd tasted, how overwhelming her response to him had been.

Marco clenched his eyes shut as a sheen of sweat broke out on his forehead. Next to him Sierra shifted and sighed, and the breathy sound made another spasm of longing stab through him. It was going to be a long flight. Hell, it was going to be a long three days. Because one thing he knew was he wouldn't take advantage of Sierra again.

He must have fallen into a doze eventually, because he woke to find her sitting up and smiling at him. Her hair was in delightful disarray about her face and she gave him a playful look as he straightened.

'You snore, you know.'

He drew back, caught between affront and amusement. 'I do not.'

'Hasn't anyone ever told you before?'

'No, because I don't snore.' And because he'd never had a woman stay the night to tell him so. Since Sierra, his love life—if he could even call it that—had been comprised of one-night stands and week-long flings. He'd had no intention of being caught again.

'Not very loudly,' Sierra informed him with an impish smile. 'And not all the time. But you do snore. Trust me.'

Trust me. The words seemed to reverberate through him before Marco shook them off. 'I suppose I'll have to take your word for it. And I might as well tell you that *you* drool when you sleep.'

'Oh!' Mortification brightened her cheeks as one hand clapped to her mouth. Marco instantly regretted his thoughtless quip. He'd been teasing and it wasn't true anyway; she'd looked adorable when she slept, her chin tucked towards her chest, her golden lashes fanning across her cheeks.

'Actually, you don't,' he said gruffly. 'But I couldn't say you snored, since you don't.'

'You cad.' Laughing, she dropped her hand to hit him lightly on the shoulder, and before he thought through what he was doing he wrapped her hand in his, savouring the feel of her slender fingers enclosed in his, the softness of her skin. Her eyes widened and her breath shortened.

Always it came back to this. The intense attraction that seemed only to grow stronger with every minute they spent in each other's company. Carefully, Marco released her hand. 'We'll be landing soon.'

Sierra nodded wordlessly, cradling her hand as if it was tender, almost as if he'd hurt her with his touch.

The next few hours were taken up with clearing Customs and then getting out of the airport. Marco had arranged for a limo to pick them up but nothing could be done about the bumper-to-bumper traffic they encountered all the way into Manhattan.

Finally the limo pulled up in front of The Rocci New York, a gleaming, needle-like skyscraper that overlooked Central Park West.

'It's gorgeous,' Sierra breathed as she stepped out of the limo and tilted her head up to the sky. 'I feel dizzy.'

'I hope you're not scared of heights.' He couldn't resist putting his hand on the small of her back as he guided her towards the marble steps that led up to the hotel's entrance. 'We're staying on the top floor.'

'Are we?' Her eyes rounded like a child's with excitement and Marco felt a deep primal satisfaction at making her happy. This was what he'd wanted seven years ago: to show the world to Sierra, to give it to her. To see her smile and know he'd been the one to put it there. No, he hadn't loved her, but damn it, he'd *liked* her. He still did.

'Come on,' he urged as they mounted the steps. He realised he was as excited as she was to see the hotel, to share it with her. 'Let me show The Rocci New York.'

Sierra followed Marco into the hotel's soaring foyer of marble and granite, everything sleek and modern, so unlike the faded old world elegance of the European Rocci hotels. This was something new and different, something created solely by Marco, and Sierra liked it all the more for that reason. There were no hard memories to face here, just anticipation for all that lay ahead.

Marco spoke to someone at the concierge desk while

Sierra strolled around the foyer, admiring the contemporary art that graced the walls, the sleek leather sofas and chairs and tables of polished wood. Everything felt clean and polished, sophisticated and streamlined. Empty, too, as the first guests would not arrive until tomorrow, after the official opening. Tomorrow night the hotel would have a gala in its ballroom to celebrate, and then the next day she'd fly back to London. But she'd enjoy every moment of being here.

Marco returned to her side, a key card resting in his palm. 'Ready?'

'Yes…' She eyed the key card uncertainly. 'Are we staying in the same room?'

The smile he gave her was teasingly wolfish. 'Don't worry, there's plenty of room for two.'

It didn't feel like there was plenty of room, Sierra thought as she stepped into the mirrored lift that soared straight towards the sky. The lift was enormous, their hotel suite undoubtedly far larger, and yet she felt the enclosed space keenly; Marco's sleeve brushed her arm as he stood next to her and Sierra's pulse jerked and leapt in response.

She needed to get a handle on her attraction. Either ignore it or act on it. And while the latter was a thrilling possibility, the former was the far wiser thing to do. She and Marco had way too much complicated history to think about getting involved now, even if just for a fling.

But what a fling it would be…

She could hardly credit she was thinking this way, and about *Marco*. What had happened to the man who had seemed so cold, so hostile? And what about the man she'd fled from seven years ago, whom she'd felt she couldn't trust? Had it all really changed, simply because he'd finally been honest? Or had *she* changed and let go of the past, at least a little? Enough to make her contemplate an affair.

Not, she reminded herself, that Marco was thinking along the same lines. But she didn't think she was imagining the tension that coiled and snapped between them. It wasn't merely one-sided. She hoped.

The lift doors opened into the centre of the suite and Marco stepped aside so she could walk out first.

'Welcome to the penthouse.'

Sierra didn't speak for a moment, just absorbed the impact of her surroundings. The penthouse suite was circular, with floor-to-ceiling windows surrounding her so she felt as if she were poised above the city, ready to fly.

Marco's footsteps clicked across the smooth floor of black marble as he switched on some lights. 'Do you like it?' he asked, and he almost sounded uncertain.

'Like it?' Sierra turned in a circle slowly, taking everything in: the luxurious but understated furnishings, nothing taking away from the spectacular panoramic view of the city. 'I love it. It's the most amazing room I've ever seen.' She turned to him, gratified and even touched to see the relief that flashed across his face before he schooled his features into a more neutral, composed expression. 'But surely this isn't the whole suite?' The circular room was a living area only. 'I don't see any beds. Or a bathroom, for that matter.'

'The rest of the suite is upstairs. But I wanted to show you this first.'

'It really is amazing. You must have a fantastic architect.'

'I do, but the idea for this suite was mine.' Sierra saw a slight blush colour Marco's high cheekbones and she felt an answering wave of something almost like tenderness. 'He didn't think it was possible, and I nagged him until he conceded it was.'

'Clearly you're tenacious.'

'When I have to be.'

His gaze held hers for a moment and she wondered at the subtext. Was he talking about them? If she'd confessed her fears to him all those years ago, would he have been tenacious in helping to assuage them, in making their marriage work? It was so dangerous to think that way, and yet impossible to keep herself from wondering. But she didn't want to imagine what life could have been; she wanted to think about what still could be.

'Let me show you the upstairs,' Marco said and took her hand as he led her to the spiral staircase in the centre of the room, next to the lift, that led to the rooms above.

Upstairs there were still the soaring views, although the space was divided into several rooms and the windows didn't go from ceiling to floor. Marco showed her the kitchen, the two sumptuous bedrooms with luxurious en suite bathrooms, and Sierra noted the small amount of hallway between them. There was room for two as Marco had assured her, but they would be sleeping right across from each other. The prospect filled her with excitement and even anticipation rather than alarm.

What was happening to her?

'You should refresh yourself,' Marco said when he'd shown her the guest room that she would use. 'Rest if you need to. It's been a long day.'

'Okay.'

'The ribbon-cutting and gala are tomorrow but if you feel up for it we could see a few sights today,' Marco suggested. 'If you're up for it?'

'Definitely. Let me just get changed.'

As she showered and dressed, Sierra gave herself a mental talking-to. She was playing a dangerous game, she knew, and one she hadn't intended to play. She was attracted to Marco and she was discovering all over again

how much she liked him. She knew he was attracted to
her; maybe he even liked her. They had plenty of reasons
to have a nice time together, even to have a fling.

It didn't have to be for ever. They'd contemplated marriage once before, a marriage based on expediency rather
than love, but they didn't have to this time. This time whatever was between them could be for pleasure. In her mind it
sounded simple and yet Sierra knew the dangers. Trusting
any man, even with just her body, was a big step, and one
she hadn't taken before. Did she really want to with Marco?

And yet the three days that stretched so enticingly in
front of her, the excitement of being with Marco... How
could she resist?

But perhaps she wouldn't need to. Perhaps Marco had
no intention of acting on the attraction between them. Perhaps he'd meant what he'd said back at the villa about never
touching her again.

With her thoughts still in a hopeless snarl, Sierra left
her bedroom in search of Marco. She found him downstairs in the circular salon, talking in clipped English on
his phone. Sierra had become fluent in English since moving to London and she could tell he was checking on the
hotel's readiness for tomorrow.

'Everything okay?' she asked as Marco slid the phone
into his pocket.

'Yes. Just checking on a few last-minute details. I don't
want anything to go wrong, not even the hors d'oeuvres.'

He smiled ruefully and Sierra laid a hand on his sleeve.
'This is really important to you.'

He gazed down at her, his wry smile replaced by a sombre look. 'I told you the truth before, Sierra. The whole
truth. The hotel is everything to me.'

Everything. Sierra didn't know whether to feel rebuked
or relieved. She decided to feel neither, to simply enjoy

the possibilities of the day. 'So what sights are you going to show me? You must have been to New York loads of times, overseeing the hotel.'

'Do you have anything you want to see in particular?'

'Whatever your favourite thing is.' She wanted to get to know this man more.

A smile curled Marco's mouth, drawing Sierra's attention to his firm and yet lush lips. Lips she still remembered the taste of, and craved. 'All right, then. Let's go.'

It wasn't until they were out on Central Park West and Marco had hailed one of the city's trademark yellow cabs that Sierra asked where they were going.

He ushered her into the cab first, sliding in next to her so their thighs were pressed together. 'The Museum of Modern Art.'

'Art!' She shook her head slowly. 'I never knew you liked art.'

'Modern art. And there are a lot of things you don't know about me.'

'Yes,' Sierra answered as Marco held her gaze, a small smile curving his wonderful mouth. 'I'm coming to realise that.'

CHAPTER NINE

Marco could not remember a time when he'd enjoyed himself more. He and Sierra wandered around the airy galleries of the MoMA and, at some point while looking at the vast canvases and modern sculpture, he took her hand.

It felt so natural that he didn't even think about it first, just slid his hand into hers and let their fingers entwine. She didn't resist, and they spent the rest of the afternoon remarking on and joking about Klimt's use of colour and Picasso's intriguing angular forms.

'I'm not an expert, by any means,' Marco told her when they wandered out into the sunshine again. It was August and New York simmered under a summer sun, heat radiating from the pavement. 'I just like the possibility in modern art. That people dared to do things differently, to see the world another way.'

'Yes, I can understand that.' She slid him a look of smiling compassion. 'Especially considering your background.'

Marco tensed instinctively but Sierra was still holding his hand, and he forced himself to relax. She knew more about him than anyone else did, even Arturo, who had been as good as a father. Arturo had known about his background a little; he'd raised him up from being a bellboy and, in any case, Marco knew his accent gave him away as a Sicilian street rat. But Arturo had never known about his father. He'd never asked.

'Where to now?' Sierra asked and Marco shrugged.

'Wherever you like. Are you getting tired?'

'No. I don't know how anyone can get tired here. There's so much energy and excitement. I'm not sure I'll ever get to sleep tonight.' Her innocent words held no innuendo but Marco felt the hard kick of desire anyway. She looked so lovely and fresh, wearing a floaty summery dress with her hair caught in a loose plait, her face flushed and her eyes bright. He wanted to draw her towards him and kiss her, but he resisted.

That wasn't the purpose of this trip...except now maybe it was. At least, why shouldn't it be? If they were both feeling it?

'I'd love to walk through Central Park,' Sierra said and Marco forced his thoughts back to the conversation at hand.

'Then let's do it.'

They walked uptown to the Grand Army Plaza, buying ice creams to cool off as they strolled along the esplanade. Sierra stopped in front of a young busker by the Central Park Zoo, playing a lovely rendition of a Mozart concerto. She fumbled in her pockets to give him some money and Marco stopped her, taking a bill from his wallet instead.

'Thank you,' she murmured as they continued walking.

'Why do you only play in private?' Marco asked. He was curious to know more about her, to understand the enigma she'd been to him for so long.

Sierra pursed her lips, reflecting. 'Because I did it for me. It was a way to...to escape, really. And I didn't want anyone to ruin it for me, to stop me.'

'Escape? What were you escaping from?'

Her gaze slid away from his and she licked a drip of ice cream from her thumb. 'Oh, you know. The usual.'

Marco could tell she didn't want to talk about it, and yet he found he wanted to know. Badly. He'd painted a rosy, perfect picture of her childhood; considering his own, how could he have not? She had two parents who adored her, a beautiful home, everything she could possibly want. He'd wanted to be part of that world, wanted to inhabit it with her. But now he wondered if his view of it had been a little too perfect.

'But now that you're an adult? You still play in private?'

She nodded. 'I've never wanted to be a performer. I like teaching, but I play the violin for me.' She spoke firmly and he wondered if she would ever play for him. He thought that if she did it would mean something—to both of them.

And did he want it to mean something? Did he want to become emotionally close to Sierra, never mind what happened between them physically?

It was a question he didn't feel like answering or examining, not on a beautiful summer's day with the park stretched out before them, and everything feeling like a promise about to be made. He took Sierra's hand again and they walked up towards the Fountain of Bethesda, the still waters of the lake beyond shimmering under the sun.

By early evening Marco could tell Sierra was starting to flag. He was, too, and although he wanted to spend the entire day with Sierra, he knew there was pressing business to attend to before tomorrow's opening. He took a call as they entered the hotel, flashing a quick apologetic smile at Sierra. She smiled back, understanding, and disappeared into her room in the penthouse suite while Marco stretched out on a sofa and dealt with a variety of issues related to the opening.

He loosened his collar and leaned his head back against the sofa as one of his staff droned on about the guest list for tomorrow night's gala. From upstairs he could hear Sierra moving around and then the sound of a shower being turned on. He pictured her in the luxurious glass cubicle, big enough for two, water streaming down her golden body, and his whole body tightened in desperate arousal.

'Mr Ferranti?' The woman on the other end of the line must have been speaking for a while and Marco hadn't heard a word.

'I'm sorry. Can you say that again?'

A short while later Sierra came downstairs, dressed in a T-shirt and snug yoga pants, her hair falling in damp tendrils around her face.

Marco took one look at her and ended his call. His mouth dried and his heart turned over in his chest. She was utterly delectable, and not just because of her beauty. He liked having her in his space, looking relaxed and comfortable, being part of his world. He liked it a lot.

'You've finished your calls?' she asked as she came towards him. She curled up on the other end of the long leather sofa, tucking her feet underneath her.

'For the moment. There are a lot of details to sort out but first I think I want to eat.' His eyes roved over her hungrily and a blush touched her cheeks. Marco smiled and gestured to the city lights sparkling in every direction. 'The world is our oyster. What would you like to eat? We can order takeaway. Whatever you want.'

'How about proper American food? Cheeseburgers and French fries?'

He laughed and pressed a few buttons on his phone. 'And here I thought you'd be asking for lobster and caviar and champagne. Consider it done.'

* * *

Sierra watched as Marco put in their order for food. She felt jet-lagged and sleepy and relaxed, and she laid her head back against the sofa as Marco tossed his phone on the table and rose in one fluid movement.

'I'm going to get changed. The food should be here in a few minutes.'

'Okay.' It felt incredibly pleasant, no, wonderful, to sit there and listen to him go upstairs. The snick of a door closing, and she could imagine his long, lean fingers unbuttoning his shirt, shrugging it off his broad shoulders. He was the most beautiful man she'd ever seen. She remembered the feel of his body against hers, her breasts crushed against his chest...

A smile curved Sierra's mouth and she closed her eyes, picturing the scene perfectly. Then she imagined going up those stairs herself, opening that door. What would she say? What would she do? Perhaps she wouldn't have to do or say anything. Perhaps Marco would see her and take control, draw her towards him and kiss her as she wanted him to.

'I think the food's here.'

Sierra's eyes flew open and she saw Marco standing in front of her, wearing jeans and a faded grey T-shirt that clung to his pecs. His hair was slightly mussed, his jaw shadowed with stubble, and she didn't think she'd ever seen anything as wonderful, as desirable.

'You look like you were about to drop off,' Marco remarked as he took the food from the attendant who stepped out of the lift.

'I think I was.' She wasn't about to admit what had been going through her head. The mouth-watering aroma of cheeseburgers and fries wafted through the room and Marco brought the tray of food to the coffee table in front of the sofa.

'We might as well eat here.'

He handed her a plate heaped with a huge burger and plenty of fries and Sierra bit in, closing her eyes as the flavours hit her. 'Oh, this is *good*.'

Marco made a choked sound and Sierra opened her eyes, her heart seeming to still as his hot gaze held hers. 'Look like that much longer and I'll have to forget about this meal,' he said, his voice a low growl, and awareness shivered through her.

'It's too delicious to do that,' she protested, her voice breathy, and Marco shrugged, his gaze never leaving hers.

'I can think of something more delicious.'

Colour flooded her face and heated her body. This was so dangerous, and yet…why shouldn't she? Why shouldn't *they*? They were in a glamorous hotel in one of the most amazing cities in the world. There was nothing, absolutely nothing, to keep them from acting on the desire Sierra knew they both felt.

Marco plucked one of her French fries from her plate. 'Your face is the colour of your ketchup.'

She laughed shakily and put her burger down, wiping her hands on the napkin provided. 'Marco…' She trailed off, not knowing what to say or how to say it.

Marco smiled and nodded towards her still full plate. 'Let's eat, Sierra. It's a big day tomorrow.'

That sounded and felt like a brush-off. Trying not to feel stung, Sierra started eating again. Had Marco changed his mind? Why did he say one thing and then do another? Maybe, Sierra reflected, he felt as conflicted as she did. Maybe a fling would be too complicated, considering their history.

Considering her lack of experience, she didn't even know if she could handle a fling. Would she be able to walk away after a couple of days, heart intact? The truth was, she had no idea.

Marco's phone rang before they'd finished their meal and he excused himself to take the call. Sierra ate the rest of her burger and then tidied up, leaving the tray of dirty dishes by the lift. She wandered around the living area for a bit, staring out at the glittering cityscape, before jet lag finally overcame her and she headed upstairs to bed. Marco was still closeted in his own bedroom and so, with a sigh of disappointment, Sierra went into hers. Despite her restlessness, sleep claimed her almost instantly.

When she woke the sun was bathing the city in gold and she could hear Marco moving around across the hall.

The ribbon-cutting ceremony was that afternoon, and it occurred to Sierra as she showered and dressed that she really didn't have the right clothes.

Back in London, her one smart day dress and second-hand ball gown had seemed sufficient but now that she'd been to the hotel, now that she cared about it—and Marco's success—she realised she didn't want to stand in front of the crowd looking dowdy or underdressed. She wanted to look her best, not just for Marco and the public but for herself.

She dressed in jeans and a simple summery top and headed downstairs in search of Marco. He was standing by the window, scrolling through messages on his phone and drinking coffee, but he looked up as she came down the stairs, a smile breaking across his face.

'Good morning.'

'Good morning.' Suddenly Sierra felt shy. Marco looked amazing, freshly showered, his crisp blue shirt set off by a darker blue suit and silver tie. His hair was slightly damp, curling around his ears, and his smoothly shaven jaw looked eminently touchable. Kissable.

'Did you sleep well?'

'Yes, amazingly. But I wondered if there was time to go out this morning, before the opening.'

'Go out? Where?'

'Shopping.' Sierra flushed. 'I don't think the clothes I brought are…well, nice enough, if I'm honest.' She let out an uncertain laugh. 'A second-hand ball gown from a charity shop doesn't seem appropriate, now that I'm here.'

Surprise flashed across Marco's face before it was replaced by composed determination. 'Of course. I'll arrange a car immediately.'

'I can walk…'

'Nonsense. It will be my great pleasure to buy clothes for you, Sierra.' His gaze rested on her, his silvery-grey eyes seeming to burn right through her.

'You don't have to buy them, Marco—'

'You would deny me such a pleasure?' He slid his phone into his pocket and strode towards her. 'The car will be waiting. You can have breakfast on the way.'

Within minutes Sierra was whisked from the penthouse suite to the limo waiting outside the hotel; a carafe of coffee, another of freshly squeezed orange juice and a basket of warm croissants were already set out for her.

'Good grief.' She shook her head, laughing, as Marco slid into the seat next to her. 'This is kind of crazy, you know.'

'Crazy? Why?'

'The luxury. I'm not used to it.'

'You should get used to it, then. This is the life you would have had, Sierra. The life you deserve.'

She paused, a croissant halfway to her mouth, and met his gaze. 'The life I would have had? You mean if I'd married you?' She spoke softly, hesitant to dredge up the past once again and yet needing to know. Did Marco wish things had been different? Did she?

'If you'd married anyone,' Marco said after a pause.

'Someone of your father's choosing, of your family's station.'

'You think I should have married someone of my father's choosing?'

'I think you should have married me.'

Her insides jolted so hard she felt as if she'd missed the last step in a staircase. 'Even now?' she whispered.

Marco glanced away. 'Who can say what would have happened, how things would have been? The reality is you chose not to, and we've both become different people as a result.'

But people who could find their way back to each other. The words hovered on her lips but Sierra didn't say them. What were they really talking about here? A fling, a relationship, or just what might have been? She didn't know what she felt or wanted

'Ah, here we are,' Marco said, and Sierra turned to see the limo pull up to an exclusive-looking boutique on Fifth Avenue. She stuffed the rest of her croissant into her mouth as he jumped out of the limo. She swallowed quickly and then took his hand as he led her out of the car and into the boutique.

Several assistants came towards them quickly and Sierra glanced around at the crystal chandeliers, the white velvet sofas, the marble floor. There seemed to be very few pieces of clothing on display. And she felt underdressed to go shopping, which seemed ridiculous, but she could not deny the svelte blonde assistants were making her feel dowdy.

But then Marco turned to her, his eyes lit up as his warm, approving gaze rested on her. 'And now,' he said, tugging her towards him, 'the fun begins.'

CHAPTER TEN

MARCO STRETCHED OUT on the sofa, handling business calls while Sierra tried on outfit after outfit, shyly pirouetting in front of him in each one. He couldn't think of a better way to spend his time than watch Sierra model clothes. Actually, he could. He'd like to spend his time taking the clothes off her.

She'd started with modest day outfits, but even tailored skirts and crisp blouses sent his heart rate skyrocketing. He wanted to slip those pearl buttons from their holes and part the silky fabric to see the even silkier skin beneath. He wanted to shimmy that pencil skirt off her slim hips.

Instead he issued a terse command to the fawning assistant. 'We'll take them all.'

Sierra was in the dressing room and didn't hear him; a few minutes later she came out, frowning uncertainly. 'I think maybe that blue shift dress might be the best choice…'

'You can decide later,' Marco answered indulgently. It amused him that Sierra thought he was going to be satisfied by simply buying her a single outfit. What kind of man did she think he was?

A man who was falling in love with her.

The words froze inside him, turned everything to ice. He couldn't be falling in love. He didn't *do* love. He'd seen what it had done to his mother. He'd felt what it had done to him. Waiting for someone who wasn't going to come back, who didn't feel the same way. His mother. *Sierra*. And he hadn't even loved Sierra, back then. Did he want to set himself up for an even harder fall?

No, he was not falling in love with her. He was just enjoying himself. And yes, he might be thinking about what might have been; it was damned hard not to. Seeing Sierra in her element, where she belonged, every inch the Rocci heiress, her desire shining in her eyes…how could he not think about it?

'What do you think about this one?' Sierra emerged from the dressing room in an evening gown, a blush touching her cheeks. Marco stared at her, his whole body going rigid. The dress was a long, elegant column of grey-blue silk that matched her eyes perfectly. A diamanté belt encircled her narrow waist, and her hair was loose and tousled about her shoulders.

Marco couldn't even think when he saw her in that dress. 'We'll take it.' He bit the words out gruffly, and Sierra's eyes widened.

'But if you don't like it…'

'I like it.' From the corner of his eye Marco saw an assistant smile behind her hand. 'Please go wrap up the other outfits,' he barked and she melted back into the boutique, leaving them alone.

'The other outfits?' Sierra frowned. 'But I thought you were just buying the blue dress.'

'You thought wrong.' He stalked towards her and to his satisfaction he could see a pulse begin to hammer in her throat. 'I'm buying them all, Sierra. I want to see you in them all.'

She pressed a hand to her fluttering pulse as she swallowed convulsively. 'There are a few more evening gowns to try on…'

'And I want you to try them on. But I think I'd better help you with the zipper on that dress.'

Her eyes had gone huge, as blue and glassy as twin mountain lakes. Her pink lips parted, and when her tongue darted out to moisten them, Marco groaned.

'The assistant…' she murmured and he shook his head, everything in him demanding that he touch her. Now.

'Is gone. I'll do it.' Gently but purposefully, he pushed her back into the dressing room, drawing the thick brocade curtain closed behind them. The space was private, the silence hushed and expectant. After a second when she just stared at him, Sierra turned and offered him her back.

Marco moved the heavy, honeyed mass of her hair, revelling in the softness of it as it slipped through his fingers. With the nape of her neck bare he couldn't keep from kissing her. He brushed his lips against the tender skin and felt her whole body shudder in response.

She swayed against him silently and he put his hands on her shoulders to steady her. Desire raged through him, a fierce and overwhelming need that obliterated all rational thought. He'd take her right in this dressing room if she'd let him, but he didn't want their first time together to be urgent and rushed. No, he'd take his time, prolong the exquisite agony.

Slowly Marco drew the zip down the dress, the snick of the fabric parting one of the most erotic sounds he'd ever heard.

The strapless dress slipped from her body, leaving her bare, her skin golden and perfect. He slid his hands around her waist, spanning it easily, and then, because he couldn't keep himself from it, he slid them up to cup her breasts, his thumbs flicking over her nipples, his hands full of her lush softness.

Sierra sagged against him, her breath coming out in a shudder. Marco pushed into her, and she gasped again at the feel of his arousal against her bottom.

When she pushed back gently, her hips nudging him with intent, he almost abandoned his resolution to take his time. It would be so easy, so overwhelmingly satisfying, to pull her dress up and bury himself inside her right then and there.

He slid his hands back down to her hips, anchoring her against him, pushing into her and having her push back, their bodies moving in an ancient rhythm. Sierra's breath caught on a gasp and her whole body went tense. Marco knew she was close to climaxing, just from this. Hell, so was he.

'Mr Ferranti?' The musical trill of the assistant's voice caused reality to rush in. Sierra stiffened and reluctantly Marco eased back.

'We're not finished here,' he told her in a low voice.

Sierra let out a laugh that sounded close to a sob. 'Dear heaven, I hope not.'

He smiled as he kissed the nape of her neck once more and then slipped from the dressing room to deal with the ill-timed assistant.

As soon as Marco had gone Sierra sank onto one of the padded benches, the dress pooling around her waist, her head in her hands. Her whole body trembled with the aftershocks of his touch. She'd been so close to losing control, and simply by the feel of his body pressing into hers. And as amazed and mortified as she felt that she'd been so shameless in a public dressing room, the overwhelming feeling she had now was a desire to rush out of this shop, jump in a limo and race back to the hotel where Marco could make good on his promise.

We're not finished.

Not, Sierra hoped, by a long shot.

'Sierra?' Marco called, his voice sounding crisply professional and not as if he were remotely affected by what had just happened between them. 'We should be getting on. You'll need to leave some time to get ready and I have a few things to finish before the opening.'

'Of course.' Hurriedly, she slithered out of the evening gown. 'Let me just get dressed.' She yanked on her jeans and pulled her T-shirt over her head, finger-combing her tousled hair as she slipped from the dressing room, her body still weak and trembling from their encounter. Marco, of course, looked completely unruffled. Maybe this was a normal experience for him. 'What about the evening gown…?' she asked, glad her voice came out sounding even.

'We're taking them all,' Marco informed her blithely. 'The assistant will have them wrapped and sent to the hotel. It's all taken care of.'

'Taking *all* of the evening gowns? But I didn't even try them on.'

'I'm sure you'll look fabulous in them. And if you don't like any of them, I'll arrange for them to be returned.' Marco took her elbow. 'Now, the limo is waiting.'

Sierra let herself be ushered out of the store, amazed by the whole experience, from the sheer number of clothes Marco had bought her to the exciting interlude in the dressing room.

'You make everything seem so easy,' she commented as she slid into the limo. 'Like the world is at your fingertips, or even your feet.'

Marco gave her a quick smile as he checked his phone. 'I've worked hard to have it be so.'

'I know you have. But do you ever…do you ever feel like pinching yourself, that this is your reality?'

For a second Marco's gaze became distant, shuttered. Then he turned back to his phone. 'Money doesn't buy everything,' he said, his voice clipped. 'No matter how many people think so, it can't make you happy.'

The honest statement, delivered as it was so matter-of-factly, both surprised and moved her. 'Are you happy, Marco?'

He glanced up with a wolfish grin. 'I was very happy with you in the dressing room. And I intend to be even happier before the day is done.'

She felt a flush spread across her body as her insides tingled. She knew Marco was deliberately avoiding a serious conversation, but she wanted him too much to care. 'I hope you do mean that.'

He paused, lowering his phone. 'I do mean it, Sierra. I want you very badly. So badly I almost lost control in a dressing room, which is something I've never done before.'

'You haven't?' she teased, trying to ignore the jealousy that spiked through her. 'I imagine you've got quite a lot of experience under your belt.'

'Not as much as you probably think, but I know my way around.' Her face heated even more and she looked away. Yes, he most certainly did. 'What about you?' he asked abruptly. 'You must have had lovers over the last seven years.' She opened her mouth to admit the truth but before she could he held up a hand. 'Never mind. I don't want to know.' His face had hardened into implacable lines, and his eyes blazed. 'But make no mistake, Sierra. I want you. Tonight.'

'I want you, too,' she whispered.

His gaze swept over her, searching, assessing. 'We're not who we were seven years ago. Things are different now.'

'I know.' She lifted her chin and met his gaze directly. 'I know what this is, Marco. We're in an amazing city for a short period of time and we happen to be attracted to each other. *Very* attracted. So why shouldn't we act on it?' She smiled, raising her eyebrows, making it sound so simple. As if she had had this kind of experience before. 'It's a fling.'

'Yes,' Marco said slowly. 'That's exactly what it is.'

Back in the hotel, Marco disappeared into the office to deal with some business before the opening while Sierra headed upstairs to the penthouse. The elegant lobby was bustling with staff as they prepared for the champagne and chocolate reception that would immediately follow the opening. And then, tonight, the ball...

Staff hurried and worked around her as she walked towards the private penthouse lift. One middle-aged man caught her eye and executed a stiff bow. 'Good afternoon, Miss Rocci. I hope you find everything to your satisfaction.'

'Yes, yes, of course,' Sierra nearly stammered. She was shaken by the way the man knew her, knew she was a Rocci. She hadn't truly been a Rocci in seven years. She'd turned her back on it all, and in that moment the memories came back in a sickening rush—the hotel openings so different from the modern elegance of The Rocci New York and yet so frighteningly familiar.

'Miss Rocci? Are you all right?' The man who had spoken to her before touched her elbow cautiously and Sierra realised she must have looked unwell. She felt sick and faint, and she reached out a hand to the lift door to steady herself.

'I'm fine. Thank you. I just haven't eaten today.'

'I'll have something sent up to your room.'

'Thank you,' Sierra murmured. 'I appreciate it.'

The lift doors opened and she stepped inside, grateful for the privacy. For a few seconds she'd heard her father's voice, felt his hand pinch her in warning as they mounted the steps of one hotel or another.

Be a good girl, Sierra. Smile for everyone.

She could hear the implied threat in his voice, the promise of punishment if she didn't behave, all against the background of a crowd's expectant murmurings, the clink of crystal…

The lift doors opened and Sierra stumbled out into the penthouse's living area, the city stretching all around her, one hand clamped to her mouth. She swallowed down the bile and then hurried upstairs to the freestanding kitchen units and poured herself a glass of water. Dear heaven, she couldn't fall apart now. Not when the opening was about to start, everyone was waiting for her. Marco was depending on her.

Sierra closed her eyes, memory and regret and fear coursing through her in unrelenting waves. She didn't want to let Marco down. How much had changed in such a short time—six weeks ago she'd been hoping never to see him again.

And now…now she was hoping he'd make love to her tonight. She wanted to stand by his side at the opening and make him proud. *She was halfway to falling in love with him.*

Sierra's eyes snapped open. *What?* How could she be? She'd always avoided and disdained love, seen how her mother had prostrated herself at its altar and lost her soul. And now she was poised to fall in love with a man she still didn't entirely trust? Or maybe it was herself she didn't trust. She didn't trust herself to keep her head straight and her heart safe.

She was inexperienced when it came to romance or sex, and here she was, contemplating a fling? For a second Sierra wondered what on earth she was doing. And then she remembered the feel of Marco's hands on her, his body behind her, and a shiver of sheer longing went through her. She knew what she was doing—and she needed to do it.

And as for the opening... She glanced at the clock above the sink and saw with a lurch of alarm that the opening was in less than an hour. An hour until she had to face Marco and the crowds of people who would be watching her, knowing she was a Rocci who had fallen from grace. Her stomach clenched and she half wished she could cry off, even as she acknowledged that she would never leave Marco in the lurch, publicly humiliated and alone. It would be almost as bad as leaving him at the altar.

She took a deep breath and willed her nerves back. Lifted her chin and straightened her shoulders. *Show no fear.* She could do this.

Marco paced the foyer of the hotel as the reporters, celebrities and guests attending the opening of The Rocci New York waited outside the frosted glass doors. It was three minutes past two o'clock and Sierra was meant to be down here. He'd already sent a staff member upstairs to check on her; she'd promised to be down shortly. He'd thought of going up himself, but some sense, or perhaps just an innate sense of caution, had stopped him. What if she didn't want to see him now?

'We should start...' Antony, the head of the hotel, looked nervously at the waiting crowds.

'We can't start without a Rocci,' Marco snapped. He felt his 'less than' status as the non-Rocci CEO keenly then, but worse, he felt it as a man. Sierra's lateness was too powerful a reminder of another time he'd been kept waiting.

Another time he'd felt the blood drain from his head and the hope from his heart as he'd realised once again someone wasn't coming back. Wasn't coming at all.

He blinked back the memories, willed back the hurt and fear. This was different. He and Sierra were both different now.

Then the lift doors opened and she stepped out, looking ethereally lovely in a mint-green shift dress—and very pale. Her gaze darted round the empty foyer and then to the front doors where the crowd gathered, waiting; she took a deep breath and threw her shoulders back. Marco frowned and started forward.

Sierra saw his frown and faltered and Marco caught her hands in his; they were icy.

'Sierra, are you all right?'

'Yes...'

'You look ill.'

'Jet lag.' She didn't quite meet his gaze. 'Everything has been such a whirlwind.'

But he knew it couldn't just be jet lag. As beautiful as she was and always would be to him, she looked awful. 'Sierra, if you're not up for it...' he began, only to stop. She had to be up for it. The security of the company and his place at its head rested on having a Rocci at this opening.

And yet in that moment he knew if she said she wasn't, he would accept her word.

'I'm fine, Marco.' She squeezed his hands lightly and gave him what he suspected was meant to be a smile. 'Really, I am. Let's do this.'

Sierra watched as Marco scanned her face like a doctor looking for broken bones. She knew she must look truly awful for him to seem so worried and she tried to dredge up some confidence and composure. It was just the memories. So many of them, crowding her in like jeering ghosts. She wanted to drown out the babble of their voices but it was hard. She hadn't been at an opening like this since she was a teenager, her father's hand hard on her elbow, his voice in her ear.

Be good, Sierra. With the awful implied *or else.*

Finally Marco nodded and let go of her hands. 'All right. The crowd is waiting.'

'I'm sorry I'm late.' She'd been trying not to be sick.

'It's fine.' He strode towards the front doors and resolutely, holding her head high, Sierra followed.

A staff member opened the doors and Sierra stepped out into the shimmering heat and the snap and flash of dozens of cameras. She recoiled instinctively before she forced herself to stop and straighten. Foolishly, perhaps, she hadn't realised quite how big a deal the hotel opening would be, bigger than any of the ones her father had arranged, but then she hadn't considered Marco's ambition and drive.

Marco had stepped up to a microphone and was welcoming the guests and media, his voice smooth and urbane, his English flawless. Sierra stood stiffly, trying to smile, until Marco's words began to penetrate.

'I know Arturo Rocci, my mentor and greatest friend, would be so proud to be here with us, and to see his daughter cutting the ribbon today. Arturo believed passionately in the values that gird every Rocci hotel. He valued hard work, excellent service and, of course, family ties.' He glanced at Sierra, who stood frozen, her stomach churning. She hadn't expected Marco to mention her father. She couldn't keep his words from washing over her like an acid rain, corroding everything.

The crowd clapped and someone pressed an overlarge pair of gilded scissors into her hand. The silver satin ribbon that stretched across the steps glinted in the sunlight.

'Sierra?' Marco asked, his voice low.

Somehow she moved forward and snipped the ribbon. As it fell away the crowd cheered and then Marco took her elbow and led her inside to the cool sanctuary of the foyer.

'You don't look well.'

'I'm sorry, it must be the heat. And the jet lag.' *And the memories.* And her father's ghost, hurting her from the grave. Marco still believing the best of him, and she could hardly fault him. She hadn't said anything, hadn't thought it was necessary. And when she'd been planning never to see Marco again, it hadn't been. But now? Now, when she was thinking of something actually happening between them?

'Do you want to sit down?' Marco asked. 'Catch your breath?'

Sierra shook her head. 'I'm fine, Marco. I came here for this, and I'll see it through.' She plucked a flute of champagne from a waiter's tray. She definitely needed some liquid courage. Guests were starting to stream into the foyer, chatting and taking pictures. 'Let the party begin,' she said, and raised her glass in a determined toast.

CHAPTER ELEVEN

A FEW HOURS into the reception Sierra finally started to relax. The memories that had mocked her were starting to recede; her father's grip not, thankfully, as tight as she'd feared it was. She avoided reporters with their difficult, probing questions and chatted with various guests and staff about innocuous things: New York, London, the latest films. She was actually having a good time.

The three glasses of champagne helped, too.

'This is the most amazing thing I've ever seen,' she told a waiter as she studied the chocolate fountain with floating strawberries. He smiled politely and a firm hand touched her elbow. Even though Sierra couldn't see who it was, she felt it through her marrow. Marco.

'You're not drunk, are you?'

'Drunk? Thanks very much.' She turned around, misjudging the distance, and nearly poured her half-full flute of champagne onto his front. Marco caught her hand and liberated her glass. 'Slightly tipsy only,' she amended at his wry look. 'But this is a fun party.'

Marco drew her aside, away from the waiter and guests. 'You seemed tense earlier. Even upset. Was it something I said?' Concern drew his straight dark eyebrows together, his wonderful mouth drawn into a frowning line.

'No,' Sierra answered. 'It wasn't something you said.'

'Are you sure?'

She nodded, knowing she couldn't explain it to him here, and maybe not ever. The deeper things got with Marco, the harder it became to come clean about her past. She didn't want to hurt him, and yet if they were to have any future at all she knew she needed to explain. He needed to understand.

But why was she even thinking about a future? They were just having a fling. And they hadn't even had it yet.

'When is the ball tonight?'

'Not for a few hours. But if you'd like to retire up-stairs and get ready, you can. You've shown your face here. You've done enough.' He paused, and then rested a hand on her arm. 'Thank you, Sierra.'

Marco watched Sierra head towards the lift, a frown on his face. She'd looked so pale and shaky when she'd first come to the opening, almost ill. Something was wrong and he had no idea what it was.

At least she'd rallied, smiling and talking with guests, her natural charm and friendliness coming to the fore. She'd maybe rallied a little too much, judging by the amount of champagne she'd imbibed. The thought made him smile.

He was looking forward to seeing Sierra tonight at the ball, and then after. Most definitely after.

'Mr Ferranti, do you have anything to say about Sierra Rocci's presence at the opening today?'

Marco turned to see one of the tabloid reporters smirking at him.

'No, I do not.'

'You were engaged to Sierra Rocci seven years ago, were you not?' the weedy young man pressed. 'And she broke off the engagement at the last moment? Left you standing at the altar?' He smirked again and Marco stiffened, longing to wipe that smug look off the man's face.

He hadn't considered the press resurrecting that old story. His engagement to Sierra had been kept quiet back then; Arturo had wanted a quiet ceremony, not wanting to expose Sierra to media scrutiny. Marco had been glad to agree.

'Well?' The reporter smirked, eyebrows raised.

'No comment,' Marco bit out tersely, and stalked off.

'You can look in the mirror now.'

'Thank you.' Sierra smiled at the stylist, Diana, whom Marco had arranged to do her hair and make-up for the ball. It had been a nice surprise to emerge from an hour-long soak in the sunken marble tub to find a woman ready to be her fairy godmother.

Now Sierra turned around and gazed at her reflection in the full-length mirror, catching her breath on a gasp of surprise.

'Oh, my goodness…'

'My sentiments exactly,' Diana agreed cheerfully.

Sierra raised one hand to touch the curls that were piled on top of her head, a few trailing down to rest beguilingly on her shoulder. Diamond clips sparkled from the honeyed mass and when she turned her head they caught the light. Her make-up was understated and yet somehow transformed her face; she had smoky eyes, endless lashes, sculpted cheekbones and lush pink lips.

'I had no idea make-up could do so much,' she exclaimed and leaned forward to peer at herself more closely.

Diana laughed. 'I didn't use that much make-up. Just enough to enhance what was already there.'

'Even so.' Sierra shook her head, marvelling. She had never worn make-up as a teenager, and she hadn't changed much during her years in London. Now, however, she could see the advantages.

Her gaze dropped from her face to her dress. She'd chosen the dress Marco had seen her in, the silvery-blue column of silk with the diamanté belt around her waist. Looking at herself in the dress made her face warm and her blood heat as she remembered how Marco had unzipped it. How he'd put his hands on her hips and pulled her towards him and she'd gone, craving the feel of him, desperately wanting more.

'I wonder if I put a bit too much blusher on,' Diana mused and, with a suppressed laugh, Sierra turned away from the mirror.

'I'm sure it's fine.'

Marco was getting ready just across the hall, and she couldn't wait to see him. She couldn't wait for him to see her, and for this wonderful, enchanted evening to begin. No matter what had happened before or might lie ahead, she wanted to truly be Cinderella and enjoy this one magical night. The clock wasn't going to strike just yet.

Marco knocked softly on her bedroom door and, with a conspiratorial grin, Diana went to answer it. 'I'll tell him you're coming in a moment. You're going to knock his socks off, you know.'

Sierra smiled back, one hand pressed to her middle to soothe the seething nerves that had started in her stomach. She didn't want anything to ruin this night.

Diana told Marco with surprising bossiness to wait for Sierra downstairs and, after taking the filmy matching wrap and beaded bag, Sierra opened the door and headed out.

She walked down the spiral staircase carefully; the last thing she wanted was to go flying down the stairs and fall flat on her face.

She saw Marco before he saw her; he was standing by the windows, staring out at the city where the sky was lit up with streaks of vivid orange and umber, a spectacular summer sunset.

Her heels clicked on the wrought iron and he turned around, going completely still as he caught sight of her. Sierra couldn't tell anything from his face; his perfect features were completely blank as his silvery-grey gaze swept over her.

She came to the bottom of the staircase, her heart starting to beat hard. 'Do I…? Is everything all right?'

Suddenly she wondered if she had lipstick on her teeth or she'd experienced some unknown wardrobe malfunction.

Then Marco's face cleared and he stepped forward, taking her hands in his. 'You have stolen my breath along with my words. You are magnificent, Sierra.'

A smile spread across her face as he squeezed her hands. 'You look pretty good yourself.'

Actually he looked amazing. The crisp white tuxedo shirt was the perfect foil for his olive skin, and the tailored midnight-dark tuxedo emphasised the perfect, powerful musculature of his body. Marco wasn't the only one who was breathless.

He touched her cheek with his fingertips, and the small touch seemed to Sierra like a promise of things to come. *Wonderful* things to come. 'We should go, if you're ready.'

'I am.'

The gala was in the hotel's ballroom, several floors below the penthouse yet with the same spectacular view from every side. Sierra stepped into the huge room with a soft gasp of appreciation. The room was as sleekly spare and elegant as the hotel foyer, letting the view be its main decoration. Tuxedo-clad waiters circulated with trays of champagne and hors d'oeuvres and a string quartet played softly from a dais in one corner of the room. Sierra turned to Marco, her eyes shining.

'Did you have some say in this room, too?'

'Maybe a little.' He smiled, taking her by the hand to draw her into the ball. 'Let me introduce you.'

Sierra had never particularly liked social occasions, thanks to her father's silent, menacing pressure. Even in London she'd preferred quiet gatherings to parties or bars, and yet tonight those old inhibitions fell away. It felt different now, when she was at Marco's side. When she felt safe and confident and valued.

But not loved. Never loved.

She pushed that niggling reminder to the back of her mind as Marco introduced her to various guests—stars, socialites, business types and the odd more ordinary people, and Sierra chatted with them all. Laughed and drank champagne and felt dizzy with a new, surprising elation.

After a few hours Marco pulled her away from a crowd of women she'd been chatting with, plucking the half-drunk glass of champagne from her fingertips and thrusting it at a waiter, who whisked it away.

'What is it...?' Sierra began, only to have her words fall away as Marco drew her onto the dance floor.

His gaze was hooded and intent, the colour of his eyes like molten silver as his hands slid down to her hips and he anchored her against him.

'Dance with me.'

Sierra felt as if the breath had been vacuumed from her lungs as she wordlessly nodded, placing her hands on his broad shoulders, the fabric of his tuxedo jacket crisp underneath her fingers.

The string quartet was playing a lovely, lazy melody, something you could sway to as you lost your soul. And

Sierra knew she was in danger of losing hers, of losing everything to this man. Tonight she wasn't going to worry, wasn't even going to care. She'd let herself fall and in the morning she'd think about picking up the broken pieces.

'It seems like the ball is going well,' Sierra said as they swayed to the music. 'Are you pleased?'

'Very pleased. The hotel is booked solid for the next three months. That's in part because of you.'

'A very small part,' Sierra answered. 'You're the one who put in all the hard work. I'm proud of you, Marco.' She smiled shyly. 'I know you told me how much your job meant to you, but I realised why tonight. You're good at this. You were meant for this.'

Marco didn't speak for a few seconds; a muscle flickered in his jaw and he seemed to struggle with some emotion. 'Thank you,' he said finally. 'That means a great deal to me.'

The song ended and another one began, and neither Marco nor Sierra moved from the dance floor. She felt as if she could stay here for ever, or at least until Marco finally, thankfully took her upstairs.

'You are the most beautiful woman in the world tonight.' Marco's voice was low, his tone too sincere for her to argue with.

'As long as you think so,' Sierra murmured.

His eyes blazed for a second, thrilling her, and he pulled her even closer to him. 'Do you mean that?'

'Yes,' she said simply. After everything that had happened, everything he'd made her feel, she knew there could be no dissembling.

Marco drew a shuddering, steadying breath and eased her a little bit away from him as he smiled wryly. 'I don't want to disgrace myself here.'

She smiled, the curve of her lips coy. 'Then disgrace yourself upstairs.'

Regret flashed across his features like a streak of pain. 'We can't leave the ball yet.'

'Do you have to stay to the end?' Some of the socialites and celebrities seemed ready to party until dawn.

'No,' Marco answered firmly. 'And even if I needed to, I wouldn't. I can't last that long without touching you, Sierra. Without being inside you.'

The huskily spoken words sent a spear of pure pleasure knifing through her. 'Good.'

Marco shook his head. 'Keep looking at me like that and I really won't last.'

'How am I looking?' Sierra asked with deliberate innocence.

'Like that.' He pulled her closer again. 'Like you want to eat me.'

'Maybe I do.' A blush pinkened her cheeks but she held his heated gaze. She could hardly believe the audacity of her words, and yet she meant them. Utterly.

Marco groaned softly. 'Do you enjoy torturing me?'

'Yes,' she answered with a shameless smile. 'It's payback for the way you tortured me this morning.'

His gaze swept over her body. 'That was torture for me, as well. Sweet, sweet torture.'

She felt as if she could melt beneath the heat of his gaze. Or maybe combust. She'd felt an intense excitement spiralling up inside her from the moment Marco had taken her onto the dance floor, and it was overwhelming now. The need for him was a physical craving, so fierce and wonderful she was helpless to its demand.

Her tongue shot out and dampened her lips as she gave him a look of complete yearning. 'Marco…'

'We're going,' Marco bit out. 'Now.' His long, lean fingers encircled her wrist as he led her purposefully from the dance floor.

In any other circumstance Sierra would have baulked at being led from the ballroom like a sulky schoolgirl or a flagrant harlot. Now the need was too much to feel even a twinge of embarrassment or anger. She just wanted to get upstairs fast.

Marco muttered a few words to one of his staff standing by the door, and then they were out in the hall, the air cool on Sierra's heated cheeks. A few guests loitering there shot them speculative looks, but Marco ignored them all. He stabbed the button for the penthouse lift and Sierra held her breath until the doors opened and Marco pulled her inside.

CHAPTER TWELVE

THE LIFT DOORS had barely closed before Marco pulled Sierra to him, her breasts colliding with his chest as his mouth came down hard on hers. He couldn't have waited another moment, not even one second, to touch her, and the feel of her lips on his wasn't the water in the desert he'd thought it would be; it was a match to the flame, igniting his need all the more.

He backed her up against the wall of the lift, his mouth plundering hers as his hands fisted in her hair. Diamond-tipped pins scattered across the floor of the lift with a tinkling sound. Marco couldn't get enough of her. He moved his hands from her hair to her hips, yanking up a satiny fistful of her dress, needing to touch her skin.

He found the curve of her neck with his mouth and sucked gently, his desire knifing inside him as Sierra groaned aloud.

'You'll ruin the dress…' she gasped.

'I'll buy you another. I'll buy you a dozen, a hundred others.'

The doors pinged open and Marco stumbled backwards into the penthouse, pulling Sierra with him. She came with him, laughing and breathless, clutching his shirt as she tried to pull it away from his cummerbund.

'I need to see you,' Marco said. He tugged at the zip at

the back of her dress. 'Now.' He tugged harder at the zip and the dress slithered off her, leaving her in nothing but a scrap of lace pants. Marco inhaled sharply at the sight of her pale golden perfection, the lights from the city gleaming on her smooth skin.

She stepped out of the dress, chin lifted, smile shy, wearing nothing but lace and stiletto heels. Marco had never seen a more magnificent sight.

'This feels a bit unequal,' she said with a little uncertain laugh. 'I'm in my birthday suit and you're completely dressed.'

He spread his arms wide. 'Then maybe you should do something about it.'

'Maybe I should.' She stepped closer to him so he could breathe in the lemon scent of her hair; it had come undone from the pins he'd pulled out in the lift and lay in twists and curls about her shoulders. She pursed her lips slightly as she fumbled with the studs on his shirt; her breasts grazed his chest every time she moved.

Finally she'd managed to release the studs; she tossed them aside with a breathless laugh and then tugged his shirt out from his cummerbund and parted it, smoothing her hands along his chest. Marco closed his eyes, his breath hissing between his teeth. It amazed him how profoundly her touch affected him. He'd been with plenty of women over the years, gorgeous women with experience and expertise and plenty of confidence, but Sierra's hesitant touch reduced all those women to a pale memory.

'You're very beautiful,' she whispered, and tugged his shirt off his body before undoing the laces of his cummerbund. He wore only his trousers now, and he saw the hesitation in Sierra's face and wondered what she'd do about it. Sometimes she seemed so innocent and inexperienced he wondered how many lovers she'd actually had. But it wasn't a train of thought he enjoyed dwelling on, and so he made himself stop thinking about it. It didn't matter. The only thing that mattered was that she was with him now.

'Well?' He arched an eyebrow, his mouth curving in a salacious smile. 'I'm not naked yet.'

'I know.' She laughed again, a soft, breathy sound, and then tugged his trousers down. Marco kicked them off his feet, and followed with his shoes and socks. Now all he wore was a pair of navy silk boxers and his arousal was all too evident.

Sierra's gaze darted up to him and she licked her lips. Marco groaned. Then she reached out a hand and touched his shaft through his boxers, her fingers questing uncertainly and then wrapping more firmly around him.

Marco clenched his jaw against the almost painful wave of pleasure that crashed over him. 'Sierra…'

'Is this okay?' She jerked her hand back as if she'd hurt him and he laughed, albeit shakily.

'More than okay. What you do to me… But I need to do some things to you.' He reached for her then, because he needed her next to him. The feel of their naked bodies colliding made them both gasp aloud, her breasts against his chest, their legs tangled.

Marco kissed her deeply and she responded with all of her clumsy ardour, tangling her hands in his hair as he fitted her body more closely to his. Marco backed her towards the wall, pressing her against the sheet of glass as Sierra let out a soft laugh.

'Half the world now has a glimpse of my backside.'

'No one can see you from up here,' he promised her, 'but, if they could, it would be the most splendid view. Not,' he added in a growl as his mouth moved down her body, 'that I want anyone to see you but me.' *Ever*, he silently added, and then pushed the thought away as he turned his attention to her breasts. Her skin was pale and gleaming in the moonlight; she looked like a statue of Athena or Artemis, naked and proud.

Sierra's head came back against the glass, her hair tumbling about her shoulders, and her legs buckled as Marco lavished his attention on each breast in turn and then moved lower.

She gasped, a ragged pant, as he parted her thighs. 'Marco…'

'I want to taste you.' Was she thinking of before, in the villa, when he'd touched her like this? Then it had been confused, born of both need and anger, a twisted revenge he hadn't wanted to articulate even to himself. Now he felt nothing but this deep physical and emotional connection he needed to act on. To show her how important she was to him. 'I want to feel you come apart beneath me,' he muttered against her. 'I want you to give me everything, Sierra.' *For ever.*

Sierra sagged against the window, Marco supporting her with one arm, as he plundered her centre. She didn't know how she could have, but she'd forgotten how intense and exquisite and *intimate* this was. Marco's hands were cupping her bottom as pleasure spiralled inside her, up and up, tighter and tighter until she felt as if she were apart from her body even as she dwelt so intensely in it. When she came, she cried out, Marco holding her to him as she slid into boneless pleasure.

A few moments passed while he cradled her and her breathing slowed and then he scooped her up in his arms and took her up the spiral staircase to his bed.

He deposited her on the navy silk sheets tenderly, like a treasure, and Sierra lay there, gazing up at him with pleasure-dazed eyes as he stripped the boxers from his body and then stretched out next to her.

Completely naked, he was magnificent, every muscle perfectly sculpted, the hard ridge of his abdomen begging for her touch. She slid her hand down his toned stomach, a thrill of wonder and pleasure shooting through her at Marco's ragged gasp. It amazed her that she affected him so much. That she had that much power. It was a heady feeling but a serious one, too, because she knew all about the abuse of power.

'You're amazing,' she whispered, and wrapped her fingers around his shaft. His skin was smooth and hot, and it thrilled her.

'*You're* amazing,' he muttered and pulled her to him, sliding a hand between her thighs, where she was still damp from his touch. 'I want you now, Sierra. I want to be inside you.'

'I want you inside me.'

He rolled on top of her, poised at her entrance as a frown furrowed his forehead. 'Birth control…'

She blushed even as she opened herself to him. 'I don't… That is, I'm not on anything.'

In one swift movement Marco rolled off her. Sierra felt the loss of him keenly. 'Marco…'

'I'm sorry. I should have thought of it sooner. I was so wrapped up in you…'

Disappointment made her feel as if she'd swallowed a stone. 'But don't you have anything?'

He arched an eyebrow, a wry smile twisting his lips. 'I wasn't expecting to need *anything* on this trip.'

'You didn't think you'd get lucky?' she teased and his expression turned serious.

'I didn't dare hope, Sierra.'

'Even so…'

'I'm not quite,' he said, 'the super stud you seem to think I am. But thanks, anyway.'

She laughed softly. 'But you must have had plenty of women...' Even if she felt like scratching their eyes out just then.

Marco's expression closed and he shook his head. 'Let's not talk about that. The past is in the past, for both of us.'

She nodded and Marco left the room. He came back seconds later, condom in hand. 'Fortunately, the penthouse is admirably stocked. Now, where were we?'

She arched her body against the sheets, eyebrows raised as a provocative smile curved her mouth. 'Right about here?'

His gaze darkened with desire as he watched her move. 'Yes, I think so. But I'd better check.'

He rolled on the condom and Sierra watched, transfixed by the sight, by the sheer beauty of him. Now would probably be a good time to tell him that she hadn't actually done any of this before. The feel of him in her hand had caused her a twinge of alarm, wondering how he was going to fit inside her. Wondering how the mechanics of this actually worked.

But she didn't want to break the moment, and she knew any explanation she gave would be clumsy and awkward. Marco had said the past was in the past. Better to leave it there.

He lay down next to her again, stirring up the embers of need into roaring flame with just a few touches, his mouth on hers, his hand between her thighs. She arched against him, a sound like a kitten's mewl emerging from her lips.

He laughed softly and then rolled on top of her, braced on his forearms as he nudged at her entrance. 'Are you ready...?'

'Yes,' she panted. *'Yes.'*

He moved inside her and Sierra stiffened instinctively at the entirely unexpected feeling. Her gaze widened and her mouth parted on a soundless gasp. She felt so…full. Invaded, yet in an exciting way. He moved again and she let out a little gasp as the first twinge of discomfort assaulted her.

Marco froze, his face twisted in a grimace of shock and restraint. 'Sierra…'

'I'm all right,' she assured him. 'Just…give me a moment.'

He stared at her in disbelief as she adjusted to the feel of him, her body expanding naturally to accommodate his. The twinges of discomfort receded and she arched upwards to take him more fully into herself. 'You can move,' she whispered. 'Slowly.'

He slid deeper inside and she gasped again, the sensation acute and overwhelming. He froze, and she let out a shaky laugh. 'This isn't quite…'

He touched his forehead to hers, his biceps bulging with the effort of holding himself back. 'Why didn't you tell me?'

'I don't know,' she confessed. 'I didn't want to ruin anything. It seemed so…' She laughed again, softly. 'I don't know.' Maybe part of her had liked the idea of Marco thinking she was experienced, worldly. Maybe part of her had wanted to match him for sophistication and expertise, even though she knew she never could. In some unvoiced corner of her heart she'd wanted to make their positions more equal.

'Are you okay?' he whispered, and she nodded. It hurt more than she'd expected, but within the hurt were flickers of pleasure, and her body arced towards those, seeking them out of instinct. Marco moved again, sliding deeper inside and then out again and Sierra tried to relax. He was so big, and he filled her so completely. It was overwhelming, both emotionally and physically, to be completely *conquered* by another person. She felt him in every nerve, every cell of her body. There was no part of her that he did not possess, and it was a complex and frightening feeling.

'Okay?' he asked again and she laughed, a hiss of sound, as she clutched his shoulders.

'Stop asking me that.'

'I don't want to hurt you.'

'You're not.' Except he was, and in a way she hadn't expected. The physical pain was nothing compared to the emotional onslaught, the sense that Marco Ferranti was battering every defence she had, leaving her completely bare. Exposed and vulnerable and *wanting*.

And even as these feelings crashed over her, pleasure came, too. Tiny at first, little whispers that promised something greater, and her body responded instinctively, arching up towards his as she wrapped her legs around his waist and drew him completely into herself. She could feel him everywhere, and it made tears start in her eyes.

Marco was moving faster now and Sierra found his rhythm and matched it, awkwardly at first and then with more grace as the sensations whirling inside her coalesced and drove her body onwards. The pain had receded and pleasure took its place, so she clutched him and threw her head back, letting out a ragged cry as she climaxed, the feeling more intense than anything she had ever experienced. Marco shuddered on top of her, his body sagging against hers even as he bore his weight on his arms.

He kissed her temple, his lips lingering against her skin. 'That was incredible.'

'Was it?' she asked, her voice trembling a little with everything she felt.

'You have to ask?' He smiled tenderly and smoothed the hair away from her flushed face.

'Well, I don't have much experience of this kind of thing. As you know.' She let out a shaky laugh and averted her face. She was, quite suddenly and inexplicably, near tears and she didn't want Marco to see.

'Sierra…' He trailed his fingers down her cheek, the gesture so tender it brought a lump to her throat. In a few seconds she'd be bawling. 'You should have told me.'

'It didn't feel like the right moment.'

'I'm not sure when a better moment would have been,' he said wryly, and then pulled out of her, rolling away to dispose of the condom. Sierra took the reprieve from his scrutiny to tidy her hair and wipe quickly at her eyes, wrapping the duvet around herself.

Marco glanced back at her, eyes narrowed. Was she so obvious? Could he see the torment and confusion in her eyes, her face? 'Are you sure you're okay?' he asked, and she nodded. 'You don't…you don't regret this?'

'No,' she whispered, because that much was true. Mostly.

He stretched out next to her, unabashedly naked, and tucked a few stray tendrils of hair behind her ear as he studied her face. 'Then why do you look like you're about to cry?'

'Because it's so *much*.' The words burst from her and a few rogue tears trickled down her cheeks. She batted at them impatiently. 'I wasn't expecting to feel so much. And I don't mean physically,' she clarified quickly. 'I'm not talking about the pleasure.'

'I hope you felt that, too.'

'You know I did,' she said, and she sounded almost cross.

Marco frowned, shaking his head. 'Then what?'

Did he not get it? But then maybe Marco hadn't felt the

emotional tidal wave that had pulled her under. Maybe she was the only one who felt so exposed, so vulnerable and needy. She felt as if Marco had stripped away everything she'd had to protect herself and left her reeling, wondering how to recover. Wondering how she would ever live without him even as terror clutched her at the thought of living with him. At being this vulnerable again, ever.

'I need to use the bathroom,' she muttered and wriggled away from him, the duvet snagging about her body.

Marco reached for her arm. 'Sierra—'

'Please, Marco.' She finally freed herself from the bedcovers and hurried towards the en suite bathroom. 'Please just let me be.'

Marco watched Sierra barricade herself in the bathroom, a frown deepening on his face. What the hell had happened? He'd had the most incredible sexual experience of his life, and he'd reduced his lover almost to tears. It didn't make sense. He knew, despite the initial pain, she'd enjoyed herself. He'd felt her climax reverberate through his own body. And he knew she'd been touched emotionally, too, but then so had he. Sex had never felt so important as it did right then.

But Sierra seemed to think that was a bad thing. She'd been tearful, cross, even angry—and why? Because she didn't want to feel those things? She didn't want to have that kind of connection with him?

The answer seemed all too obvious. Swearing under his breath, Marco rose from the bed and reached for his boxers. The intimacy they'd wrapped themselves in moments before was already unspooling, loose threads they might never knit back together, which was just as well. This was a fling, nothing more. No matter what he'd felt moments before.

And yet it still stung that Sierra was withdrawing from him. The possibility that she might regret what had happened filled him with a bitter fury he remembered too well. This time he'd be the one to walk away first. He'd make sure of it.

CHAPTER THIRTEEN

BY THE TIME Sierra emerged from the bathroom twenty minutes later she'd managed to restore her composure. Cloak herself in numbness, just like she used to during her father's rages. Strange that she was using the same coping mechanisms now, after the most intimate and frankly wonderful experience of her life, as she had then.

She unlocked the door to the bathroom and stepped out, thankfully swathed in an enormous terry-cloth dressing gown. Marco was sitting in bed, his back propped against the pillows, his legs stretched out in front of him, his arms folded. His face was unsmiling.

'Better?'

'Yes.' She tucked her hair behind her ears and came gingerly towards the bed. What was the fling protocol now? Should she thank him for a lovely time and beat it to her own bedroom? That was what she wanted to do. She wanted an out, even if the prospect filled her with an almost unbearable loneliness.

Marco arched an eyebrow. 'You're not actually thinking of leaving my bed, are you?'

It disconcerted her that he could guess her thought processes so easily. 'I thought... I thought maybe it was best.'

'Best? How so?' There was a dangerous silky tone to Marco's voice that she remembered from when she'd first seen him at the lawyer's office, and then at the villa. It made alarm prickle along her spine and she took an instinctive step backwards.

'You no doubt want your space, as do I. We know what this is, Marco.'

'What is it?'

'A fling.' She forced herself to say the words, to state it plainly. 'We're agreed on that. Nothing's changed.' Even if she felt as if her whole world had shattered when Marco had made love to her.

Love... How had she not realised how dangerous this would be? How had she not seen how much a so-called fling would affect her?

'And does having a fling mean we can't sleep together?' Marco bit out. 'Does it mean you've got to hightail it from my bed as if you've been scalded?'

Sierra stared at him in surprise, understanding trickling through her. He was *hurt*. He'd taken her sprint to the bathroom as a personal slight. The realisation softened her, evened out the balance of power she'd felt so keenly had been in his favour.

'Maybe you ought to tell me what the rules are. Since I've obviously never been in this situation before.'

'I haven't either, Sierra.' Marco rubbed a hand across his jaw as he gazed at her starkly. 'No other woman has made me feel the way you do.'

Sierra swallowed hard, a thousand feelings swarming her stomach like butterflies. Disbelief. Fear. Hope. Joy. 'Marco...'

'Don't,' he said roughly. 'Like you said, we both know what this is. But you can still stay the night.'

'Is that what you want?'

He hesitated, his jaw tight. 'Yes,' he finally bit out. 'It is.'

'It's what I want, too,' Sierra said softly.

'Good.' Marco held out his arms and she went to him easily. Suddenly it seemed like the simplest thing in the world to accept Marco's embrace. Moments ago she'd wanted to escape, but now she felt there was no other place to be.

Sierra closed her eyes and snuggled against him, wondering how a supposed fling could be so confusing and make her feel so much.

Marco woke slowly, blinking in the sunlight that streamed through the huge windows. Sierra lay curled up in his arms, her cheek resting against his bare chest. They'd slept in each other's arms all night, and Marco had marvelled at how good it had felt, how much he didn't want to move. Even if he should. No matter what he'd said last night, this felt like more than a fling…to him.

Now he eased slowly from Sierra's sleepy embrace and stole downstairs to the living area; dawn was streaking across the city sky and the first rays of sunlight were touching the skyscrapers of midtown in gold.

He gazed out of the window at the beautiful summer morning, but his thoughts were with the woman he'd left upstairs in bed. Sierra was supposed to fly back to England this afternoon. He'd booked her ticket himself. A few weeks ago it hadn't seemed an issue. He'd convinced himself that he wanted her only to open the hotel, not in his bed. In his life. *Maybe even in his heart.*

Marco let out a shuddering breath and pressed his fists to his eyes. He couldn't be in love with Sierra. He'd written off that useless emotion. He'd seen how people who supposedly loved you were able to walk away. His father. His mother. And even Sierra, seven years ago, although at least no love had been involved then. No, then it had only been a lifetime commitment. And if Sierra had been able to walk away from him then, how much more easily could she do it now?

He should let her go. Kiss her goodbye, thank her for the memories and watch her walk onto the plane and out of his life. That would be the sensible thing. It also made him recoil with instinctive, overwhelming revulsion. He didn't want to do that. He wasn't going to do that.

So what was he going to do?

Marco turned away from the window and reached for his laptop. He'd leave the question of Sierra for a little while, at least until she woke up and he got a read on what she was feeling.

He clicked on his home news page, freezing when he saw one of the celebrity headlines: *A Rocci Reunion?*

Quickly, he scanned the article, which covered the hotel opening yesterday. Very little was about the hotel; the journalist was far more interested in lurid speculation about the relationship between him and Sierra. There was even a blurry photo of him and Sierra slow-dancing last night, which infuriated him because no paparazzi had been invited to the private ball. It looked, he decided, like a snap someone had taken on their phone and then no doubt sold to the press.

Marco swore aloud.

'Marco?'

He turned to see Sierra standing in the doorway, an uncertain look on her face. She was wearing that ridiculously huge dressing gown, her hair about her shoulders in tousled golden-brown waves. She looked delectable and yet also nervous.

'Is something wrong?' she asked, and she took a step towards him.

Marco glanced back at his laptop. 'Not exactly,' he hedged. He realised he had no idea what Sierra's reaction to the news article would be. He didn't even know what *his* was. Irritation that someone had so invaded his—their—privacy. And anger that someone was plundering their shared past for a sordid news story. And, underneath all that, Marco realised, he felt fear. Shameful, hateful fear, that Sierra would see this article and be the one to walk away first.

'What does "not exactly" mean, Marco?' Sierra's gaze flicked to his laptop and then back to his face. He'd closed the browser window, thankfully, so she hadn't seen the article. But he knew he couldn't, in all good conscience, keep it from her.

'We've made the news,' he said after a pause. 'Someone must have snapped a photo of us on their phone.'

'On their phone? But why?'

'To sell to a celebrity tabloid.'

'A celebrity tabloid...' She shook her head, bewilderment creasing her forehead. 'But why would a celebrity tabloid want photos of us? I mean...I know I opened the hotel, but it's not as if I'm actually famous.' Her gaze widened. 'Are *you* famous? I mean, that famous?'

'We're famous,' Marco stated flatly. 'Together. Because of our past.'

'You mean...'

'Yes. That's exactly what I mean.' He bit out each word, realising he was sounding angry, but he couldn't keep himself from it. This was the last thing he wanted to have happen now.

'What does it say?'

After a moment's hesitation, Marco clicked to enlarge the browser window. 'See for yourself.'

Sierra stepped forward, her mouth downturned into a frown as the gist of the article dawned on her. '"Will these star-crossed lovers find happiness off the dance floor?"'

she quoted, and then shook her head. 'Goodness,' she murmured faintly.

'I'm sorry. Press were forbidden from coming to the ball. I had no idea something like this would happen.'

'I had no idea our engagement seven years ago was so well known,' Sierra said slowly. 'I thought it had been a quiet affair.'

'Not that quiet. Your father made a public announcement at a board meeting. It was in the papers.'

'Of course. It was business to him. And to you.' She spoke without rancour, and Marco let the comment pass.

The last thing he wanted to talk about now was what had happened all those years ago. He wanted to take Sierra back to bed and he wanted, he knew, for her to stay past this afternoon.

Sierra took a deep breath and turned to face him directly. 'Do you mind? About the article?'

'It's an annoyance. I value my privacy, and yours, as well.'

'Yes, but…' She hesitated, fiddling with the sash of her robe. 'Having it all in the papers? The fact that I… that I left you?'

Tension knotted between his shoulder blades. 'It's not something I particularly relish having bandied about,' he answered, keeping his voice mild with effort. 'But I'm not heartbroken, Sierra.' He'd refused to be.

'Of course not,' she murmured and then nodded slowly. 'I should get ready for my flight.'

'Don't.' The word came out abruptly, a command he hadn't intended to give.

She gazed at him, her eyebrows raised. 'Don't?'

'Don't get ready for your flight. Don't go on your flight.' He held her gaze, willing her to agree.

'But the opening is over, Marco. I'm not needed here any more.'

'Not needed, maybe.' He paused, trying to find the right words. 'We're having fun, though, aren't we?'

Her gaze widened. 'Fun…'

'Why should we end it so soon?' Smiling, he reached for the sash of her robe and tugged on it gently, pulling her towards him. She went, a small smile curving her lips, and triumph roared through him. 'Stay with me,' he said when she'd come close enough for him to slide his hands under her robe, around her waist. Her skin was warm and silky soft. She let out a breathy little gasp of pleasure. 'Stay with me a little while longer.'

'I have a job, you know,' she reminded him, but she didn't sound as if it mattered much.

'Teaching a few after-school lessons? Can't you reschedule?'

She frowned slightly but didn't move away. 'Maybe.'

'Then reschedule.' He pulled her close enough so their hips collided and she could feel how much he wanted her. 'Reschedule, and come with me to LA.' A few more days with her, nights with her, and then perhaps he'd have had enough. Perhaps then he'd be willing to let her go.

It was amazing how tempted she was, and yet not amazing at all because what woman on earth could resist Marco Ferranti when his hands were on her skin and his smile was so seductive?

And yet…to leave her job, her obligations, her life back in London and go with him wherever he beckoned?

'Sierra?' Marco brushed her neck with his lips in a kiss that promised so much more. 'You will come?' He nibbled lightly on her neck and Sierra let out a helpless gasp of pleasure as she reached up to clutch his shoulders so she could steady herself.

'Yes,' she managed, knowing there had never really been any doubt. 'Yes, I'll come with you.'

Later, lying amidst the tangled sheets while she admired the view of Marco's bare and perfect chest, Sierra finally summoned the mental energy to ask, 'Why are you going to LA?'

'I'm hoping to open the next North American Rocci hotel there.'

'Hoping?' Lazily, she ran her hand down the sculpted muscles of his chest, her fingers tracing the ridge of his abdomen before daring to dip lower.

Marco trapped her hand. 'Minx. Wait a few minutes, at least.'

'A few minutes?' Sierra teased. 'And here I thought you were some super stallion with superhero capabilities in the bedroom.'

'I've just proved my capabilities in the bedroom,' Marco growled as he rolled her over so he was on top of her, trapping her with his body. 'But I'll gladly prove it again.'

She smiled up at him, feeling sated and relaxed and happy. Happier than she'd been in a long time, perhaps ever. 'So have you started plans for a hotel in LA?'

'Preliminary plans.' Marco released her, rolling onto his back, but he kept one hand lying on her stomach and Sierra found she liked it. She'd had so few loving touches in her life. Her mother had hugged her on occasion, and her father only in public, but to be caressed and petted and stroked. She felt like a cat. She could almost start purring.

'What's got you looking like the cat who's just eaten the cream?' Marco asked as he shot her an amused look and Sierra laughed.

'I was just comparing myself to a cat, as it happens.'

'Comparing yourself to a cat? Why?'

'Because I like being touched. I feel like I could start purring.'

'And I like touching you.' Marco moved his hand from her stomach to her breasts and then Sierra almost did start purring. 'Very much.'

They spent the day in bed. Although not technically in bed; some time around noon Marco ordered food in and they ate it downstairs in the living area, in their dressing gowns. And some time in the late afternoon Marco ran a deep bath full of scented bubbles and just as Sierra was about to sink into all that bliss he actually joined her.

Water sloshed out of the tub as Sierra scooted to one side and Marco settled himself comfortably, seeming undaunted by the bubbles that clung to his chest.

'I didn't realise you were going to get in with me,' Sierra exclaimed, her voice coming out in a near squeak, and Marco arched an eyebrow.

'Is that a problem?'

'No, but…' How could she explain how it felt even more intimate to share a bath with this man than what they'd done in the privacy of the bedroom? And the things they'd done…

Quickly, Sierra realised she was being ridiculous. 'No, of course not,' she said and slid over so she was next to Marco, their legs tangling under the water. 'Actually, I can think of some interesting ways to wash.'

His gaze became hooded and sleepy as he watched her reach for the soap. 'Can you?'

'Oh, yes.' Her embarrassment and uncertainty, after a day's worth of thorough lovemaking, had fallen away. She felt confident, powerful in her knowledge of how much Marco desired her. 'Yes, indeed,' she murmured and she slid her soapy hands down his chest to his hips. After ev-

erything they'd done together that day she was amazed
that Marco still desired her. But how could she be amazed,
when she still desired him?

'Sierra…' His voice came out on a groan as she stroked
his shaft. She loved giving him pleasure, loved knowing
that she made him this way.

'You're going to kill me,' he muttered and stayed her
hand.

She arched an eyebrow. 'But wouldn't it be a good way
to go?'

'Yes indeed, but I have a lot more life in me yet,' he answered, and then showed her just how much.

Twilight was falling over the city several hours later
as Sierra lay in bed and watched Marco get dressed. 'Are
we going somewhere?' she asked as he pulled on a crisply
ironed dress shirt.

'I have a business meeting,' he said with one swift,
apologetic look towards her. 'It's been wonderful playing
hookey today, but I've got to make back sometime.'

'Oh.' Sierra pulled the rumpled duvet over her naked
body. 'Of course. So you're going out?'

'You can order whatever you like from room service,'
Marco said as he selected a cobalt-blue tie.

Sierra watched him slide his tie in his collar and knot
it with crisp, precise movements. She felt uneasy, almost
hurt, and she wasn't quite sure why. Of course Marco had
business meetings. Of course she couldn't tag along with
him, nor would she want to.

'So.' He turned back to her with a quick smile that didn't
reach his eyes. 'I'll see you later tonight. And tomorrow
we'll go to LA.'

'I haven't even dealt with my plane ticket…'

'I cancelled it.'

She jerked back a little. 'You did?'

Marco was sliding on his jacket and checking his watch. 'Why should you worry about it?'

'But I need to book an alternative return flight...'

He gave her a wolfish smile. 'We don't need to think about that now.' Then he was dropping a distracted kiss on her forehead and hurrying out of the suite, all while she lay curled up in a crumpled duvet and wondered what she'd got herself into.

'A fling,' she said aloud. Her voice sounded small in the huge empty suite. 'You know very well what this is. A fling. You're here for sex.' What had seemed simple and safe now only felt sordid.

She got out of bed, trying to shake off her uncertain and grey mood, and dressed. She didn't feel like ordering takeaway and eating it alone upstairs; she'd go out, explore the city on her own for a bit.

Twenty minutes later Sierra headed downstairs and out of the modern glass doors of the hotel. The foyer was buzzing with guests; clearly the opening had been a success. A few people clearly recognised her, but Sierra ignored their speculative looks. She wasn't going to care about the tabloid article that had come out this morning. It would be forgotten by tomorrow, no doubt.

She strolled down Central Park West towards Columbus Circle, enjoying the way twilight settled on the city and the traffic started to die down. She found a little French bistro tucked onto a side street and went inside. As she sat down and glanced at the menu she realised she was ravenous. She supposed that was what making love all day did to you, and the thought made her smile. She ordered a steak and chips and ate it all and was just heading back outside, feeling replete and happy, when a reporter accosted her.

'Excuse me... Sierra Rocci?'

'Yes?' she answered automatically, before the flashbulb

popped in her face, making her momentarily blind, and the reporter started firing questions.

'Why are you out alone? Have you and Marco Ferranti had a lovers' tiff? Is it true you're staying in the same suite? Why did you jilt him seven years ago—'

'No comment,' Sierra gasped out and hurried away. The reporter kept yelling his awful questions at her, each one sounding like a horrible taunt.

'Did Ferranti cheat on you? Did you cheat on him? Are you together now merely as a business arrangement?'

Finally Sierra rounded the corner and the reporter's questions died away. She kept up a brisk pace all the way to the hotel, only slowing when she came to the front steps. Her heart was thudding and she felt clammy with sweat. She'd thought she could handle the press, but she hadn't been prepared for that.

She'd managed to restore her composure by the time she got into the penthouse lift, and she felt almost normal when the doors opened.

That was until she stepped out and Marco loomed in front of her, his face thunderous, his voice a harsh demand.

'Where the *hell* have you been?'

CHAPTER FOURTEEN

MARCO COULDN'T REMEMBER the last time he'd felt so furious—and so afraid. He'd come up to the penthouse suite expecting to see Sierra still lounging in bed, waiting for him. Instead, the place had been echoing and empty, and when he'd called downstairs the concierge had said she'd left hours ago.

He'd paced the penthouse for a quarter of an hour, trying to stifle his panic and anger, but rational thought was hard when so many memories kept crowding in. He told himself she hadn't taken her clothes and that she wouldn't just leave.

But she'd taken hardly anything when she'd left the night before his wedding. And the possibility that she might have skipped out on him again made everything in him clench. Damn it, he would be the one to say when they were done. And it wasn't yet.

'Well?' he demanded while she simply stared at him. 'Do you have an answer?'

'No,' Sierra stated clearly, her voice so very cold, and she stalked past him.

Marco whirled around, disbelieving. '*No?* You're gone for hours and you can't even tell me where you went?'

'I don't have to tell you anything, Marco,' Sierra tossed over her shoulder. 'I don't owe you anything.'

'How about an explanation?'

She walked up the spiral stairs, one hand on the railing, her head held high. 'Not even that.'

Marco followed her up the stairs and into the bedroom and then watched in disbelief as she took out her suitcase and started putting clothes into it.

'You're packing?'

She gave him a grim smile. 'It looks like it, doesn't it?'

'For LA?'

She stilled and then raised her head, her gaze clear and direct. 'No. For London.'

Fury and hurt coursed through him, choking him so he could barely speak. He didn't want to feel hurt; anger was stronger. 'Damn it, Sierra,' he exclaimed. He raised his hand to do what, he didn't know—touch her shoulder, beseech her somehow—but he stilled when she instinctively flinched as if she'd expected him to strike her.

'Sierra?' His voice was low, her name a question.

She straightened, her expression erased of the cringing fear he'd seen for one alarming second. 'I'm going.'

Marco watched her for a few moments, forcing himself to be calm. He'd overreacted; he could see that now. 'Were you planning on returning to London before you got back to the penthouse?' he asked quietly.

She gave him another one of those direct looks that cut right to his heart. 'No, I wasn't.'

He took a deep breath and then let it out slowly. 'I'm sorry I was so angry.'

She made a tiny shrugging gesture, as if it was of no importance, and yet Marco knew instinctively that it was. 'You flinched just then, almost as if...' He didn't want to voice the suspicion lurking in the dark corners of his mind. And maybe that flinch had been a moment's instinctive reaction, and yet…she'd had such a look on her face, one of terrible fear.

'Almost as if what?' Sierra asked, and it sounded like a challenge.

'Almost as if you expected me to…' He swallowed hard. 'Hit you.'

'I wasn't,' she said after a moment. She took a deep breath and let it out slowly. 'But old habits die hard, I suppose.'

'What do you mean?'

She sighed and shook her head. 'There's no point having this conversation.'

'How can you say that? This might be the most important conversation we've ever had.'

'Oh, Marco.' She looked up at him, and everything in him jolted at the look of weary sorrow in her eyes. 'I wish it could be, but…' She trailed off, biting her lip.

'What do you mean? What aren't you telling me?' She didn't answer and he forced himself not to take a step towards her, not to raise his voice or seem threatening in any way. 'Sierra, did a man…did a man ever hit you?'

The silence following his question seemed endless. Marco felt as if he could scarcely breathe.

Finally Sierra looked up, resignation in every weary line of her lovely face. 'Yes,' she said and then Marco felt a fury like none he'd known before—this time at this unknown man who had dared to hurt and abuse her. He'd *kill* the bastard.

'Who?' he demanded. 'A boyfriend…?'

'No,' she said flatly. 'My father.'

Sierra watched Marco blink, his jaw slackening, as he stared at her in obvious disbelief. She kept packing. Having him yell at her like that had been the wake-up call she needed, and in that moment she'd realised why she'd felt so uneasy earlier, when Marco had left her alone in the suite. She was turning into her mother. Dropping her own life at a man's request, living for his pleasure. There was no way she was walking even one step down that road, and when Marco had shouted at her, looking so angry, Sierra had realised the trap she'd been just about to step into. Thank God she'd realised before it was too late... even if the thought of leaving Marco made her insides twist with grief.

'Your father?' Marco repeated hoarsely. 'Arturo? No.'

'I knew you wouldn't believe me.'

He was shaking his head slowly, looking utterly winded. Sierra almost felt sorry for him.

'But...' he began, and then stopped. She reached for the dress she'd worn to the opening yesterday. 'Sierra, wait.' He grabbed her wrist, gently but firmly, and she went completely still.

He stared at her for a moment, his face white, and then he let her go and backed away, his hands raised like a man about to be arrested. 'You know I would never, ever hurt you.'

'I know that,' she said quietly. She believed it but even with that head knowledge she couldn't keep from fearing. Trust was a hard, hard thing.

Slowly, Marco dropped his hands. Sierra resumed packing. He watched her for several moments and his scrutiny made her hands tremble as she tried to fold her clothes. 'Do you mind?' she finally asked, and to her irritation her voice shook.

'What did you mean—that he hit you?' Marco asked.

'Does it really need explaining?'

'Sierra, your father was as good as my father. I loved him. I trusted him. Yes, it needs explaining.' His voice came out harsh, grating, and she forced herself not to flinch.

'Then let me explain it for you,' she said coolly. She was surprised at how much a relief it was to tell him the truth. She'd been keeping this secret for far too long, first out of fear that he wouldn't believe her, and then because she hadn't wanted to hurt him. Both reasons seemed like pathetic excuses now. 'My father hit me,' Sierra stated clearly. 'Often. He hit my mother, too. He played the doting father and adoring husband for the public, but in private he heaped physical and emotional abuse on us. Slaps, pinches, punches, the lot. And the words…the insults, the sneers, the mockery.' She shook her head, tears stinging her eyes as a lump formed in her throat. 'My mother loved him anyway. I've never been able to understand that. She loved him and wouldn't hear a word against him, although she always tried to protect me from his anger.'

Marco was shaking his head, his body language refuting every word she'd said. 'No…'

'I don't care if you believe me or not,' Sierra said, even though she knew that for a lie. She did care. Far too much. 'But at least now I've said it. Now you know, even if you don't want to.'

She closed her suitcase, struggling with the zip. Marco placed a hand on top of the case. 'Please, Sierra, don't go like this.'

'Why should I stay?'

'Because I want you to stay. Because we've been having a fantastic time.' He took a deep breath. 'Look, this is a tremendous shock to me. It's not that I don't believe you, but give me a few moments to absorb it. Please.'

Slowly Sierra nodded. She could see the sense in what he was saying, even if her instinct was to run. And in truth there was a part of her, a large part, that didn't want to leave. 'Okay,' she said, and then waited.

A full minute passed in silence. Finally Marco said hesitantly, 'Why...why didn't you tell me?'

'Would you have believed me? You hated me, Marco.' It hurt to remind him of that.

'I mean before.' The look he gave her was full of confusion and pain, and it made guilt flash through her like a streak of lightning. 'When we were engaged.'

'Even then you were his right-hand man.'

'But you were going to marry me. How could we have had a marriage, with such a secret between us?'

'I realised we couldn't.'

'Your *father* is why you left?' Marco stared at her in disbelief, his jaw tight.

'In a manner of speaking, I suppose.'

'I don't understand, Sierra.' He raked his hands through his hair and even now, in the midst of all this confusion and misery, Sierra watched him with longing. Those muscled arms had held her so tenderly. She'd nestled against that chiselled chest, had kissed his salty skin. She averted her gaze from him. 'Please help me to understand,' Marco said, and underneath the sadness Sierra heard a note of frustration, even anger, and she tensed.

'I don't know what you want me to say.'

'Anything. Something. Why did you agree to marry me?' The question rang out, echoing through the suite.

Sierra took a deep breath and met his gaze. 'To get away from my father.'

Marco's face paled as his jaw bunched. Sierra kept herself from flinching even though she could tell he was angry. She didn't completely understand why, but she felt it emanating from his taut body. 'That's the only reason?' he asked in a low voice.

Wordlessly she nodded, and then she watched as Marco turned and strode from the bedroom. Alone, she sank onto the bed, her legs suddenly feeling weak. Everything feeling weak. She felt nearer to tears now than she had a few moments ago, and why? Because she'd lost Marco? It was better this way, and in any case she'd never really had him. Not like that.

But it still felt like a loss, a gaping wound that was bleeding out. Another deep breath and Sierra turned to her suitcase. She struggled with the zip, but she finally got it closed. And then she sat there, having no idea what to do. Where to go, if anywhere.

After a few moments she worked up the nerve to lug her suitcase down the spiral staircase. Marco stood in the living room, his back to her as he stared out at the darkened city. She hesitated on the bottom step because now that she was here, she didn't really want to go. Walk out like she did once before, into a dark night, an unknown future.

Yet how could she stay?

The step creaked beneath her and Marco turned around, his dark eyebrows snapping together as he saw her clutching the handle of her suitcase. 'You're still planning to go?' he asked, his voice harsh.

'I don't know what to do, Marco.' She hated the wobble in her voice and she blinked rapidly. Marco swore under his breath and strode towards her.

'Sierra, *cara*, I've been an utter ass. Please forgive me.'

It was the last thing she'd expected him to say. He took the suitcase from her and put it on the floor. Then he stretched out his hands beseechingly, his face a plea. 'Don't go, Sierra. Please. Not yet. Not till I understand. Not till we've made this right.'

'How can we? I know what my father meant to you, and I hate him, *hate* him—' She broke off, weeping, half amazed at the emotion that suddenly burst from her, tears trickling down her cheeks. 'I always have,' she continued, but then her voice was lost to sobs, her shoulders shaking, and Marco had enfolded her in his arms.

She pressed her face into his hard chest as he stroked his hand down her back and murmured nonsense endearments. She hadn't realised she had so many tears left in her and, more than just tears, a deep welling of grief and sorrow, not just for the father she'd had, but for the father she'd never had. For the years of loneliness and fear and frustration. For the fact that even now, seven years on, she was afraid to trust someone. To love someone, and the result was this brokenness, this feeling that she might never be whole.

'I'm sorry,' she finally managed, pulling away from him a bit to swipe at her damp cheeks. Now that the first storm of crying had passed, she felt embarrassed by her emotional display. 'I didn't mean to fall apart...'

'Nonsense. You needed to cry. You have suffered, Sierra, more than I could ever imagine. More than I ever knew.' Sierra heard the sharp note of self-recrimination in Marco's voice and wondered at it. 'Come, let us sit down.'

He guided her to one of the leather sofas and pulled her down next to him, his arm around her shoulders so she was still nestled against him, safe in his arms. Neither of them spoke for a long moment.

'Will you tell me?' Marco finally asked.

Sierra drew a shuddering breath. 'What do you want to know?'

'Everything.'

'I don't know where to begin.'

He nestled her closer to him, settling them both more comfortably. 'Begin wherever you want to, Sierra,' he said quietly.

After a moment she started talking, searching for each word, finding her way slowly. She told him how the first time her father hit her she was four years old, a slap across the face, and she hadn't understood what she'd done wrong. It had taken her decades to realise the answer to that question: nothing.

She told him about how kind and jovial he could be, throwing her up in the air, calling her his princess, showering her and her mother with gifts. 'It wasn't until I was much older that I realised he only treated us that way when someone was watching.'

'And when you were alone?' Marco asked in a low voice. 'Always…?'

'Often enough so that I tried to hide from him, but that angered him, too. No monster likes to see his reflection.'

'And when you were older?'

'I knew I needed to get away. My mother would never leave him. I begged her to, but she refused. She'd get quite angry with me because she loved him.' Sierra shook her head slowly. 'I've never understood that. I know he could be charming and he was handsome, but the way he treated her…' Her voice choked and she sniffed loudly.

'So why didn't you run away? When you were older?'

She let out an abrupt yet weary laugh. 'You make it sound so simple.'

'I don't mean to,' Marco answered. 'I just want to understand. It all seems so difficult to believe.'

How difficult? Sierra wondered. *Did* he believe her? Or even now did he doubt? The possibility was enough to make her fall silent. Marco touched her chin with his finger, turning her face so she had to look at him.

'I didn't mean it like that, Sierra.'

'Do you believe me?' she blurted. The question felt far

too revealing, and even worse was Marco's silence after she'd asked it.

'Yes,' he said finally. 'Of course I do. But I don't want to.'

'Because you loved him.'

Marco nodded, his expression shuttered, his jaw tight. 'You know how I told you my own father left? He was hardly around to begin with, and then one day he just never came back. And my mother…' He paused, and curiosity flared within the misery that had swamped her.

'Your mother?'

'It doesn't matter. What I meant to say is that Arturo was the closest thing to a father that I ever had. I told you how I was working as a bellboy when he noticed me… I would have spent my life heaving suitcases if not for him. He took me out for a drink, told me he could tell I had ambition and drive. Then he gave me a job as an office junior when I was seventeen. Within a few years he'd promoted me, and you know the rest.' He sighed, his arm still around her. 'And all the while he'd encourage me, listen to me… accept me in a way my father never did. To now realise this man I held in such high esteem was…was what you say he was…' Marco's voice turned hoarse. 'It hurts to believe it. But I do.'

'Thank you,' she whispered.

'You don't need to thank me, Sierra.' He paused, and Sierra could tell he was searching for words. 'So you wanted to escape. Why did you choose me?'

'My father chose you,' Sierra returned. 'I was under no illusion about that, although I flattered myself to think I had a bit more discernment and control than I actually did.' She let out a sad, soft laugh. 'Do you know what convinced me, Marco? I saw you stroking a cat, the day I met you. You were in the courtyard, waiting to come in, and one of the street cats wound its way between your legs. You bent down and stroked it. My father would have kicked it away. In that moment I believed you were a gentle man.'

'You sound,' Marco said after a moment, 'as if you now think you were wrong.'

'No, I…' She stopped, biting her lip. It was so difficult to separate what she'd felt then and what she felt now. 'I was going to marry you for the wrong reasons, Marco, back then. I realised that the night before our wedding. No matter what is between us now—and I know it's just a fling—it would have never worked back then. I needed to find my own way, become my own person.'

'So what happened that night?' Marco asked. 'Really?' He sounded as if he were struggling with some emotion, perhaps anger. Sierra could feel how tense his body was.

'Just what I told you. I overheard you talking with my father. I realised just how close you were. I…I hadn't quite realised it before. And then I heard my father give you that awful advice.'

'"I know how to handle her",' Marco repeated flatly. 'I see now why that would have alarmed you, but…couldn't you have asked me, Sierra?'

'And what would I ask, exactly?' The first note of temper entered her voice. '"Will you ever hit me, Marco?" That's not exactly a question someone will answer honestly.'

'I would have.'

'I wouldn't have believed you. That's what I realised that night, Marco. I was taking too great a risk. It was about me as much as it was about you.'

'So you ran away, just as you could have done before we'd ever become engaged.'

'Not exactly. My mother helped me. When I told her I didn't love you…' Sierra trailed off uncertainly. Of course

Marco knew she hadn't loved him then. He hadn't loved her. And yet it sounded so cold now.

'Yes? When you told her that, what did she do?'

'She gave me some money,' Sierra whispered. 'And the name of a friend in England I could go to.'

'And you just walked out into the night? Into Palermo?'

'Yes. I was terrified.' She swallowed hard, the memories swarming her. 'Utterly terrified. I'd never been out alone in the city—any city—before. But I hailed a taxi and went to the docks. I waited the rest of the night in the ferry office, and then I took the first boat to the mainland.'

'And then to England? That must have been quite a journey.' Marco didn't sound impressed so much as incredulous.

'Yes, it was. I took endless trains, and then I was spat out in London with barely enough English to make myself understood. I got lost on the Tube and someone tried to pickpocket me. And when I went to find my mother's friend, she'd moved house. I spent a night at a women's shelter and then used a computer in a library to locate the new address of my mother's friend, and she finally took me in.'

'So much effort to get away from me,' Marco remarked tonelessly and Sierra jerked away from him.

'No, to get away from my father. It wasn't about you, Marco. I keep telling you that.'

He gazed at her with eyes the colour of steel, his mouth a hard line. 'How can you say that, Sierra? It most certainly was about me. Yes, it was about your father, as well, I understand that. But if you'd known me at all, if you'd trusted me at all, you would never have had to go to London.'

She recognised the truth of his words even if she didn't want to. 'Understandably,' she answered stiffly, 'I have had difficulties with trusting people, especially men.'

Marco sighed, the sound one of defeat, his shoulders slumping. 'Understandably,' he agreed quietly. 'Yes.'

Sierra stood up, pacing the room, her arms wrapped around her body. Suddenly she felt cold. She had no idea if what she'd told Marco changed things. Then she realised that of course it changed things; she had no idea how much.

'What now?' she finally asked, and she turned to face him. He was still sitting on the sofa, watching her, his expression bland. 'Should I leave?' she forced herself to ask. 'I can go back to London tonight.'

Marco didn't look away; he didn't so much as blink. 'Is that what you want?'

Was it? Her heart hammered and her mouth went dry. Here was a moment when she could try to trust. When she could leap out and see if he caught her. If he wanted to. 'No,' she whispered. 'It isn't.'

Marco looked startled, and then a look of such naked relief passed over his face that Sierra sagged with a deep relief of her own.

He rose from the sofa and crossed the room, pulling her into his arms. 'Good,' he said, and kissed her.

CHAPTER FIFTEEN

MARCO GAZED OUT at the azure sky, his eyes starting to water from staring at its hard brightness for so long. The plane was minutes away from touching down in LA and he'd barely spoken to Sierra for the six hours of the flight.

He'd wanted to. He'd formed a dozen different conversation openers in his mind, but everything sounded wrong in his head. He had a feeling it would sound worse out loud. The trouble was, since her revelation last night he hadn't known how to approach her. *How to handle her.*

Guilt churned in his stomach as he replayed in his mind all that Sierra had told him. It was a form of self-torture he couldn't keep himself from indulging in. A thousand conflicting thoughts and feelings tormented him: sadness for what Sierra had endured, guilt for his part in it, confusion and grief for what he'd felt for Arturo, a man he'd loved but who had been a monster beyond his worst imaginings.

In the end, beyond a few basic pleasantries about the trip and their destination, he'd stayed silent, and so had Sierra. It seemed easier, even if it made him an emotional coward.

'Please fasten your seat belts as we prepare for landing.'

Marco glanced at Sierra, trying for a reassuring smile. She smiled back but he could see that it didn't reach her eyes, which were the colour of the Atlantic on a cold day.

Wintry grey-blue, no thaw in sight. Was she angry at him? Did she blame him somehow for what had happened before? How on earth were they going to get past this?

Which begged another question—one he was reluctant to answer, even to himself. Why did they need to get past this? What kind of future was he envisioning with Sierra?

A few days ago he'd wanted to be the one to walk away first. But a realisation was emerging amidst all his confusion and regret—he didn't want to walk away at all.

But how could they build a relationship on such shaky, crumbling foundations of mistrust and betrayal? And how could he even want to, when he had no idea what Sierra wanted? When he'd been so sure he'd never love someone, never want to love someone?

'Are you looking forward to seeing Los Angeles?' he asked abruptly, wanting to break the glacial silence as well as keep from the endless circling of his own thoughts.

'Yes, thank you,' Sierra replied, and her tone was just as carefully polite. They were acting like strangers, yet maybe, after all they hadn't known about each other, they *were* strangers.

The next hour was taken up with deplaning and then retrieving their luggage; Marco had arranged for a limo to be waiting outside.

Once they'd slid inside its luxurious leather depths, the soundproof glass cocooning them in privacy, the silence felt worse. More damning.

And still neither of them spoke.

'Where are we staying?' Sierra finally asked as the limo headed down I-405. 'Since there isn't a Rocci hotel here yet?'

'The Beverly Wilshire.' He managed a small smile. 'I need to check out my competition.'

'Of course.' She turned back to the window, her gaze

on the palm trees and billboards lining the highway. The silence stretched on.

Sierra admired the impressive Art Deco foyer of the hotel, and when a bellboy escorted them to the private floor that housed the penthouse suite, Marco experienced a little dart of satisfaction at how awed she looked. It might not be a Rocci hotel, but he could still give her the best. He wanted to give her the best.

And the penthouse suite *was* the best: three bedrooms, four marble bathrooms, a media room, plus the usual dining room, living room and kitchen. But best of all was the spacious terrace with its panoramic views of the city.

Sierra stepped out onto the terrace, breathed in the hot, dry air of the desert. She glanced up at the scrubby hills that bordered Los Angeles to the north. 'It almost looks like Sicily.'

'Almost,' Marco agreed.

'I don't know if we need such a big suite,' she said with a small teasing smile. 'Three bedrooms?'

'We can sleep in a different one each night.'

Her smile faltered. 'How long are you planning on staying here?'

Marco noted the 'you' and deliberately kept his voice even and mild. 'I'm not sure. I want to complete the preliminary negotiations for The Rocci Los Angeles, and I don't need to be back in Palermo until next week.' He shrugged. 'We might as well stay and enjoy California.' *Enjoy each other.* He only just kept himself from saying it.

'I have a job to get back to,' Sierra reminded him. 'A life.'

And she was telling him this why? 'You have a freelance job,' Marco pointed out. 'What is that if not flexible?'

Her eyebrows drew together and she looked away. So he'd said the wrong thing. He'd known he would all along.

Sierra walked back into the suite and after a moment Marco followed. When he came into the living area he saw how lost she looked, how forlorn.

'I think I might take a bath,' she said without looking at him. 'Wash away the travel grime.'

'All right,' Marco answered, and in frustration he watched her walk out of the room.

Could things get more awkward and horrible? With a grimace Sierra turned the taps of the huge sunken marble tub on full blast. She didn't know what she regretted more: telling Marco the truth about her father or coming with him to LA. The trouble was, she still wanted to be with him. She just didn't know how they were going to get past this seeming roadblock in their relationship.

Whoa. You don't have a relationship.

She might be halfway to falling in love with him, but that didn't mean Marco felt the same. He'd made it abundantly clear that they were only having a fling and, in any case, she didn't even *want* him to feel the same. She didn't want to be in love herself. Not when she'd seen what it had done to her mother. Not when she'd felt what it could do to herself.

Since meeting Marco again her whole world had been tangled up in knots. Since making love with him she'd felt happier and yet more frightened than she ever had in the last seven years. Happiness could be so fleeting, so fragile, and yet, once discovered, so unbearably necessary. How much was it going to hurt when Marco was gone from her life?

Better to make a quick, clean cut. She'd told herself that yesterday and yet here she was. She was more like her mother than she'd ever wanted to be. Filled with regret and uncertainty, Sierra closed her eyes.

She almost didn't hear the gentle tapping at the bathroom door. She opened her eyes, alert, and then heard Marco call softly, 'Sierra? May I come in?'

She glanced down at her naked body, covered by bubbles. Everything in her seemed to both hesitate and yearn.

'All right,' she said.

Slowly the door opened. Marco stepped inside the steamy bathroom; he'd changed his business suit for faded jeans and a black T-shirt that clung to his chest. His hair was rumpled, his jaw shadowed with stubble, his eyes dark and serious.

'I haven't known what to say to you.'

Sierra gazed at him with wide eyes. She felt intensely vulnerable lying naked in the bath, and yet she recognised that Marco had come in here for a reason. An important reason. 'I haven't known what to say, either.'

'I wish I had the right words.'

'So do I,' she whispered.

Slowly Marco came towards her. Sierra watched him, her breath held, her heart beating hard. 'May I help you wash?' he asked and she stared at him, paralysed by indecision and longing. Finally, wordlessly, she nodded.

She watched as Marco reached for the bar of expensive soap the hotel provided and lathered his hands. He motioned for her to lean forward and after a moment she did and he began to soap her back. His touch was gentle, almost hesitant, and it felt loving. It also felt incredibly intimate, even more so than the things they'd done together in bed. Yet there was nothing overtly sexual about his touch as he slid his hands up and down her back. It felt almost as if he were offering some kind of penance, asking for absolution. Almost as if this act was as intimate and revealing for him as it was for her.

She let out a shuddering breath as he pressed a kiss

to the back of her neck. Desire, like liquid fire, spread through her as he kissed his way down the knobs of her spine.

'Marco...'

'Let me make love to you, Sierra.'

She nodded her assent and in one easy movement he scooped her up from the tub and, cradling her in his arms, he brought her back to the master bedroom. Sierra gazed up at him with huge eyes as he laid her down on the bed and then stripped his clothes from his body.

She held her arms out and he went to her, covering her body with his own, kissing her with a raw urgency she hadn't felt from him before. And she responded in kind, kiss for kiss, touch for touch, both of them rushed and desperate for each other, until Marco finally sank inside her, buried deep, her name a sob in his throat as they climaxed together.

Afterwards they lay quietly as their heart rates returned to normal and honeyed sunlight filtered through the curtains.

She would miss this, Sierra thought, when it was over. And despite the tenderness Marco had just shown her, despite the fierce pleasure of their lovemaking, she knew it would be over soon. She felt it in the way Marco had already withdrawn back into the shuttered privacy of his thoughts, his eyebrows drawn together as he stared up at the ceiling. She had no idea what he was thinking or feeling. Moments ago he'd been the most loving, gentle man she could have imagined, and now?

She sighed and stirred from the bed. 'I should dress.'

He barely glanced at her as he reached for his clothes. 'We can order room service if you like.'

'I'd rather go out.' She wanted to escape the oppressive silence that had plagued them both since last night.

'Very well,' Marco answered, and he didn't look at her as he started to dress.

An hour later they were seated at an upmarket seafood restaurant off Rodeo Drive. Sierra perused the extensive and exotic menu while Marco frowned down at the wine list.

'So what business do you have to do here exactly?' she asked after they'd both ordered.

'I'm meeting with the real estate developers to agree on the site for the new hotel.'

'Where is it?'

'Not far from here. A vacant lot off Wilshire Boulevard.' He drummed his fingers on the table, seeming almost impatient, and Sierra couldn't help but feel nettled.

'Sorry, am I wasting your time?' she asked tartly and Marco turned to her, startled.

'No, of course not.'

'It's just you seem like you can't wait to get away.'

'*I* seem…?' Now he looked truly flummoxed. 'No, of course not.'

Sierra didn't answer. Maybe the problem was with her, not with Marco. She could feel how his changing moods affected her, made her both worry and want to please him. Had her mother been like this, wondering if her husband would come home smiling or screaming? Bracing herself for a kiss or a kick?

She couldn't stand the see-sawing of emotions in herself, in Marco. The endless uncertainty. It had been better before, when she hadn't cared so much. That was the problem, Sierra realised. She really was starting to love him. Maybe she already did.

Cold fear clawed at her. *So much for a fling.* How had she let this happen? How had he slipped under her defences and reached her heart, despite everything? She'd never wanted love, never looked for it, and yet it had found her anyway.

'Is something wrong?'

Sierra jerked her gaze up to Marco's narrowed one. 'No...'

'It's just that you're frowning.'

'Sorry.' She shook her head, managed a rather sick smile. 'I'm just tired, I suppose.'

Marco regarded her quietly, clearly unconvinced by her lie. 'My business should only take a few days,' he said. 'I'll be done by the day after tomorrow. Maybe then we could go somewhere. Palm Desert...'

For a second Sierra imagined it: staying in a luxurious resort, days of being pampered and nights spent in Marco's arms. And then, after a few days, what would happen? Maybe he would ask her to go with him to Palermo. Maybe there would be more shopping trips and fancy restaurants and gala events. But eventually he would tire of her tagging along with him, leaving her own life far behind, just as her mother had. And even if he didn't tire of her, what would she be but a plaything, a pawn?

And yet still she was tempted. *This was what love did to you.* It wrecked you completely, emotionally, physically—everything. It took and took and took and gave nothing back.

Marco frowned as he noted her lack of response. 'Sierra?'

'How long would we go to Palm Desert for?'

Marco shrugged. 'I don't know—a few days? I told you, I have to be back in Palermo next week.'

'Right.' And never mind what she had to do. Of course. Sierra took a deep breath. This felt like the hardest thing she'd ever said, and yet she knew it had to be done. 'I don't think so, Marco.'

His mouth tightened and his eyes flashed. She knew he'd taken her meaning completely. Before he could respond the waiter came with their wine, a bottle of champagne that now seemed like a mockery, the loud sound of the cork popping a taunt.

The waiter poured two flutes with a flourish, the fizz going right to the top. Marco took one of the flutes and raised it sardonically.

'So what shall we toast?'

Sierra could only shake her head. She felt swamped with misery, overwhelmed by it. She didn't want things with Marco to end like this, and yet she didn't know how else they could end. Any ending was bound to be brutal.

'To nothing, then,' Marco said, his voice hard and bitter, and drank.

CHAPTER SIXTEEN

HE WAS LOSING HER, and he couldn't even say he was surprised. This was what happened when you loved someone. They left.

And he loved Sierra. Had loved her for a long time. And even though he'd been telling himself he would walk away, Marco knew he didn't want to. Ever. He wanted to love Sierra, to go to sleep with her at night and wake up with her in the morning. To hold her in his arms, hold their child in his arms. To experience everything life had to offer, good and bad, with her.

Marco put down his empty champagne flute, his insides churning with the realisation. He loved Sierra and she was slipping away from him every second.

'I think perhaps I'm not hungry after all,' she said quietly. Her face was pale, her fingers trembling as she placed the napkin on the table and rose from her seat.

She was leaving him, in a public restaurant? The papers would have a field day. Quickly, Marco rose, taking her elbow as he steered her out of the restaurant.

She jerked away from him the moment they were out on the street. '*Don't* manhandle me.'

'Manhandle?' he repeated incredulously. 'There were bound to be reporters in there, Sierra. Paparazzi. I was just trying to get us out of there without a scene.'

She shook her head, rubbing her elbow as if he'd hurt her. He suddenly felt sick.

'You think I'd hurt you? After everything?'

'No,' she said, but she didn't sound convinced. She'd never trust him, Marco realised. Never mind love him. Not after everything that had happened with Arturo, and not with how close he'd been to the man. The memories ran too deep. No matter what either of them felt, they had no chance.

'Let's go back to the hotel,' he said tersely and hailed a cab.

Back at the penthouse suite, Sierra turned to face him. 'I think I should leave,' she said, voice wobbling and chin held high.

'At least you had the decency to tell me this time,' Marco answered before he could keep himself from it. He felt too emotionally raw to be measured or calm.

Her face paled but she simply nodded and turned away. He sank onto a sofa, his head in his hands, as he listened to her start to pack.

He told himself it was better this way. The past held too much power for them to ever have a real relationship, if that was even what Sierra wanted.

But it was what he wanted. What he needed. Was he really going to let Sierra walk out of his life a second time?

The force of his feelings felt like a hammer blow to his heart, leaving him breathless. He *loved* this woman, loved her too much to let her walk away. Again.

But that was what people did. His father, his mother, Sierra. They'd all left him, slipped out without saying goodbye, leaving him with nothing to do but wait and grieve.

But this time he had a choice. He had a chance to talk to Sierra honestly, to ask or even beg her to stay. He wouldn't be proud. He loved her too much for that. The realisation sent adrenaline coursing through him and he rose from the sofa, pacing the room as panic roared through him. What if she said no? What if she still left?

Sierra emerged from the bedroom, her face still pale, her suitcase clutched in one hand. 'I can call for a taxi…'

'Don't.' The word came out like a command, and far too aggressive. Sierra blinked, then set her jaw. She didn't like him ordering her around, and he could understand that. He respected it, liked her—no, *loved* her—more for it.

'Please,' he burst out. 'Sierra, I don't want you to walk out of my life again.'

She hesitated and he took the opportunity to walk towards her, take the suitcase from her unresisting hand. 'Please listen to me for just a few minutes. And if you still want to leave after I'm done, I won't stop you, I promise.' His voice was hoarse, his heart beating painfully hard.

Sierra nibbled her lip, her wide eyes searching his face, and then finally she nodded. 'All right,' she whispered.

He led her over to the sofa and she sat down but he found he couldn't. He had too much raw energy coursing through him for that. 'I don't want you to go,' he said as he paced in front of her. 'I don't want you to go today or tomorrow or the day after that.' The words burst from him, a confession that hurt even though he knew he needed to make it. For once in his life he was fighting for what he wanted, who he loved, and even in this moment of intense vulnerability it made him feel powerful. Strong. *Love* made him strong. 'I don't want you to go ever, Sierra.'

'It hasn't been working, Marco.' Her voice was soft and sad. 'There's too much history…'

'I know there is, but we're giving the past too much power.' He dropped to his knees in front of her and took her cold hands in his. 'I love you, Sierra. I only realised how much when you were about to walk out that door. I've been a fool and an ass and whatever other name you want to throw at me. I deserve it. When you told me about your father, I didn't know how to handle it. I felt guilty and hurt and betrayed all at once, and I was afraid you'd always associate me with him, you'd never be able to trust or love me. And maybe you won't but I want to try. I want to try with you. Not just a fling, but something real. A relationship. Marriage, children—the fairy tale if we can both believe in it.'

Tears sparkled in her eyes and she clung to his hands. 'I don't know if I can. My mother loved my father and look what it did to her. It killed her in the end, maybe not literally, but she was never the person she could have been. She was like a shadow, a ghost—'

'That wasn't love. Love builds up, not breaks down. I have to believe that. I want the best for you, Sierra—'

'To follow you around from one Rocci hotel to another?' she burst out. 'I don't want to live in your shadow, Marco.'

'And you don't have to. We can make this work. I realise your life in London is important. I won't ask you to drop it to follow me around. I want you to be happy, Sierra, but I want you to be happy with me. If you think you can.' He held his breath, waiting for her answer.

'I want to be,' she finally said, her voice hesitant.

'I know I've made a lot of mistakes. I've let the past affect me more than I wanted it to. Not just your leaving, but my father's. And…' He paused because this was something he'd never told another person '…my mother.'

Sierra frowned. 'Your mother?'

'She left when I was ten,' Marco admitted quietly. 'After my father walked out she tried to hold things together, but it was tough as a single mother in a conservative country. She ended up taking me to an orphanage in Palermo, run by monks. She said she'd come back for me, but she never did.'

Tears filled Sierra's eyes. 'Oh, Marco...'

'I stayed until I was sixteen, and then I got the job at The Rocci. I tried never to look back, but I've realised I was looking back all the time, letting the past affect me. Control me. That's why I took your leaving before so badly. Why I've been afraid to love anyone.'

She bit her lip, a single tear sliding down her cheek, devastating him. 'I've been afraid, too.'

Gently, Marco wiped the tear from her cheek. 'Then let's be afraid together. I know it might be hard and there will be arguments and fears and all the rest of it. But we can find the fairy tale, Sierra. Together. I believe that. I have to believe that.'

Sierra gazed at him, her eyes filled with tears and yet also a dawning wonder, a fragile hope. 'Yes,' she said. 'I believe that, too.' And then, as Marco's heart trembled with joy, she leaned forward and kissed him.

EPILOGUE

Three years later

SIERRA STOOD AT the window of their London townhouse and watched as Marco came inside, whistling under his breath. A smile softened her features as she watched him, loving how light and happy he looked. There had been so much happiness over the last three years.

Not, of course, that it had been easy or simple. She and Marco had both had so many fears and hurts to conquer. So many mountains to climb. And yet they'd climbed them, hand in hand, struggling and searching, together.

They'd married in a quiet ceremony two years ago, and then decided to split their time between Palermo and London; Sierra continued with her music teaching, using holiday time to travel with Marco to various hotels all over the world. The Rocci Los Angeles had opened last year and Marco already had plans to open another hotel in Montreal, although he'd promised to reduce his work schedule in the next few months.

'Sierra?' His voice floated up the stairs and Sierra called back.

'I'm in the nursery.'

Grinning, Marco appeared in the doorway, his warm glance resting on the gentle swell of Sierra's bump. They were expecting a baby girl in just over three months—a new generation, a wonderful way to redeem the past and forge a future together.

'You're feeling all right?' he asked as he came towards her.

Laughing, she shook her head. 'You don't have to coddle me, Marco.'

'I want to coddle you.' He slid his arms around her, resting his hands over her bump. She laced her fingers with his, savouring his gentle touch.

That had been another mountain to climb: forcing her fears back and trusting in Marco's love and goodness. And he'd been so good, so gentle and patient with her in so many ways. It had taken her a few years before she felt brave enough to start a family, to trust Marco not only with her own heart but the heart of their child's.

The reality of their baby, their joined flesh, had made their marriage all the stronger. Sierra had never looked back.

As if agreeing with her, their baby kicked beneath their joined hands. Marco laughed softly. 'I felt that one.'

'She's a strong one,' Sierra answered with a little laugh and leaned her head back against Marco's shoulder.

'Just like her mother, then,' Marco said, and kissed her.

* * * * *

BEST MAN
FOR THE
BRIDESMAID

JENNIFER FAYE

For Linda

To an amazing lady who has
a heart as big as Texas.

Thanks for your guidance and support
over the years. This one is for you!

CHAPTER ONE

ALWAYS A BRIDESMAID...

Jules Lane lifted her chin and smiled broadly.

Her steps grew quicker as she made her way past the other departing passengers. At last she was in Rome. Rome, Italy, to be exact. She continued to grin and resisted the urge to pinch herself just to make sure this wasn't a dream.

On the other hand, this wasn't exactly a vacation. She was here for an important job—to help plan her foster sister's wedding. This wouldn't be Jules's first time down the aisle. She'd been a bridesmaid more times than she could count on one hand.

However, this time around she had the privilege of being the maid of honor. It was a role she eagerly anticipated. She liked to take charge —to provide order to chaos. She wasn't a closet romantic. She didn't dream about finding Prince Charming. She didn't fantasize about her "big day." But she did have a thing for pretty dresses and cake—cake was definitely her weakness.

Actually now that she thought about it, Lizzie, her foster sister, hadn't been into romance, either...at least not until she'd flown here three months ago for a television show—a reality segment about cooking. Cupid sure seemed to have hit the mark with Lizzie and Dante.

For most of Jules's life, Lizzie had been the keeper of her secrets, her protector and her only family. Jules loved her with all her heart. But that security came with a steep price tag for both of them—learning at an early age that they only had each other to lean on.

Now it was time for a change—if only Jules could find a way to tell Lizzie her news.

Jules sighed as she made her way through the Leonardo da Vinci terminal. She'd find the right time. She just had to have patience.

The strap of her carry-on dug into her shoulder, and she struggled to adjust it. The black-and-white cloth bag was weighted down with a wedding planner, a big bag of sour candies and plenty of bridal magazines with dog-eared pages and sticky notes. She had everything necessary to plan the perfect wedding—except for one very important but necessary ingredient: caffeine. But no worries—Lizzie had been raving about the delicious coffee Rome had to offer.

Considering no details about the wedding had been tacked down, there would be long conversations over this now-infamous coffee. First, they had to nail down a wedding date. Jules was thinking a spring wedding next year. It'd be perfect as Lizzie had mentioned something about an Italian vineyard as the backdrop. Talk about some amazing photos.

This wedding-planning stuff shouldn't be too hard. After all, Jules had most of it memorized by this point. Now she'd be able to put all of that knowledge to good use.

Boisterous voices filled the terminal as friends greeted each other. An American family called frantically for their son, who stood ten steps away checking out the cell phones that a beautiful woman with long dark hair and a brilliant smile was eager to show the teenager. Jules took it all in as she strode through the congested concourse, following the signs to the baggage claim.

She couldn't wait to see Lizzie. It felt like an eternity since they'd seen each other. And she was looking forward to meeting her future brother-in-law, Dante. Lizzie swore the photos she'd emailed didn't do him justice. That was hard to believe since Jules had found him quite handsome.

She walked over to the luggage carousel, hoping her suitcase had made the journey and hadn't been lost along the way. All the while, she kept glancing around for Lizzie. Where could she be? It wasn't like her to be late.

Jules's gaze strayed across to a tall dark-haired man at the other end of the luggage return area. He spoke to a pretty young woman, who shook her head and turned away. And then he moved on to the next young woman. What was that all about?

Jules shrugged and turned away. She pulled the phone from her pocket, hoping a message from Lizzie would pop up, but instead a dead battery symbol flashed on the screen and then everything went black. Jules sighed. This couldn't be happening to her while she was all alone in a foreign country. She'd charged it before she left New York, hadn't she?

"*Scusi.* Are you Ms. Lane?" A deep male voice immediately drew her attention.

She turned to find the same dark-haired man speaking to a woman a couple of people down from her. Was he looking for her? How did he know her name?

When the blonde woman wearing a pastel flowered dress shook her head, he moved on. He skipped over an older woman, not even bothering to ask her. And then his gaze skimmed over Jules's pigtails, long-sleeved black top, purple-and-black plaid miniskirt and knee-high platform black boots. His facial expression remained neutral, but he didn't say a word to her as he moved on down the line.

Seriously? He was that put off by her appearance that he wasn't even going to speak to her? She turned her back to him. Then she realized he might have a message from Lizzie. Jules turned back around.

He stopped at the next young woman. "*Scusi*, are you Julianne—"

"Hey, mister." When he turned to her with a raised brow, she had to fight back a laugh. "I'm Julianne Lane."

He apologized to the young lady before backtracking and stopping directly in front of Jules. His forehead was creased. "*Signorina*, you are Lizzie's sister?"

She nodded. Her pigtails bobbed. He wasn't the first person to be surprised by her unconventional appearance. She'd given up a long time ago trying to live up to everyone's expectations. And she'd been dressing this way so long now that it came naturally.

The same couldn't be said about him. He looked as if he'd just walked off the cover of a men's fashion magazine. His navy blue suit was perfectly tailored to show off his broad shoulders, and the gray dress shirt was unbuttoned just enough to show off a hint of his muscular chest.

Jules swallowed hard. *Wow!* No wonder Lizzie lost her heart here. They sure made them hot and sexy in Italy.

With effort, she forced her gaze upward to meet his serious stare. "Is there a problem?"

"Umm…no." The lines on his forehead smoothed. "Lizzie is your sister, isn't she?"

Jules's chest tightened. "Yes. Is she all right?"

His dark brows rose as his warm brown eyes seemed to hold her captive. "Yes, she is."

Jules breathed out a pent-up breath. "Don't do that."

"Do what?"

"Scare me. I thought something had happened to my sister."

"I assure you that she's perfectly fine. But something came up and she asked me to pick you up."

"You should have said that part first." She glanced over at the luggage carousel, which had started to move. Before she could ask him anymore questions, the luggage appeared on the conveyor belt. "I'll be right with you. I just need to grab my bag."

She could feel the man's curious gaze boring into her back. She wondered what he was thinking, but something told her she was better off not knowing.

And then her black suitcase with the large white circle pattern dropped onto the conveyer belt. She shifted her carry-on so that it was resting against her back and out of her way to grab the large piece of luggage.

As she reached for it, the man stepped between her and the belt. "Let me grab that for you. Which is it?"

"Don't bother. I've got it." She didn't need him going out of his way for her. She wasn't some spoiled rich girl. Not by anyone's imagination. She'd been taking care of herself for a long time. Maybe that's what always scared men off. She didn't need them.

The man's eyes widened as he backed away. "Ms. Lane, I only meant to help."

She grabbed the suitcase and swung it around to place it on the floor beside her. "I appreciate your offer, but I'm used to taking care of myself. And, by the way, I prefer to go by Jules. Who would you be?"

"I'm Stefano DeFiore. Dante's older brother."

Lizzie had mentioned in passing that Dante had a brother, but she'd never mentioned how good-looking he was or that he would be meeting her at the airport. "Nice to meet you."

She smiled and stuck out her hand. He hesitated for a moment before glancing quickly to the left and then to the right before his hand encased hers. Was he looking around to see if anyone noticed that he hadn't gotten her luggage for her? Really? He was that worried about what everyone thought?

And then the smile slipped from her face. Her stomach plummeted. She realized the real reason for his awkwardness. He was embarrassed to be seen with her.

What kind of family was Lizzie marrying into?

Stefano DeFiore found himself utterly mesmerized—and that was something that he never let happen.

He struggled to keep his gaze anywhere but on the delicate tiny blue—or was it purple?—butterfly body art flirting with the beginning of the swell of her breasts... just above the diving neckline of her black top. He found it and her absolutely fascinating. And that was not good.

He swallowed hard and drew his focus back up to her face. His brother and his soon-to-be sister-in-law should have picked up Jules—not him. But family takes care of family.

Jules was undeniably intriguing but not in the usual manner. Her goth style was unique, to say the least. And then there was the purplish lipstick, heavy black eyeliner and the stuff on her eyelashes that set off her look. He was anxious to see the woman beneath it all.

He certainly didn't know what to make of Julianne—erm—Jules. Lizzie hadn't given any hints that her sister was so different from her in every way. Lizzie was tall, fair and blonde; Jules was the opposite. She was shorter in stature with dark brown hair in twin ponytails and long sweeping bangs that she brushed off to the side.

Realizing he was staring, he said, "We should get moving. Lizzie should be done with her meeting when we get there."

"Get where?" Jules eyed him as though she wasn't planning to budge.

She didn't trust him. It was a new experience for him. There had been a time in his life when he didn't have a problem putting the female persuasion at ease. But he wasn't exactly acting like the old smooth-talking guy he used to be. Things had changed a lot in recent years.

Combine that with his concerns over his younger brother's sudden wedding announcement and the fact that he'd been elected to play chauffeur today without so much as waiting for him to agree and he was left feeling out of sorts.

Stefano swallowed down his agitation and tried to soften his tone. "I'm dropping you off at Dante's place, Ristorante Massimo. It's not that far from here."

She gave him one last hard look as though making up her mind about him. "Sounds like a plan. Let's get moving."

He reached for her suitcase but then hesitated, recalling how she'd expressed her desire to remain independent. He returned his hand to his side as she extended the handle on her luggage. He merely shook his head and turned away. His lack of understanding where women were concerned had cost him dearly not so long ago. Since then he'd learned to refrain from flirting with them. Relationships were a thing of the past for him.

So then why did he find Jules so intriguing? He couldn't help casting her the occasional glance. It had to be her pigtails. Did grown women really wear those? He smiled. They did look cute on her.

But it was the butterfly that kept him distracted. He pictured it in his mind's eye. He had to admit that he'd never been intrigued by a tattoo before. His late wife had had a fear of needles, so getting any sort of body art wasn't even a possibility. And they'd lived out in the country where that sort of thing wasn't popular in the nearby village.

When his shoulder collided with someone, he glanced up. *"Scusi."*

He could feel Jules's gaze on him, but he pretended not to notice. He wasn't about to let on that her little butterfly had him distracted to the point of not watching where he was walking. After all, he was a DeFiore. DeFiores didn't allow themselves to be distracted.

Once they were situated in his sleek black luxury sedan, which he only used when escorting around special guests of the DeFiore Vineyard, he turned to Jules. Her body was stiff and her hands were clasped in her lap. He supposed that was to be expected. He hadn't exactly made her feel welcome. He really needed to try harder. After all, it was important to Dante that this visit go well.

Stefano was about to say something when that darn butterfly once again snagged his attention. It rose and fell with her every breath. He was being ridiculous. It was just an inconsequential tattoo—that teased and taunted him.

He turned and stared blindly out the windshield. "Is this your first trip to Rome?"

"Yes, it is." Jules turned to him, but he kept his gaze directly ahead. "What happened? I mean, Lizzie was supposed to pick me up."

"She didn't tell you?"

"No. My phone battery died, so I haven't been able to talk to her."

This was his chance to see what Jules thought of the impending nuptials. He was curious to see if she thought they were a bit rushed. "When Dante called, he said that the announcement of their engagement made a big splash with the paparazzi, and the studio heads wanted to figure out how to work the wedding into an upcoming show."

"What does their wedding have to do with a cooking show?"

"My thoughts exactly. Maybe it'll delay the wedding."

"Why would you say that?" Suspicion laced every syllable.

This is where he had to move carefully. He sensed Jules's defenses kicking into gear, and he didn't blame her. He'd react the same way if he thought someone was about to jeopardize his brother's happiness.

Again Jules's taunting butterfly came to mind as well as her different taste in clothes. Something told him that she wasn't a traditionalist like his family was. Maybe she was one of those live-on-a-whim types? Even if it meant letting people set themselves up to get hurt?

Like he'd done to himself.

Like he'd done to his late wife.

CHAPTER TWO

THE SILENCE STRETCHED OUT.

The longer it took Stefano to answer her, the more concerned Jules became. With her sister's happiness at stake, Jules couldn't let the subject drop. Not without some answers.

She turned in her seat in order to gauge Stefano's expression. "Why do you want them to delay the wedding?"

He sighed. "I just think they are rushing into this without thinking it through."

"It sounds to me like you're opposed to the wedding." Jules sank back against the leather seat. Surely she had to be jet-lagged and reading too much into his reserved demeanor and hesitant words. Perhaps she needed to be more direct. "Will you try and stop the wedding?"

Jules studied his handsome face with its aristocratic features for some indication of his thoughts. Because there was no way she'd let anyone come between Lizzie and her happiness. Over the years, when they'd fantasized about the future, Lizzie had always dreamed of meeting Mr. Right. But neither of them had ever invested much hope in those dreams. Until now. This was Lizzie's chance to live out her dream.

Though that meant breaking up their small family and the thought saddened Jules, she refused to dwell on it.

Lizzie's happiness had to be the priority. And on a positive note, this meant Jules would at last gain her freedom to make all her own choices. They'd been making decisions together since they were kids, but now it was time they each stood on their own. And for Jules that meant making her own career choice—one Lizzie wouldn't approve of.

And if Jules was ready to see her foster sister—her only family—move an ocean away so that she would be happy, what possible reason could Stefano find to object to the wedding? Or was she reading him wrong? It was so hard to tell—his tanned face wasn't giving her any clues about his thoughts.

"I'm waiting for an explanation." She crossed her arms. No way was she going to drop the subject until they sorted it out.

"Fine. I'll admit it. I'm not a fan of marriage."

"This particular marriage? Or just marriage in general?" She could have sworn that Lizzie had mentioned he was married. Maybe that was it. Maybe he and his wife had hit a rough patch. "Aren't you married?"

"I was." His knuckles on the steering wheel gleamed white. "She died."

"Oh. Sorry." *Great job, Jules. Talk about opening your mouth and inserting your size-six boot.*

"And for the record, it's not my place to say whether the wedding should go on or not. My brother has a mind of his own."

"Good." She settled back against the smoky-gray leather seat. "I don't want anything ruining this wedding for them." She gave him a pointed look, but Stefano didn't give her the satisfaction of looking her way. "We have a lot to plan between now and next spring or summer. Have they mentioned to you if they've picked a date?"

"No. But it sounded to me like it is going to be sooner than next year."

"They can't move up the wedding. That would be a nightmare. There's just too much to arrange. Besides, if they were doing something like that, they'd have told us. After all, you're the best man."

Stefano sighed. "I suppose I am. But that just means they'll tell me when and where to show up."

"You really think you'll get off that easily?"

"Why wouldn't I? Men don't care about all of that stuff. Weddings are for women."

"We'll see about that." Did he really believe that? Was he that jaded? Or was it grief over losing his wife?

"I guess we will."

She pressed her lips firmly together. She'd been in Rome less than an hour. It wouldn't do to wage war with Lizzie's future brother-in-law.

Jules inhaled a deep, calming breath and noticed the very fine automobile had a wonderful new car scent. Her gaze strayed to the dash, where Stefano's long, lean fingers were adjusting the controls on a large touch screen. Soon the velvet sounds of an Italian baritone replaced the oppressive silence.

She leaned her head back and turned to the window. She took in the golden glow of the sun over the city. People were out and about—neighbors filling each other in on the events of the day. Children were running around laughing and playing. Jules smiled, liking what she'd seen so far.

She couldn't believe that she was truly in Italy. Her friends back at the New York City coffee shop where she worked were never going to believe this. She'd definitely have to get lots of photos before catching her flight in a week.

When the car pulled to a stop, Stefano turned to her. "We're here."

So this was Ristorante Massimo.

Jules stared out the window at the line of patio tables with red umbrellas. And the double red doors with large brass handles that led to the dining area. This was where her sister had lost her heart—this was where Lizzie intended to spend the rest of her life.

The breath caught in Jules's throat. She might at last be gaining her freedom, but at what cost? She blinked repeatedly. She'd told herself the whole flight here that she wouldn't melt into a sobbing mess.

A hand pressed against her shoulder. "Julianne...um, Jules, are you okay?"

She nodded and blinked, tucking her emotions into that trusty box she'd been using since the days of being shuttled in and out of foster homes. She swallowed down the lump in her throat, hoping that when she spoke her voice wouldn't waver. "I'm fine."

"Why don't you go inside? I'm sure Lizzie is anxious to see you. I'll grab your luggage and meet you in there."

She agreed and made her way inside. The restaurant was quite large, and a wall of photos was the first thing to grab her attention. There were framed photos of various sizes and all manner of frames starting at the ceiling and trailing down to the floor. As she passed by, she noticed some famous faces. *Wow! This place must be really upscale.*

"Jules, is that you?" Lizzie came rushing toward her.

In no time, they were wrapped in each other's arms. It felt so good to be with her sister again. They both started to talk at once. It wasn't until they glanced around and saw Dante and Stefano observing them with amusement dancing in their eyes that both women realized their lack of manners.

Lizzie stepped in the middle of everyone. "Jules, I'd like you to meet Dante, my future husband. Dante, this is my sister, Julianne, but everyone calls her Jules."

"Hello, Jules."

"Hi." When she went to hold her hand out to him to shake, he pulled her forward and gave her a big hug.

She hesitated at first. This wasn't the sort of greeting she was accustomed to. It certainly wasn't the sort of greeting she'd received from Stefano. When Dante let her go, she gazed up at him. He was almost as tall as Stefano. But he wasn't nearly as disarmingly handsome as his older brother.

"Don't frown at me," Dante said lightly. "We're family and you'll soon find that the DeFiores are huggers."

"Thanks for the warning."

From what Lizzie had told her most of the family lived outside the city on a vineyard. Too bad there wouldn't be time to visit, but Jules didn't want to overstay her welcome or crowd the lovebirds. Her mission was to check out the groom, catch up with Lizzie and get wedding details—lots of details. It was never too soon to plan the perfect wedding, and Lizzie deserved no less.

"Let's go upstairs and get you settled." Lizzie started for the front door of the restaurant.

"Where exactly are we going?" Jules asked, looking around and trying to get her bearings.

Dante spoke up. "There are apartments above the restaurant. And the entrance is outside."

"Sounds good. We can get started right away on the wedding plans. We don't have time to waste." Jules grabbed for her purse. Before she could reach for her carry-on, Stefano had it in hand. She turned back and followed Lizzie out the door. "Do you have a date picked out? Say, next spring? Or summer?"

"That's what we wanted to talk to you about." There was hesitation in Lizzie's voice.

Jules's hand gripped the strap of her purse tighter. She sensed trouble. Were they calling the wedding off? They didn't seem to be fighting or anything. So what was the matter?

"Lizzie, at least let your sister get settled in before you get into it." Dante maneuvered her suitcase in through a side door and over to a waiting elevator.

"You're right. My head is just spinning at the moment." Lizzie turned to Jules. "Wait until you see the penthouse. It's amazing. I think our entire apartment would fit in the guest room alone."

Jules watched as Lizzie leaned over and placed a kiss on Dante's lips. A look came over her sister's face—a look of utter happiness and love. Suddenly the impact of what was about to happen struck Jules. The thought made her stomach plummet. How had she missed this before?

First, there'd been the eviction notice. Their New York apartment building was converting to expensive condos. That shock had been closely followed by the panicked search for affordable housing combined with trying to find a way to tell Lizzie that she'd had a change of heart about her future. All in all, she'd been pretty caught up in the drama that was her life.

But even with all of that, she couldn't hide from this piece of reality forever. The backs of her eyes stung, and she blinked repeatedly. The life she'd always known— Lizzie and Jules joined at the hip—was over.

She was now alone in this great big world.

The smiles.
The I-love-you looks.
The kisses.

Stefano couldn't wait to bolt for the door. His younger brother certainly had it bad for Lizzie. Whatever was going on with the wedding, they certainly weren't about to call it off. Maybe they'd already eloped. Stefano ground his teeth together. The thought of his brother doing something so impulsive—so reckless—had Stefano's whole body tensing up.

He knew what it was to love and lose. He knew the pain...and the guilt that ate at him. He didn't want Dante to end up like him or their widowed father. DeFiore men inevitably ended up alone—one way or the other. Dante knew all of this; he just chose to ignore it. Avoidance, it was a DeFiore trait. So was stubbornness. And he couldn't forget to toss in a driving need for independence.

"What has you so quiet this evening, big brother?" Dante clapped him on the back.

"I have a lot on my mind."

"Really? Do tell?" Dante moved through the open floor plan from the ultramodern black-and-white living room to the stainless steel galley kitchen.

"Nothing you'd be interested in hearing."

"Aka it's vineyard business." Dante pulled open the fridge and perused the contents. "Want something to drink? Looks like Lizzie stocked up on everything for her sister's arrival."

"I'm good."

Dante withdrew a bottle of water and unscrewed the top. "Okay, what's eating you?"

Before Stefano could think up something to tell his brother besides the truth, the women returned. *Thank goodness.* He could now escape before the lovey-dovey stuff started again.

"Isn't it wonderful?" Lizzie smiled. When her eyes landed on Dante, she glowed with happiness.

"It really is amazing." Jules twisted her hands together, looking a bit uncomfortable as the lovebirds radiated toward each other as if by magnetic force. "Well, don't keep us in suspense—what did you have to tell us about the wedding?"

Stefano's gaze moved from Jules, with her now sad eyes and her drawn face, to the happy couple who looked as though they belonged on the front of a Valentine's Day greeting card. With their arms draped around each other's waist, they looked lovingly into each other's eyes. Stefano glanced away. He truly wanted it to last for them, but the DeFiore statistics were against them.

"Shall we tell them everything now?" Lizzie stared adoringly up at his brother.

Stefano's gut rolled nauseously. There was only so much sugary sweetness he could stomach before he became ill. Had he and Gianna ever looked that ridiculously in love? If they had, he couldn't recall.

"Tell them," Dante prodded. "It isn't like it's a secret. And to pull this off, we're going to need their help."

The smile faded from Lizzie's face. "I guess you're right—"

"Guys, what is it?" Stefano hadn't meant to lose his patience, but he really did want to get out of there. He needed to head back to the vineyard, where he could lose himself in work and forget the lovey-dovey stuff as well as Jules's little purple butterfly that still tempted and teased.

He felt Jules's narrowed gaze on him. He ignored her as he crossed his arms, willing this to be over. Soon.

"Well, the thing is," Lizzie began, reaching for Dante's hand, "the reason we couldn't pick you up at the airport is that the studio contacted us for a teleconference."

Jules implored her sister with her big emerald eyes. "Would you just tell us what they said?"

"They want to spotlight our wedding on the show—our very own cooking show."

"That's wonderful!" Jules rushed over and hugged her sister.

Stefano held his place. His gut grew uneasy. There was more to follow. He was certain of it.

When the girls pulled apart, Lizzie continued, "The thing is we have to have the wedding in the next two months—"

"What?" Jules's eyes grew round. "That's not possible. Do they know what it takes to plan a wedding?"

"They were really excited about the idea. They said it could really boost ratings." Lizzie clutched Dante's hand. "I...I told them we could do it."

"You did what?" Jules's face filled with color as she pressed her lips together.

Stefano didn't know if Jules was going to yell or cry. And Lizzie looked upset, too. Honestly, he didn't know what the big deal was. The only thing you needed was the bride and groom, and the rest was a bunch of froufrou.

"Jules, you don't understand. This is the opportunity of a lifetime."

His gaze ping-ponged between the two women. Tempers were rising. If someone didn't do something, this happy reunion was going to end up in a fight. And he didn't want to see that happen—especially when the disagreement would be over something so stupid.

"Ladies, I'm sure it can be worked out. After all, it's only a wedding. How hard can it be?"

Suddenly everyone's attention was on him. The two women looked as though they would send poisonous arrows his way if they could. Dante smiled and shook his head, but he didn't say a word. So much for receiving any support from his own flesh and blood.

Jules marched over to him. She planted her hands on her hips and lifted her chin. "Exactly how many weddings have you planned?"

He wasn't about to get into that debate, but when he opened his mouth there was a distinct disconnect between his brain and his vocal cords. "It can't be that hard. After all, the venue is all taken care of."

"The venue is only one part of a wedding."

"So you pick out some pretty dresses and order a cake. Nothing to stress out about."

Jules glared at him and turned away. "Said like a man who has never planned a wedding."

Lizzie nodded as though in total agreement. "I know this is short notice. But Dante and I were talking, and we really don't want to wait a whole year, anyway."

Jules's brows lifted. "Is there some other news we should know?"

Color rose in Lizzie's cheeks. "No. Nothing like that. We're just anxious to get on with the rest of our lives."

"But I'm leaving in a week." Jules worried her bottom lip.

"I know. But if Dante and I buy you an airline ticket for a later date, to make up for the one you'll be forfeiting, would you consider staying until after the wedding? Please."

Stefano's focus zeroed in on Jules. Part of him wanted her to stick with her original plans and leave soon. But a much stronger part of him wanted a chance to check out the butterfly tattoo a little closer—

No! What was he thinking? He didn't want anything to do with her. Butterfly or no butterfly. He had no intention of getting too close—of feeling too much. The price was too steep. And on top of it all, he didn't deserve a second chance at happiness.

"Yes, I'll stay." Jules crossed her arms and gave Lizzie a firm look. "You know that this is the craziest thing we've ever done. Whoever heard of putting together a wedding in two months?"

"We can do it." Lizzie looked over at Dante. "Didn't I tell you she's amazing?"

"Yes, you did."

Dante swept Lizzie into his arms and kissed her like there was no tomorrow. Stefano averted his gaze and ended up staring at Jules. She looked just as uncomfortable as he felt. No one should be as much in love as them. Thankfully he was leaving.

At the DeFiore Vineyard there were no couples in love—no uncomfortable moments. Only memories of mistakes that couldn't be undone.

CHAPTER THREE

WAS THAT WHAT it was like to be hooked on someone?

Jules gave a slight shake of her head. She wouldn't know. She'd never let herself get that close to anyone. She glanced at the engaged couple, who were gazing longingly into each other's eyes. It was as though they had forgotten that anyone else was in the room. She considered making a joking comment, but she couldn't bring herself to do it. She'd never seen Lizzie so happy...ever. And she didn't want to do anything to ruin it.

"I should be going." Stefano hedged his way toward the door.

"Wait." Jules sent him a desperate look. He couldn't just leave her there. "Could you give me a ride?"

She may not want to ruin Lizzie's happiness, but that didn't mean she wanted to be subjected to it in large quantities. No way was Stefano escaping this den of love and leaving her trapped. There was only so much she could take of this sugary sweetness. And her teeth already ached.

Lizzie pulled away from Dante. "A ride where?"

"To get a hotel room."

"Why would you do that?" V-shaped lines formed between Lizzie's brows. "After all, this will be your home during school breaks."

"What?" This was news to her.

Before Jules could find the words to set her sister straight, Stefano stepped forward. "Jules might enjoy staying at the villa. It's quite spacious, and it'll be helpful for her to see where the wedding will take place."

Lizzie's mouth opened, but nothing came out. Jules had the feeling she was wearing a similar expression. The man who didn't approve of her appearance and who thought weddings were a waste of time was now suggesting she stay with him? She wasn't so sure how she felt about his offer.

Lizzie's gaze narrowed as it darted between Jules and Stefano. "Thank you, Stefano. But I'm sure Jules will be more comfortable staying here."

Jules swallowed and straightened her shoulders. "I think a hotel would be best."

"You really don't want to stay here?" Lizzie's voice grew soft, eroding Jules's resolve.

Dante stepped up and pulled Lizzie close. Her head tilted against his shoulder as if they'd been leaning on each other for years.

Dante met Jules's gaze. "You are welcome here. Anytime. For as long as you want. It's your home now, too."

"Thank you." It really meant a lot coming from him, but it still didn't change her mind. She couldn't impose on them. But she didn't have the money to stay in a hotel indefinitely. She turned to Stefano. "How far is the vineyard from here?"

"It's a bit of a drive."

"But my brother will be happy to get you back and forth." Dante smiled as though he really liked the idea.

Jules worried her bottom lip. It was only logical that she go home with Stefano, and he seemed fine with the idea. So why was she throwing up roadblocks?

"I guess Stefano's right. With the wedding being pushed

up, we need to get started right away." And then Jules got
an idea and turned to her foster sister. "Maybe you should
come with me."

Lizzie's expression filled with worry. "I'd really like to,
but I have to stay here as they want to start filming this
week. I'm sorry."

"Oh. I see." It was going to be challenging planning a
wedding without the bride constantly on hand, but somehow they'd make it work.

"But I do have some notes." Lizzie rushed back the
hallway and soon returned with a notebook. She handed
it over. "I wrote out a bunch of ideas and attached pictures
I cut out from magazines. How about you look over these
and then we'll talk?"

"Sounds good. But what about your dress? Will you be
able to get something in such a short time frame?"

Lizzie sent her a knowing smile. "I had the same worry.
I ran out as soon as the studio proposed the idea, and I
found exactly what I wanted. It's being altered right now."

"Great." Check the most important item off the list.
"Did you happen to find one for me?"

"Actually I found three that will work. All you have to
do is try them on and see which looks the best."

Okay, so maybe this rushed wedding wasn't going to be
as horrible to plan as she'd initially envisioned. It wasn't
like Lizzie would turn into bridezilla or anything. Her foster sister had never been a prima donna.

"Are you sure you won't stay here?" Lizzie begged her
with both word and look. "I was really hoping we could
catch up on everything and watch some old movies together."

If it were only Lizzie in the apartment, she wouldn't
hesitate to stay. But even now she noticed how Dante
and Lizzie gravitated together. They couldn't keep their

hands off each other. And if she were perfectly honest, she wanted to see the vineyard. From everything she'd heard, it was gorgeous. Who would pass up a chance to stay at an Italian villa?

Once you got past his solemn attitude, her host wasn't too bad, either. She glanced over at Stefano, who was talking with his brother. Okay, so he was a lot more like drool-worthy. Her stomach fluttered. Thankfully the attraction was a one-way avenue. He'd already made it perfectly clear that she wasn't his type.

She glanced away—but not soon enough. Lizzie raised her eyebrows, followed by a questioning look. Jules rolled her eyes and shook her head. The last thing she needed was Lizzie thinking that she had a thing for Stefano. He was much too serious for her. And she didn't have time for a guy. She had other things on her mind—like planning a rushed wedding and figuring out what to do with her future once she withdrew from grad school.

"How are things coming with school?" Lizzie stepped closer to her.

"Uh…good." That was strange. It was as if Lizzie could read her mind. She considered telling Lizzie her decision and getting it over with, but not with the guys in the room. This delicate conversation was going to require some uninterrupted privacy.

"Are you ready to go?" Stefano sent her a direct look that said he wanted to escape honeymoon central.

"Yes, I am. Just let me grab my bag."

"I've got it." Stefano gripped the handle.

Jules turned back to Lizzie, who had an expectant look on her face. "We'll talk later. I'm so happy for you. And don't worry about a thing. I promise we'll plan the best wedding. Ever."

Lizzie's worried expression eased. "Thank you. You're the best."

"I'll remember that you said that." Jules smiled, so happy to see her sister again. "We have a lot of work ahead of us."

What in the world had he been thinking?

Stefano shook his head. Obviously he hadn't been thinking, at least not clearly. What he knew about playing host wouldn't even fill up his mother's thimble—a memento that his father kept on his dresser. And what Stefano knew about making women happy was practically nonexistent. His wife could attest to that—if she were still alive. Guilt weighed heavy on his shoulders.

It was just one more reason that taking Jules home with him wasn't a good idea. Because once you got past all the makeup and distinctive clothes, there was something special about Jules—something that intrigued him. And that was definitely not a good thing.

But he couldn't just leave her stranded there with those two. His brother could barely keep his hands off Lizzie. Not that he could blame him.

But there was no way anyone could convince Stefano to stay in that apartment—no matter how spacious it was. There was only so much of that mushy stuff that one could handle. Regardless of his hesitation, Jules didn't deserve to play the third wheel.

"Thank you."

Her voice startled him out of his thoughts. "What?"

"Thank you for helping me out back there. I don't think I could have stood to watch them much longer. Did you ever see such a happy couple?"

He shook his head. At last, they had something in common. "They certainly have it bad for each other."

"You noticed that, too?"

He nodded, keeping his eyes on the road. "What do you think about their rush to say *I do*?"

"I was beginning to think that Lizzie was never going to settle down with a family of her own, especially after—well, anyway, it's full steam ahead."

After what? He wanted to ask, but he didn't. He just hoped that Dante knew what Jules was referring to. He wasn't crazy about the rushed engagement and even less so about the hurried wedding. He wished Dante would take his time and give the whole marriage idea more thought.

Perhaps now Stefano wasn't the only one with reservations. He'd noticed the brief frown that had crossed Jules's face back at the love nest when she thought no one was looking. Maybe she'd had a change of heart about this whirlwind romance.

Could it be he had an ally—someone who thought the happy couple should slow down and see reason? Sure, the television people were anxious for the wedding. The only thing that mattered to them was their ratings. But marriage was about so much more than a popularity contest. It was a lifelong commitment—one that could have devastating consequences if you weren't careful.

He cleared his throat. "That sure was a surprise about them pushing the wedding up so far. It's only a matter of weeks away. I wonder if they're doing the right thing."

He took his focus off the road for a moment and glanced over to find Jules studying him suspiciously. Definitely not a good sign. It would seem that he'd read her reactions all wrong.

"What are you worried about?" she asked. "Don't you like Lizzie? Don't you think she's good enough for your brother?"

"Whoa! Slow down. That isn't what I meant." Why in

the world had he even opened his mouth? He should have just left well enough alone.

He kept glancing between Jules and the road. She crossed her arms and arched a brow at him. She was waiting for an explanation, and he didn't know exactly what to say. He didn't want to open his mouth and insert his freshly polished dress shoe. But she didn't look as though she was about to let him off the proverbial hook anytime soon.

He sighed. "What I meant was that if it's real between them, there's no need to rush—no matter what the television studio says. They can take their time—"

"That's not the real truth, is it?" When he didn't have an immediate denial, Jules barreled on. "The truth is you know about Lizzie's past and you don't think that she's good enough to marry into the DeFiore family."

"That's not true." He wished that was the case. If his disapproval was the only obstacle Dante and Lizzie had to face, their future would be paved in rose petals. But the truth was he thought they made a great couple—a couple totally in love with each other. The problem with love was that it was blind and deaf to the truth. And sooner or later, devastation would plan a sneak attack—it always did. But how did he explain any of that to Jules? Unless you had lived through it—twice in his case—you just couldn't truly understand.

Marriage to a DeFiore ended with dire consequences.

"Then what is it?" Jules continued to stare at him. "Why are you against this wedding?"

"I'm not. At least not as far as them being together."

"But…"

He couldn't do it.

Telling Jules the whole truth wasn't an option. He couldn't pry open that door to his past—to relive the pain. And though he barely knew her, he couldn't stand the thought of Jules turning those luminous green eyes on him in judgment, followed by condemnation. Gianna's family still looked at him that way. He'd finally accepted that they'd always blame him.

Pain and worry drowned out his common sense, and he spoke from his tattered heart. "I don't think they know each other well enough yet. Heck, even when you've known someone for years, there's still so much adjustment you have to make."

"You sound as though you know this firsthand."

He shrugged off her comment.

There he'd gone and done it. He'd cracked open the door to his past. And now he just hoped he could get it closed again before too many memories leaked out. The painful image of his wife's mangled car being towed away had him gripping the steering wheel tighter.

He choked down the jagged lump in his throat. "The point is that I like Lizzie. I think she's great."

"You do?" There was a note of surprise mingled with happiness in Jules's voice. "Really?"

He nodded and then switched on the turn signal as they neared the entrance to the vineyard. "I just don't want them to rush things and then find out later that they made a mistake."

"Is that what you think they're doing? Making a mistake?"

He shrugged again. "I think love is a two-edged sword. And if you aren't careful, you'll get cut."

He didn't look at her this time, but he could feel her steady gaze on him. He wasn't going any further with this conversation. He didn't owe her any other explanations. None whatsoever.

CHAPTER FOUR

HONESTY RANG OUT in Stefano's voice.

But could Jules believe her ears?

Did he truly like her sister? Or was he just telling her what he thought she wanted to hear? Jules wanted to believe him. Truly she did. But there was something more to his hesitation than the wedding being bumped up. And that made her intensely curious.

"Here we are." Stefano's deep voice with its heavy accent drew her out of her thoughts.

With the setting sun at her back, Jules stared out over the vast sloping green fields. It was the most gorgeous evening she'd ever seen. Brilliant pinks and purples painted the sky, while the symmetrical rows of bountiful grapevines were shadowed against the horizon. It was a little piece of heaven on earth.

"You live here?"

"The DeFiore family has lived here for generations."

He turned the car down a small lane. Off to the side sat a painted wooden sign. Gold letters on a deep purple background spelled out DEFIORE WINERY. It was very stylish. Something told her this villa was going to be more impressive than she'd been imagining. Already the landscape had an essence of romance and blissful happiness written all over it.

What exactly had she gotten herself into by agreeing to stay here?

A sexy Italian by her side, the poshest car she'd ever ridden in and the most magnificent countryside added up to trouble. She was certain of it.

Then again, why fight it? Why not enjoy it? This was her treat for working so hard to graduate with high honors from college. Granted she'd been a couple of years older than her classmates, a result of enrolling late because of a financial hardship. But none of that meant the classes had been any easier for her.

"Here we are." Stefano slowed the car to a stop outside a sprawling villa. "I hope you'll be comfortable here."

"I...I'm certain I will be."

She gazed up at the sprawling three-story villa. This was more like a colorful mansion than a cozy country home. She caught herself gaping and pressed her lips together. Bright blue shutters adorned each window and door. The color contrasted well with the sunny yellow walls and the red tile roof. Someone sure appreciated vibrant colors. And she couldn't blame them. It made a happy, welcoming statement.

The various balconies beckoned to her. Was it possible that her room would have one? She hoped so. She envisioned strolling out there to enjoy her morning coffee. *Wow.* People really lived like this?

She couldn't help but glance around looking for someone with a video camera. But there was no one in sight. Somehow it was hard to imagine that this villa was someone's home and not a prop on a television show about the rich and famous. And Stefano could easily fit the part of a sexy movie star who set women's heart's racing—except hers. She was immune to his charms.

Stefano opened the car door for her, and she stepped out. "This place is amazing."

"Thank you."

"It'll be the perfect backdrop for the wedding." She glanced around, searching for the ideal spot for Lizzie and Dante to say their vows.

"You're thinking of having the ceremony outside?"

A gentle breeze tickled her skin. "Of course. With such a beautiful setting, it's not even worth considering any other place."

"If you don't mind me asking, what do you know about planning a wedding? Are you—I mean, have you been married?"

She laughed. She couldn't help it. The thought of her making such a commitment was akin to asking her if she could sprout wings and fly. Sure, she hoped that Lizzie would live happily ever after, but, as for herself, she didn't believe in putting her future in someone else's hands.

"I'm a confirmed bachelorette."

His dark brows lifted. "Really?"

"Don't look so shocked. Men don't have the market cornered on staying single."

He rubbed the back of his neck. "I guess I just never met a woman that didn't believe in roses, platitudes and promises of forever."

"Well, now you have."

"So I have."

Though she'd never admit it, standing here in this little piece of heaven on earth with a man whose thoughts extended beyond his zipper, she could at last understand why some women went the romantic forever route. She turned, and their gazes connected. She should glance away, but she didn't want to. Not yet. Her stomach quivered. She'd never experienced such a sensation around a man. What was it about him that had her body betraying her?

Whatever it was, she'd have to be careful around him. No way was she going to fall for some unrealistic fantasy. She knew for a fact that the people you were supposed to trust the most were the first to let you down—the first to inflict pain. Her father had done it first. And then her mother had let her down in the worst way.

Jules refused to let herself get close enough to a man for him to hurt her.

The following morning, Stefano found himself lingering in the updated kitchen longer than necessary. Instead of his normal one cup of *caffè*, he'd just finished his second when he turned to refill his cup and found the pot empty.

Oh, this was ridiculous. He was stalling, and by the look on Maria's face, their cook/housekeeper knew it, too. Thankfully she didn't say a word about his beautiful houseguest. Maria turned her back to him and set about making a fresh pot.

He carried his empty cup to the sink.

Maria tilted her head to look at him. "If you wait, you can have more *caffè*."

"No, thanks." He forced a smile before gazing out the window at the brilliant morning sunshine casting a golden glow over the ordered rows of grapevines. "I'm just tired today. I was up late last night catching up on some paperwork for the winery. Harvest time will be here soon. We need to be prepared."

Maria's dark head nodded before she moved to the fridge. *Just great.* Now he was talking like a blathering fool. He shouldn't be standing around—waiting for Jules. She'd be fine on her own. He'd shown her all around the villa yesterday.

The less he thought about the woman who wore far too much makeup, the better. His work was waiting for him, and it wasn't getting done standing here.

"Thanks for breakfast."

"Don't worry so much. Everything will work out."

Before he could ask what she meant, he heard footsteps. He turned to find Jules standing there in black shorts and a sheer long-sleeved black top. But what sent his heart slamming into his ribs was the black bra that was visible beneath her top. Wait. It was more than a bra, but not much more. There was a strip of stomach visible, and the spaghetti straps left her arms bare beneath the sheer top.

His first instinct was to get her one of his long-sleeved shirts to put on. What if one of the workmen saw her like this? His gut knotted up. Then again, why should he care what clothes she wore? Or who looked at her? But he couldn't shrug off the unsettling feeling of protectiveness. He didn't want other men ogling her.

The thought brought him up short. He couldn't be jealous. That was ridiculous. He had no claim on her. Nor would he. She could traipse around in her birthday suit and it'd mean nothing to him.

So then why was the sight of her in that sexy little outfit warming his blood? His jaw tightened, and his body tensed. It'd be best if he thought of something else—and quick.

"Good morning." She smiled as though she didn't have a care in the world. "I didn't mean to sleep in so late. I guess all of the traveling is catching up with me."

Stefano's mouth went dry, and his mind went blank. He should say something. Yet his tongue stuck to the roof of his mouth. He was staring. And he couldn't tear his gaze from her.

Maria stepped between them and offered Jules breakfast

—a hearty one. As Jules dug in, the fact that the slip of a woman had such a hearty appetite didn't escape his attention. When her eyes met his there was a twinkle of amusement in them.

He swallowed past the lump in his throat. "Did you sleep well?"

"I did. I opened the window and a cool breeze put me straight to sleep."

He sure hadn't slept well—not at all. Thoughts of the little butterfly tattoo had fluttered through his mind. His attention strayed to her chest, but the material obscured his view. Just as well. He was better off not thinking of it at all.

Work. Concentrate on today's tasks.

"I'm heading out to the fields."

Jules's eyes lit up. "Are you going to pick grapes? It looks like such fun on television."

He chuckled. It was refreshing having someone around who didn't think she was an expert when it came to the vines. "No. It's not that time of the year. But at harvest time, you're welcome to come back and join us."

"Thanks." The enthusiasm in her voice made him smile. "I just might take you up on the offer. But is it hard to learn?"

"No. Anyone can do it. I'm sure you'll take right to it."

Her lips pursed together. "I'll definitely keep it in mind. Thank you for the invite."

He mentally kicked himself for extending such a ridiculous invitation. Like she was going to fly all the way back to Italy to pick grapes. Yeah, right. But what if she did? Hope ballooned in his chest, and he immediately squelched it.

"If you aren't picking grapes, what do you do?"

"There's always something that needs tending. Right now, I'm going to thin the shoots."

"Interesting." Her brows scrunched together. "Sorry. I don't know much about making wine. Actually I don't know anything at all about it except how to drink it."

It was on the tip of his tongue to offer to show her the basics, but spending time with her wasn't a good idea. Besides, she was only feigning interest in the grapes to be nice. After all, why would this city girl be interested in a bunch of plants? He assured himself that she had plenty of wedding stuff to keep her occupied.

His grandfather shuffled into the kitchen using a walker to assist him. Ever since Nonno had a stroke, forcing him to hand over the reins of Ristorante Massimo to Dante, he'd been living at the villa. Nonno was his mother's father and the only grandfather Stefano had even known. He loved him dearly and was so relieved to find that Nonno was starting to pull himself out of that dark place he'd briefly visited after being forced into retirement.

Stefano spoke up. "Nonno, this is Jules, Lizzie's sister. She got in last night. Jules, this is my grandfather, Massimo."

"I'm old, not deaf." His grandfather frowned at him before turning a lopsided smile to Jules. "Welcome."

Stefano smiled and shook his head. His grandfather still had an eye for women. Some things didn't change. Stefano watched as his grandfather interacted with Jules. The frown lines on his face eased, and that took years off his appearance. Obviously Stefano wasn't the only one to find a special quality in Jules that made the world a brighter place.

Jules smiled brightly at Nonno. "Lizzie has told me a lot about you, too."

"All good, I hope." His grandfather's speech was still a bit slurred, but Stefano was either getting used to it or his grandfather's therapy was helping him.

"Only the best. She told me you are quite handsome and a wonderful conversationalist."

Nonno joined Jules at the table. He reached out and squeezed her hand. Her smile lit up her eyes. Jealousy poked at Stefano. She never smiled that brightly at him. She always remained reserved, as if she were prepared for him to bite her at any moment. And now that his grandfather was there it was as though she'd forgotten he was even in the room.

"Well, I'll let you eat your breakfast." Stefano needed to get away—to get some fresh air to clear his thoughts.

His grandfather didn't say a word as he sipped at his *caffè*.

At last, Jules turned to Stefano as though she'd just remembered his presence. "I shouldn't have slept so late. Lizzie will be here at lunch so that we can get started with the wedding plans."

"Then I'll leave you to your planning." He slipped out the door feeling torn between the relief of escaping and the disappointment that he wouldn't see her again until dinner.

CHAPTER FIVE

"I WAS BEGINNING to think that I'd never find you." Jules strode up to Stefano. She'd just about given up when she spotted him checking the vines.

He furrowed his brow. "I thought you'd be inside making wedding plans with Lizzie."

"She canceled it."

"The wedding—"

"No. It's still on." Heat rushed up and filled Jules's face. "I meant she canceled our plans for today. She said that she had to stick around the restaurant for a video conference with the people at the studio. Something about finalizing some details for next week's taping. They sure have a lot of meetings for a reality show."

Stefano stepped away from the grapevines and joined Jules in the rutted dirt path. "That show seems to take up more and more of their time. When my brother started coming home less and less on the weekends, he blamed it on filming conflicts. Me, personally, I thought it was because he wanted alone time with Lizzie, but it seems now he's been telling the truth."

"That's too bad. But at least they're happy. And I suppose it won't last forever. This is their fifteen minutes of fame."

He dusted his hands off on his faded jeans. "I was just heading back to the barn."

"The barn?"

He pointed to a large building off in the distance with a stone facade. "It's where we produce the wine. Beneath it is the barrel cellar."

"Do you mind if I tag along? There's something I want to ask you." Since Lizzie couldn't drive out to the vineyard, she'd asked if Jules would mind meeting them in Rome the next day. It sounded important, but Lizzie had been very closemouthed and said they'd talk at dinner.

"Sure. Come on." They fell in step, side by side. "What's on your mind?"

The thought of begging him for a ride into the city didn't sit well with her. She didn't like relying on others. Lizzie had said to bring Stefano along, but with all the work he had to do, would he want to drive all that way just to have dinner? She decided to put off asking him. She was enjoying his good mood, and this was her chance to get to know him a little better.

"It's big." She pointed to the wine barn. "Really big."

"It wasn't always that size. My father and I have done a lot to expand the business. Although we made a point of keeping the outside looking traditional, the inside has been totally modernized. We want to grow DeFiore winery into a household name. Hopefully it can be passed on from generation to generation."

"I'm sure your children will appreciate all of your efforts—"

"I don't have kids." His quick response caught her off guard.

"I kinda guessed that. But you will as soon as you meet the right woman. Isn't that what all of this is for?"

"No." He rubbed the back of his neck. "Maybe Dante's kids will take an interest in the business."

Jules glanced over at him, noticing the strained look

on his face as he kept his line of vision straight ahead. She wondered about his strong reaction to the thought of having kids.

Maybe it had something to do with her surprise in finding that she was the only woman aside from Maria living at the villa. Where were the women? Stefano was very handsome. In fact, if she were looking for fun beneath the Italian sun, he'd be first on her list. Was he still mourning his wife? Not that it was any of her business. But still she was curious.

"How about you?" Stefano's voice drew her out of her thoughts.

"What?"

"Are you interested in having a family?"

He was the first person to ask her that question. Not even Lizzie had asked her. And she supposed she owed him some sort of answer since she'd brought up the subject in the first place.

"Do I look like mother material?"

"Sure. I guess."

"You aren't even looking at me."

He stopped walking and turned to her. Silence ensued as he stared at her. "I think that beneath all of that makeup lies a beautiful woman who can have whatever she sets her mind on."

Her heart stopped. He thought she was beautiful? This was yet another thing that no one had ever said to her. What did she say now?

She moved her tongue from where it was stuck to the top of her mouth, hoping her voice would work. "Thanks. But you don't have to say that just to make me feel better."

"I'm not." His eyes darkened as he continued to stare at her as though he was truly seeing her. "There's something special about you."

A fluttering sensation filled her chest, and all she could think about was sinking into his arms and finding out if his kisses were as romantic as the ones she watched in the black-and-white movies that played late at night when she was alone while her friends were out on dates.

"I'm out of the loop on what's in style as far as women's fashions. I suppose that the makeup and dark clothes are a fashion statement."

Jules glanced down at her black-on-black ensemble. She never really stopped to think about her appearance. She'd been dressing like this for so many years that it was just natural for her. It hid the ugly scars that lurked beneath—a reminder of a part of her life that was best left hidden and buried.

"Actually, it's just my style."

"I see. It...it's different from how the women in these parts dress. In the village, things are more simplistic than you'll find in Rome or Milan."

Normally she'd have taken that as an insult, but he'd already said he thought she was beautiful...beneath the makeup. So maybe he was just stating a fact. She stood out around here. But she didn't have anything else to wear—anything that would make her fit in better. Not that she planned to—fit in, that is.

She toyed with a loose thread on the hem of her top. "It's just so different back in New York. It's like a melting pot of styles and trends."

"I can imagine. But I'm confused. What does your appearance have to do with you becoming a mother?"

Back to that subject—the one she didn't want to delve into. "I'm not having kids."

"As in ever?"

"As in never ever. I wouldn't have a clue how to be a good mother." And there she'd gone and blurted out more than she'd intended to say—more than she normally shared with anyone.

Stefano started walking again toward the barn, and she fell in step beside him, waiting and wondering what he'd ask next. They moved along quietly for a few minutes. A gentle breeze brushed over Jules's face and made her pigtails flutter. But it was the man to her left that had her chest all aquiver. He really thought she was beautiful? Her heart tumbled.

As they neared the large stone structure, Stefano cleared his throat. "You'd be surprised at what people are capable of when their hearts are involved."

She shook her head. "Trust me. I didn't have a good role model."

"I'm sorry to hear that."

Not as sorry as I am.

Just then she heard something. A squeak? A squeal? A cry?

She stopped walking. "Did you hear that?"

Stefano stopped and glanced back at her. "I don't hear anything. What is it—"

"Shhh…" Her gaze darted around the foundation of the building, where the grass was higher.

If it was a rat, she was going to scream and jump on Stefano's back. She may be pushing to gain her independence from her foster sister, but that didn't mean she didn't have a weakness or two. And rodents gave her the willies. Still curiosity drove her on.

Squeak.

"Did you hear it that time?"

He nodded. "I wouldn't worry about it. I'm sure it's just some sort of wildlife that can take care of itself. Come on. I'll give you the unofficial tour of the winery."

"We can't leave. Not yet. What if it's hurt?"

Stefano arched a brow. "Didn't you just get done telling me that you weren't the motherly type?"

"I'm not." Though deep down she wished someday she could be the kind of mother that she'd dreamed of. "But that doesn't mean that I'm heartless. The creature might be starved or worse."

She didn't want to think about the worse part. She'd always had a tender spot for animals, even though she'd never been able to have a pet. Her foster homes wouldn't allow animals. And then the apartment lease forbade them. But now that she was moving, perhaps she'd look for a pet-friendly apartment.

She hunched over and started searching around the shrubs and through the greenery along the side of the building. When she glanced over her shoulder, she found Stefano standing there staring at her.

"Don't just stand there. Help me." She didn't wait for his response as she turned and continued her hunt.

There was a distinct sigh from Stefano followed by the sound of his approaching footsteps. She wished whatever it was would squeak again. She couldn't see any signs of life. What was it? And where was it?

"Is this what you're searching for?"

Jules immediately straightened and turned. Her gaze landed on a fuzzy ball of orange fur. "What is it?"

Stefano chuckled. "Don't you city girls know a kitten when you see one?"

"A kitten?" Her mouth fell open, and she forced it shut. She moved closer. "Is it yours?"

He shook his head. "Not mine."

"Then how did it get here?" She glanced around, not seeing any nearby houses.

"Sometimes when people don't want animals, they drop them off. I don't know why they think this is a good place to leave animals, especially cats. It isn't like we're a dairy farm or anything."

She stuck out her hand to pet it, then paused just inches from the ball of fluff. "Is…is it okay?"

"I'm no vet but…" He lifted the little thing up and gave it a once-over. "I think it's scared to death and starved. Otherwise, I think it's okay."

Jules blew out a breath she hadn't known she'd been holding. "Can I pet it?"

His brow crinkled. "Sure. It isn't that fragile."

Her fingertips stroked the dirty and tangled fur. She could feel its little ribs as they moved in and out with each breath. And then it turned to look at her. Its crusty little blue eyes peered at her. In that moment, Jules's heart melted. How could anyone dump such a sweet little thing?

"Do you want to hold it?" Stefano held out the kitten to her.

"Sure. But…but I don't want to hurt it."

"Trust me—you'll be fine."

She held out her hands, and then there was a little pile of fur in them. She didn't know that anything could be so featherlight. Her fingers instinctively stroked the fur. She could so relate to this kitten. She knew what it was like to be abused by those who are supposed to care for you.

"Aww…it's so sweet." She lifted the kitten until they were face-to-face. "Don't worry. You're safe now."

As she started back toward the house, Stefano called out to her, "What about the tour of the winery?"

"It'll have to wait. Apricot needs some food."

"Apricot?" There was a pause and then the sound of him catching up to her. "What are you planning to do with…Apricot?"

"Feed her, of course." What did he think she was going to do with the poor little thing?

"I meant after that. Do you really think it's such a good idea to name it?"

She saw the concern in his eyes. What was he worried about? That she didn't have a clue what she was doing? That somehow she'd hurt Apricot? Maybe he was right. She didn't know what she was doing, but she was willing to learn.

"We can't keep calling her 'it.' That's not a name. And I may not know anything about cats, but I can learn. That's what the internet is for." And then a worrisome thought formed. "Or are you worried about having the cat in the house?"

"The cat in the house is fine. It's a big place, and if you keep it in your suite of rooms, no one will even know it's there."

As they walked on in silence, Jules's nerves kicked up. She really didn't know what she was doing. What if she did hurt the kitten? After all, she'd never taken care of anyone but herself, and even then Lizzie had always been around.

This is why she wasn't having children—ever. She didn't know thing one about taking care of others. And judging by the worried expression on Stefano's face, he agreed. She glanced down at Apricot. Someone had to do his or her best for the kitten. And for the moment that was her.

"What did you want to talk to me about, you know, before the whole cat thing?"

That's right. She still had to spring the idea of a trip into the city on him. "What exactly are you doing tomorrow?"

CHAPTER SIX

W<small>HY EXACTLY HAD</small> he agreed to dinner out?

Stefano sat stiffly in a chair in one of Rome's finest hotels. Jules and Lizzie were chatting nonstop about wedding preparations. And he wanted to be anywhere but listening to things like guest lists, linen choices and table settings. All it did was stir up long-forgotten memories.

His wedding to Gianna had started with such promise. Then the problems had set in—inconsequential things at first. A comment about a forgotten toothpaste cap seemed so minor. Then things escalated to a litany of how he'd lost interest in her. He'd thought it was what every married couple went through as they adjusted to married life.

He tried to do better. He started taking Gianna to Rome as often as his work would allow him to be away. She'd always loved the city. And he'd loved spoiling her. But when he'd mentioned starting a family, she'd gotten angry. She didn't want to be trapped at the vineyard with a baby. She wasn't ready to settle down into family life. She wanted the money the vineyard provided, but she didn't want anything to do with a quiet country life. Stefano tried, but he just couldn't understand why she didn't want a family of their own. Wasn't that just a natural progression of marriage—having babies?

"Hey, man, what has you so quiet?" Dante leaned back

in his chair after the server removed the now empty dishes from the table.

"Nothing." He shrugged off the unwanted memories.

"Don't tell me that. I know you. And something is eating at you."

It was true. His brother could still read him quite well. He'd really been there for him after Gianna's death. And the fact that Dante had witnessed what he'd gone through after losing Gianna either made Dante brave for going ahead with this wedding or foolish. Stefano wasn't sure which was the case.

"Are you really serious about wanting to move the wedding to this hotel?" Stefano wanted to turn the conversation away from himself. "I thought you wanted to get married at the vineyard. What changed?"

Dante raked his fingers through his hair. "The television people. They're making it nearly impossible to do what we want with the wedding."

"Then quit the show." Stefano never did understand why his brother was so anxious to turn his life upside down for a television show.

Dante shook his head. "I can't do that. We have a contract."

"I'm confused. What does the show have to do with your wedding?"

"A lot." Lizzie spoke up. All eyes turned to her. "That's why we asked you guys to dinner. We had a long meeting with the executives, and they need us to step up our filming."

"But why move the wedding here?" Jules echoed Stefano's question.

Lizzie fingered the edge of the white linen napkin. "Because the time I have available to plan the wedding is very limited. I don't know how often we'll be able to get out to the vineyard before the big day. So if we have the wedding here in Rome, it'll be more convenient."

"But will it be what you truly want? After all, it's your big day—the biggest of your life. Shouldn't it be what you want and not what's easiest?" Jules sent her foster sister a determined look.

Stefano didn't think this wedding was such a great idea, but he had to agree with Jules. If it was going to take place, it should be what they wanted and not just what was most convenient.

"Jules is right." Stefano could feel her wide-eyed stare, but he kept his vision on Lizzie before turning to Dante. "I don't hear you saying anything."

"I'm fine with whatever Lizzie decides. I want this wedding to be everything she ever dreamed it would be, whether it's here or at the vineyard."

"Thank you." Lizzie squeezed Dante's hand and gazed lovingly into his eyes. Then she turned to Jules and Stefano. "You're right—you're both right. The vineyard would be ideal. But—"

"No buts." Jules crossed her arms. "We'll make it work."

Stefano shifted in his seat. Who was this "we" that she referred to? He didn't say anything as he waited to find out exactly what she had in mind.

Lizzie peered at her sister. "I couldn't ask you to do more than you're already doing."

"You aren't asking. I'm offering."

Stefano was starting to like the sound of this. If Jules was off planning a wedding, she'd be out of his way, and maybe then he wouldn't think about those short skirts, the knee-high black boots or that little butterfly, whose purple wings at this very moment were peeping out over the plunging neckline of Jules's purple top.

"And my brother will be around to drive you back and

forth to the city. And whatever other help you'll need."
Dante clapped him on the back and grinned at him as if
he'd just caught him in a trap.

Stefano choked. How dare his brother automatically
assume he'd be willing to continue his role as chauffeur.
With all eyes on him, Stefano struggled for a neutral tone.
"I have a business to run."

"Papa will help out. After all, it isn't harvest season.
There shouldn't be anything too pressing."

Jules turned to him. Her eyes pleaded with him. And
his resolve began to crack. Would it really be so bad? One
or two trips to the city. Maybe three at most. It wasn't like
he'd be doing anything but driving Jules around. How hard
could that be?

"I'd really appreciate your help." Jules's lips lifted at the
corners, brightening the softly lit dining room.

And in that moment, the last of his resolve shattered.

"Just let me know what you need me to do." Had he really just spoken those words?

Jules reached over and squeezed his hand. "I will. There
shouldn't be too much."

Her smile reached her eyes and made them sparkle like
gems. His chest filled with a funny sensation. Must be
indigestion. No way was he falling for Jules. Of that he
was certain.

What was up now?

Jules followed Lizzie to one of the hotel's terraces with
a marble statue and a beautiful view of the city. With no
other people around, they could talk openly for the first
time since she'd arrived in Italy. But what did her sister
want to talk about privately?

"Lizzie, what's going on?"

Her sister moved to the stone rail and stared out at the

lights of Rome. They twinkled like rare jewels. But there was something more pressing on Jules's mind—Lizzie. The longer her sister remained quiet, the more worried Jules became.

At last, Lizzie turned to her. "I just want you to know that nothing between us is going to change—"

"What? Of course they're going to change. They have to." Jules took a deep breath. It was time for a healthy dose of reality. "It's time we both make lives of our own. Yours is here in Italy. Mine...well, I'm not sure where mine will be—"

"Yes, you do. Your future is in New York, getting your master's degree. Have I told you lately how proud I am of you?" Without waiting for a response, Lizzie continued, "I've been telling everyone who would listen what a smart sister I have. I even mentioned it on an upcoming television segment."

"You didn't?" Jules's stomach sank. Now the whole world would know when she dropped out. They'd all realize she was a failure.

Lizzie smiled and nodded. "I want everyone to know how proud I am of you."

Jules knew she should tell Lizzie the truth right now, but as she looked into her sister's eyes, her courage failed her. She just couldn't formulate the words to tell Lizzie that she was never going to live up to those dreams. Everything was different now. She wasn't the same girl with thoughts of changing the world.

"Don't look so sad." Lizzie squeezed her hand. "We'll stay in close contact. We can get an international phone plan." She smiled as though she'd just discovered the solution to world peace. "And we can text, email, chat on social media. It'll be just like nothing changed."

Jules pressed her lips firmly together as she sent her

sister an I-don't-believe-you look. Change was the only way either of them was going to be able to truly be happy. It was scary; that was for sure. But big changes always were unsettling. Right at this moment, Jules had to be the strong one.

"The truth is—" Lizzie's eyes glistened with unshed tears "—I don't know if I can do this."

"Are you getting cold feet?" Whatever the problem was, they'd deal with it together, just like they'd been doing most of their lives.

Lizzie shook her head. "I love Dante. I love him more than I ever thought was possible."

"Then what is it?"

"It…it's you and me." Lizzie sniffled. "It's always been us against the world, and now I'm destroying that. I feel like I'm abandoning you."

Jules gave her what she hoped was a reassuring hug and then pulled back. "Our family isn't breaking up. It's expanding. I'm excited to be gaining a brother. You know I've never had one of those, and I think it's about time I did."

Lizzie sniffled again. "You're really happy about this? You aren't just saying that to make me feel better?"

Jules's finger crossed over her heart. "I swear."

Lizzie dried her eyes and smiled. "Thanks. Now what's this about you taking in a kitten?"

Stefano had mentioned it at dinner, and she'd known by the look on Lizzie's face that it had piqued her curiosity. "Apricot is adorable." Except when she tried to steal her pillow at night. "I can't wait for you to meet her. You're going to love her."

Lizzie's forehead wrinkled. "I didn't even know you wanted a cat."

The truth was she'd always loved cats, but with getting bounced around from home to home pets were out of the question—unless they were the plush stuffed ones. She was certain she'd mentioned wanting a cat in the past, but she hadn't gone on and on about something that couldn't be. What would be the point?

Jules shrugged. "I guess I'm full of surprises."

"I guess we both are. Who'd have ever dreamed I'd be getting married and moving to Rome?" Lizzie sent her a hesitant look. "Are you sure about this? I mean, I could put the wedding off. You know…until you finish grad school."

And the truth was that Lizzie would do that if Jules asked her to make the sacrifice. She just hated how insistent Lizzie was on her going to grad school. Maybe now was the time to tell her that she'd changed her mind. That she wasn't up for any more school at this point in her life, and that after doing an internship at the social services office, she knew that she wasn't cut out to be a social worker. She just couldn't stuff her feelings in a box and do what was expected of her.

As it was, she'd spoken up one too many times and was asked not to return. But she just couldn't stand by and watch as government guidelines overruled common sense. It was frustrating. Infuriating. There had to be another way to help deserving children in this world, and she hadn't figured out how yet. But she would. One way or another.

"Lizzie, listen. About grad school, I was thinking—"

"That we haven't thrown you some sort of celebration." Lizzie smiled, and her eyes sparkled with happiness. "I'm sorry. I didn't mean to steal your thunder with the wedding and all."

"You didn't. Honest." The wedding was the best thing to happen as far as Jules was concerned. Her sister had more things to worry about than just her. "Getting married was something you and I never thought would happen for us. This is your chance to have a real family. You have to make the most of this—for both of us."

Lizzie hugged her tight, and Jules blinked repeatedly, trying to keep the tears from splashing onto her cheeks. She'd been kidding herself. Sure, gaining the freedom to make her own choices would be great, but the price of giving up this close relationship was almost more than she could bear.

Lizzie pulled back. "Does this mean that we're okay?"

Jules nodded while stuffing down the torrent of emotions churning inside her. She wouldn't ruin this for Lizzie. After all Lizzie had done for her, she deserved every bit of happiness she could find in this life.

"We're perfect. Now let's go see what the men are up to."

"Knowing those two, we might have to break up a sparring match."

Jules gaped. "They don't get along?"

"Oh, no. They get along. But when Stefano starts his big-brother routine, Dante takes matters into his own hands. They end up acting like two-year-olds." Lizzie smiled and shook her head. "If only Stefano would realize that Dante is all grown up now and not in need of his brotherly advice."

Jules wanted to say that it was like the pot calling the kettle black, but she refrained. She knew it all came from a special place in Lizzie's heart. And now wasn't the time to delve into that messy subject. It could wait until later.

CHAPTER SEVEN

THIS COULDN'T BE HAPPENING.

The next day, Stefano stood in the office of Ristorante Massimo while Dante took a business call. They'd just returned from getting measured for new tuxes while the women were out shopping. He figured with his one and only brother getting hitched, it was time to pull out all the stops. After all, it was his duty to look his best with Jules on his arm—for the ceremony, of course.

From the disgruntled tone of Dante's voice, the phone conversation wasn't going well. And the way his brother was frowning told him that his brother was losing the argument.

Dante slammed the phone down and turned to him. "Lizzie isn't going to like this. At all."

"She isn't going to like what?" Lizzie glided into the room and into Dante's arms as though they'd been together for years.

Stefano's gaze moved to Jules, who stood hesitantly in the doorway. He imagined what it'd be like for her to rush into his arms. He longed to pull her petite form to him. He inwardly groaned imagining her soft curves pressing against him.

Jules's eyes met his. Was that a questioning look? Was it possible she had caught on to his wayward thoughts?

Impossible. His guilty conscience was just getting to him. He had no business fantasizing about her—or anyone.

He turned to Dante and Lizzie, who'd drifted apart. The smiles had faded and a serious undercurrent ran through the room. He wished Dante would just spill the news instead of letting the tension mount. Then again, maybe Dante was waiting for some privacy to talk with Lizzie alone.

"Maybe we should go," Stefano said to Jules.

"Uh..." Her glance swung back and forth between Lizzie and Dante. "Okay. Call me."

"No, wait. This involves both of you. Might as well tell everyone at once. Close the door, Lizzie."

Without a word, she did as he asked, closing out the noise of the kitchen staff. Stefano straightened. This wasn't going to be good. Maybe this was the last straw for Dante. Perhaps the setbacks had made him realize that the DeFiore men weren't meant for marriage.

The bad part about all of this was that Stefano had grown to really like Lizzie. She had spunk and a fire in her that you just couldn't help but admire. And she was good for his brother. Just like Gianna had been good for him. She *had* been good for him, hadn't she? At some point, they had been good together...hadn't they?

The memories stuck a sword of guilt through his gut. Her death was on his hands. He may not have done it, but he was the cause of it. If only he had kept his mouth shut. If only they hadn't argued—

"Dante, you're worrying me." Lizzie stepped up to him. "What is it?"

"That was the studio on the phone."

"But didn't we just talk to them yesterday? I thought everything was settled."

"It was. And then the execs looked at the footage we

filmed this past week for the upcoming series." Dante ran a hand over the back of his neck. "They don't like it. They say that it isn't fresh enough. They want to change the backdrop and the menus."

"What?" Lizzie stepped back. Her mouth fell open, and her eyes widened. "They can't do that."

"They can. And they have."

Well, this certainly wasn't the news Stefano was expecting. And he was surprised to feel a huge wave of relief. Though he believed his brother was headed for trouble, he didn't want to see him get hurt. It wasn't his place to say anything. Dante would have to make his own decisions— for better or worse—all by himself, just like Stefano had done with Gianna.

He relaxed and settled on the couch in the office. He didn't know why his brother had wanted him and Jules to stick around. She moved to the couch and sat down, too. Even at this respectable distance, she skewed his thinking. His only tangible thought was how her gentle floral scent reminded him of sunny days and grassy fields. And that was not good. He'd forfeited his right to enjoy a woman's presence the night Gianna had died.

"Do you have any idea why we're here?" Jules leaned closer to him.

"You're here because this impacts the wedding," Dante said before turning to Lizzie. "There's no way we can do what they want for the show and complete the wedding preparations in time."

Lizzie's hands settled on her hips. "But they said they wanted the wedding for the show."

"They said a lot of things, but we can't do everything. I'm sorry. We'll have to reschedule the wedding."

Stefano didn't want to say that this was an ominous sign—a warning—but he did think it was a chance for his brother to slow down and think through his choices. Still, the crushed look on Lizzie's face dug at him. They really didn't deserve so many problems, but it wasn't as if he could do anything to help.

"Are you saying you don't want to get married anymore?" Lizzie's voice wavered.

"Of course I do." Dante reached out and caressed her now pale cheek. "You know I love you. Maybe we can just make it something quick and simple."

Jules moved as if to stand up, and Stefano grabbed her arm, stopping her from interrupting. They really needed to figure this out for themselves. Certainly if there was such a serious problem between him and Jules, he'd want to figure it out for himself. Not that they'd ever be planning a wedding or anything.

When Jules's puzzled gaze turned to him, he shook his head. Her frosted lips pressed into a firm line, and her brows drew together. But she remained seated. Together they waited to see what their siblings would decide.

"But I have my dress picked out." Lizzie pulled away from Dante. "This isn't fair. This television show is messing everything up. We should quit."

"You're forgetting we signed a contract. And I don't think you really want to walk away from this. I see how you light up in front of the cameras. You're a natural."

Lizzie sighed, and her shoulders slumped. "But it's our wedding. What are we going to do?"

This time when Jules went to stand up, she gave Stefano the death stare when he reached out to her. Boy, that woman was as stubborn as she was beautiful. What exactly was she going to offer to this conversation? He had to admit that he was quite curious. Still, it wasn't for them to interfere.

Jules's mouth started to open, but he beat her to the

punch. "Jules and I should be going. Let us know what you decide to do."

All eyes turned to him. There were also two sets of raised brows and one frown. Everyone's face held an unspoken accusation. What in the world had he said that was so bad?

"Don't mind him." Jules turned her back to him. "We're here to help you. I think the real question is, do you still want to go through with the ceremony as planned?"

Dante and Lizzie gazed into each other's eyes.

"Yes." They spoke in unison.

Somehow that answer did not come as a surprise to him. Love made people do foolish things and gave them the illusion that they could overcome anything. But there were some things in life that even love couldn't conquer.

"Then let me help." Jules pressed her hands to her slender hips.

Lizzie raised her brows. "What do you have in mind?"

"Do you trust me?" Jules looked directly at her sister.

"Of course."

"Good. Then let me take over your wedding for you. All you'll have to do is your final dress fitting and make sure you show up for the ceremony." Jules grinned at her sister, lightening the mood.

"But there's so much to do. We couldn't ask you to do it all yourself—"

"Why not? I am the maid of honor, you know. And this isn't my first time helping with a wedding. And you know how I enjoy organizing things."

Lizzie turned a questioning gaze to Dante. "What do you think?"

He shrugged. "Whatever makes you happy is fine by me."

Lizzie turned to Jules. "You'd really do this for us?"

"Consider it my wedding gift."

"And," Dante piped up, "I'm sure my brother can give you lots of help. He has great taste. Isn't that right, Stefano?"

All eyes turned to him. Stefano struggled not to choke on his own tongue. They wanted him to help with the wedding preparations? Were they serious? "I don't think that's a good idea."

That response only succeeded in gaining him yet another round of frowns. He swallowed hard while keeping his chin high. He knew he was fighting a losing battle, but he just wasn't ready to concede to picking out flowers and whatever else went into a wedding.

Dante walked over and clapped him on the shoulder. "This experience will do you good. Maybe it'll give you some new ideas for your wine-tasting events."

Stefano resisted the urge to roll his eyes. His brother was really digging deep to come up with ideas of why he should waste his time planning some froufrou event. But he knew better than to vocalize his thoughts. He had no doubt that Jules and Lizzie would pounce on him like two lionesses going after fresh meat. Inwardly, he cringed at the thought.

"And what do you expect me to do about work at the vineyard while I'm out planning your nuptials?"

"I'm sure Papa won't mind taking over the vineyard in your absence."

"That's the second time you've said that. What do you know that I don't?"

"He's hinted that he's feeling a bit left out. Ever since Gianna's accident...well, um, you've been doing more and more of the work."

"And he told you this?" Then it all clicked into place. He recalled how Dante and their father had repaired their strained relationship. Their father must have confided his true feelings to Dante.

"All I'm saying is that you don't have to worry about the vineyard—it'll be handled. And I'm sure you don't want Jules to have to rely on public transportation when time is so vital."

Didn't his brother understand that it wasn't just the work? Planning a wedding would bring back unwanted memories. Thinking of Gianna still brought with it a truckload of guilt. If he hadn't married her and if he hadn't been expecting a life like the one his mother and father shared—a traditional lifestyle with the man working in the fields and the wife at home tending to the children— then maybe they wouldn't have started fighting. Maybe then she wouldn't have torn off in an angry huff that stormy night...

"I know Stefano won't let us down," Dante said confidently. "He's always there when the family needs him."

No, he wasn't. Otherwise he'd have been there for Gianna. But that was beside the point right now.

And so was how he felt about his brother tempting fate with this wedding. The only truly important thing now was that his brother was counting on him and he couldn't let him down. It'd been a long time since Dante had asked him for anything.

"Yeah, I'll help. As long as Papa is okay with the plan."

Dante smiled broadly. "Good. I'll call him as soon as we're done talking here."

Stefano couldn't believe he was going to help plan a wedding. Surely they didn't expect him to do more than drive Jules around. Even that would be a challenge. Though she was not his type, he couldn't deny her beauty. And those short skirts that she wore that showed off her toned legs were such a distraction. Jules's clothes were nothing like Gianna would have worn, no matter how modern his wife wanted to be. And what amazed him most was now that he'd gotten over the shock of Jules's trendy wardrobe, he was really starting to like the way she dressed.

But her makeup still made him pause. He wished she wouldn't apply it so heavily. He thought she was beautiful, but to be honest, it was hard to tell with all the makeup. And it taunted him, making him long to wipe it away and get to the real woman beneath it all.

The dresses were done. *Check.*

Well, not exactly. They were picked out, which in Jules's opinion was the hardest part of any wedding. Lizzie had her heart set on a stunning full-length oyster-colored gown. The fitted bodice was hand-beaded with crystal embellishments. The sweetheart neckline accentuated Lizzie's long neck, and the asymmetrical pleating that draped up over her waist was to die for. Jules thought it was absolutely perfect—befitting Cinderella herself.

For herself, they'd agreed on a knee-length strapless dress. The part she liked the best was the color: jazzberry jam. A black sash set off the whole dress and tied at the side. And they both agreed on a pair of black strappy sandals to go with it.

That was one thing she admired about her sister. Lizzie wasn't afraid of making decisions and going for it. She knew what she liked, and she didn't waver after her decision was made. Jules wished she was more like her. But maybe there was hope for her. Lately she'd noticed that she was more willing to make a decision without any input, and it felt good.

Armed with a wedding guide, a day planner and a credit card, Jules was ready to get to work. She glanced over at

Stefano as he navigated his way through the congested streets of Rome.

"Is traffic always like this?" she asked.

"Like what?"

"So busy."

"Not always, but we've hit the morning commute. I told you we should have waited a bit before coming to the city."

She shifted uncomfortably in the leather seat. "I thought you were just putting me off because you didn't want to come with me."

"Why would you think that? I agreed to help, didn't I?"

She glanced down at her black-and-white plaid mini-skirt. It was the tamest thing she owned. For the first time she felt out of place. The truth was she used her clothes as a defense mechanism. If people were busy talking about the length of her hemline, they weren't noticing how the heavy makeup camouflaged her facial scars.

But right now she wondered what it would be like to let down her guard and dress like everyone else—like Lizzie. It would definitely be different. Maybe it'd make Stefano less hesitant to escort her around Rome. It was a thought. One she'd take into consideration. She just wasn't so sure that she was ready to let down her tightly held defenses just yet.

"I…I just know that your brother gave you a healthy shove into agreeing to this."

"Here's a lesson in DeFiore men. When we don't want to do something, we don't do it. And nothing and no one will change our minds."

She took in his serious expression. Maybe she was reading too much into his reluctance to leave the vineyard that morning. Perhaps she should have believed him when he'd said he didn't want to get stuck with the morning commuters.

But she still found herself thinking of visiting a boutique or two while they were shopping. She couldn't afford off-the-rack fashions. Unlike her sister, who shopped at secondhand stores, Jules found most of her stuff at the back of stores on the clearance racks. When your tastes were a bit eclectic, it made discount shopping a lot easier. But that would have to wait. She had other, more important, business to deal with first.

"I was just going over the wedding checklist, and we might just pull this off."

"Might?" He chanced a quick glance her way.

"Well, yes. It's going to be a lot of work, but we already have the venue and the dresses, and Lizzie found a place online that will print her invitations and mail them for her. Those will go out this week. Let's see. What else is there?" Her gaze skimmed down over the master list. "Lizzie mentioned something about you being able to supply tables and chairs."

Stefano nodded. "We have plenty we keep on hand for large events at the winery."

"Great." One more thing checked off her long list. "Are we almost at the next florist?"

"Yes, it's right ahead." Stefano braked for a traffic light. "I still don't know what you didn't like about the last florist."

She turned a narrowed gaze his way. "They were trying to pawn their overstock on us. They wanted to make an easy sale, and I don't want that. Lizzie and Dante deserve more than that. Lizzie and I don't exactly come from a traditional background. And now that she's found her Prince Charming, she—they—deserve to have a perfect day. And if that takes you and I driving all around this city to find the right florist, then that's what we'll do."

"I didn't know you were that invested in this wedding."

"There's a lot about me that you don't know."

"I'm listening if you want to tell me."

For a moment, she was tempted to let down her guard and open up to him about the loss of her mother and the string of foster homes. But what would that accomplish? Nothing. She had to stay focused. "This isn't about me. It's about Lizzie and Dante."

The traffic surged forward, and Stefano followed. "It doesn't look like there's any parking. I'll drop you off. You have my cell number, right?"

"Yes, but aren't you coming in?"

"The last time you were in and out so fast that I'd just walked up in time to hold the door as you stormed out—"

"I wasn't that bad. Was I?"

A smile tugged at his lips. "Let's just say that everyone knew you weren't a satisfied customer."

"But what if these people don't speak English? You have to come with me. After all, you told your brother that you would help with everything. You don't want to go back on your word, do you?" Jules reached down and grabbed her oversize purse, which contained pictures of the dresses and color swatches. Without waiting for his response, she added, "I'll see you inside."

CHAPTER EIGHT

WHAT IN THE world had his brother gotten him into?

Stefano's feet felt weighted down as he made his way to the florist. The last thing he needed to be doing was escorting Jules around. She made him think things and feel things he shouldn't. And when she looked at him with those big green eyes, his common sense took a hike. His raging hormones took charge and left him longing to steal a kiss. A long, passionate one.

He was in so much trouble.

He half hoped Jules would already be waiting for him on the sidewalk. They could head back to the villa, and he could lose himself in his work. It'd keep his mind from straying back to Jules's sultry lips or tempting butterfly. He inwardly groaned.

And no matter what Dante said about his father wanting to get more involved with the business side of things, Stefano had made a lot of changes since his father had last run DeFiore Winery. Stefano was certain he'd have questions.

When Stefano neared the front of the shop, he peered in the big showroom window. Colorful blooms in various arrangements stared back at him, and he saw no sign of Jules making a hasty exit. Could it be that this place lived up to her high standards?

He sighed in relief. Once they placed a quick order,

they'd be back on the road. Maybe this day wasn't going to be a complete waste of time after all.

A little bell above the door chimed as he entered the shop. He was surprised to find so many people inside. There were men with bouquets of long-stemmed red roses. Others had arrangements of pink carnations. And yet another man had a bouquet of lilies, some sort of bright green pom-poms, brilliant pink roses and tiny deep purple flowers. And then there were a cluster of young women pointing at the cooler cases that held a wide array of flowers in black buckets. He couldn't help but wonder if this place was always this busy. Perhaps he'd gone into the wrong business.

He found Jules at the back of the shop, studying a cooler case of flowers he didn't recognize. "Did you find what you need?"

"I think so."

"Good." This had gone even easier than he'd imagined. "Ready to go?"

"Go? Are you kidding?" When she looked at him with those big green eyes, he could feel himself melting. "I haven't even talked with a salesperson yet."

"You haven't? What have you been doing?" It wasn't until the words were out of his mouth that he realized how they sounded.

She frowned. "You might get things done by pushing to the front of the line, but there are those of us who believe in waiting our turn."

His head lowered. She was right. "I just didn't realize there'd be such a demand for flowers." Well, he wasn't going to do any good just standing there taking up space. "It looks like it's going to be a while. I've got some things to do. I'll be back—"

"You're leaving me?"

The way she said it made him feel as though he was shirking his duties as best man. "I was just trying to make good use of the time. I don't know a dandelion from a carnation."

"You can help me pick out some flowers. Lizzie told me the main flower she wants in her bouquet is a dahlia. If possible it should have a yellow center with deep pink tips. She said they have a sentimental meaning for her and Dante." Jules shrugged her slender shoulders. "I see that they have some here, so it shouldn't be too much of a problem to get them to order more. I hope."

"Great. It sounds like you have the flowers all figured out." He turned toward the door, feeling extremely uncomfortable as a grandmotherly woman gave him a smile and a nod as though she thought that Jules and he were…were a couple. "I'll just wait outside."

Jules reached out and caught his arm. "Not so fast. I still need some other flowers to complement the bouquet. I thought about baby's breath, but everyone uses that. Lizzie needs something different. Something that will make the colors in the bouquet pop. You know this whole thing will be on television. Well, not the whole thing, but highlights of the wedding. And it just has to be perfect."

Stefano stifled a groan as Jules pulled him around to look at the variety of flowers. Though she mainly wore black and white, she appeared to have a fondness for other colors, too. *Interesting.*

"I'm sorry it took me a bit to get to you two." The saleswoman was an older lady who spoke perfect English with an Italian accent. "With summer here, romance is in the air."

"It certainly is." Jules smiled broadly. "We're here to order flowers for a wedding."

Stefano was caught off guard by the ease of her smile

and the twinkle in her eyes. Was it possible that Jules was a closet romantic? She certainly seemed to know enough about this stuff.

The woman's face lit up. "What do you have in mind?"

Jules turned to him and asked if he'd hold her purse. He quickly scanned the area. Relieved to find no male witnesses, he reached out for the very large black leather purse. He was shocked by its weight. What did she carry in there? Barbells?

He watched as Jules opened her wedding planner and flipped to a page with colorful pictures, but before he could focus in on the images, she lifted the notebook out of his view. Whether it was intentional or not, he didn't know and he wasn't about to ask. He didn't need her thinking that he was interested in any of it. He was doing his duty as best man. Nothing more.

The saleswoman produced various stems of tiny flowers from white to pink to deep purple. In the beginning, Jules would turn to consult him. He generally shrugged and said they were nice. After he kept repeating the same response, she gave up asking for his input, which was fine with him.

"Don't worry, honey." The woman patted Jules's arm. "If it were up to most men, they'd pick some wildflowers from the side of the road as a wedding bouquet. That's why you have me."

"Thank you so much. I really appreciate all of your help. And I know it's short notice, but the wedding is next month. Will we be able to get the flowers in time for the ceremony?"

"Let me check." The woman pulled out a day planner and Jules read off the date. "*Non c'è problema.* You two are such a cute couple." The woman beamed at them.

Without warning, Jules leaned over, wrapped her hands around his arm and leaned her head against his shoulder.

His body stiffened. What was she doing? He would have asked, but his heart in his throat kept him from breathing, much less speaking.

"You really think so?" Jules lifted her chin and smiled broadly up at him.

"Oh, definitely. Just wait until you have children. They'll be real darlings."

"Hmm…I hadn't thought about it."

Jules gave him a quick once-over as though inspecting his physical attributes to see if he would make good father material—a father to their children. When her gaze met his, her lips lifted into a smile that lit up her eyes. His jaw tightened. She was having fun at his expense. But what bothered him the most was he could easily envision a little girl with Jules's big green eyes—his daughter. He stopped his thoughts from meandering down that dangerous path.

What in the world was going on? He and Jules were barely even friends, much less planning a life together. That was not going to happen.

Jules pulled away. Although he should have felt relieved, he found himself missing her touch. It killed him to admit even to himself, but he'd enjoyed the softness of her hands pressing against his bare arm. The warmth of her gaze was powerful stuff. A man could get swept away and forget all about logic. He'd have to be careful around this one. He wasn't going to fall in love again. No way. The price was too high.

The saleswoman continued to beam at them. "Don't you two worry about flowers for your big day. As soon as I looked at you I knew there was a love connection. You'll make a wonderful bride and groom."

Stefano cleared his throat, at last feeling as though he'd regained his ability to speak—he must clear up this misunderstanding. He couldn't continue to play along with Jules's game any longer.

"We aren't together." His voice came out gruff.

Both women turned to him with startled looks. It had to be from the tone of his voice because there was no way that Jules was surprised by his admission. It wasn't as if she even liked him.

Did she?

"This isn't for our wedding." Stefano had to correct the woman since Jules didn't seem the least bit interested in doing it. He couldn't let the woman go on about them being such a great couple.

Jules's perfectly plucked brows drew together into a formidable line and her lush red lips pressed together as though she were holding back a heated reprimand. Let her fume. He'd merely corrected a glaring error. End of story.

The saleswoman's puzzled gaze moved from him to Jules. "I don't understand." The woman's face took on a very serious expression. "These flowers you've picked out, if they aren't for you two, who are they for?"

Jules sent him a this-is-your-fault look. But he didn't feel the least bit guilty. Why should he?

She shifted her weight in those sky-high black-heeled boots that made her look as if she'd just stepped out of some rock-and-roll video. Not that he'd watched many. But he had seen a few in his time, and, well, she was definitely gorgeous enough to star in them if only she'd lighten up on the makeup so people could really see her. But right now there was no mistaking that she was upset. Not even that thick makeup could hide her frown lines.

Jules clasped her hands together. "The thing is we're picking out flowers for another couple."

"You're what?" The saleswoman looked taken aback. "Where's the bride?"

"Working. She had an emergency come up and asked if we'd step in and help with the plans."

"Will she be in later to approve the order?"

"I'm afraid not." Jules clenched her hands together. "I don't think we can take your order—"

"But you must." Jules's voice cracked with emotion. "We're running out of options. I promise everything will be to the bride's liking."

The saleswoman shook her head. "We can't do it."

"What's the big deal?" Stefano came to Jules's defense. "They're flowers, for goodness' sake. They all pretty much look the same except for the colors. And Jules showed you the color of the dresses. Now we'd like to buy some flowers."

"You might want to, but that doesn't mean it's going to happen. Listen, I just got burned on a really big order where the bride was too busy with her dress or some such thing to come in and approve what her mother picked out for the wedding. I'm still sorting out that mess." She shook her head. "I'm not doing that again. Either the bride comes in or you'll have to go elsewhere to buy your flowers."

The woman couldn't be serious. He glanced at Jules, who looked upset. "Listen here, you can't do that—"

"What he meant to say is we understand. Thank you so much for your time." She pulled on his arm to leave.

He refused to be turned away. "I want to talk to the owner."

The saleswoman pressed her hands to her generous hips. "You're speaking to her. And it's time you left."

"Thanks again." Jules tugged harder and finally he gave in, letting her lead him from the flower shop. He didn't know why she was retreating. The woman was there to sell flowers and they were there to buy them, not cater to the woman's wishes. This was ridiculous.

Once outside and down the sidewalk a ways, Jules spun around and got in his face with her finger pointing at him. Her face was filled with color. Her eyes narrowed on him. This wasn't going to be pretty. Not at all.

"Do you know what you just did in there?" Her heated tone left no doubt about her agitation.

"Yes, I corrected the woman. You let her think that we were a couple. I couldn't let her think that."

"Why? Is it so awful to think that you and I might be involved?"

He rubbed the back of his neck, trying to avoid the curious looks as people passed by. "Can we talk about this later? People are starting to stare."

"Let them. You owe me some answers."

"Fine. I don't like to lie. And letting that woman believe we're something we're not was a lie."

Jules's gaze narrowed even more. "And you are the pillar of honesty?"

He lowered his head as memories of his not so distant past started to pound him. No, he wasn't the pillar of anything. In fact, he was the exact opposite. If he'd been more of a proponent of the truth while he was married, he might still be married—well, he wouldn't go that far. But Gianna would still be alive.

He'd give anything to erase that awful night. Anything at all.

"Lying only leads to regrets." He looked at Jules. She didn't seem as hostile now. In fact, the way she was gazing at him it was as if she was trying to read him. "What does any of this matter, anyway? They were just flowers. I'm sure there are lots of other shops that would be more than willing to take our business."

"Not if you keep shooting your mouth off like that.

These people like to know that they are dealing with the person in charge—"

"And that's you—"

"Not in this case. This is a wedding. The bride is always in charge. It's her wedding. Her big day. The whole thing revolves around her. And these people have been down the aisle enough times to know how it works."

"So if that's the case, why's Lizzie dumping it all in your lap instead of delaying the wedding?"

"Because she trusts me. We're the only family each other has. We know each other better than anyone in the world, and she knows that I will plan the perfect wedding for her."

"I hope you're right. About knowing her so well."

Jules's lips lifted in a small smile. "You don't have to worry." She lifted her phone and waved it in his face. "I've been texting and sending photos on top of talking to her every day. She's on top of things. I'm just acting as her mouthpiece."

That bit of news sent a wave of relief through him. But they still had to find flowers, someplace without such a picky saleswoman.

"Well, Ms. Mouthpiece, any ideas where we should go next?"

"I don't know. Let me see." She started typing on her smartphone.

When she turned to start walking, he called out, "You're going the wrong way."

She glanced up, confusion reflected in her beautiful eyes. "Oh."

Quietly they retraced their steps. Her focus was on her phone. And his attention was on keeping her from walking into other pedestrians. When they reached the car, she had another florist for them to try. But it was nearing lunchtime, and he really needed a break before they set out again.

He turned to Jules. "How about lunch?"

"Already?" When she glanced at the time on her phone, her lips formed an O. "I didn't realize it was so late. Would you mind if we had lunch at Ristorante Massimo? I have a couple of things to go over with Lizzie."

"Sounds like a plan. Why don't you call ahead? Dante can have something waiting for us so it won't take so long. Those two stops this morning took forever. I hope we don't have to wait that long in the next shop." He didn't know if he had the patience for this wedding shopping. It was like watching a grape ripen—painfully slow.

"I hope so, too, or the shopping is going to take us more than a week. And with time being of the essence, we have to move quickly. We still have the cake to pick out."

"Why didn't we do that first?"

Jules grinned at him. "Because the cake tasting is the best part of this whole adventure. It's like a reward."

He smiled and shook his head. "I don't know how someone as slender as you can gorge on cake."

"You just watch, and I'll show you." Her eyes twinkled with mischief.

Jules was a breath of fresh air. She was nothing like the women that lived in the nearby village, who enjoyed a more sedate way of life. And yet she wasn't like some of the posh urban women who attended the wine-tasting events and were always in such a hurry. Jules had an air about her, but it was all her own.

The more time he spent with her, the more he was beginning to like her—really like her. And that just couldn't happen.

CHAPTER NINE

A DELICIOUS LUNCH could change one's perspective.

If Jules had known food could put a smile on Stefano's face, she'd have suggested it ages ago. He'd actually started a conversation, but it was directed at Dante, not her. And it was about one of his favorite subject—grapes. Still it had been nice watching him let down his guard and relax.

But as soon as they climbed back in the car, the walls around him went back up, blocking her out. She didn't understand what she'd done to get him to hold her at arm's length. Surely he still wasn't upset about the salesclerk thinking they were a couple.

Jules glanced down at her black skirt, black stockings and black boots. Okay, so maybe her color choice was a bit somber, but her styles weren't.

She gave herself a mental jerk. What was she doing? Reevaluating her clothes because of a guy that barely tolerated her? She was fine just the way she was. And black was her favorite color.

She needed to focus on the wedding, not pleasing Stefano. With that thought, she realized it might be best to tell him exactly what she had in mind as they visited this florist.

She leaned over and said, "Just follow my lead. Can you do that?"

He maneuvered the car into a parking spot. "Depends. Are you going to lie?"

"Stefano, do you want this wedding to be nice for your brother?"

"Yes, but he isn't going to care about flowers."

"He might not, but his bride will. If she's not happy, do you really think that he'll be happy?"

There was a strained pause. "I suppose not."

She didn't say a word as he alighted from the car. While she gathered her purse and wedding planner, Stefano rounded the front of the car. She reached for the door handle, but Stefano beat her to it and swung it open. He was a gentleman, something she wasn't accustomed to. But she could get used to this. After all, if they were about to create a little bit of make-believe, she might as well enjoy some of the benefits.

Inside there was one man working the shop, and he was already busy with someone at the register placing an order. That would give her time to scope out his supply and find out if he was a viable candidate.

"Oh, look—they have dahlias." She rushed over to take a closer look. "And there are some in the right color." She couldn't resist smiling and gently clapped her hands. "So far, so good."

Stefano pretended to be interested, but she could tell by his reserved reaction that he was less than impressed. She wasn't going to let his mood ruin this for her. She intended to enjoy this wedding as much as possible. It was quite possibly the last thing that Lizzie would ever ask her to do…especially after Lizzie learned that she wasn't going to grad school.

"Are you finding what you're looking for?" The salesman approached them.

This was where she had to play her cards just right.

There was no way she was going through all the pain and effort to select the flowers only to have the man turn them away. They didn't have the time to waste.

She slipped her hand in Stefano's. When he tried to pull away, she tightened her grip. Silently she willed him to play along with her. She would do her best not to outright lie. The impression the salesman made would be his own responsibility.

After all, she certainly wasn't expecting anything to come of this. Sure, she'd dated in the past, but she'd always insisted on keeping things casual—except one time. It had been a blind date set up by her lab partner. His name was J.T. It had been a case of infatuation from the get-go. As they'd started to see each other on a regular basis, she'd thought they were building the solid foundation for a committed relationship. She had been certain of it.

With J.T's graduation just weeks away, he'd asked her to dinner. He'd said that he had something he wanted to say to her. She recalled how excited she'd been. While Lizzie had done her utmost to talk sense into her, all Jules could think about was a diamond ring. At last, someone in her life who would love her and never leave.

In the end, the dinner had been a thank-you for tutoring him in a philosophy class. He had told her that he couldn't have passed the course without her help. And, as she'd tried her best to suck up her disappointment, he'd capped off the evening with an announcement that he was moving across the country to California. He was leaving, and she wasn't invited to go with him.

It wasn't until after a couple of tissue boxes—the jumbo size—that she had realized it had worked out for the best. It reaffirmed her belief that love didn't exist. It was a fleeting notion. Something that she never planned to explore ever again. But now, after witnessing Lizzie and Dante's relationship, she thought maybe her assessment hadn't been quite so accurate.

Jules presented her best smile to the salesman. "We'd like to order some flowers for a wedding."

"Excellent." The man glanced around as though searching for something. "Let me just grab something to write on." He rushed back to the counter and returned with a clipboard and a pen. "When is the wedding?"

"The middle of next month."

The smile faded from the man's face. "Oh, that soon."

"Is that a problem?"

"Why don't you tell me what you have in mind, and we'll go from there."

Not wanting to press her luck, she released Stefano's hand. She chanced a quick glance at him to find a frown pulling at his lips. Disappointment wiped away her own smile. Not exactly the look a bride would want from her intended bridegroom, but it wasn't as if they were even involved. So then why did his scowl dig at her?

After reviewing each flower on Lizzie's list, the man assured her he'd be able to order them all. The bridal bouquet would be quite extravagant. And the changes the florist suggested, although small, were just enough to set off the flowers.

With the deposit made, Jules and Stefano turned to the door. She slipped her hand back in his. She didn't have to, she knew that, but she wanted to feel his strong fingers entwined with hers. It had been a long time since she'd dated. Maybe she was lonelier than she'd thought. Or maybe all of this focus on the wedding was making her realize how alone she'd be without her sister.

"Don't worry," the salesman called out. "You two will have a marvelous wedding."

She turned and waved goodbye. His words drove home

her loneliness. Maybe always being the bridesmaid wasn't all she'd convinced herself it would be.

Jules sucked in an unsteady breath. She'd promised herself on the flight over that she wouldn't fall apart. She would be happy for her foster sister. No matter what.

"Are you okay?" Stefano stopped on the sidewalk to look at her.

"Umm…yes, I'm fine." When she realized that her hand was still in his, she tried to pull away, but this time he was the one to tighten his grip.

She gave up the struggle and took comfort in the innocent touch. Instead of dwelling on her loneliness, she turned her thoughts back to Apricot. She desperately wanted to take the kitten home with her. She'd soon be known as the spinster cat lady, she mused. She wondered what Stefano would say if he knew about the direction of her pathetic thoughts.

As for the kitten, she wasn't so sure it was a good idea to transport it such a long distance. And if she didn't know better, she'd swear that Apricot was working her way into Stefano's heart. Perhaps finding Apricot a home wouldn't be as hard as she'd originally thought.

She still had a handful of weeks until the wedding to make up her mind about the cat. One way or another Apricot would have a loving home.

More than a week had passed since the whirlwind, otherwise known as Jules, had blown Stefano's routine life off course. Nothing was the same with her around. She'd befriended his father. Nonno thought the sun rose around her. And Maria had taken her under her wing, showing her some of her favorite recipes. It was as though Jules fit right in.

But she didn't belong at the vineyard. And she never

would. Nothing good would come of him imagining any other scenario.

So if that was the case, why had he immediately noticed Jules's absence from the breakfast table? He forced himself to stay there and eat. After all, she wasn't his responsibility. It was enough that he had to babysit her on their numerous ventures to Rome, but the line had to be drawn somewhere. He couldn't risk getting involved.

Once he'd finished his *caffè*, he quietly emptied his barely picked-over breakfast into the trash. He had no appetite even though Maria was a fine cook. At last he escaped to the silence of the outdoors, but it was no easy task. His father was in quite a chatty mood. In fact, he hadn't seen his father this animated in a long time. Maybe Dante had been right. Maybe Stefano had unintentionally cut his father out of more of the business than he'd intended. At least one of them was happy.

Once outside, Stefano hesitated. His thoughts turned back to Jules. Maybe he should check on her. After all, something could be wrong. He assured himself that it was his duty to be a good host. With his mind made up, he made his way around to the front of the house, preferring to avoid the prying eyes in the kitchen.

In no time at all, he was standing outside Jules's room. He rapped his knuckles on the door. "Jules, are you there?"

"Come in."

He didn't know what to expect when he opened the door, but it wasn't the sight that greeted him. There was Jules sitting on the floor, surrounded by an array of various shades of purple-and-white tissue paper. And the kitten was scurrying around, chasing bits of paper. What a mess.

In the middle of it all, Jules smiled up at him. "Hi. Did you need something?"

"I didn't see you at breakfast. I thought maybe you weren't feeling well."

"No, I'm fine. I'm just busy." She held up a tissue-paper flower for his inspection. "What do you think?"

"Um…" He wasn't so sure what to say. "It's nice."

Her smile broadened. "Thanks. I'm a bit of an expert at these by now. But I've never had to make them by myself before. Usually the bridal party gets together for some fun and we make the flowers. By the end of the night, there's hundreds of them. But since Lizzie wants a small wedding, I guess it's up to me to make them."

"But I don't understand. Isn't that what we went to the florist for?" He'd never figure out women, no matter how long he lived.

"This is different. These are for decorations."

"If we need to buy more flowers, just say so." By the looks of this room, she'd been here forever making flowers.

"Thanks. But it's not necessary. I want both types of flowers."

This wedding business was way more involved than he'd imagined. Jules was going to wear herself to a frazzle. There had to be a better way to go about it. And that's where he could help her out.

"You can't do everything yourself."

With a paper punch in one hand and tissue paper in the other, she paused and glanced up at him. "Why, Stefano, is that your way of offering to make flowers with me?"

"Definitely not." When her smile dimmed, he hurried to correct himself. "I mean, I can hire someone to do this stuff. I can hire as many people as it takes. Just tell me what you need."

Jules unfolded her legs and stood. "I don't want strangers doing Lizzie's wedding."

He was obviously missing something, but he had no

clue what it might be. Back when he was married to Gianna when he didn't understand her logic, he'd just shrug and walk away. Maybe if he'd asked more questions and tried to understand her better, their life wouldn't have careened out of control.

"Why in the world not?"

"It doesn't matter."

Okay, he probably could have worded that better. He cleared his throat to try again. "Talk to me. Obviously there's something I'm missing and I'd like to understand."

Surprise reflected in her green gaze. "I...I don't have money to buy them a proper wedding gift. I know it's silly, but I want to create a cozy wedding with a personal touch. Lizzie doesn't know I'm doing all of this. And don't you tell her."

He felt like such an unfeeling lowlife now. The money aspect had never even crossed his mind. And he had to admit Jules's gift would surpass even the most expensive offering because it came from the heart.

"Your gift will be their favorite." And he meant it. "What can I do to help, aside from making flowers? I don't think mine would be suitable for anything but the garbage."

Jules's stance eased, and she asked if she could use his computer to order some favors. She listed off things he never would have thought of, including wedding bubbles and sparklers. It would definitely be a wedding to remember.

"You're welcome to use my computer anytime. Now, how about taking a break to eat?"

She settled back on the floor, right in the middle of the mess. "I'll get to it later. I'm excited to see how many of these I can get done today. And Apricot is being a big help."

Stefano looked dubiously at the kitten running around

and batting at the scraps of colorful tissue paper. Well, as long as Jules was happy, he was fine with it.

"I've got some work at the barn that I need to do. If you need me, I'll be there."

She gathered a stack of tissue paper and pushed a round punch through the sheets. "We're good. Huh, Apricot?"

The kitten gave her a quick glance and then returned to playing.

Stefano felt guilty as he walked away. But seriously, having him make tissue-paper flowers would have been an utter disaster. Maybe he could help with her internet shopping. That was something he could do.

With a plan in mind, his steps toward the barn grew quicker. She didn't want help from strangers, but that didn't include him. They'd moved past being strangers a while back. Where they were headed he wasn't quite sure.

He walked into the office just in time to find his father shutting down the computer. "Calling it a day already?"

Papa jerked his salt-and-pepper head up. "Sorry. I didn't hear you come in. Umm...yes. I thought I'd take a break."

"You feeling all right?"

"Of course." Frown lines creased Papa's tanned face. "Am I that much of a workaholic that you think because I am out of the office something must be wrong?"

Since when did his father become so defensive?

Stefano shrugged, trying to take a neutral stance. "Is there anything around here that needs my immediate attention?"

His father rubbed his jaw. Instead of the gray stubble that normally dotted it, it was clean shaven. "Not that I can think of. I've calculated the number of new barrels we'll need for the fall harvest, and I've ordered the supplies. They should be here in a few weeks."

"What about the email? Is it backed up? It always seems they come in faster than I can respond to them."

"No, I just finished responding to the last email. Things are pretty quiet right now. I was thinking that perhaps we should consider increasing the number of wine-tasting events we host. It'd be good for the business, and I think it'd be well received."

Stefano nodded. "You know we have one coming up before the wedding."

"I do. I just think that we can do more."

It'd been one of those things that he'd been meaning to get to, but there was always something else that needed his attention first. But it seemed his father was on top of everything. Good for him. Right now, Stefano was actually kind of enjoying this downtime.

"You headed out to the fields?" Stefano asked, feeling obligated to accompany him. "I can give you a hand."

Papa's bushy brows rose. "Um...no, that isn't necessary. I'm going to have some *caffè* first. Why don't you take the day off?"

That was the problem; he didn't want to slow down because then his thoughts would take over and that would do nothing but get him in trouble. He'd start remembering his past mistakes. Or worse yet, he'd start thinking about Jules in all the wrong ways. The last thing he needed to do was to start caring about her.

His father clapped him on the shoulder. "It's a beautiful day. Don't spend all of it in here."

After his father walked away, Stefano sat down at the desk. Out of the corner of his eye, he spied the coffeemaker. It was still on, and the pot was full. *What in the world?* Why was his father heading to the house for *caffè* when there was plenty here?

Stefano shook his head and gave up trying to figure out

his father. He turned on the computer and found the email was in fact under control. The office was in decent shape. And there was absolutely no business requiring his attention. *Good.* Now he had time to help Jules with the wedding. His fingers flew over the keypad.

A little later, he headed back to the house, excited to tell Jules what he'd ordered. His steps grew faster the more he thought of her sitting on the floor in those short shorts with her bare legs showing and that contagious smile on her face. He didn't know what it was about her that drew him in. She was unlike any other woman he'd ever known.

Maybe his problem was he spent too much time alone at this vineyard. But that was his punishment for what had happened to Gianna. He didn't let himself go out and have a good time. He didn't let himself think about the future because she didn't have one.

However, now, for the first time since his wife's tragic death, he wanted to live again. He wanted to feel alive. And that's how Jules made him feel—heart-poundingly, soul-stirringly alive.

It was a strange sensation after living so long in self-imposed exile. He'd cut himself off from most of the outside world. He'd unknowingly followed in his father's footsteps, even though he'd sworn that he would be different. Yet another thing he'd failed at, but he wouldn't fail Jules. He'd do his best to help her make this wedding special.

As he drew close to the house, he saw someone exit the kitchen door. It was Maria, and she was laughing. In the past eleven or so years that she'd been tending to the house, he didn't recall ever hearing her laugh like that—unrestricted and joyous. What could have put her in such a good mood—

His father.

Papa's deep chuckle drifted through the air. Stefano came to a halt. What in the world was going on?

Stefano watched in amazement as the two, not noticing him, started off toward the vines as though they were going for a stroll—together. If he hadn't seen it with his own eyes, he never would have believed his father was interested in Maria. How long had this been going on? And how had he missed it until now?

Did this explain the recent change in his father? The easiness Papa had taken on? The not working until all hours of the night? The added pep in his step?

Stefano raked his fingers through his hair as he tried to come to terms with the fact his father was back among the living. There was a mixed ball of emotions churning in his gut. He truly wanted to be happy for his father, but it nagged at him that he and his brother had suffered through their childhoods with an emotionally detached father. If only his father had made this change long ago, he could have saved everyone so much misery.

When his father and Maria were far enough off, Stefano made the rest of his way to the house. It seemed as though everyone was getting on with their lives—except him. But how did he do that? How did he forget what he'd done?

He didn't have any answers, just more questions. The one thing he could do was get into the spirit of his brother's wedding. Maybe Dante was right to roll the dice and see what life handed him.

The thought of Jules making all those silly paper flowers alone tugged at his conscious. He was the best man. And since there was no other bridal party, it fell to him to help her. Whether he was any good at it or not, he could try his best.

Spending some time with Jules was not silly—not at all.

Besides, it would keep his mind off the fact that his father was changing—right before his very eyes. Suddenly Stefano felt as though he was standing still in life and soon he'd be left behind.

CHAPTER TEN

JULES RAN THE brush through her damp hair, pulling the dark strands back in a single ponytail. The cool shower felt rejuvenating. She'd just sat down on the bedroom floor to make some more flowers when there was a knock at the door.

Her chest tightened. She wasn't expecting anyone to come looking for her. She thought everyone was out and about doing their own thing.

She scrambled to her feet. The door was locked, so it wasn't like anyone would just come walking in on her.

"Jules, are you in there?" Stefano's deep tones vibrated through the door.

"Did you need something?"

"I have news. You know, it's easier to talk when there isn't a piece of wood standing between us."

Jules pressed her hands to her cheeks. She hadn't had a chance to do her makeup yet. She couldn't have him seeing her like this—with her scars exposed. Her heart beat rapidly. She didn't think she could stand to have him turn away in repulsion.

She stepped closer to the door. "Could we talk at lunch?"

There was a slight pause. "Is everything okay?"

What could be so important? She didn't have a clue. She had to admit that she was quite curious to know what was so urgent.

"Jules?" The doorknob jiggled. "Jules, what's going on? Why is your door locked?"

She sighed. He wasn't going to just give up and go away. She'd already witnessed his stubborn streak at the florist. This time he might just break down the door to see for himself that she was okay.

This might be just what she needed to end the silly crush she had on him. Once he saw the scars on her face, he'd turn tail and run.

"Jules, come on. You're starting to worry me."

She sucked in a steadying breath, leveled her shoulders and released the lock on the door. With a twist of the knob, she pulled it open. Stefano stood there, all six-plus feet of him, with his forehead wrinkled with worry lines. He stepped into the room, and she backed up so he could enter the whole way.

"See, nothing to worry about." She felt a little off center that he was actually worried about her. Aside from Lizzie, no one worried about her.

His gaze slid over her fuzzy black robe with purple polka dots. She suddenly wished it was a little longer. As it was, it barely reached midthigh, and the only thing beneath it was a lacy black bra and matching undies. Though she was modestly covered, she still felt fully exposed. She lowered her head, staring at her purple toenails.

"You aren't dressed yet?"

She shrugged. "I've been busy."

"I noticed. That's what I wanted to talk to you about—"

"If this is about hiring help, I told you to forget it."

"Actually, what I wanted to say is I know in the beginning I wasn't a fan of helping with this wedding, but I want to help now. I want to do whatever it is that you need. Just give me a task, and I'll get it done. Or at least I'll try my best."

Jules crossed her arms. "Do you mind if I ask what brought about this change of heart?"

He paused and stared at her. Was it her scars? Did he at last see her defects? That crescent moon scar that wrapped around the side of her left eye and the long scar that trailed down her jaw. They were so ugly.

She couldn't stand him staring any longer. She felt as though she were under a spotlight. Pretending to be intent on picking up some of her flower-making supplies from the floor, she kept her back to him.

"I'm sorry. I didn't mean to stare."

"I should have put on my makeup, but I didn't get to it yet."

"Don't." When she turned a questioning look his way, he added, "Don't put the makeup on."

She straightened and turned to him. "You've got to be kidding."

"No, I think you look beautiful without all of that stuff."

He couldn't be serious. There was no way someone could find her scarred face beautiful. She shook her head. "Don't lie."

"I'm not." He stepped closer to her. When she wouldn't meet his gaze, his thumb moved beneath her chin and raised her face until she was looking directly at him. "You are beautiful."

"But...but what about my scars?"

"The one by your eye is hardly noticeable. It's your green eyes that draw my attention. The gold flecks in them catch the light just right. And your pert nose is just perfect. And then there's your lips—they are quite fascinating. They look as though they are just ripe for kissing."

The breath hitched in her throat. He was seducing her with his words. No one had ever done that before, and all she wanted him to do now was put some action behind his compliments.

Then in the next breath his hand pulled away from her chin, and he stepped back. "If that's the only reason you wear all of that makeup, then don't. You are much more beautiful without it. Trust me. I wouldn't lie to you."

Maybe he wouldn't. He'd just lead her on and then leave her wanting a kiss that wasn't coming. How in the world was she ever going to concentrate on anything but him?

"I'll consider it." She'd been wearing makeup since she was a teen, hiding her scars.

"Are you still making flowers?" He glanced around at the array of papers on the floor.

"The shower gave me renewed energy, and I thought I might make some more before lunch."

"I see your helper faded away."

"Apricot wore herself out chasing the paper and then sliding across the floor. When she got bored of that I rolled a piece into a ball. She batted it everywhere until at last it went under the bed. Instead of going after it, she clawed her way up the bedspread and laid down."

There in the middle of her bed, in a pink fuzzy blanket Jules had bundled up into a circle with a divot in the middle, was Apricot—belly up and sound asleep. The kitten was so sweet. She didn't know how she'd ever leave her behind.

"Seems as if she couldn't be happier." He turned back to Jules. "You're really good with her. Someday you'll make a great mother."

"It's not going to happen."

She waited, but he didn't say anything else on the matter.

Deep inside she wanted to believe him. She wanted to believe that she could someday be a mom. Lizzie wasn't the only one who'd dreamed of having her own family.

But knowing she wasn't cut out to raise children, Jules had turned her focus to social work. She thought she could care for the kids from a distance. Until she'd found out that she was unable to maintain a professional distance. Frustration knotted her stomach.

Stefano made himself comfortable on the floor and started to gather a stack of papers. "So how do you do this?"

"You really want to make a flower?" She surely hadn't heard him correctly. There was nothing about this jean-clad, muscle-bound businessman that said he had a crafty bone in his body.

"Of course I do. I told you that I would do everything I could to help with this wedding. Speaking of which, I ordered those wedding favors."

"You did?"

He nodded. "You wouldn't believe all of the party favors they offer. I hope you don't mind, but I ordered a few other things. Of course, you get final approval."

Impressed with his new attitude toward the wedding, she sat down next to him. "Thank you. I can't wait to see them."

She went on to instruct him about making flowers by taking eight sheets of tissue paper and aligning them with the round paper cutter. For a while she gave him her undivided attention, but he was a quick learner. His flower wasn't perfect, but it impressed her—he impressed her. It wasn't just his flair for crafts, but his ability to put aside his misgivings about the wedding for his brother's happiness.

"Not exactly like your flowers," he said, surveying his rather limp effort.

"But not bad for your first try." She gave him some pointers, and he tried again.

"That's better."

"Yes, it is."

He turned to her. "Now that I have this flower stuff figured out, how about you tell me more about your decision not to have a family? I see the motherly instincts come out in you every time you gather that little bundle of fur in your hands."

But Apricot was so easy. She wasn't stressful. Jules didn't have to worry about messing her up for the rest of her life.

Jules punched another set of papers. "You don't want to hear this."

"Yes, I do. If you'll tell me." He sat there holding a stack of deep purple papers in his hand, staring at her with such compassion in his eyes.

What did it matter now if she told him the bitter truth? He knew the answers already; he just hadn't put it all together. But delving into those deep, dark memories made her heart pinch. It was a subject that she didn't share with anyone. She'd learned how to push those painful memories to the far recesses of her mind.

So why did she feel the temptation to open up to Stefano? Why did she want him to understand her?

"It's okay." His voice was gentle and filled with understanding. "If it's too painful, you don't have to say anything. I won't mention it again."

He was letting her off the hook just like that, with no probing questions about her scars—no judgments. Stefano was a complex man. She had the feeling he had his own ghosts hanging in the closet.

Maybe he would understand her story.

Her mouth grew dry as she struggled to swallow. "My mother, she…she tried her best. But she was a very unhappy soul. When I was little, my father left us. She did her best to find work, but without much education, her choices were limited and minimum wage doesn't pay for much. It was a tough life, and she took her frustrations out on me."

The memories of her childhood came to her in snippets. Flashes of her mother crying. The sense of insecurity. Her stomach growling when she went to bed. Over the years, Jules had tried to forget the details, but some refused to fade away.

Still she'd promised herself that she wouldn't end up like her mother. She wouldn't trust her future to a man, only to have him pull the rug out from under her. She wouldn't take her anger and frustration out on her child. And she wouldn't just quit on life.

"I'd been removed from my mother's care a few times. But I was always returned. Each time she promised that she'd get it right. But the last time…" Her voice drifted away as those dark memories resurfaced. "The last time she did this to me." Jules pointed to her scars.

She couldn't say any more. She didn't want to dissolve into a tearful mess. Perhaps she'd kept the memories locked up for too long. Stefano's presence had her letting down her defenses, leaving her vulnerable to the pain she'd neatly tucked away in the back of her heart.

She swallowed down the lump of emotions. "We should get these flowers done."

Before she could reach for the papers, Stefano moved to her side. His hands reached out, cupping her shoulders. "I'm so sorry that happened to you. No child should ever go through what you did."

She glanced away, not wanting to see the sympathy in his eyes. "It was a long time ago."

"But it still hurts. I know."

Their gazes collided, sending her heart beating out of control. "You truly get it, don't you?"

He nodded. "We didn't have the same sort of childhood,

but I know what it's like to lose a parent and hope they'll come back. And I know what it's like to be forgotten by a parent."

In that moment, she knew that she'd found someone else besides Lizzie who understood her and didn't judge her by her past. The breath hitched in her throat as her focus slipped to his mouth—his very kissable mouth. She wondered what it'd be like to be held in his strong arms and to have his lips press to hers. Would his kiss be swift and passionate? Or would it be slow and tantalizing?

She didn't have to wonder any longer as he pulled her close. Her hands grabbed hold of his broad shoulders to steady herself. When his head dipped toward her, her eyelids fluttered closed.

Her heart beat so loudly that it was all she could hear. Could Stefano hear it, too? Did he know how much she wanted him?

And then he was there, pressing his lips to hers. The hunger and need in his kiss answered her questions. He wanted her as much as she wanted him.

He tasted of coffee. Caffeine might provide a jolt of energy, but it didn't compare with the rush of adrenaline from Stefano's kiss. A moan swelled in her throat. His touch was so much better than anything she'd conjured up in her imagination.

But this wasn't right. Getting involved with Stefano would only complicate things. She had to stop before it went any further.

With every bit of willpower she could muster, she pressed her palms to his solid chest. The *thump-thump* of his heart vibrated through her fingers. Ignoring the delicious sensations that zinged up her arms, she pushed him away.

She looked at him, finding bewilderment in his eyes.

Perhaps he, too, was caught off guard by the intensity of that amazing kiss.

"I...I should be going." Stefano jumped to his feet.

He beat a path through the colorful paper to the door without even a glance back. Why was he acting as though he couldn't get away from her fast enough? Was she the only one to feel anything? No, she was certain that he'd felt it, too. Then she realized that it must have unnerved him, as well.

Just then Apricot stood up, stretched and gave off a little baby *murr*. She strolled across the bed to where Jules was leaning against it and rubbed her head against Jules's hair, which was drying into an unruly mess of spiral curls.

Maybe opening up to him hadn't been the wisest move. She'd have to be careful going forward and keep a safe distance. Because his kiss was much too tempting, and she might just forget that she wasn't interested in starting up anything with him.

CHAPTER ELEVEN

"WHAT DO YOU MEAN, Lizzie canceled?"

Stefano's irritated tone echoed through the car, catching Jules's full attention.

She turned in her seat, noticing the distinct frown lines marring his face as he skillfully maneuvered them through the busy streets of Rome. Why in the world was he so upset about Lizzie's change of plans? Or was something else bothering him? Something to do with the kiss that neither dared to mention?

It didn't matter. She refused to let Lizzie's call or Stefano's gloomy mood ruin this day. This was the very best part of planning a wedding—picking out the cake.

"Lizzie mentioned that there is a special party in the dining room tonight and it's all hands on deck. You should be happy. Your grandfather's restaurant is thriving again."

"I am." Stefano sighed as he slowed to a stop for a red light. "I'll find a place to turn around and we'll head back to the vineyard."

"Why would we do that?"

"Why not? The only reason we were heading into the city was to help the bride pick out a cake."

"And that's exactly what we're going to do."

"What?" He chanced a quick glance her way. "You've got to be kidding, right?"

"No. I'm quite serious."

He'd barely spoken to her since they'd kissed two days ago. Was it because she'd pushed him away? Or was it something more? Maybe he wasn't over the loss of his wife. Jules had spied a snapshot of him and his wife in a collage in Massimo's room. When she'd mentioned the particular photo, Massimo would only say that Gianna had died a couple of years ago. It made Jules wonder if there was more to the story—more behind Stefano's hesitation to let himself live again.

From the photo, she gathered that Stefano's wife had been nothing like her. Or perhaps it'd be better to say that Jules was nothing like his wife. Gianna had worn her long hair pulled back into a conservative braid, her face had been devoid of makeup and her clothes were quite modest and not the least bit showy. She was the quintessential wholesome, modest wife—something Jules would never be.

For the first time ever, Jules wanted to change. She wanted to be the woman who could make a simple dress look amazing. She wanted to be comfortable in her own skin and not feel the need to hide behind a wall of makeup. But more than anything she wanted a man to look at her with love and desire like Stefano had been looking at his wife in the photo. Correction: she wanted Stefano to look at her that way. But that was never going to happen.

Now he barely glanced her way—not since she'd lost her head and let things go too far. She missed the friendship they'd been building. If only she could undo that moment.

She couldn't let that stand between them doing their duty as maid of honor and best man. She was a grown-up, and so was he. They could move past this. Somehow.

She swallowed her uneasiness and hoped her voice would sound more confident than she felt inside. "We promised to do everything we could to make this wedding a success. Can you still do that?"

"But it's their wedding, not ours."

Jules's mouth opened but nothing came out. Him mentioning them and a wedding all in the same sentence caught her off guard. She wondered if it was unintentional, or if his thoughts had been straying back to the brief but heated kiss they'd shared.

His knuckles gleamed white as he gripped the steering wheel. "You know what I mean." His body visibly stiffened. "Not that you and I are getting married—I mean not that we're even involved—"

"It's okay. I know what you mean." She watched as the tension eased out of his shoulders. "But that doesn't change things. We still have to do this for Lizzie and Dante."

"I sure hope you know what you're doing."

"Trust me. I do." She grabbed her wedding planner from her purse and perused the photos of cakes that Lizzie preferred. "I know what she likes. Trust me."

"You keep saying that, but I just don't know."

"If it makes you feel any better, Lizzie picked out photos of cakes. We weren't sure what the baker could produce on such short notice, so I had her line up her choices in order of what she liked best." Jules flipped to the section where she'd taped the pictures of the cakes. "None of these look too elaborate."

"If you say so. Now where exactly am I supposed to be going?"

She read off the directions to the first bakery. While he navigated the congested roadway, she settled back in the comfortable leather seat and thumbed through her organizer. There was still so much to do for this quickly approaching wedding, but it was her escort that kept distracting her. The memory of his kiss was always lurking at the edge of her thoughts. Why couldn't she forget it? Why did this one have to stand out in her mind?

Going forward, she had to be careful not to let it happen again. These DeFiore men came armed with irresistible smiles, alluring dark eyes that drew you in, and when they talked to you, it was as if you were the only person that existed. Lizzie had already fallen hook, line and sinker. But Jules was smarter than that. She wasn't going to let her heart do the thinking for her. She knew too well that the L word wasn't enough.

Her father had told her that he loved her and that he was doing what was best for her. Then he'd left. She never saw him again. It wasn't until she was a teenager that she learned he'd died in an auto accident. Then there was her mother, who would tell her that she loved her, but when times got tough, her temper would flare and she'd turn to alcohol.

If that was love, she didn't want any part of it. Growing up, Jules and Lizzie never talked about love. They both quietly acknowledged that they cherished each other like sisters but neither could bring themselves to say the L word. It was as if vocalizing the emotion would jinx their entire relationship. Jules had since avoided the word altogether.

Jules was grateful for the distraction as they pulled up to Sweet Things Bakery. Her anticipation was short-lived—they were booked. Soon they found that Spagnoli's Bakery, Antonio's Bake Shop and Cake Haven were also booked. Weddings were a big business. And it was first come, first served.

"This isn't looking too good." Stefano started the car.

"Thank you, Captain Obvious."

He glanced at her with surprise written all over his face. And then, instead of grouching at her, he started to laugh.

And laugh. To be honest, she didn't know what there was to laugh about. How in the world were they supposed to have a wedding without a cake?

Stefano gathered himself. "So how are you at baking?"

"You've got to be kidding." He was kidding, wasn't he? She looked him in the eyes and saw a glint of seriousness. "I'm awful. I can't even make a box cake, not without it falling. My baking skills are not pretty at all. We have to find a bakery to do the wedding cake, even if it means visiting every single bakery in this city."

When they pulled up in front of Tortino Paradiso—Cupcake Heaven—Jules knew they were in the right place. It may not be the wedding cake that Lizzie was dreaming of. But in times of desperation, there had to be compromises.

The building was a dark-chocolate brick. The striped awning was the color of pink-and-pearl-white frosting. And the large windows held various cupcake towers as well as cupcakes displayed in the shape of a smiley face. The display that truly caught Jules's attention was one of cupcakes decorated as various brightly colored flowers and placed in a garden setting with a white picket fence. It was detailed, imaginative and fun. The bakery radiated a sense of cheerful creativity where the sky was the limit.

"This is it!"

Stefano turned a puzzled look her way. "This is what?"

"This is the place where we'll find Lizzie and Dante's cake."

"Maybe your Italian isn't so good. This is a cupcake shop. I don't think that's what they had in mind for their wedding cake."

"Just trust me."

"That's what I'm afraid of."

She jumped out of the car before Stefano could say

more. She pulled off her sunglasses and smiled at a customer who'd just exited the bakery. In their hand was a cute bag with the picture of a chocolate cupcake with pink frosting on the front. It appeared that this place was all about the details. Now they had to pass one last test—the taste test.

Stefano rounded the car and joined her on the sidewalk. She leaned toward him and whispered, "Just follow my lead. Or else."

Without waiting for his response, she reached out and slid her hand in his. Goose bumps raced up her arm, and a warm sensation swirled in her chest. She resisted the urge to glance his way to see if he noticed her reaction to his touch. She willed herself to breath regularly and act nonchalant. She assured herself that the reaction had nothing to do with that much-too-short kiss.

"Is this really necessary?" He glanced down at their clasped hands, but he didn't pull away.

"Most definitely." She swallowed the lump in her throat. "I'm not about to let this place slip through our fingers. So to speak."

"Shouldn't you call Lizzie and let her know what you have in mind?"

"I will."

"When?"

"When I know that this place can fit the wedding on their calendar. Otherwise there's no point in consulting Lizzie. She may not be here, but she's still the bride and brides do get nervous. If she knew how many bakeries had turned us away, she'd start to panic. Is that what you want?"

"No, but—"

"That's what I thought. Now let's get moving. The only way to find out anything is to ask."

They walked up to the bakery hand in hand. Jules hoped that she looked more confident than she felt. It bothered her that the only way he'd hold her hand was by way of a threat. He probably would rather do a hundred other less desirable things than act as if they were a happy couple. But he was doing his best to be a good brother and keep his word to Dante—not many people would go to this length.

Like the gentleman she knew him to be, Stefano opened the glass door for her. When she passed by him, she caught a hint of his spicy cologne. She'd never been one to pay much attention to those sorts of things, but in Stefano's case, she found the inviting scent quite appealing. In fact, she was quite tempted to pause and get a much better whiff.

The chime above the door startled her from her day-dream. What was she thinking? She wasn't in Italy to get involved with a man, casually or otherwise. Her lips pressed firmly together as she held back a frustrated sigh. When the store clerk spotted them, it was with great effort that Jules forced her mouth into a smile.

"Showtime," she whispered to Stefano. "Remember this is for your brother and my sister." She didn't know if the warning was more for him or her.

"Hi," the saleswoman with a pink-and-brown-striped apron said from behind the counter. "If there's anything I can do to help you, just let me know."

"Actually, there is something." Jules led the way to the counter. "We want to know if you have an opening for a July wedding."

"Let me just pull up my calendar." The woman had a friendly smile and a bouncy ponytail. She typed in the information. "Any particular date?"

Jules read off the date as the woman's fingers clicked over the keyboard. Then an ominous silence came over the showroom. Jules's chest tightened as she waited for the verdict. The woman said nothing, and then she typed a little more. Behind her dark-rimmed glasses, her eyes narrowed and her forehead creased.

"This summer is so busy. It seems like everyone is getting married."

Jules wanted to press her for an answer, but she used every bit of willpower not to sound overbearing and pushy. "Yes, it's a great summer for a wedding."

Was that a sigh she heard from Stefano? She glanced his way, but he was still wearing that stoic expression as he pretended to be totally absorbed in the array of cupcakes in the display case.

The silence was unnerving. If this place couldn't help them, she didn't know what they were going to do. Chances were really good that at this late date every bakery was booked. Lizzie would be crushed. After waiting all this time to find her soul mate, this wedding had to go on without a hitch—or at least go on.

"We'll take anything you can do." Jules didn't care at this point if she sounded desperate. She was desperate.

When Stefano flexed his fingers, she realized that she had a death grip on him. She loosened her hold and lifted onto her tiptoes to peer over the counter, but she was at the wrong angle to read the computer monitor.

The woman glanced over at her. "I know you're anxious for an answer, but I have a bit of a conflict. I'm checking to see if there is a way around it. If you just give me one more minute."

"Sure. Whatever it takes. I know this is short notice, but it's so important."

The saleswoman smiled. "I understand. You two are a cute couple."

Jules felt Stefano's gaze on her. He wanted her to correct

the woman, and she would, just not yet. They needed a spot on the calendar before Jules would risk rocking the boat.

"Okay, I can make this work. It just took a bit of juggling."

Jules released Stefano's hand and clapped her hands together. She was more wound up about this than she'd realized.

"If you could just give me your name, I'll add you to the calendar."

Jules supplied the necessary information. The last part that might mess up this arrangement was the location of the wedding. She hesitantly informed her that the wedding and reception would be outside the city at the vineyard, but the woman barely batted an eye except to tell her that there'd be an additional delivery fee. Jules told her that would be perfectly fine.

They now had dresses, flowers and a cake, of sorts. This wedding was going to come together. And Jules had already figured out what to do about the food. Dante's family had been anxious to help; they could do covered dishes. From what she'd learned in her short time in Rome, the DeFiore family was a group of accomplished cooks. She couldn't imagine buying anything that tasted anywhere as good as the dishes they made in the restaurant.

Right now was Jules's favorite part of the wedding preparations—a chance to sample mouthwatering cakes from dark chocolate to angelic white. Or in this case, sample the wide array of cupcakes. Jules grinned like a little kid as she eyed the display case filled with cupcakes decorated in every imaginable color.

"Relax." The woman smiled at Stefano. "I promise this won't hurt at all. In fact, you might enjoy it. If you two would just have a seat at the table over there, I'll grab some samples."

"Thank you." Jules took Stefano's hand and led him to the table. Once they were seated, Jules turned to him. "Would you relax? You're making everyone uncomfortable."

"What?" Stefano glanced across the little white café-style table at her.

"Cheer up. This won't take long, and you get to taste some delicious cupcakes."

"Sorry. I was thinking about something else."

"I'm sure you were," she mumbled.

"I was." His gaze narrowed in on her. "I was thinking about the vineyard."

Apparently she hadn't spoken quite as softly as she'd thought. "Are you that bored that you'd rather be working?"

"Why must you jump to conclusions?"

She shrugged. Was she wrong? Was it possible he wasn't wishing he was anywhere but here with her?

"Then why were you thinking about the vineyard?"

He leaned the little chair back on its two rear legs and crossed his arms as though trying to decide if he should take her into his confidence. That bothered her. After everything she'd told him about her past, he really had to decide if she was trustworthy?

Before she could say a word, he spoke up. "It was brought to my attention that I've been cutting my father out of the business side of things at the vineyard. I guess I was so intent on keeping busy after Gianna died that I hadn't noticed that he felt cut out. That was never my intention."

"And you think your father wants more responsibility."

Stefano nodded. "He's succeeded in keeping everything under control while I've been helping you with the wedding. And he seems happier. But then again, I don't know if it's the winery or if he's falling in love."

"What? With whom?"

Before Stefano could answer, the saleswoman returned with a tray full of cupcakes. Jules's mouth started to water just looking at the beautiful little cakes. With a knife they cut the cupcakes in half. The flavors ranged from lemon with buttercream frosting to red velvet with cream cheese frosting to banana crème. All in all there were eight flavors to choose from.

Jules didn't know how she was going to make such a truly difficult decision. All of them tasted divine except maybe the vanilla. It was good, but in comparison to the others, it was a bit boring.

"Well, did you make a decision?" the woman asked after returning from helping some other customers.

"I don't know. They're all so good." Needing some help, she turned to Stefano. "What do you think?"

She didn't normally turn to a man for advice. Typically the men she'd dated never wanted to involve themselves in decision making of any form. It was easier to stand on the sidelines and let someone else do the problem solving. And she wouldn't bother asking for Stefano's input, but this decision was a big one. She didn't want to get it wrong.

Who was she trying to kid? She valued Stefano's opinion a lot. He had good taste and…she liked him. Even though he wasn't crazy about weddings, he'd turned his life upside down to help her out. Someday when he was ready to get on with his life, he'd make somebody a good husband.

She glanced across the table at him. He smiled at her, and her heart gave off a fluttering sensation. What were they talking about?

His gaze moved to the tray, now littered with crumbs. "I think I like the espresso with buttercream."

"You do? Really?" He was a man after her own tastes.

When he nodded to confirm his choice, she countered with, "But what if not everyone cares for coffee flavor?"

The young woman spoke up. "That's not a problem. You know that we can do two flavors."

"That would be great." Since he'd stepped up and picked out one flavor, now it was her turn. "I think the other should be strawberry with the cream cheese."

The woman started typing in the information. She paused and looked at Stefano. "And the groom's name?"

Jules wasn't about to let him mess this up. "The thing is he isn't exactly the groom."

"Really?" The woman's brows rose beneath her bangs. "But you two look so perfect together. I would have sworn—oh, never mind. It's none of my business. If you'll just tell me your groom's name, I'll put it in the computer."

She didn't want the woman to get the wrong idea. "I'm not the bride. We—" Jules pointed back and forth between her and Stefano "—are the maid of honor and the best man."

The woman's eyes lit up and the worry lines left her face. "That makes sense, because I could sense that you two are a couple. And quite in love with each other. I can always tell these things."

Stefano leaned forward and opened his mouth. Before he could utter a single syllable, Jules kicked him under the table. His mouth snapped shut, and his brows drew together as he glared at her. She smiled broadly back at him, hoping to soothe his ruffled feathers.

"Now that we have that straightened out, if you'll just give me the name of the bride and the groom, we'll get this order in the system."

When they finally walked out the door, Jules was amazed at how laid-back and easygoing the woman was about the wedding. She had actually been sympathetic about Lizzie having to work instead of getting the chance to do the actual planning of her wedding.

Now if only everything else would fall into place. And Jules didn't just mean for the wedding. No, she had something else in mind. A chance for people to see her as something more than a scarred-up goth chick.

But to do that, she'd have to let her guard down. She'd have to do away with the things that after all these years were inherently her. Could she do it? And would it make a difference to Stefano?

CHAPTER TWELVE

WHAT WAS UP with Jules?

More importantly, what was up with him?

Stefano stared blindly at the blinking cursor on the computer monitor. Ever since they'd kissed, things had shifted between them. He'd lost his footing where Jules was concerned. And try as he might to get back to that solid ground of casual acquaintances, he couldn't quite reach that plateau.

Instead, he'd tried losing himself in his work, like he'd done ever since Gianna's tragic death, but that wasn't working, either. His father was quite productive. By the time Stefano got back from his excursions to Rome with Jules, there wasn't much for him to do, certainly nothing comprehensive requiring his full attention. And time on his hands at this point was not a good thing. All he could think about was kissing Jules. A definite no-no.

Resisting her was getting harder and harder, especially when she slipped her soft hand in his. Did she have any clue what her touch did to him? And then she'd lift her chin and smile up at him, and his heart would careen into his ribs. His common sense fizzled and shorted out. His only saving grace had been that she always pulled away before he could act on his impulses.

With a frustrated sigh, he glanced at the clock, finding

it was almost lunchtime. He shut down the computer. It'd been a waste of a morning as he'd barely gotten a thing done for thinking about his beautiful houseguest.

Yesterday after they'd left the bakery, Jules had wanted some time to do a little shopping. He hadn't minded. He'd needed some time alone before sharing the small confines of the auto with her. He especially needed a break after that lady at the bakery kept going on and on about them being a couple. And it didn't help that sometimes when Jules turned her green gaze on him, it was as though she was trying to tell him something—as if she wanted more from him than what he could offer her...or anyone.

Or was he seeing what he wanted to see? That thought stopped him in his tracks as he made his way from the barn to the house. Was it possible Jules, with her outrageous makeup and hip clothes, had somehow gotten to him? His steps faltered. After all this time telling himself that he'd had it with love, was he starting to fall for the girl from New York?

He gave his head a shake. Wasn't going to happen. He resumed his trek to the villa. Suddenly his appetite for lunch had disappeared. All he could think about was Jules and how her green eyes spoke to him—telling him of her past emotional wounds. His gut reaction was to protect her and show her that life didn't have to be so hard. But how could he do that when he knew for a fact that life was unpredictable and quite unfair?

No, the best thing he could do for both of them was to back away. He'd been wrong to get so invested in this wedding. He might be the groom's brother and best man, but he didn't do wedding planning. By now Jules should know how to get into the city on her own and with all the electronic wizardry on her phone, she'd find her way around.

Yes, that's what he'd do. He'd back out of this wedding

froufrou and submerge himself in work. After all, there was a tour and wine-tasting event on the calendar. He could think of ways to expand it, perhaps by adding some tales from his family's colorful history. He didn't have anything specific in mind, but he'd think on it.

He'd just neared the house when Jules stepped outside. His thoughts screeched to a halt as he took in her appearance. Her very different appearance. He blinked to make sure he wasn't seeing things.

She was wearing a pale blue cotton dress. It was short, just above the knee, and the skirt flared out a bit. The waist was snug and hinted at her curves. Her very fine curves. He struggled to keep his mouth from gaping open. His gaze traveled up over the white stripes of the bodice and stopped at her bare shoulders and arms. The only things holding up that scrap of a dress were two thin straps. A lump formed in his throat.

She smiled at him, and the whole world seemed to glow. "Do you like my new purchase?"

"It's um…very nice." He forced his gaze to meet hers.

"Walk with me."

Her request wasn't a question, but rather a honeyed command—one he wasn't about to disobey. She passed by him, and all he could do was stare. It was then that he noticed her hair. There were no ponytails. Instead her dark wavy hair was loose and flowing down her back. *What in the world?* She'd never worn it like that before, but he certainly approved.

He took long strides to catch up to her. "Where are we going?"

"To the barn. I still haven't seen it, and I thought… well, I hoped that you might have a few minutes to show me around."

She wanted to see the winery? And she wanted him to

show her around? What could it hurt? Maybe this would be a good prelude to him letting her know that he'd changed his mind about working on the wedding planning with her.

"Sure. Is there anything in particular that you want to see?"

Her sun-kissed shoulders rose and fell. "Whatever you want to show me will be fine."

She was actually interested in his work—in his heritage. That was an area where Gianna had never showed any interest. The only thing that she had to say about the vineyard was that it took up all his time and that it kept them from moving to the city. He hadn't realized when they'd married that she expected a different sort of life. He figured that marrying a local girl would ensure that they both wanted a quiet way of life. He'd been so wrong.

He gave Jules the grand tour, starting at the office, and then they moved on to the processing room, where during the harvest the grapes were hand sorted. He showed her the barrel room where the wine was aged. The tour concluded in the spacious wine-tasting room with its long, thin table for the guests.

"We should head back for lunch." He guided her outside.

"Thank you for the personal tour. I really enjoyed it. I'm just sorry I'll miss seeing all of the activity during the harvest."

"You always have an open invitation to return anytime."

She peered deeply into his eyes, and his heart thumped hard and fast. When she glanced away, her butterfly tattoo caught his attention. Just the tips of the wings peeked out of the dress's neckline. He longed to see all of it. He'd never seen anything so captivating. A struggle warred within him—common sense versus his raging testosterone. And the testosterone was taking the lead.

Jules turned away and started to walk. "This estate is so big. You certainly don't have to worry about bothering any of your neighbors."

The land was the last thing on his mind, but he struggled to make intelligent conversation. "Over the generations, it has grown. Buying more of the surrounding properties was a priority."

"Are you still looking into expanding?"

"If the opportunity presents itself, sure. But it isn't my focus." His only interest now was finding out if her lips were as sweet as the finest brachetto grape.

"What is your priority?"

It was on the tip of his tongue to say that it was her—that making her deliriously happy was his priority. But he bit back the ridiculous words before he could utter them. What in the world was getting into him?

He cleared his throat as he searched for a reasonable answer. "The quality of the wine. And broadening our interaction with the public."

Her footsteps were muffled by the grass. "Sounds exciting."

"You think so?"

"I do. I love the vineyard. I'm sure others will love it, too. It's so peaceful and relaxing. I can see why you stayed on and continue to work with your father."

"But surely you wouldn't do the same thing if roles were reversed." She was a city girl, born and bred. The tranquility was just a novelty thing. Sooner or later she'd want to move on...just like his late wife.

"I could definitely see me living here. In another world, I'd have a big family with lots of room for the kids to play. And cats. And dogs. And maybe a horse or two."

"Talk about a menagerie. Are you sure you'd be up for all of that?"

She shrugged. "It isn't like it's ever going to happen. I don't live here, and as you well know I'm not exactly the poster girl for motherhood. But sometimes it's nice to dream."

"I don't see why you have to dream when you can make it a reality. Well, at least the part of being a mother and having a menagerie of cats and dogs."

She stopped and stared up at him. "Look at me."

He did as she asked. His heart started to pound again. He held his body rigid, resisting the urge to pull her close. He recalled vividly how soft her curves were, and his resolve wavered.

"No, really look at me." Her serious tone snapped him to attention. "What do you see?"

"I see your beautiful face without all of that makeup."

"I didn't see much point in it without air-conditioning. I end up wiping most of it off throughout the day."

"That's good." When her brows lifted in a questioning fashion, he added, "I mean it's good that you gave up on the makeup. You don't need it."

The truth was that she was even more beautiful without it. She had such a fresh young face, and it needed no enhancement at all. He was captivated by her natural beauty. And with her hair loose and blowing in the breeze, she had a down-to-earth appeal. No longer did she look like she'd just walked off a rock video. Now she looked like someone who might actually belong in his world. But part of him missed her hip, chic look. That in and of itself surprised him.

Her head tilted to the side, but her gaze never left his. "What are you thinking?"

He hadn't realized he'd gotten so caught up in his thoughts. "I was thinking about you."

"And what did you decide?"

"That you are beautiful." He looked deep into her eyes and saw disbelief. He'd have to prove it to her. "Your green eyes are a shade or two deeper than the grape leaves. And your long, dark lashes make your eyes very alluring. Your skin is smooth and makes me long to run my fingers down its velvety softness."

Color rose in her cheeks. "You're missing the point. The scars. You can't miss them. And they're ugly."

"They aren't ugly. You aren't ugly."

She shook her head. "You're just saying that to make me feel better."

"I'm speaking the truth." He desperately wanted her to believe him.

"No, you aren't." She let out an exasperated sigh. "I didn't tell you the details before, maybe I should now. Maybe then you'll understand why I find the scars so ugly."

He opened his mouth to protest but then closed it without saying a word. Perhaps talking about it would be good for her.

"I told you that my mother did this to me, but what I didn't tell you was that it was during one of her drunken bouts. She was angry because she'd run out of vodka. I was on my way home from playing with the neighbor. She smacked me and I lost my balance at the top of the porch steps. Down I went, hitting…hitting my head on the edge of the steps and landing on the cement sidewalk."

Stefano clenched his hands. How could a mother do that to her own child? It was inconceivable. And yet the only words he could find to convey his sympathy seemed so inadequate. And it really didn't matter because no words could make up for what she'd experienced at the hand of the one person who was supposed to love and protect her.

"I'm so sorry."

"Don't be. It was the best thing to happen to me." Her

eyes were shiny with unshed tears, but she kept it together. "When I lived with my mother, there was never enough to eat. Rarely was there clean laundry. And the longer it went on, the meaner she became. If they hadn't taken me away, I'd have never met Lizzie." Jules stopped and drew in an uneven breath. "My mother wasn't strong enough to take care of both of us. Eventually she turned to drugs and OD'd. Now do you finally understand why I shouldn't be a mother?"

"I think that you're amazing and the strongest person I know." He meant every single word. She had impressed him before this, and now he was just in awe of her. "And above it all, I still believe you can achieve whatever you set your mind on. But none of that changes what I see when I look at you. You're beautiful. From the wrinkle in your forehead when you're confused to the tip of your nose to your rosy lips that are just ripe for tasting."

And without thinking of the ramifications of what he was about to do, he leaned forward and lowered his head. The only thing that mattered now was making her feel better. He had to let her know that those scars didn't define her. She was beautiful in spite of them. And her beauty resonated from the inside out.

His lips gently brushed against hers. He didn't want to scare her off. When he pulled back a little, he heard her undeniable sigh of enjoyment. She liked his touch, and he liked touching her. What would it hurt to follow up that kiss with another one?

He sought out her lips again. They were sweet like chocolate. His hands slipped around her waist, and she leaned into him. He'd been waiting so long to do this again. And it was even better than what he'd remembered.

The kiss went on and on. She should be kissed like this and often. Jules deserved to be cherished and loved. And if somehow he could convince her of this, he would. He couldn't imagine her throwing her life away because of some scars that weren't even that noticeable.

Her soft curves molded perfectly to him. And when a soft moan reached his ears, he wasn't so sure which of them had made the sound of pure pleasure. Not that it mattered as her fingers wrapped around his neck and raked through his hair, sending a whole new wave of excitement through him. Every nerve ending stood at attention.

"Beautiful day, isn't it?"

The sound of his father's distant voice sent them flying apart as though lightning had struck the ground between them. Her cheeks turned a dusty pink and her lips a shade of deep rosy red. She looked as if she'd been ravished. And he'd never seen her look more beautiful.

Stefano gave himself a mental jerk. What in the world had he just let happen? His gaze sought out Jules. He meant to send her a sympathetic look, but her eyes wouldn't meet his. Instead of making things better, he'd only succeeded in making them worse.

Him, the man who'd sworn off relationships, was standing in the open, drowning in the sweetest kiss. Not that the kiss constituted a relationship. He combed his fingers through his hair. Somehow he had to put things back on track between them. He promised himself that he wouldn't lose control around her again.

With his father just far enough down the path, Stefano lowered his voice to say, "That shouldn't have happened. I don't know what I was thinking. It…it was a mistake. I know neither of us is looking for a relationship."

He steeled himself and turned to his father, who was making his way to the house from the winery. His father's eyes danced with merriment, but his face was devoid of the mischievous smile that Stefano could only imagine would materialize after he passed them.

"I...we were just on our way back from a tour of the winery."

His father nodded. "I guess I don't need to ask how it went."

Stefano couldn't believe he was having such fun at his expense. This was something his father never would have bothered with when he was a kid. Back then his father was quite stoic and didn't joke around. But lately he'd been seeing more and more changes in him. Any other time Stefano would have welcomed this transformation, but not now—not with Jules. And not when he'd made such a monumental mistake. Whatever made him think that kissing her was such a good idea?

"Stefano, did you hear me?"

His father was staring at him expectantly, but Stefano hadn't heard a word. "What?"

"I said you better hurry or you'll never catch up to her."

Stefano glanced around, finding that Jules had taken off toward the house. *Great!* Could this get any worse? He stopped that line of thought as he knew all too well that things could always get worse. He swore under his breath.

He started after her. He didn't have a clue what he would say to her. Maybe it'd be best to just let her go. She'd get over the kiss quickly enough. After all, it hadn't meant anything. Nothing at all. Except it felt as if it had been the beginning of something—something profound. His teeth ground together as he stifled a groan of frustration.

His world had been orderly until Jules had entered it. He was a widower of his own making. Being alone was punishment for his actions. If he hadn't been so stubborn, if he hadn't pushed Gianna into marrying him, she'd still be here—still be alive. His footsteps faltered.

The problems came after they'd married and he'd found out that they wanted different things in life. She wanted excitement and fun. He wanted stability and routine. Where he enjoyed kicking back in front of the large-screen television to watch football, she wanted to dress up and go to the theater. The love they'd initially felt started to dwindle with each passionate disagreement. And then that fateful night.

He couldn't let the past repeat itself. Though he highly doubted that Jules would take off in his car, he couldn't take the chance. He couldn't let this misunderstanding linger between them. There had to be a way to fix what he'd broken. Maybe if he'd have done that with Gianna, she'd still be alive.

When he entered the kitchen, Jules was nowhere to be found. Maria stood at the counter, stirring a pasta salad. She turned to him. It wasn't often just the two of them stood in the kitchen. He was tempted to ask her if there was something going on between her and his father. He resisted, still unsure how he felt about the idea of them hooking up.

"Did you need something?" Maria wiped her hands on a little white apron trimmed with purple grapes.

"Um, no." Now wasn't the time to get into it. He had enough problems on his hands.

"Are you sure? Because if you're looking for Jules, she tore through here a minute or two ago." Maria sent him a disapproving look before pointing to the upstairs.

"Thanks. I'll check on her." He rushed past Maria and headed for the spiraling staircase. He took the steps two at a time. He didn't know what he'd say to Jules when he found her. He'd have to wing this one.

What a fool she'd been.

Jules picked up Apricot and snuggled her nose down

into the downy soft fur. A loud purr vibrated through the little kitten's body. Tears stung the back of her eyes, but she refused to let them fall.

What had she been thinking back there in the field? It was as if she were a kid with the biggest crush in the world. When Stefano had looked at her with desire in his eyes, she'd forgotten everything but feeling the excitement and passion of his lips moving over hers.

Then to have him push away from her and try to dismiss the moment as though it meant nothing hurt more than the rude comments she'd received back in school about her scars. The cruel comments kids threw out about how she was defective and that's why her own parents didn't even want her had cut deeply. But Stefano's actions had surpassed that pain.

Why, oh, why did she ever think that he might be different? Just because his brother had accepted Lizzie with her less-than-stellar past didn't mean that Stefano would be as open-minded. Sure he said all the right things, but that was just because he was a gentleman. It didn't mean that everything he said was true—not when it came to her scars or her past.

A knock at her door had Apricot squirming to get out of her hands. Jules moved next to the bed so that the little one would have a soft landing.

"Who is it?"

"It's Stefano. We need to talk."

"No, we don't." She was being childish, and she knew it. She just didn't know what to say to him at the moment. Her emotions were raw and conflicting.

"I hope you're decent because I'm coming in."

She started for the door, but before she could get to it, it swung open. And there stood Stefano. His large physique filled the doorway. There was no getting past him even if she wanted to. His forehead was creased, and his dark brows were drawn together. His gaze zeroed in on her and made her want to turn away, but she refused to let on how much he'd hurt her.

She leveled her shoulders and crossed her arms. "What do you want?"

"I told you we need to talk."

"And I told you I don't want to talk. I…I have stuff to do."

"Such as?"

"I need to make more paper flowers." Deciding that it would be good to have something to do with her hands, she moved to the dresser and started gathering the items she'd need.

She heard the door swing shut, followed by his approaching footsteps. His fingers encircled her arm. "Those can wait. This can't."

She glanced at his hand on her bare arm and then lifted her chin. "You make it sound like life or death."

"It could be." He sighed and shook his head. "I need to apologize."

"Wait. Why might this be life or death?" What was she missing? Obviously it was something big.

"Because…oh, it doesn't matter. I want to apologize for kissing you—"

"Why? It isn't your fault that this—" she pointed to the half-moon scar next to her eye "—is so ugly that it repulses you." She started to turn away.

He gripped her shoulders in his strong hands and pulled her around so that they were face-to-face. "It doesn't repulse me. How many times do I have to tell you that you're beautiful before you believe me?"

She shook her head, fighting back the tears that were

threatening to fall. "But the scars *are* ugly. I'm ugly. That's why I wear the makeup. It hides things."

"You don't have to hide." His voice was deep and soothing.

"Yes, I do." She pulled away from his hold. "Look at me. I tried to play this your way. I tried to look like everyone else around here. I bought different clothes. I didn't put on my makeup. I even brushed out my hair and wore it loose. And still it doesn't work. I'm still different."

He smiled at her. "You're right—you are different."

If this was his way of making her feel better, he was doing a lousy job. "Just go."

"Not until I tell you this." When she didn't look at him, his thumb moved to her chin and lifted it. "Being different isn't bad. Being different is something to be proud of. Just make sure you're doing it because it's what makes you happy and you aren't doing it just to make a statement or to hide."

"I wanted to dress like the other women in your life. I wanted to be like everyone else."

"You'll never be like everyone else. You are special. To me."

And then his head dipped and his lips pressed to hers. Her heart tumbled in her chest. He did care about her, scars and all. She knew that life wasn't that easy and that she shouldn't fall for him, but the reasons to hold back and keep him at a safe distance were eluding her at the moment.

His kiss was filled with heat, leaving no doubt in her mind that he desired her. And she wanted him, too. She wanted him more than she could say. But when he lifted his head and looked her in the eyes, the doubts started to crowd in.

"They'll be looking for us at lunch." Her feet refused to cooperate. She stayed right there in his very capable arms.

"They won't wonder about us for long."

Heat rose to her cheeks. "They know you're up here with me?"

He nodded. "Maria pointed out your whereabouts. Don't worry—no one will disturb us."

Suddenly she felt like a kid making out in her boy-friend's house with his parents in the next room. She knew she was being ridiculous. This was a massive villa. The dining room and kitchen were at the other end. And they were consenting adults. Still…

"I want you." Stefano's voice was husky with desire, leaving no doubt in her mind about his intention.

"I want you, too."

CHAPTER THIRTEEN

"WHAT'S GOING ON between you and Stefano?"

"Nothing." Jules avoided meeting Lizzie's inquisitive gaze as they sat on the living room floor of the villa. "Whatever you're thinking, just let it go."

Why did Lizzie have to pick today of all days to drive to the vineyard to help with the wedding details? Jules held back a yawn as she reached for the glue.

She didn't want to lie to Lizzie about Stefano. But she didn't know what to tell her sister because quite honestly she didn't know what was going on herself. She'd been awake most of the night replaying everything between them. How could she explain something when she didn't understand it herself?

After she and Stefano had made love, he'd kissed her goodbye and spent the rest of the day and evening at the winery. He said they were preparing for a wine-tasting event that weekend. She told herself that his absence meant nothing. That he was just taking care of his responsibilities.

But a nagging voice kept telling her that he was intentionally avoiding her. Instead of their lovemaking bringing them together, it had driven them apart. But why?

"There's something going on between you." It was on the tip of Jules's tongue to deny it when Lizzie continued, "You aren't falling for him, are you?"

Jules shook her head vehemently. "You don't have to worry. Just because you found your Prince Charming doesn't mean that I want the same thing."

Lizzie straightened and eyed her from across the coffee table. "I know that it's easy to get caught up in all of this wedding stuff and start to daydream about falling in love."

Jules stopped gluing together another fan with the wedding program printed on it. "You don't have to worry. Stefano has been nice and all, but my future isn't here—"

"You're right. I don't know what got into me. You're too smart to throw away your exciting future for anything or anyone." Lizzie's stiff posture eased. I'm just so proud of you for getting into grad school. You'll see—the time will fly by."

This was Jules's opening—a chance to tell Lizzie that she'd had a change of heart. But she'd have to do it gently. She could tell Lizzie was already nervous about the wedding. "What if I didn't go back to school?"

Lizzie's head lifted. Her focus narrowed in on Jules. A long moment of silence passed, and then Lizzie smiled. "You know, you scared me. Don't do that. For a moment, I thought that you were serious."

Jules's palms grew moist. "You make it sound like grad school is the only worthwhile option."

"It is." Lizzie leaned forward, her elbows resting on her knees. "I don't understand. I thought this is what you wanted—what we've been working toward."

"But what if I changed my mind?" She prayed Lizzie would understand. "What if I don't have what it takes to get through the program?"

"So that's what this is all about." Lizzie leaned back and sighed. "Jules, you don't have to worry. You're going to do great. You're the smartest person I know."

"I'm not that smart." Still it felt good knowing that her sister thought that highly of her.

"Smart enough to get honors in college and get accepted to your first-choice school. To me that's very impressive. Just don't stress yourself out. You can do anything you set your mind on."

"But what if—"

"Lizzie, are you ready to go?" Dante strolled into the room, rubbing his hands together as though he was ready to hit the road.

"Yeah, I'm ready." Lizzie put her supplies in a nearby box. "Did you remember to pack the recipes your aunt gave me?"

Dante nodded. "I got them."

"And the photos your father gave me of when you were little."

"I got those, too. Mind telling me what you plan to do with all of that stuff?"

Lizzie smiled up at him, and he just shook his head. "Well, you better get moving. We have to get ready for tomorrow's filming, and I want to do some prep work tonight on the menu."

Lizzie turned to Jules. "I'm sorry I can't stay longer and help more."

"Don't worry. I've got this."

"And make sure you ask my brother for help," Dante told her as he offered Lizzie a hand to help her off the floor.

When Lizzie got to her feet, she leaned forward just as natural as could be and pressed a quick kiss to his lips. The look that passed between them spoke of their boundless love. Jules smiled. This just confirmed that all her hard work for the wedding was so worth it. This truly was her sister's happily-ever-after.

Lizzie turned back to her. "I'm taking the rest of the fans with me to finish. And I have the heavy paper for the place cards. I'll run them off on the printer in the office once we have a finalized guest list."

Jules placed the rest of the programs in the box and closed the lid. "I don't think you have to worry about that. My guess is everyone will attend. No one wants to miss the celebration."

"You don't think they're all coming because it's supposed to be filmed for television, do you?"

Dante wrapped an arm over his future wife's shoulders. "My family is all about the celebrating and it has nothing to do with television."

Lizzie gazed into Dante's eyes. "I hope you're right."

"Trust me. They're happy for us."

Lizzie reached up and squeezed his hand.

"I wouldn't trust him." Stefano stepped into the room. "If there's one thing I learned growing up with him, it is to be wary when he says 'trust me,' especially if it involves the last of the gelato."

Dante smiled and turned to his brother. "Hey, I can't help that you were so gullible."

"What did you expect me to do when you said Papa was looking for me and to trust you that there'd be some gelato left when I returned?"

"See? You learned a valuable lesson—eat your gelato first." Dante smiled broadly over the memory of outsmarting his older brother. "We've got to go."

"Don't worry." Lizzie turned back to Jules. "Everything will work out."

And with that Lizzie and Dante carried the wedding supplies out the door, leaving her alone with Stefano. He turned a puzzled face her way.

"What did she mean about everything working out?"

Jules shook her head and got to her feet. "It's nothing."

She turned her back to him and bent over, picking up her supplies. She wasn't going to get into another discussion about her education. He'd probably side with Lizzie anyhow, and she didn't need people ganging up on her. When were people going to trust her to make her own decisions?

He stepped forward and wrapped his hands around her shoulders, and turned her around to face him. "I know that something is bothering you. Did you tell her? You know, about us?"

"No. Why would you think that?"

"I don't know. Women like to confide in each other, and I thought that you might have said something."

"I wouldn't know what to say." Her frustration and insecurities came bubbling to the surface. "You and I never talked about what it meant. You've made yourself scarce since then."

He arched a brow. "You make it sound like I've been hiding from you—"

"Haven't you?" She dropped down on the couch, and he joined her.

"I've been busy. You know that."

"Uh-huh." He surely didn't think she was going to buy that he didn't have one spare moment to speak to her, did he?

"It's the truth. There's a wine-tasting event this weekend, and I've been helping my father nail down the details. But don't change the subject. We were talking about what your sister said. What's going to work out?"

Jules sighed. "I was trying to tell my sister that I'm not so sure that I still want to go to grad school."

"And…"

"And she thinks I have cold feet. She's certain I'll get over it and things will go according to plan."

"Is that how you feel?"

"No." It was the truth, and she was tired of holding it all inside.

His tone softened. "Then talk to me. Tell me what's on your mind."

Maybe Lizzie wasn't ready to hear what she was feeling, but Stefano genuinely seemed interested. And she felt as though she could confide in him. Maybe he'd surprise her and be in her corner.

"The truth is I no longer want to go to grad school."

"That's a big decision. What changed your mind?"

"Are you really interested?" She didn't want to go on and on if he was only being polite.

His tone held a definite note of sincerity. "I wouldn't have asked if I wasn't interested."

She leaned back on the couch and folded her hands in her lap. "I just finished a session as an intern with social services before I flew here."

Then again, maybe she didn't want to get into it all. Stefano was the picture of success. His winery was thriving. She'd been awed by all the awards he'd won. They were displayed in the wine-tasting room. His wine had worldwide recognition. He'd never understand failure. And she didn't want him to think less of her.

"Jules, are you going to make me drag it out of you a little at a time?"

"No. Never mind. It's not important." She attempted to get up, but Stefano reached out to her.

"It is important." His tone was filled with concern. "If it wasn't, you wouldn't be trying to tell your sister about it with the wedding so close. Since you can't talk to her, talk to me. Maybe I can help."

She glanced up at him and wanted to believe that he could actually understand. That he wouldn't think less of her. Jules's heart told her one thing, but her mind said the opposite. She decided to follow her heart.

Unable to look him in the eyes, she ducked her head. "I got fired from my position. Well, I don't know if you can get fired from an internship, but I was asked not to return."

There. It was out there. The embarrassing truth. She was a failure.

When Stefano didn't say anything, she glanced up. In his eyes, she didn't see any signs of judgment—just compassion.

"I'm sure there has to be more to the story than that. What aren't you telling me?"

"I…I couldn't do things the way they wanted. The kids…they needed someone in their corner. And I couldn't stand by and say nothing. When I spoke up one too many times, the supervisor determined I wasn't suited for the position."

"Sounds to me like you were just following your heart."

"But don't you see, I can't do that type of work. I can't follow their rules and regulations blindly when they just don't make sense in every case. I know the rules are there for a reason, but sometimes exceptions need to be made."

"Did you ever think that you're letting your injured ego override everything else? You could help so many kids. I agree with your sister. You need to keep going and get your degree. Maybe you can bring about change to the system."

Why did she ever think that opening up to him would be a good idea? He wasn't any different from her sister. Sure, it hurt getting fired. No matter how nicely the woman at the office stated it, a firing was a firing. She was certain there were other occupations that she could be just as good at or better.

But switching her focus made her feel as though she

were copping out somehow. And she didn't want to turn her back on those kids who didn't have a voice. She wanted to do her part, but how could she do that without compromising who she was and what she believed in? She'd never be a yes-girl.

Guilt chewed at her as she considered doing something other than being a social worker. Why the guilt? Was it projected on her from her sister and now Stefano? She didn't know, but she sure wanted to figure it out. And she'd do it on her own, without his input or her sister's. This was a choice only she could make.

"Maybe you're right," she said. When he smiled broadly as though he'd just solved the world's economic crisis, she added, "But maybe you're not. That's why I haven't pressed the subject with Lizzie. I want to be sure before I get into it with her."

"And that's why what happened between us can't happen again."

Jules forced her mouth closed as a hundred thoughts struck her all at the same time. "You think me changing my mind about grad school is somehow related to us making love?"

"I think that you don't know what you want in life, and I don't want to confuse matters. It isn't like I can offer you anything serious. I've done that, and it didn't work out. You're still young. You have your whole future ahead of you."

A future without him. The thought tore through her, making the backs of her eyes sting. She blinked. He was right. They didn't have a future, but it had nothing to do with her being young or his first marriage ending. It had to do with her not being wife and mother material. Maybe he realized that, too, but didn't want to point it out.

Jules sucked in a steadying breath. "You're right. I have

my whole future ahead of me. And right now that consists of creating the most amazing wedding for my sister."

She got to her feet and started for the door. No matter his reason for rejecting her and their lovemaking, it still hurt. She didn't want him to see how much it bothered her.

"This isn't how I meant for things to go between us." His voice was gentle and thick as honey. "Don't go away mad."

"Just go away," she mumbled.

She fled from the room as quickly as her legs would carry her. Her heart was heavy. He regretted their love-making, while she'd been replaying it over and over in her mind. She'd been such a fool to think that it'd been special for the both of them.

She wouldn't make that mistake again. And she didn't have time to dwell on her foolish mistake. The wedding was getting close—a wedding to top all others. It'd be so romantic that it'd have couples falling in love all over again.

Except for her and Stefano.

CHAPTER FOURTEEN

HE'D MADE A mess of everything.

Stefano's hands balled up and pounded the desktop, rattling the mug of pens as well as the computer keyboard. A few days had passed since he'd ended things with Jules. She still spoke to him, but it was at a bare minimum. And now that the wine-tasting event was over, he had far too much time on his hands.

What had gotten into him to let things get so out of control?

How could he have forgotten that his solitary life was one of his own making? His penance. If Jules had a clue he was to blame for his wife's death, she'd hate him. And that's how it should be. He didn't deserve another chance at love. And he certainly didn't deserve it at the expense of Jules's education. He couldn't stand to be responsible for the demise of her dreams. He'd done enough damage for one lifetime.

If only he'd kept his hands to himself. His thoughts strayed back to the amazing time he'd spent with her wrapped in his arms. The strawberry scent of her hair. The velvety smoothness of her skin. He drew his tormenting thoughts up short. How could their lovemaking be so wrong when it felt so right?

It had to be all the talk about the wedding. It was messing with his mind, reminding him that he was all alone. Any other time that wouldn't have bothered him, but right now it sounded so grim and miserable. He was going to end up like his father. Old and alone.

But the memory of his father and Maria squeezed into his mind. Something told him that his father was starting to live again, step-by-step. He was happy for him, but that wasn't possible for Stefano. It was different.

Stefano had driven his wife from the house in the middle of the night with his unwillingness to compromise—his unwillingness to see that his wife was not the same woman he thought he'd married. Or that he'd only seen what he'd wanted to see when they'd said their vows. Either way, they'd both become disillusioned.

Her last words to him ran through his mind. *The man I thought I loved doesn't exist. He was a man I made up in my mind. We don't belong together. We never did.*

"Are you busy?"

The sound of Jules's voice had him turning to find her standing in the doorway of the winery office. "What are you doing here?"

Her eyes widened at his unintentionally brusque tone. "I wanted to know if you'd have time to run into the city tomorrow. But don't worry about it. I'll find another ride."

"Don't be silly. It's my responsibility to get you around." He hadn't meant to be so rough with her. He was frustrated with himself, not with her.

"I don't want to put you out. With you being busy, I can get there on the train."

In truth, he didn't have that much to do. This wasn't their busy time, and his father was moving around the vineyard like a man half his age. If it was because of Maria, he would be the first to admit that love suited his father. "I said I'd take you."

"Fine." She turned to walk away.

Guilt gnawed at him. He couldn't let her leave with things so tense between them. He couldn't stand the thought of her hating him. After all, they were going to be family.

He jumped to his feet and took off after her. "Hey, I'm sorry. I just have a lot on my mind right now."

She shrugged. "Don't worry about it. I know I've been a bother. Always getting in the way—"

"No, you haven't. You haven't done a thing wrong." He didn't want this cold indifference to drag on. "I know I've been tough to live with lately. Let me make it up to you."

"You don't have to bother."

"But I want to."

"I don't know." She wrung her hands together. "What do you have in mind?"

He thought back to what she'd said about wanting a family and a menagerie of animals. He couldn't help her with the family, but there were animals at the vineyard. "How would you feel about a horseback ride around the grounds?"

She worried her bottom lip. "But I've never been on a horse before."

"I'll teach you."

Her eyes lit up. "Are you serious?"

He nodded. "Does this mean you agree?"

"I suppose."

Was that a hint of a smile pulling at her very tempting lips? He sure hoped so.

He suddenly found himself anxious to show her the ropes. Jules could be a lot of fun—when she wasn't upset with him. She had a way of making him smile, and it'd been a long time since he'd done that. The guy he used to be—the one who used to talk smoothly with the women and make them smile—now seemed like a stranger to him. Maybe it was time he brushed up on his skills. After all, there was no reason to make Jules miserable. She hadn't done anything wrong except get involved with him.

And how could things go astray while taking a horseback ride? After all, they'd be on separate horses. It wasn't like he would have a chance to wrap his arms around her and pull her close. Her lips wouldn't be right there in front of him, ripe for the picking.

He squelched the titillating thoughts. He had to see Jules like he saw other women. He couldn't keep lusting after her. Her future was in New York.

Jules was proud of herself.

After some coaching from Stefano and the patience of a mild-mannered horse, she was feeling at ease as Stefano guided her around the vineyard. The place was even bigger than she'd imagined. Acres and acres of vines stretched out in every direction. Stefano regaled her with stories of his family's history on the land and how they'd been able to expand onto neighboring lands.

She really enjoyed listening to him talk. She wasn't so sure if it was the honeyed tones of his voice or the entertaining twist he put on the tales—each story bigger and more outrageous than the last. He got her to laugh, and it felt good. It was as if a dark cloud had rolled away, letting the warm sunshine rain down on them.

They stopped on a distant hillside overlooking the villa. She wished that she'd brought her camera. This was a scene worthy of being on the back of a postcard. On the other side it should read: heaven.

Stefano alighted from Bandit, his chestnut mare with the fiery mane. The horse was spirited just like her master. And when they rode, it was if they could read each other's thoughts. Their ride had been smooth, and Jules had enjoyed watching them.

Stefano glanced her way as though waiting for her to get down. She wasn't about to budge, not a chance. Not without his help. She didn't relish the thought of falling on her backside, especially in front of him. She'd never live it down.

He started toward her. "Would you like some help?"

"Yes. Thank you."

When he stood before her, she leaned over. His hands gripped her waist as though they belonged there. Her fingers pressed to his muscled shoulders. The heat of his body permeated his shirt and warmed her hands. Her gaze met his. Her heart *tap-tapped*. She felt herself drowning in his bottomless eyes. The breath hitched in her throat as her body slid slowly, agonizingly, down over him.

When they stood chest to chest, there was a distinct unsteadiness in his breath. And then there was a nudge behind her. The horse had given her a healthy shove until her entire body was pressed against Stefano's unmoving form. In the next instance, his mouth pressed to hers. It was only then that she was willing to admit how much she'd longed for this moment.

His mouth moved passionately over hers as though he was starving for this kiss—for her. Her heart pounded in her chest. And the only thought in her head was the L word. Dare she admit it? How could she not?

She loved Stefano!

When had that happened? She wasn't sure. But she knew it'd been growing and evolving for a while now. And she couldn't deny it any longer. She was in love with Stefano DeFiore. Her heart soared as she met his kiss with her own vigor and excitement.

She felt as though she were floating on a fluffy cloud.

She didn't want to mess up this moment. She'd been waiting her whole life for him. Wrapped in his arms, it felt as though anything was possible. And it didn't matter how steep the climb—she would reach the summit. She could do it.

Before she lost her nerve, she had to tell him. She had to let him know that she loved him with all her heart. Her insides quivered, and she didn't know if it was the excitement of his kiss or the trepidation of vocalizing the L word—something she hadn't said since she was a naive kid.

Using every bit of willpower, she braced her hands on his solid chest and pushed. Her mouth tingled, but she resisted the urge to smooth her fingers over the whisker-worn skin. There was a far more important task ahead of her. She hoped he felt the same way about her.

His confused gaze met hers. She couldn't let him say anything. He'd ruin the moment, and she'd lose her nerve.

"I love you."

Those three ginormous words hung there. Stefano didn't move. He didn't speak. She wasn't even sure if he was still breathing.

As the silence stretched on, she started to question whether she'd truly uttered the words or just imagined the whole thing.

"Did you hear me?" She didn't have the courage to repeat the words.

His eyes darkened. He'd heard her. And he wasn't going to respond the way she'd imagined—the way she'd hoped he would.

His hands fell away from her, setting her free. In fact, it was as though he'd quickly erected a fortress around himself. He didn't even have to say anything; she already felt the coldness of rejection.

She refused to let him off that easily. She'd never spoken those words to another man in her entire life. He at least owed her an explanation of his feelings. A simple apology because he didn't feel the same way. Anything but this damnable silence that was about to drive her crazy.

"Say something!" She clenched her fists. "Don't just ignore me."

He cleared his throat. "I'm not."

"Aren't you going to say anything in response?"

His hands moved to his waist and he stared down at the ground. "I can't tell you what you think you want to hear."

Wait. Did he just say what she thought he'd said? She replayed his words in her mind.

"What I *think* I want you to say. What does that mean?"

He sighed. "You're a long way from home. Your sister is moving half a globe away from you. And you're at a crossroads in your life. It's natural that you'd want to reach out to someone and hold on tight. It would be an easy fix."

With every word out of his mouth her face warmed, but it wasn't embarrassment. It was anger. He was diminishing this moment—the first time she'd trusted a man with her heart. And he was shredding it before handing it back to her.

Unable to formulate words, she stood there. Tears stung her eyes, and she blinked repeatedly, refusing to let them fall. She was stronger than that. Stefano didn't deserve to witness her tears.

"You don't love me." He shifted his weight from one foot to the other. "I'm flattered that you think so highly of me, but if you really knew me, you wouldn't love me."

He wasn't getting off that easily. "Tell me. Tell me every reason that would make you unlovable."

He shook his head and then rubbed the back of his neck. "I don't think so. We need to get back to the villa before people start to wonder what happened to us."

"I'm not going anywhere until you talk to me." She walked over to a tall tree filled with fluttering green leaves and sank down on the lush grass beneath it.

"Jules, be reasonable."

"I am. I was honest about my feelings. Now you need to be honest with me. I'm not going anywhere until you do."

Resignation filtered across his tanned face. He led the horses over to a nearby tree and tied them up before returning to her side. He sat down next to her.

She steeled herself for whatever he was about to say. The way he'd been acting and holding himself back told her that it was pretty serious. Whatever it was, they'd deal with it together.

"Talk to me, Stefano. I've told you about my past."

"I know you did, and I appreciate how brave you were to do that, but this isn't the same thing. I…" He plucked a piece of tall grass and twirled it between his fingers. "I've done things—things that can't be forgiven."

She wanted to understand, but he wasn't giving her much to go on. "Does this have to do with your wife?"

He nodded. "We were high school sweethearts. She had this special way about her. All the guys turned to watch when she passed by, but she only had eyes for me."

"What was she like?"

"A dreamer. She'd love to lie back in the grass and stare up at the blue sky and talk about her dreams for the future." He leaned back against the trunk of the tree. "Taking those dreams from her changed her."

"How did you do that?"

"I married her. She thought by marrying a DeFiore that my money would bankroll her dreams. The truth is she never wanted to live here at the vineyard. She longed for the city and the high life."

"And you didn't see things that way?"

"No." Stefano gazed straight ahead. "After the honeymoon ended, the arguments started. She wanted to travel, and I kept putting her off, hoping she'd adjust to our new life together."

"But she never did."

He shook his head. "And I thought if we had a baby that it'd help things." He raked his fingers through his hair. "I don't know what I was thinking. A baby is no answer to problems in a marriage, but I was desperate. We were becoming more distant by the day."

Jules knew that it was important for him to get this off his chest and for her to hear it. She also knew how difficult and painful it could be to peel back the scab on a deep wound. She reached out and squeezed his hand, giving him what reassurance she could.

He cleared his throat. "Nothing I said or did was right. And I was losing hope that somehow we'd find the light at the end of the tunnel."

"Oh, Stefano. I'm so sorry. It must have been so hard for you."

"But that's just it—it shouldn't have been so hard. If only we'd talked before we got married. I mean really talked about what we were feeling and what we wanted out of life. But we were always so busy with this or that. I kept putting it off, figuring that we were in love and that life would just work itself out. But I was so wrong. I really messed things up."

"I'm sure you aren't the only one who thought that love was enough to iron out all of the wrinkles in life. Sometimes love runs out of steam and the wrinkles are all that remain."

He turned to her, his eyes full of turmoil. "But it's more than that. When I learned that Gianna wasn't interested in having kids or living here at the vineyard, I didn't take it well. I thought when we married that it was understood that we would start a family and I would keep working at the winery."

"But she wanted her dreams, and they were a long way from the vineyard."

He nodded. "She wanted to travel the world and write stories of our experiences. She said there were people that became professional bloggers for a living. She thought since I did well in English class that I would be able to do this. What she didn't consider was that I hate to write. I can do it for the winery blog, but it is out of necessity, not want."

To Jules, he was a hands-on guy, one who didn't mind rolling up his sleeves and getting dirty—actually he probably preferred it. As for kids, Jules imagined he'd make an excellent father. He had the patience and the temperament to help them reach their full potential. If only she could be like that... But this wasn't about her, and there was more to his story. Of that she was certain.

"What happened to your wife?"

"Things had been deteriorating between us for a long time. I'd finally moved into the bedroom next to hers. She'd threatened to leave numerous times, and I always talked her out of it, certain that there had to be a way to fix things. But I just didn't know what the answer was." He sighed deeply as though he'd been carrying around the weight of the world on his shoulders. "Then one stormy night, she prepared dinner, but I could tell that she had something on her mind. Neither of us ate much, and when my father made a quick exit to his room, her anger and frustration came tumbling out. She said that she got an email from one of our classmates, and he was about to set sail around the world."

Jules's insides tensed with foreboding. His tone grew

softer as though he had disappeared back in time to that fateful night. She wanted to pull him back to her—back to the present—but she couldn't. If they were ever going to make a future for themselves, then they had to get this all out in the open.

"What...what happened next?"

He gave Jules a quick glance as though she'd startled him back to reality. Then, in a hollow, pained voice, he continued, "Gianna said that she was tired of waiting for me. She was losing time, time that she could be off exploring the world, discovering new things. I...I asked her if she still loved me."

Jules's heart pinched. She knew the answer, and she was willing to bet that he'd known the answer before he had even asked the question. The backs of her eyes stung again, and she blinked repeatedly to keep her tears of sympathy from splashing down her cheeks. She didn't want to make this any harder on him.

He drew in an unsteady breath. "She said she didn't love me. She...she didn't know if she ever truly did because I wasn't the man she thought she'd married."

Jules squeezed his hand tight. She wanted to offer words of comfort, of encouragement, but they clogged up in her throat. This story was going to get worse, much worse. She lifted her head and tried to subdue her emotions. In the otherwise clear blue sky, one lone cloud floated over them, blocking out the sunlight.

Stefano massaged the back of his neck. "I was hurt and I was angry. Most of all, I was tired—tired of all the fighting. Tired of trying to find a way out of the mess. Tired of feeling so miserable. And that's when I made the worst mistake of my life."

The air was trapped in Jules's lungs as she waited for what happened next—what had turned this fine man into a shadow of the outgoing person everyone told her he used to be.

"I told Gianna that I wasn't a man to skip off into the sunset and forget my responsibilities. And that she might as well quit waiting around for that to happen. If she didn't love me or our life at the vineyard, then she could use the door. I told her I was done...with her." He rubbed a hand over his eyes. "And with our marriage." He dropped his face into his hands. "Why did I do that?"

"You can't blame yourself for being honest with her."

His head jerked up, and his distraught gaze needled her. "You don't know what you're saying. If only I hadn't lost my patience—if I'd tried to reason with her, none of it would have happened."

"What happened?"

The only sound was the breeze rustling the leaves overhead and a couple of birds singing. Stefano stared off into the distant horizon as though in his mind he was back in that stormy night. Jules waited for the ominous conclusion to his heart-wrenching story.

"For the first time ever, she didn't fight back." His voice cracked with emotion. "It was as though my words had knocked the fight out of her. Gianna ran out of the kitchen. I didn't want to go upstairs. I didn't want to confront her again. So I started cleaning up the dinner dishes. I don't know how much time passed when I heard the car start and the engine rev as she gassed it out of the driveway. I went to the door and ran outside after her. The rain was coming down in sheets, and the wind was turbulent. It wasn't a night fit for driving. But I couldn't stop her."

Jules's wrapped her arm around his back and leaned her head against his shoulder. "You didn't force her out into the storm—"

"But I did. I was the reason she ran off that night. I didn't give her any reason to stay. If only I'd…"

"Nothing you could have said would have made a difference. She was only waiting for you to give her a reason to follow through with her threats. She wanted to go."

"But not that night." His voice cracked with emotion. "It wasn't too much later when the phone rang. The car had hydroplaned…Gianna lost control. The…the car went over an embankment."

How awful. Now Jules understood the shadow that seemed to follow him around and the way he pulled back when he was having a good time.

"It's not your fault," she repeated, willing him to believe her. "She knew what she was doing."

"But she wouldn't have been out there if I had thought before opening my mouth. I had all of those months to tell her how I was feeling. Why did it have to be that night?"

"Because she was backing you into a corner. She wanted to go, but she just hadn't worked up the courage to do it."

"So you agree. I'm responsible—"

"No. That's not what I'm saying. You'll never know exactly what she was thinking that night. But she was a grown woman plenty capable of making her own choices and the accident was just that—an accident."

"They said that she died instantly." His voice was so soft that she strained to hear him. "The coroner said she was pregnant. She was going to have my baby." A tear splashed onto his cheek.

Jules leaned forward and wrapped her arms around him. At first, he hesitated, and then his body pressed against hers. Her heart was breaking for him. When he finally got himself together, he pulled back. She reluctantly let him go.

She looked into his bloodshot eyes. "And this is the guilt

you've been carrying around with you, isn't it? Every time we start to get close, you pull back because you're still blaming yourself for Gianna and the baby?"

"Yes." His voice took on a weary, broken tone. "I don't deserve to have you in my life."

"I disagree. I think I'm exactly what you need."

When he glanced at her, she ducked her head and pressed her lips to his. He didn't move at first. She brushed her mouth over his, hoping he'd respond—that he'd reach out to her. He'd been so alone for so long and piling on the guilt for his wife's untimely death. She couldn't imagine what that would feel like. He was a good guy, and he deserved to move on with his life.

His lips moved over hers like a drowning man sucking in some much needed oxygen. He pulled her over onto his lap. His hands on either side of her head. Her hands resting on his powerful shoulders. Lip to lip and tongue to tongue, the love dance of a lifetime started.

At last the wall between them had come crumbling down. Jules knew what she wanted—Stefano. She wanted all of him, his past and his future. She loved him.

CHAPTER FIFTEEN

"WE SHOULDN'T HAVE done that." Stefano rushed to button his shirt.

He swore under his breath. Every time he was alone with Jules all his common sense evaporated. Guilt consumed him. He'd meant to explain to her why they couldn't be together and he'd ended up making love to her instead.

He raked his fingers through his hair. He didn't dare look at her. It would be so easy to believe this was the beginning of something—not the end of something very special. *Wait.* Why was she taking this so well? She should be yelling at him—calling him every rotten name in the book. After all, he'd be the first to admit that he deserved it.

Maybe she hadn't heard him. That had to be it. He opened his mouth to repeat himself, but nothing came out. He pressed his lips together. Deep down he didn't want to push Jules away—he wanted to pull her close and keep her there. But that was impossible. And now, after reliving how his lack of good judgment had cost Gianna and their unborn child their lives, he couldn't do the same thing with Jules's future. He couldn't let her wreck her future over him.

No matter how much she'd end up hating him, he had to set Jules free. It was for the best. "I'm sorry—"

"Don't be. You were amazing." Jules pulled on her boots and strode over to him. She smiled up at him. "And I—"

He pressed a finger to her soft lips, not letting her finish. He knew what she was going to say, and he didn't think that he could bear to hear her say again that she loved him. If she uttered those words, he was afraid the last of his resolve would crack, and that couldn't happen.

"You aren't understanding me." He averted his face to avoid witnessing the inevitable hurt in her eyes. "You and I aren't meant to be."

"Yes, we are."

"No, we aren't. Your life is back in New York. You have grad school to attend."

"Grad school was Lizzie's idea, not mine. I want to stay here with you."

He couldn't keep arguing with her. She had to understand that this thing, whatever it was, wasn't going to happen again. She had a life to lead, and it wasn't with him.

Stefano grasped her shoulders. "You have to hear me. This thing between us is over. After the wedding, you'll get on a plane back to New York and I'll be busy preparing for the harvest."

Her eyes opened wide. "You're serious, aren't you?"

"Yes, I am."

"But we just shared—"

"A special moment that I'll never forget. But we have to be realistic. We both want different things in the future. And you don't even know for certain what that's going to be."

She drew her shoulders back. Her eyes glittered with strength and determination. "I know I want you. And you punishing yourself for your wife's accident isn't going to change what happened. You're a good man, and you deserve to be happy again."

"I will be when I know that you aren't throwing away your future. You have the whole world at your feet. All you have to do is choose your path."

"I choose you."

He refused to accept her words. She didn't mean them. In time, she would realize that they were a mistake. "Don't let your experience as an intern scare you away from grad school. This world needs people who see things that need changing and aren't afraid to speak up. The key is not to give up in the face of adversity. Sometimes you just have to regroup and take a different approach. Be the voice of those children who can't speak for themselves."

She hadn't thought of it that way. Was she turning her back on helping countless children who didn't have a voice? The thought tumbled through her mind.

"And if you want to be a mother, you can do that, too. Don't let your past hold you back. I know your life with your mother wasn't good, but use it as a lesson in what not to do as a parent."

Jules worried her lush bottom lip. "But what if I'm no good at it?"

"Follow your heart. It won't lead you astray. You have good instincts. If you do that, you can't possibly fail. But remember that no one is perfect. You'll make mistakes along the way. Everyone does. Just learn from them."

She tilted her head to the side and gave him a hard stare. "You know, you're awfully full of good advice for a bachelor."

"You forget I come from a very big family, and they are all full of advice. I guess some of it rubbed off on me."

She was going to make someone an amazing wife. And when the time came some child was going to be showered in love. The image of her with a husband and baby flashed in his mind, causing his gut to knot up.

"To bad you can't accept advice as well as you hand it out." Her lips pressed into a hard line.

His hand rubbed over his stubbled jaw as a war raged inside him. "I wish I could tell you what you want to hear. But I can't."

"And here's my advice to you. Don't let the past dictate your future. Live in the moment. Otherwise you're going to miss everything that is good in life." When he didn't say anything, she glared at him. "Why do I even try? I give up."

The pained look in her eyes stabbed deep into his heart. He'd rather have dealt with some female hysterics than the defeat that was reflected in her expression. She turned, glanced over at the horses and then started walking back to the villa.

"Don't you want to ride?" he called out to her retreating form.

She shook her head and picked up her pace.

He started after her. He couldn't let it end this way. He had to tell her that their lovemaking had meant so much more than he was letting on. It had moved his world and left him wanting more of her.

His steps slowed down. He couldn't do that. He'd be encouraging her to stay here with him. She'd sacrifice everything. And maybe not today or tomorrow but someday she'd regret it. And she'd blame him.

He stopped. His gaze followed her. He assured himself that this was best for both of them. No matter how much the sacrifice would cost him.

Because beneath it all, he loved her.

In the days that ensued, Jules resolved to hold Stefano at arm's length.

How could she have been so foolish to think that he felt

the same way about her? How many times had she been told that men and women looked at relationships two different ways? She knew better. While she was busy letting her heart fill with love for him, he was enjoying the moment. He wasn't picturing a future with a picket fence, two-point-five kids and a cat or two or three.

She nuzzled Apricot close to her neck. "You know I'm leaving soon. The wedding is next week. And then my time here will be over."

Apricot purred and used her tiny pin-like nails to climb up on Jules's shoulder, where she liked to perch. The kitten's happy meter went all the way to the top, and all Jules could hear was the sound of purring. Jules loved the sound. It was comforting and reassuring. Boy, was she going to miss Apricot, this vineyard and—

She brought her thoughts up short. She refused to miss Stefano. He was the one to turn away from her—to dismiss their lovemaking as if it meant nothing. And to think that she'd blurted out that she loved him. She blinked rapidly. No way was she going to cry. He didn't deserve her tears.

Wedding or no wedding, she didn't know if she'd be able to face him again. There were just some things that you couldn't take back once they were spoken. A frustrated growl rose in her throat. Why, oh, why had she thought Stefano had been the exception to her rule about not trusting people with her heart?

Her fingers ran over Apricot's downy-soft fur. There was something so comforting and reassuring about a fur baby's presence. It calmed her and let her realize that she was wasting her time standing around thinking about Stefano. He was going to be Lizzie's in-law, and that was all. She'd probably never see him again. Well, that might be stretching it a bit, but their run-ins would be few and far between.

Speaking of which, she was supposed to ride with him to Rome for the final dress fitting. Her stomach knotted up thinking of sitting next to him—alone with him—for the entire ride. That wasn't going to happen. She'd get to Rome some other way.

A glance at the time told her that she had to get a move on. A red-and-white-striped sundress flirted just above her knees. The new white-heeled sandals perfectly complemented the dress. She had to admit that it was a big stretch from her usual black-and-purple ensembles, but she was finding that she was having fun with colors. Maybe she'd hemmed her fashion choices in too tightly. She was actually quite comfortable in the dress. Of course, she'd applied makeup to cover up her scars, but she hadn't gone so heavy with the eye makeup. Maybe when she went back to New York, she would maintain this makeover. Or at least switch up her wardrobe now and then.

She reached up and removed Apricot from her shoulder. "You have to be good, okay?"

Those big blue eyes stared at her, looking as innocent as could be. But Jules knew what trouble this fur baby could get herself into from climbing up on furniture and being unsure how to get down to sticking her paw in a glass of water and tipping it over.

"We'll just see if Massimo is up to keeping an eye on you. He'll make sure you don't get into too much trouble while I'm gone. And you can entertain him. I don't know why, but he certainly seems to like you, little miss."

Apricot mewed as if she knew what Jules had said to her.

With a smile, Jules headed downstairs in search of Massimo. Since his stroke, his room was on the first floor, and he spent a lot of time in the living room with the large glass wall that made the room bright and cheery. And that's exactly where she found him. He was sitting on the couch doing a crossword puzzle. He glanced up and sent her a lopsided smile.

"I see you brought the fuzzy one to visit."

"Yes, Apricot is feeling particularly energetic. I was wondering if you could keep an eye on her while I go to Rome. Today is our last dress fitting."

"Ah, my grandson will be driving you."

"I think I'll take the train. He has work to do."

"DeFiore men don't put work ahead of their obligations to beautiful women." Massimo reached out and squeezed her hand. "I know something is troubling you. Just remember that anything worth having is worth fighting for. Life isn't easy, and the good stuff doesn't just land in your lap. You have to work for it and never give up."

"Are you ready to go?"

She turned to find Stefano standing in the hallway. His face was a mask of indifference. It was the first time they'd spoken to each other since their moment on the grassy hillside.

"If you'd just drop me at the train station, I'll be fine."

"Don't be ridiculous. I said that I would take you, and I'm ready to go. Besides, there isn't another train until much later."

She sighed. The last thing she wanted to do was end up in a fight with him. "I was just asking your grandfather if he'd keep an eye on Apricot."

"I'd love to." Massimo reached out for the fluff ball, and she gently placed the squirming kitten in his hands.

"I should run and get her food bowl."

"No need. I'm sure Maria won't mind getting some food."

Jules glanced around, spotting the litter box in the corner of the room. "And water. I forgot the water."

"Don't worry. We'll be fine together."

"Are you sure?"

Massimo sent her a reassuring smile. "Go before you're late for your appointment. Did you say this was the last fitting?"

She nodded. "We're taking our dresses home today. Well, I guess I'm bringing both dresses here as Lizzie doesn't want to take any chance on Dante spotting it."

"All the more reason for me to drive you," Stefano piped in. "The dresses would get wrinkled on the train or worse."

He did have a good point. "Then we best get going."

This was going to be the longest ride of her life. There was tangible tension between them, and she didn't know how to get around it. She didn't even know if she wanted to resolve it. After all, she hadn't started any of this. It was Stefano. One minute he wanted her, and the next he was shoving her away and spouting out every reason why they shouldn't be together.

If he thought she was the only one who didn't know what she wanted, then he should take a good look in the mirror. His mouth said one thing. But his body said another.

CHAPTER SIXTEEN

WHAT WAS TAKING SO LONG?

Stefano sat alone in the front of the bridal boutique. The oval table in front of him was littered with every bridal magazine published. No matter how bored he was, there was no way he was picking up one of those periodicals. He'd had his fill of flowers, dresses and cakes.

He glanced at his wristwatch for the second time in five minutes. Jules and Lizzie were supposed to try on their dresses and then they'd be on their way. Not that he was anxious to repeat the car ride with Jules. The whole ride to Rome had been nothing but tense silence. What should he say to her? That he was sorry? That when he was around her he couldn't think straight? That he cared so much about her that he was trying to protect her from himself?

It was all true. But he couldn't take back his words. She'd never believe him. And if she did, where would that leave them?

His temples started to throb. Oh, it didn't matter what he felt for her. Just speaking the words that she meant something to him would only spur her on to stay here, and then what? One day she'd wake and realize that she'd sacrificed everything for him, and then she'd leave. She'd go off to follow her dreams.

It was best to let her go now before they got in too

deep. He knew that she cared for him, but it wasn't as if they'd made promises to each other. The exit door was still wide-open for both of them. By giving her a healthy shove through it, he was doing her a big favor. She may not realize it now, but in time she would understand.

She'd return to her life in New York—to grad school—and she'd soon forget about him. His gut churned. With her beauty, she could have her choice of men.

At last, the women stepped into the waiting area. Each was carrying a white zippered garment bag. They were chatting back and forth. Neither even seemed to notice him. He didn't know why it should bother him. He was, after all, just the chauffeur. And this was what he wanted—Jules to forget about him—wasn't it?

He shifted uncomfortably in his seat, not sure if they were leaving or if there was more that needed to be done. When Lizzie's phone buzzed, she held up a finger to Jules to wait a moment.

Jules glanced over at him. When she didn't move, he did. He strode over and held out his hand. "Let me take that for you."

She didn't say a word as she handed over the dress. Once she'd adjusted it so that it wouldn't wrinkle, she turned and picked up a bridal magazine. As though he wasn't even in the room, she thumbed through the glossy pages.

He'd been privy to all the other stuff for the wedding except the dresses. He had to admit he was really curious to see what Jules would be wearing. Would it be purple like the paper flowers he'd helped her make? Or would it be another color? Was it short, showing off her legs? Or was it longer on the bottom with the top scaled back and showing off her bare shoulders and that butterfly on her chest?

He cut off his thoughts. They were only going to get

him in trouble. What Jules wore to the wedding made no difference to him. He inwardly groaned, wishing that were the case.

"Are you ready to go?" He hoped so. The tension was starting to give him a headache.

She glanced up. "Are you that anxious to get away from me?"

"Of course not."

She turned back to the magazine. "I could take the train back. You don't have to wait if you're that anxious to go."

"Would you stop putting words in my mouth? I just wanted to know if I should take the dress to the car."

"Oh." She glanced down at the earth-tone swirls of the plush carpeting.

How in the world had they gone from laughter and kissing among other delicious things to this awkward silence? Agitation churned in his gut. He knew the answer, and he didn't like it one bit. He'd let things get out of hand. When he'd tried to fix it, it was too late. And he'd only made things worse.

Lizzie approached them. "That was Dante. He needs me right away at the restaurant. Something's come up. Do you think you could handle picking out the candles for the tables? I'm really sorry about this."

More time together. More stress and tension. Stefano's body grew rigid.

"Sure." Jules wore a smile that didn't reach her eyes. "Do you need anything else?"

"Not that I can think of." Lizzie gave her a hug. "You've been great. I don't know what I'd have done without you. I'm really going to miss you when you leave for school."

"I'm sure you'll be so busy being a newlywed that you won't even notice."

Lizzie beamed. "I think you're right. Oh, there is one

more thing. Would you mind stopping by the florist? They called and said that one of the flowers they ordered is out of stock or some such thing. Anyway, they said they had a suitable replacement, but I haven't had a chance to stop by. Would you mind?"

This was the last straw. Stefano just couldn't take it anymore. Everyone was acting as if everything was perfect, and it wasn't. Nothing about this was right. Jules was hiding the truth from her sister, and her sister was taking advantage of Jules's guilt and generosity.

"Yes, she minds," he heard himself say. "She's been running herself ragged for you because of that television show, and she can't do everything. You need to stop taking advantage of Jules and listen to what she needs and wants."

Both women gaped at him as if he'd just sprouted another head. But he didn't care at this point. Lizzie didn't know how much it was costing Jules to spend time in the car with him. He could tell that she just wanted to get away from him.

Jules stepped up to him and poked a finger at his chest. "You're the pot calling the kettle black. Who are you to tell Lizzie that when you refuse to hear what I've been telling you? You are so caught up in trying to make up for the past that you can't see what's right in front of you. You're squandering your future, and it's for nothing. You did nothing wrong." Her shoulders hunched as she shook her head. "I don't know why I'm wasting my time. You refuse to accept anything I say."

He wanted to object, but he couldn't. Was she right? Was it time to let go of the past? Could he move past the guilt?

Jules snatched the dress from him and turned her back to him. "Come on, Lizzie."

At the sight of her retreating back, he once again found his voice. "Jules, wait."

She stopped and turned, giving him an icy, pointed stare that stabbed straight through to his heart. "Lizzie, I need someplace to stay tonight."

"Umm...sure. Whatever you need." Lizzie frowned at him. When he went to approach Jules, who was already pulling the front door open, Lizzie held up her palm, stopping him in his tracks. "Let her go."

He blew out a pent-up breath as he raked his fingers through his hair. He'd blown it. He'd meant to help Jules and instead he'd opened his mouth and inserted his size-twelve shoe. Once upon a time he'd been good at talking to the ladies, but lately he just never seemed to say the right thing. At least not where Jules was concerned.

Still he couldn't stand the thought of her hating him. He had to say something. Whether or not it would help things he didn't know. "I'm sorry."

The glass door swung shut, and his words were lost in the warm breeze. Oh, man, what had he done? He rubbed the back of his neck, trying to gather himself. How had things ended up in such a jumbled mess? The truth was he'd ended up causing Jules the very same pain he'd been trying to save her from.

He had to stop them. He had to try again to apologize. But he was too late. He stopped on the sidewalk and didn't see the women anywhere. It was as though they'd vanished.

When Dante heard about this he'd be lucky if he didn't drive to the vineyard and kick him around the villa. And, frankly, he couldn't blame his brother. He'd utterly screwed up everything.

Late the following morning, Jules strolled to the living room of Dante and Lizzie's very spacious apartment. She hoped that she'd slept late enough that her sister would be downstairs at Ristorante Massimo.

"About time you woke up." Lizzie's voice echoed across the room. "I was starting to get worried about you." She held up a mug. "Would you like some caffeine?"

Jules yawned as she nodded her head. She'd been up most of the night thinking about Stefano and wondering what his outburst at the bridal boutique had been about. What in the world had gotten into him to say those things?

And what was Lizzie thinking? Yesterday her sister had been unusually quiet and hadn't brought up Stefano at all. Of course, some of that might have had to do with Jules fighting back tears. Maybe she didn't want to make matters worse.

But today was a new day, and Jules could feel her sister's inquisitive gaze on her. Jules wished she'd just speak up and get it over with. She wasn't good with hedging around subjects. It just ended up unnerving her more.

"Say it." Jules plunked down on the couch.

"Say what?" Lizzie said innocently as she approached her with a steaming mug of coffee.

"Don't go acting like nothing happened. You want to know what was up with Stefano and me yesterday, don't you?"

"Since you brought it up, yes. I'd like to know how far this thing between you two has gone. Are you in love with him?"

Wow! Way to go straight to the heart of the matter. Pride refused to let Jules admit that she was in love with a man who didn't love her back. She'd already made a fool of herself in front of him; she couldn't do the same with her sister.

"No. I'm not." Guilt rained down on her.

Lizzie stared at her as though trying to make up her mind. "And you still plan to attend grad school, right?"

What else did she have waiting for her back in New York? She might as well stick to her original plan. "Of course."

"Good. Because I just sent in the tuition payment."

Jules had totally forgotten about that. Well, it appeared that everyone was getting what they wanted. She would soon be out of Stefano's life, and she'd be going back to school just like her sister wanted. She should be happy that she was being offered such an amazing opportunity. Not everyone was so blessed. But somehow she just couldn't work up the excitement.

Now wasn't the time to dwell on things, not with the wedding in a matter of days. "Now that we have that settled—"

The phone rang, and Lizzie held up a finger, stopping Jules in midsentence. Jules was glad to have a small reprieve. She could use a healthy dose of caffeine before she dealt any more with her sister.

Jules swallowed another mouthful of the fragrant brew with a touch of cream and sweetener. She did have to admit that Italian coffee was quite good. In fact, she could easily get used to drinking it.

Over the rim of her cup, she noticed Lizzie had moved to the galley kitchen. Her back was to her, and Jules could only make out a word here and there—not that she was trying to eavesdrop. She had enough of her own problems without dabbling into someone else's. As it was, she was quite certain that the Stefano issue hadn't been laid to rest that easily. Lizzie was never satisfied that quickly when she was concerned about something.

A few minutes later, Jules set her empty mug on the

glass coffee table. Lizzie returned, taking a seat on the couch opposite hers. "That was Stefano on the phone."

Jules was tempted to ask what he wanted, but she resisted the urge. Her sister's inquisitive stare bore into her. She had no doubt that Lizzie knew how much it was killing her not to ask about him, but she had to play this right or Lizzie would turn into a protective mother bear. She'd make matters worse for everyone. And with the wedding just around the corner, drama was the last thing any of them needed.

Lizzie curled her feet up on the black leather couch and sipped her coffee. Waiting for her sister to speak was pure torture. At her breaking point, Jules asked, "What did he want?"

"He called to apologize."

"That's good. He should. He knows nothing about you and me."

Lizzie's lips pressed together in a firm line and her brows gathered. "He wanted to talk to you, but I told him that you didn't want to talk to him yet. That is right, isn't it?"

He wanted to talk to her? She wondered what he wanted to say. Then she realized with the pending wedding that he probably just wanted to apologize and smooth things over before the big day. The thought dashed her hopes that he might have miraculously come to his senses.

"That's fine. I can talk to him when I get back to the vineyard, anyway. I have a lot to do when I get there. The temporary flooring and tent will be arriving tomorrow, and I have to figure out the most level spot to set everything up. I should grab my planner and we can go over the final details."

She went to stand when Lizzie said, "Wait. We aren't done talking."

Jules sighed as she settled back on the couch.

"What did Stefano mean by I don't listen to you?"

No way was she getting into all of this with Lizzie on the week of her wedding. This was Lizzie's moment to shine. There would be a better time and place for this talk.

Jules shrugged. "I don't know. I think he was just frustrated. This running around for the wedding while trying to keep his business going has been a lot for him. I think he just needed to blow off some steam."

"That's interesting because he said almost the same thing on the phone."

"He did? I mean—see? I was right. Don't worry. Everything will be fine. All you have to do is show up for the big day." She forced a smile.

"You better not be falling for him." Lizzie gave her an I-mean-business look. "You can't mess up grad school. You worked too hard for it."

And you already paid the tuition.

Jules stifled a frustrated sigh. Time to change the subject.

"By the way, where's Dante?"

CHAPTER SEVENTEEN

"Are you trying to ruin everything?"

Stefano's body tensed at the sound of Dante's voice. His brother was the last person he wanted to deal with right now. He glanced up as Dante crossed the patio in his direction. Stefano turned away and stared blindly out over the sun-drenched rows of grapevines. The only vision in his mind was Jules's beautiful face.

"I'm not up for it today, Dante," Stefano warned.

"Too bad." The footsteps behind him stopped. "You have some explaining to do, big brother."

So he'd heard about the incident yesterday at the bridal boutique. He wasn't surprised, but the fact Dante had driven to the vineyard while the *ristorante* was open for business was a worrisome development.

Stefano sighed and turned to face his brother. "Shouldn't you be in Rome working?"

"I would be if my brother wasn't trying to wreck my wedding."

"What? I'm not doing any such thing."

"That's not what I hear." Dante's hands rested on his waist, pushing his suit jacket back. "I know that you're not a fan of weddings after what happened to you and Papa, but I thought you were man enough to step aside and let me make my own choices."

"I am. I did." How did he explain away yesterday? Jules wasn't even speaking to him. "How's Jules?"

"First, I think you owe me an explanation before I withdraw my request for you to be my best man."

The serious glint in Dante's eyes left Stefano no doubt about his sincerity. But he needed to know Jules was okay after the way she'd disappeared. "This is important. How's Jules? Did she say anything to you?"

Dante's brows arched. "You've fallen for her, haven't you?"

"No, I haven't. We're...we're friends. That's all."

"You have it real bad for her, and you're fighting it. That's what yesterday was about. And judging by Jules's tears, she has it bad for you, too."

"She was crying?"

His brother nodded.

Stefano ran a hand over his stubbled jaw. He hadn't bothered to shave. This was worse than he'd been imagining. He wanted to go to her and take her in his arms. But he couldn't do that. It'd only succeed in making things worse. She'd get over him. She surely didn't love him, did she? It was a crush. Nothing more.

"You need to make this right." Dante's tone left no doubt about his sincerity. "And I don't mean by playing the part of Romeo. That's already gotten us in enough trouble."

He waved away his brother's unwanted advice. "I know. I know. You don't have to lecture me, little brother."

"Really? Because from where I'm standing you've made a mess of things. And this is my wedding week. My bride is not happy, and this should be the best time of her life."

"Okay. I hear you. I'll fix this."

"I'm glad to hear you say that." The stress lines on his brother's face eased. "Then quit messing around with my soon-to-be sister-in-law. You know she's supposed to go off to some grad school, don't you?"

"Yes, I know. I've been telling her that's what she should be concentrating on."

"I bet you have." Dante sent him an I-know-better-than-that look. "And Lizzie just paid the tuition. She's counting on Jules following through with this. Don't ruin this for Jules, or you'll have me to answer to."

Stefano had no doubt that Dante meant business. His brother wasn't about to let anything ruin his wedding, and Stefano couldn't blame him. He'd be the same way if he was marrying Jules—not that he would ever be walking down the aisle again.

The first thing he had to do was talk to Jules, but since she wasn't answering her phone and Lizzie was running interference, he'd have to wait until she returned to the villa.

He didn't know what he'd say to her aside from apologizing for making a fool of himself. Maybe that would be enough. He hoped.

Jules's insides quivered. She'd rather be doing anything but this. Even a trip to the dentist sounded good to her at this point.

Her footsteps were slow but steady as she entered the winery. Lizzie had loaned her a car to transport the dresses to the villa without incident. No one wanted to trust the dresses on the train. And now that the wedding gear was stowed away safely in a spare room, Jules had to face Stefano. Things couldn't linger like this. She'd promised Lizzie there would be peace for the wedding.

She'd made a fool of herself over Stefano, but she would be fine without him. She sucked in an unsteady breath. Her heart disagreed, but her mind kept telling her to do what was easiest for everyone.

When she found Stefano, he was in the barrel room, testing some wine. He glanced up and surprise registered in his dark eyes. Then it was as if a wall came down, making it impossible to know what he was thinking. She was shut out once again.

She refused to let it stop her. "Can we talk?"

He nodded. "I needed to talk to you, too."

"I promised my sister that you and I would make peace."

"I promised my brother the same thing."

That was a good sign, right? It was so hard to tell. He didn't smile. Did she always have such a hard time reading him?

She twisted her hands together. "I just wanted to let you know that I'll stay out of your way from now on. And I'll be leaving right after the wedding."

She turned to go, and he reached out for her arm. His touch was warm and gentle. It sent a current of electricity zinging its way to her bruised heart.

"Wait. I need to say something to you."

His hand dropped away as she turned back to him. Had he at last come to his senses and realized that what they had was worth fighting for? The breath caught in her chest as she waited for his next words.

"I was a fool. I shouldn't have said those things to you in front of your sister. Please forgive me."

She nodded. "It's forgotten."

There had to be more. Anticipation had her stomach twisted in a knot. What was he waiting for? This was the part where they were supposed to kiss and make up. It's how it worked in the black-and-white romantic movies that she loved to watch late at night when she couldn't sleep.

"Do you want me to walk with you back to the villa? I can if you just give me a couple of minutes to finish filling out this form."

It wasn't going to happen. Their happy ending was not to be. She expelled a trapped breath and pulled her shoulders back. "No need. Finish what you were doing. I have some calls to make. I'll see you at dinner."

Her feet felt weighted down as she walked away. Since when had she become such a romantic? It wasn't good. Not good at all. She had to forget Stefano and her Roman holiday. In just a few days she'd catch her flight back to reality, but first she had to make sure this wedding went off without a hitch.

CHAPTER EIGHTEEN

ALL DECKED OUT in a new tux, Stefano stood at the altar.

He resisted the urge to pull at his collar. His brother stood next to him as the wedding music started to play. Dante had a permanent smile tattooed on his face. It was as it should be, but Stefano struggled to keep from frowning over the way he'd messed up with Jules.

He missed the gentle chime of her laughter. The way her eyes twinkled when she smiled.

Who was he kidding? He missed everything about her. She was so close and yet so far away. They were cordial to each other but nothing more. No teasing banter. No easy conversation.

Amid everything, Jules hadn't let it distract her. She had worked tirelessly from the time she got up until she called it a night. She'd been driven to make the wedding perfect. And it was amazing. She was amazing.

As though his thoughts had summoned her, Jules started up the aisle between the rows of white chairs with purple bows. Guests dressed in their finest turned to watch her walk up the aisle. She looked absolutely stunning in a knee-length purple dress with a black sash accentuating her narrow waist. And the fitted bodice snuggled to her curves just perfectly while leaving the butterfly tattoo peeking over the top. Stefano stifled a groan of frustration. He forced his eyes upward, noticing how the strapless dress left a clear and enticing view of her sun-kissed shoulders. It was impossible for him to look away from her.

Jules didn't appear to have a similar problem. She kept her gaze straight forward. Was she purposely avoiding looking at him? Or was she nervous about standing in front of a large group of his extended family while television cameras were pointed at her from almost every angle?

She held her chin high. With her dark hair swept up, her slender neck was left exposed with only a gold chain adorning it. Stefano's mind meandered back in time to when they'd made love. He knew exactly where her ticklish spot was, right there in the gentle curve that sloped into her shoulder. He halted the tantalizing thought.

When she neared him, she glanced his way. He expected to find fury—or anger—at the very least pain, but there was no sign of those emotions reflected in her emerald eyes. That was good, right? She'd already gotten over him. So why didn't he feel relieved?

As she took her position opposite him, the guests rose to their feet as the wedding march played. Lizzie started down the aisle on the arm of Massimo. His grandfather had surprised everyone when he'd announced that he'd worked extra hard at his therapy so he could walk Lizzie down the aisle without the aid of his walker. Stefano wasn't sure who beamed brighter, the bride or Massimo. It seemed as though it was a day for happy endings...or beginnings, depending on how you looked at it.

When Lizzie joined hands with Dante, the minister cleared his throat. "Welcome. We are gathered today to celebrate the joining of two hearts..."

As the ceremony continued, Stefano became distracted by the smile on Jules's face. It lit up her eyes and made them sparkle like fine gems.

Even though he was happy for his brother, Stefano couldn't shake the dark cloud hanging over him. He knew what it was—it was Jules's impending departure. He'd been pretending that there was plenty of time to make peace between them before she left, but now the moment had arrived, and he didn't know what to say to make things better.

The minister clasped his hands together. "And now the bride and groom will share the vows that they've written for each other."

Her hand in his, Lizzie peered up at Dante. "I never ever intended to fall in love with you. When we met, you were so stubborn and irritating." She smiled at him. Happiness danced in her eyes. "And did I mention stubborn?"

Dante's brows rose, but he didn't say a word as he continued to stare at his bride. Stefano's focus strayed back to Jules, whose eyes looked a bit misty as Lizzie continued to recite her vows.

"But then you showed me your patience, your generosity and your heart. It was then that I knew I'd at last found what I've been looking for my whole life—a home."

Stefano's heart leaped into his throat, blocking his breath. It was as though Lizzie had looked inside his heart and read his feelings for Jules. She was his home. How in the world was he going to live without the sound of her voice, the contagiousness of her laughter or the excitement he found in her kiss?

Stefano had no clue what his brother's vows were because the next thing Stefano knew the minister was saying, "And do you, Dante DeFiore, take Elizabeth Addler to be your wife, to have and to hold, from this day forward, for better, for worse, for richer, for poorer, in sickness and health, as long as you both shall live?"

Without hesitation and in a loud, clear voice, Dante said, "I do."

The minister smiled. "I now pronounce you husband and wife. You may kiss the bride."

Dante didn't waste any time gathering his bride in his arms. A round of applause filled the air. If the heat of their first married kiss was any indication, it wouldn't be long until he was a proud, doting uncle. They made a great couple. And he couldn't be happier for them.

As the reception kicked off with tissue-paper flowers everywhere and upbeat music filling the air, Stefano stood off to the side. His gaze followed Jules around the dance floor. It appeared he wasn't the only one to notice her beauty. He'd swear every one of his male relatives had paid her a compliment or two. And the single ones were all lining up to dance with her.

He'd done nothing but think of her this past week to the point of his father chasing him out of the office after screwing up an order for an important customer. Stefano didn't make mistakes—well, he hadn't before Jules stepped into his life. Now he seemed to be making one after the other.

Jules truly was something special, and he'd let her get away because of his guilt over Gianna's death. He didn't think anything could wipe that memory away, but Jules might be right, too, that this self-imposed punishment wouldn't help Gianna or himself. Nothing would bring her or their baby back. It was time that he let the past rest and move forward. After all, there was plenty of room in his heart for both the past and the future.

Dante gestured to him from the side of the dance floor. What could his brother possibly want now? Stefano had smiled for all the pictures even though there wasn't an ounce of him that was in a jovial mood.

Like the dutiful best man, he made his way across the crowded dance floor, trying not to stare at Jules as his cousin Roberto held her a little too close. Stefano made a mental note to have a talk with his cousin later. Averting his gaze, it came to rest on Papa smiling broadly as he held Maria in his arms. It would seem that his father truly was giving love a second chance and in public for all the extended family to see.

"What do you need?" Stefano asked his brother.

"Have you forgotten that you're the best man?"

"No." His focus was drawn like a magnet to Jules, wishing that he was the one holding her close and that she was smiling up at him.

Dante shoved a champagne flute in his hand. "Stefano, did you hear anything I said?"

"What? Sorry I was distracted."

"So I noticed. Well, don't worry—you'll have your turn to dance with her soon."

"Really?" He realized too soon that he'd let his anxiousness show, and that was not a good thing around his brother. He glanced over to see Dante laughing. Stefano frowned at him. "What's so funny?"

"You are, big brother. Looks like I better take some notes tonight about being the best man because you have it worse than I first thought—much worse."

Stefano turned away. He didn't like being the center of Dante's amusement, especially not when he knew that his time with Jules was severely limited.

"I'm not dancing with her." He wasn't going to torture himself. Standing here watching her in the arms of these other men was enough torture.

"Yes, you are. As soon as you give the toast."

He'd forgotten about the speech. He'd taken the time to write one out. He searched his pockets. The note card. It was missing. And the words escaped him.

"You do have the toast memorized, don't you? Because

they're going to make an announcement as soon as this dance is over."

"Yes, I've got it." Stefano lied as he frantically searched his memory for what he'd been planning to say before he let himself get distracted.

The music stopped. Before he was ready a microphone was shoved in his hand. He cleared his throat and hoped he could think of a toast on his toes.

"Could I have everyone's attention?"

Silence fell over the crowd. He immediately spotted Jules. She was staring at him. His heart slammed into his chest, and his palms grew moist.

"I know you're all having fun, and I promise this won't take long. I'd introduce myself, but seeing as most of you are family, I'm guessing you already know my name. At least I hope you do." The audience laughed and a few hassled him.

"I'd like to take a moment and thank the maid of honor for her tireless effort to make this day perfect. Everyone, give Jules a hand." They gazed into each other's eyes as the applause rose.

"And now for the happy couple. Don't they just make the perfect pair?" Another round of applause filled the air, and the couple kissed. "Now, with me being the older brother, it's my responsibility to keep Dante on the right path, so I'm going to give him the only advice he'll ever need to maintain a happy marriage. Are you ready, Dante?"

Dante laughed and nodded. "Give it to me."

"Okay, repeat after me, 'Yes, dear.'"

"Yes, dear."

"There. You've got it. That's all you have to remember."

Lizzie smiled. "Very good." The guests laughed some more.

"And that is the extent of my knowledge about women.

You're on your own for the rest of it, little brother. Now for the toast." He raised his glass. "To Lizzie, for never giving up on my brother. And to Dante, I don't know how you got so lucky, but you've gotten yourself a great lady. Never forget it. Here's hoping both of you have a lifetime of happiness."

In that moment, as his brother kissed his bride, a revelation came to Stefano. He realized that in all his effort to push Jules away, it hadn't been about her happiness. Sure, he wanted her to fulfill her dreams, but his inability to hear what she was telling him was due to the fact that if he let her into his heart, then she might later realize that he wasn't what she wanted. The thought of her rejecting him scared him senseless. He couldn't stand the thought of not being able to make her happy.

But as Dante looped his arm through his bride's so that they were linked as they sipped their bubbly, Stefano realized that love was a leap of faith. Without trust there could be no love. And he trusted Jules. Somewhere along the way he'd gotten to know the girl hiding behind all the makeup and funky clothes.

Life was full of risks. And life could change in a heartbeat. If his father and brother were willing to put themselves out there, even though they knew the risks, what was he doing playing it safe and letting the woman he loved get away?

His mouth grew dry, and he took a sip of champagne. In the next moment, someone whisked the mic out of his hand. When he looked up, Jules was headed his way. His heart pounded, his pulse raced and his hands grew clammy.

This was his moment—his chance to win over the woman he loved. The thought didn't strike him as sudden or earth-shattering. Instead the acknowledgment came easily and calmly. It'd been growing over time, but he'd been doing everything to fight it.

Jules clenched her teeth tight as she forced a smile on her face. This was going to be the last time she was in Stefano's arms. She blinked rapidly. Now wasn't the time to get emotional.

All too soon, he stood before her. He was so tall that his gaze went over her head. She didn't know what to say to him. Did she try again to make him see sense? Or did she just let it go and accept that this wasn't going to happen for them?

Before she could make up her mind, a photographer was in her face snapping their picture. As they started to dance, she chanced a glance at Stefano, who surprisingly looked at ease. His smile made her heart flip-flop. Eventually he was going to make some woman a good husband. Too bad it wasn't going to be her.

"I've been wanting to talk to you." The sound of Stefano's voice startled her from her thoughts. "But you've been busy dancing."

"Yes. It's been nice, especially since I'll be stuck on a plane tomorrow."

"You've decided to go ahead with grad school?" When she nodded, it was like a light went out in his eyes. "I'm sure you'll be happy with the choice."

She shrugged. "We'll see. Anyway, I have to get back and find someplace cheap to live before classes start." When he adjusted his hold, her heart did a rapid *tap-tap-tap*. "What did you want to talk about?"

"Uh, nothing important. I just wanted to offer you a ride to the airport."

"Thanks, but I'm getting a lift with Dante and Lizzie."

"Have a safe trip home."

This was killing her. The last thing in the world she wanted to do was say goodbye to him. "Is that what you really want? Me to leave?"

They stopped dancing, and his hand lifted to her cheek. His long, lean fingers caressed her as he stared into her eyes. "I—"

A round of applause drew her attention. *What in the world?* She looked around and realized the music had stopped a while ago and they were the only couple left on the dance floor. Heat rose in her cheeks. She didn't know if it was because she hadn't noticed the music stopping or if it was because she'd broken down once again and asked Stefano to change his mind about them.

But what she wanted to know more than anything was what he was about to say. "Say it. Say whatever it is."

"Come on, Jules! It's time for the bridal bouquet toss." Lizzie waved frantically to her from the other end of the dance floor, where a group of single females was anxiously waiting.

"Go. You are needed. We can talk about this later."

Later? How was she supposed to concentrate on anything until she knew what he was going to say? Her intuition told her that he was about to say he loved her. But was that just wishful thinking?

She walked closer to the group of excited young women. Their faces were all aglow with hopeful smiles, but there was nothing but turmoil lurking behind Jules's smile. The wedding may be in Italy, but Lizzie insisted on mixing traditions between those of Dante's family and what they were used to in New York. That had included the Chicken Dance, which had succeeded in getting everyone laughing.

Catching the bridal bouquet was one tradition that Jules could do without. A happily-ever-after didn't appear to be in the cards for her. As if fate wanted to teach her a lesson, the bouquet of pink, orange and white blossoms landed squarely in her hands.

While everyone clapped, her gaze strayed to Stefano. He wasn't clapping, but he was staring directly at her. She wished she could read his mind.

CHAPTER NINETEEN

STEFANO'S HEART SLAMMED into his chest as he stared at Jules's holding the bridal bouquet. She stared right back at him.

She was trying to tell him something, but what? He had to get this right. He couldn't afford to make any more mistakes.

Had she forgiven him? Was she willing to give him another chance? *Live in the moment*—her words echoed through his mind. He needed to trust her and her decisions—no matter what direction they led her. Although he prayed that it would be toward him.

Stefano straightened his shoulders. This had been put off long enough. He would let her know that he loved her and then he'd accept whatever decision she made.

He started toward her only to have her pulled aside for more wedding photos, this time holding the bridal bouquet. There was no way he was intruding on that moment. He'd had enough photos of himself taken to last him the rest of his life. But he also wasn't letting her out of his sight.

He didn't know how much time passed as he talked to one distant relative after the other—some he didn't even recall their names and had to fake it. And every time he was free, Jules was having more photos taken or being escorted around the dance floor. Even his father had taken his turn dancing with her.

"What are you waiting for, boy?"

He turned to find Nonno behind him. His grandfather's gaze moved from him to Jules, who was getting a drink of punch. How did his grandfather know what he was waiting to say? Was it that obvious?

"I…I didn't want to bother her."

With the aid of a walker, his grandfather moved next to him and lowered his voice. "You aren't going to bother her. I've seen the way she looks at you. Don't let her get away."

"You…you think she'll want me after I messed up?" His grandfather nodded and Stefano added, "Thanks, Nonno."

"Go. Be happy."

Jules didn't see him approaching, and she started to walk in the opposite direction. He wasn't going to turn back, not until he got this off his chest. He continued following and inwardly groaned when she approached Dante and Lizzie. The last thing he wanted to do was lay his heart on the line in front of his brother. There had to be a better way, but he was running out of time. Determined not to lose his chance, he continued over and joined the small group. They were deep in conversation.

Jules looked directly at her sister. "I wanted to let you two know that I won't need a ride tomorrow morning to the airport."

"What?" Lizzie's eyes opened wide. "But why not?"

"You know I love you." Jules's tone was low and firm. "And I know that if it wasn't for you I wouldn't be standing here. You've been the most amazing sister, but there's something I've been trying to tell you. For one reason or another it was never the right time. I'm beginning to think there'll never be a right time, so I'm just going to say it."

No one moved. Stefano wasn't even sure that Lizzie

breathed as she stood transfixed on her sister. Mentally he urged Jules onward. It was finally time that she spoke up for herself.

"It's past time I start making my own decisions and for you to respect them."

Lizzie sent her a worried look. "I have a feeling I'm not going to like this."

"Probably not. But here it goes, anyway. I'm not going to grad school." Lizzie opened her mouth, but Jules held up her palm, silencing her. "I know that you already paid the tuition. Whatever isn't refundable, I'll pay you back."

Lizzie looked more stunned than upset. "But why? I thought this is what you wanted—to help the kids like us."

"I do. But social work isn't for me." Jules glanced down and wiggled her sandaled foot on the floor. "The thing is I can't follow all of their rules all of the time. Sometimes they just don't make sense. And, well, I spoke up one too many times, and they let me go from my internship early."

"Oh. Jules, I'm sorry. But that doesn't mean—"

"It means that I wasn't happy there. And I will find another way to help less fortunate children. I already have some ideas."

Concern creased Lizzie's face. "I...I don't know what to say. Are you sure about this?"

"I'm absolutely certain. This isn't a decision I made lightly. I've thought about it for a long time."

"Then I guess there isn't anything else to say, except I love you. And I'm here if you need me."

They hugged. And though everyone else wore serious expressions, Stefano couldn't help but smile—his first genuine smile that day. He was so happy for Jules to speak up for herself. Now it was time that he did the same thing. Whether his brother witnessed his groveling or not, he was speaking his heart, here and now.

He cleared his throat. "Jules, can I speak with you?"

She spun around, and her expression was perfectly serious. "Not before I have my say." She pointed a finger at him. "And I've made a decision about you." She poked at his chest. "I've decided that you are stubborn and irritating, but that I love you, anyway. And I'm not giving up on you because I think you love me, too."

The way she gazed at him, it was as if she could read his every thought. And though not so long ago that would have scared him, now he found comfort in someone knowing him so well.

Stefano wrapped his hand around hers and pressed her palm to his pounding chest. "Thank you for being so insistent and giving me a chance to come to my senses because I do love you. I love you with all my heart."

"You do?"

"I do."

She smiled broadly. "Just remember those words because you'll be saying them again soon."

"I can't wait." He could already envision their future, and it was going to be a happy one. He'd never again become disconnected. He'd make Jules's happiness and their marriage his top priority.

Jules leaned up on her tiptoes as he leaned down. Their lips met in the middle. The empty spot in his heart flooded with love. He wrapped his arms around her and swung her around in a circle. He never planned to let her go.

EPILOGUE

One year later...

"IT'S OFFICIAL."

Jules smiled up at her very sexy husband and gave off a squeal of excitement. The noise of the family picnic in the background covered up her excitement. She'd never been so happy in her life. She almost had everything she wanted. Almost...

Stefano gathered her in his arms and swung her around as his lips pressed to hers. It didn't matter how many times he kissed her, her heart still fluttered with excitement.

"And what's going on over here?"

Stefano set her feet back on the ground. She straightened her purple top and black miniskirt. When she glanced up she found Lizzie looking expectantly at both of them as she rested a hand over her expanding midsection.

"Your sister is now an official Italian citizen," Stefano said proudly.

"Is that so?" Lizzie radiated with a motherly glow. "Well, if you two aren't careful with the celebrating, you'll end up like me. Swollen ankles. And a backache to boot."

"And you look so miserable," Jules teased her, knowing full well that Lizzie was absolutely thrilled with her handsome husband and their impending bundle of joy.

"What can I say? I'm deliriously in love." Lizzie grinned.

"Are you talking about me?" Dante sauntered up and put an arm around his wife's expanding waist, pulling her close.

"Don't worry," Jules spoke up. "We've got an announcement to make, too."

Lizzie straightened. Her eyes widened. "Jules, are you preggers?"

She shook her head, sending her pigtails swishing back and forth. Both Dante and Lizzie sent her a puzzled look. When she just grinned at them, they turned to Stefano for answers.

He smiled and shrugged. "She'll tell you."

"Well, tell us—we're dying to know."

Stefano's arms slipped over her shoulders. She loved the feel of him next to her. He was her best friend. Her lover. Her soul mate. With him by her side anything was possible.

"We're going to be parents, too."

Lizzie's forehead wrinkled. "But you said you aren't pregnant."

"I'm not. We're going to adopt some of the older kids that need a loving home. We have this big place and think it would be nice to share it with some children that don't have a home."

Lizzie's eyes filled with tears. "You found a way to help kids like us, after all. You are amazing. Both of you are amazing."

Jules gazed lovingly into her husband's eyes. They were amazing together. And Jules couldn't think of anything better than living and working next to Dante while opening their hearts and home to some less fortunate children.

Their journey was just beginning, and she knew that it wouldn't be all roses. There'd be a few thorns along the way, but together they'd work their way past them.

* * * * *

LET'S TALK
Romance

For exclusive extracts, competitions
and special offers, find us online:

- **f** facebook.com/millsandboon
- 🐦 @MillsandBoon
- 📷 @MillsandBoonUK

Get in touch on 01413 063232

For all the latest titles coming soon, visit
millsandboon.co.uk/nextmonth